Homicide detective Jake Carrington has an engagement that can't wait—with a killer.

Haunted by the murder of his sister, Lieutenant Jake Carrington struggles to control his personal demons as he stands over the brutalized body of a young woman found dead on the railroad tracks. The victim disappeared on July 6th, the fifth woman in as many years to go missing on that date. The fifth happy bride-to-be. The only one whose body has turned up.

Soon the killer is sending personal messages to Jake. They refer to an unidentified brother he believes Jake hates as much as he does. With his partner distracted by turmoil at home, Jake is on his own. Drawn deeper and deeper into a murderous family feud, his mission is to find out who the killer's brother is—and stop him before another innocent woman's life is cut tragically short.

Books by Marian Lanouette

Jake Carrington Thrillers
All the Deadly Lies
All the Hidden Sins
All the Pretty Brides

Published by Kensington Publishing Corporation

All the Pretty Brides

A Jake Carrington Thriller

Marian Lanouette

LYRICAL PRESS
Kensington Publishing Corp.
www.kensingtonbooks.com

LYRICAL UNDERGROUND BOOKS are published by
Kensington Publishing Corp.
119 West 40th Street
New York, NY 10018

All Kensington titles, imprints, and distributed lines are available at special quantity discounts for bulk purchases for sales promotion, premiums, fund-raising, educational, or institutional use.

Special book excerpts or customized printings can also be created to fit specific needs. For details, write or phone the office of the Kensington Sales Manager: Kensington Publishing Corp., 119 West 40th Street, New York, NY 10018. Attn. Sales Department. Phone: 1-800-221-2647.
Lyrical Underground and Lyrical Underground logo Reg. US Pat. & TM Off.

First Electronic Edition: December 2018
eISBN-13: 978-1-5161-0479-6
eISBN-10: 1-5161-0479-X

First Print Edition: December 2018
ISBN-13: 978-1-5161-0480-2
ISBN-10: 1-51-610480-3

Printed in the United States of America

To my wonderful brothers, Jimmy, Albert, Michael, and in loving memory of Eddie and Timmy; you've always been there for me with your encouragement, advice, and love.

Praise for Marian Lanouette's Jake Carrington Thrillers

ALL THE PRETTY BRIDES

"Tense and authentic—a suspenseful page-turner!"
—Leo J. Maloney, bestselling author of the Dan Morgan Thriller Series

ALL THE DEADLY LIES

"All the Deadly Lies is a rawly rendered thriller that toes the line between feisty and fierce without ever losing its underlying sense of fun."
—*Criminal Element*

"The dead cannot cry out for justice.
It is a duty of the living to do so for them."
—Lord Miles Vorkosigan,
Diplomatic Immunity,
Lois McMaster Bujold

Before the Altar, bowed, he stands
With empty hands;
Upon it perfumed offerings burn
Wreathing with smoke the sacrificial urn.
—*Before the Altar,*
Amy Lowell

Prologue

Another disappointment—why does she continue to deny me? Not once has she kept her promise. I've kept mine. She continues to refuse my terms. How many times must I make the wedding preparations before there is a wedding? This one's like the rest of them. She cries all day and all night long. What more could she possibly want? We have each other.

She lies. Tells me she's not my Ciara. I can see in her eyes that she's planning to run away again. Not this time, bitch. You made me a promise. A promise you will keep one way or another. You will not humiliate me again. We're mated for life. That's what marriage means. If I can't have you, no one else will.

She must die. It's that simple. Though I've explained all this to her time and time again, she doesn't listen. Not one of them has kept their promise. Don't they understand when you commit, there's no turning back? Our wedding day has come and gone—five long years alone. I thought she'd be back by now. Each time I find her, it turns out to be a cheap copy. No marriage, no children. I'll give her one last chance. But deep down in my heart I understand it's a useless gesture. She's not Ciara—Ciara would never cry. My Ciara's independent, wild, strong, and beautiful.

I will not...cannot live without her. I must end this charade with the imposter downstairs and find Ciara.

Exhausted, he pushed himself from the chair and went down the stairs. On the bottom step, he stopped, stood, listened, and shut down his emotions. He studied her as he moved closer. For the first time in weeks the differences glared out at him. *A weak copy of Ciara—how did I miss it? Oh, how she made a fool of me. Not anymore—she'll join the others.*

Calmer, he walked over to her, unhooked the chains that bound her wrists and legs. With no fight left in her, she was easy for him to handle. He dragged her up off the basement floor, spun her around, and spooned her to his body. He caressed the side of her face with his knife before pressing the sharp blade to her throat and drawing a fine line until a trickle of blood appeared. He licked the wound as he brought his head up to rest on hers. Ciara's fragrance wafted to him. Though her hair had been washed in Ciara's shampoo, her neck drenched in Ciara's perfume, this imposter was not his beloved Ciara.

I've searched for you, Ciara darling, for five long years. How did you disappear off the face of the earth? Where are you? You bitch! You humiliated me in front of our families and friends when you left me stranded at the altar on our wedding day. I waited hours for you to show up, to explain, but you never came. What an idiot I'd been...worrying something bad had happened to you. God, how I wished it had. Not one word from you, no explanation, no apology. Not a whisper or trace of you in all these years.

Your parents moved away—left me no forwarding address—but I got it anyway. I've traced them through the Internet. It seems you don't live with them. My tracers on your social security number, your credit cards haven't turned up one clue. I thought I had you once. You screwed up when your mother's credit card was used in both her state and a different state on the same day. I jumped on a plane, searched the area where the purchases were made, but never sighted you. Did I just miss you? You're not working, or if you are, you're using a different social security number and name. I'll find you though, you wait and see.

"What is your real name?" he demanded of the limp woman in his arms.

* * * *

"It's...it's Nadia. I keep telling you. My name is Nadia," she said hoarsely. Broken, she almost couldn't remember her own name. She hated the woman named Ciara, a woman she had never even met.

"It's not Ciara?"

"No." Nadia knew this was the end.

She sent her prayers, her good-byes and love to Donny, her parents, and her sister.

"Say good-bye, Nadia." He ran the knife across her throat, left to right. After weeks of torture, she barely felt the final insult.

Chapter 1

September 1

"What an excellent way to be awakened. But next time, put Brigh's bed in the living room." Mia pushed away from Jake as his cell phone started to ring.

He rolled to his side and picked up the intruding phone. The caller ID had him swearing under his breath as he answered it. There went his day off. He picked up the pen and notebook he kept on his nightstand and started writing as he listened to dispatch.

"Thanks. Notify Sergeant Romanelli and have him meet me at the scene." Jake disconnected, turning to Mia. It was strange to have her back in his bed. Life…wasn't it bizarre?

"Who's dead?"

"Dispatch didn't say. Sorry, I had hoped to spend the day with you." He got out of bed, pulled a pair of jeans from the bottom drawer, his socks and underwear from the top one.

"I understand. Call me later."

"Will do. Go back to sleep."

He took his shoulder and ankle holsters off his dresser, placed them on top of his clothes on the chair, then opened his closet safe for his guns.

Mia was sitting up in bed staring at him.

"What?" he asked.

"You've got a lot of hardware there—doesn't it bother you to carry it?"

"It would bother me more if I was in a situation and didn't have my weapons with me. Don't worry."

"It comes with the territory. Will I see you tonight?"

"I hope so. Give me a call when you're through." He bent down, glided his lips over hers and lingered—something positive he'd take with him to the scene.

Ten minutes later, showered and dressed, he brewed a quick cup of coffee, toasted a bagel, and headed to his car.

* * * *

As he pulled into the parking lot at the Metro station, he couldn't help but notice the crowd. There had to be ten cruisers with their lights flashing. *Nothing like advertising in the lot shared with the newspaper,* he thought. *Whatever happened to common sense? I bet the reporters got better pictures than we did.*

He emptied his coffee cup and wiped his mouth before climbing out of the car and stepping into the thick, humid air. *Exactly how many bodies were there that it required such a large police presence,* he wondered. The crowd consisted of not only the patrol car officers; there were a few who patrolled on foot as well as CSIs, uniformed Metro employees, and strangers he assumed were commuters who got more than a ride to work today. The crime scene tape had been placed around the area to control the lookie-loos. He recognized a couple of the uniforms as he ducked under it. Scanning the bystanders, he searched for anyone who stood out. It was never easy, but one could hope. Some killers got a kick out of watching the police process the scene.

Dispatch had reported two kids cutting school had planned to walk along the tracks to a favorite party spot that was not accessible by car. It was difficult for the cops to patrol there. Instead of enjoying the late summer day, the kids had found a body. *They might think twice about cutting class the next time,* he thought.

"This way, Lieutenant," Officer Martin Gregory said as he approached Jake.

"How contaminated is my scene, Marty?"

Jake followed him down the slight incline to the tracks while he surveyed the area. Not an easy dump site, he noted. Someone had lots of muscle if he had carried a body this far. Jake pulled out his notebook and wrote down his first impressions before listing the standard questions. What would it take to carry a body this far? How strong would a man have to be to walk two hundred or so yards to discard it? Did he drag it? How much did the body weigh? It would have had to be done early, before people headed into work. But he couldn't be positive he wouldn't be seen. Where had he parked? Where had he entered the area?

"You got kids running around, the homeless, plus all the druggies," Marty said.

"Grab a couple of uniforms and walk the perimeter. See if there are drag marks or tire tracks in case he drove it."

Jake swept his gaze over the downhill area in front of him still not able to spot the crime scene. "And see if you find any bags down there large enough to transport a body."

"Yes, sir."

"Did Sergeant Romanelli get here yet?"

"He's already with the victim, sir. My partner's with him."

Knowing Louie was in control, Jake's apprehension evened out.

"Lieutenant, is she the missing girl from July sixth?" someone shouted.

Anger burned a hole in his stomach as he turned to face the speaker. Reporters in general annoyed him. They were cretins, in his opinion. They only cared about their next headline, not the victims or their survivors. Matthew Hayes was the worst of the bunch.

"Stay off my crime scenes. This is your last warning." Hayes was on the scene too early—again. Someone had tipped the bastard off. Jake turned to Marty. "Escort this person behind the lines with the rest of the gawkers. If he asks you any questions, even one, arrest him." Turning, he headed toward the victim.

"Lieutenant, a little cooperation might help you solve the Bride Murders," Hayes shouted.

Jake knew better than to engage him, but he'd had enough of Hayes. He turned back to the reporter. The Bride Murders, as labeled by the sensationalist press. *If I find out who's letting Hayes onto my scenes, there'll be hell to pay. The victims deserve everyone's respect. They aren't headlines. Someone stole their lives, their futures.* If he let it, anger would dig deep under his skin and push his sister, Eva, into his head. She didn't belong in the here and now.

"The other women are still listed as missing, not murdered." He continued on to the body.

* * * *

"What have you got?" Jake asked his partner.

"And good morning to you too, sunshine," Louie said and continued when Jake didn't react. "A Caucasian woman in her early twenties with dark brown hair, brown eyes, weight approximately one-twenty. She fits the description of the most recent missing woman." Louie wiped the sweat from his brow.

"Same date?"

"Yes."

"Don't confirm Hayes's suspicions. It'll only give him more ammunition to tag the victim. And I don't want these crimes referred to as the Bride Murders by any officer."

"You're a little touchy this morning," Louie said for Jake's ears only.

"Hayes is on our scenes before we are. We need to find out who's feeding him."

Louie bent down to pick something up with gloved hands, placed it in an evidence bag, and labeled it.

Jake searched the faces of the cops around him—some young, some more experienced—as he pulled on his own gloves. He had put on his booties in the car. It was as good a time as any to address the issue. "You all heard what I said to the reporter. I want every victim treated with respect. It starts by referring to her by name. Not a nickname given by the press. Understood?" He didn't move until he got a nod of understanding from each of them.

"Let's get to work."

Sympathy, pain, and memories flooded him as he crouched down to examine the woman's face. It never failed to amaze him, what human beings did to one another. Animals fought and killed to survive. Humans fought and killed for many reasons—sport, food, trophies. What kind of satisfaction did the killer get from torturing a beautiful young woman? What switched on in a person's mind to cause this kind of brutality? After twelve years of being a cop, he understood self-defense, even instant rage. But murder, and especially this kind of killing, he never would. To abduct, hold, and torture a person took planning and organization. It said something about the killer.

"You ran her fingerprints through the car computer and there's no mistake?" he asked Sergeant Louie Romanelli, his partner for the last ten years, who also happened to be his best friend from childhood.

"Yep, it's Nadia Carren. According to the missing persons file she was age twenty-two at the time of her disappearance. She worked over at Feinberg & Feinberg as a paralegal. The date's the same as the other missing women. Want to speculate?" Louie asked.

"Not here. We need more information."

Jake knew questions like this would be directed at him from the brass. Last year he'd taken an FBI profiling course at Quantico. Would it offer any insight or help? That remained to be seen, though he certainly could use an edge. His recent promotion to lieutenant would make him the lead on the case. During an election year, the candidates vying for the mayor's office could be a nuisance as they often put on the pressure to solve cases.

"I don't have a clue. We'll find out when we catch him. But it will never make sense to anyone but the killer."

"None of the other victims have been found. He obviously wanted this one found. But why? And is it the same guy?" Louie asked.

"All good questions, but without the other bodies, we can't be sure."

"I'm only throwing them out there for discussion." Louie scratched his head.

Jake was used to Louie voicing his opinions and thoughts out loud. A lot of times it helped find the answers. "Maybe someone came upon him dumping the body and forced him to change his MO." They had nothing to link the killer's modus operandi to anything yet. Though deep down, in the pit of his stomach, there was no doubt about it—it had to be the same perpetrator. Nothing else made sense.

"Maybe he's tired of not getting the credit for his work." Jake heard the frustration in his own voice.

"It's a good thing she was discovered quickly. With this putrid weather the body would've decomposed in no time," Louie said.

Every July 6, for the past four years, a young woman had disappeared. Four beautiful young women ready to start their lives, all gone without a trace…until now, with number five. And Louie was right, it was a big question. Why now? What had changed?

"I hate when it ends this way, but at least now we have something to work with. Maybe she'll lead us to the other women," Louie said.

Always the optimist, Jake thought.

With a rhythm born from years of partnership, Jake and Louie worked side by side in silence, directing, gathering, and bagging evidence. Together they examined the train tracks in the area where Nadia's body was found. Jake stood beside the splayed body, eyeing the different ways the murderer could have brought her in without being noticed. If he'd done it himself, he would have parked beneath the underpass.

This location, covered in empty crack vials, cigarette butts, fast-food containers, cheap wine and liquor bottles, along with used condoms, was a favorite teen hangout. The area around the body had been cleared of debris—staged as if it were a shrine—but to who—the victim? They were probably dealing with an organized killer. Fingernails and hair had been recently washed. Bending down to get closer to the body, he took a sniff. Yep, there went his trace, damn it. *The criminals learned how to spoil evidence from television. Why here, why now,* kept popping back into his head. The killer had a reason for dumping her where she'd be found fast. What was it? Jake's stomach churned. Whoever washed the body was familiar with police procedure. Or could it be a cop? He hoped not. The department had had its share of scandals recently. It didn't need more.

Disease Haven, he'd dubbed this place years ago. It was bad enough he had a contaminated scene, between the homeless and the emergency response team. It was obvious she was dead. But it was standard procedure to call in the EMT wagon, though when they viewed the scene they should have stayed back. *Why didn't they?* Jake wouldn't be able to get any decent footprints, and the garbage in the area would hinder them further.

He directed the CSIs to pick up every bit of litter they saw. Told them he'd assign uniforms to help if necessary. He wasn't taking any chances—didn't want to miss a piece of important evidence due to laziness. One gum wrapper and maybe he'd be able to nail the suspect. Louie had a couple of officers taking swabs from Neil McMichaels, the railroad safety inspector who'd called in the report after the kids ran into his office to notify him of what they had found. Jake took samples from any of the homeless they could pin down, to eliminate them from the mix. They had to wait for the parents before they could take the kids' samples.

* * * *

After overseeing the collection of evidence, Jake walked back to the body and joined the assistant medical examiner. Louie had already bagged the hands and feet. Doc McKay pronounced the victim dead on scene and made a notation of the time. Once he completed the other necessary tasks, McKay signaled to the morgue drivers. Turning from the corpse, he took off his gloves, rolled them together, then placed them in an evidence bag so as not to contaminate any of his other instruments. Next, he wiped his hands with an alcohol wipe, then swiped the wipe over his tweezers before putting them back into his bag.

"I heard what you said to your team," McKay said, his eyes meeting Jake's before he continued. "It's one of the reasons I like working with you. You respect the victims."

"Thanks, Tim." Embarrassed, Jake asked, "Do you have an approximate time of death?"

"No, I don't even want to guess. With the wild weather and heat we've been having it could've been last week or a month ago. I'll give you a heads-up when I'm done posting."

Doc McKay stood about five-ten, with thinning hair, and his paunch hung over his belt. He handled the dead with care. On his scenes, Jake only wanted Lang or McKay.

"Good enough, Doc." He watched as the morgue assistants loaded up the body for transport.

* * * *

He and Louie headed to the west end of town, to an affluent neighborhood and a house lined with cheerful, multicolored flowers dancing along its border. After they delivered their news, it would be a false facade. He hated this part of his job. Cop families knew when another cop knocked on their door the news wouldn't be good. Civilians stalled, hoping to delay the notification. Today he would dash the hopes of the Carren family and change their lives forever.

Jake knocked harder than intended. An attractive, petite brunette in her late forties, who resembled the pictures of her missing daughter, answered the door. The welcoming expression dropped off her face when she spied their badges.

"You found Nadia? Is she okay? Where has she been?" Hope lived in her eyes.

"Mrs. Carren, is your husband home?" Jake asked.

"Yes, come in." She stepped back. Once they were inside, she turned and showed them into the living room. "I'll get him." She ran up the staircase located outside the room.

Mr. Carren walked in, followed by his wife and a young woman Jake thought must be his other daughter. The man towered over his family. Shoulders squared, his face an emotionless mask, his body language told Jake he expected the worst.

"Officers, my wife said you have news of Nadia."

"Mr. and Mrs. Carren, I'm sorry to inform you Nadia's body was found this morning."

Mrs. Carren let out a scream as she collapsed into her husband's arms. Their daughter sank into the nearest chair, tears pooling in her eyes.

"Are you sure it's Nadia?" the daughter asked.

"Yes. I'm sorry for your loss."

Useless words, but he had no others. The family's grief coated him like motor oil on an engine. It reminded him of his own family's devastation over his younger sister Eva's death. The bastards of the world preyed on the young and innocent.

"Can I get you anything?" Louie asked.

"No, we need time to process this. We prayed—we hoped—we'd find her alive. I knew this was a possibility, but still...I can't believe it," Mr. Carren said, never letting go of his wife. "Your children are supposed to outlive you."

"Mr. Carren, I understand this is a difficult time, but we have a few questions we need to ask to help us find her killer."

Weeping louder, Mrs. Carren curled into her husband. The daughter walked over and wrapped her arms around her mother's shoulders, then patted her father's back. *They're a unit,* Jake thought.

"Ask. I'll answer what I can," the daughter said.

"I'm sorry, I didn't get your name. Are you Nadia's sister?" Jake asked.

"Yes, I'm Rori."

The girl wiped tears from her face while she tried to gather her composure.

* * * *

They asked their questions but got nothing new from the family. Everything they supplied was already in the Missing Persons case file. Rori offered to fax over a list of the phone numbers and addresses of Nadia's friends. Leaving the family to their grief, Jake and Louie climbed into Jake's car and headed back to the scene.

"How's Brigh?" Louie changed the subject to a lighter matter. A tactic he'd developed over the years to combat other people's grief.

"Good. She still shakes when strangers come to the door. It's something I've learned to live with," Jake said.

"Are she and Mia getting along?"

"Yep. Want to grab lunch before I drop you back at your car?" They both needed a break after the emotional scene with the Carrens.

"That sounds good. Where do you want to eat?"

"You pick it today."

"Excellent, then let's go to the chicken place on West Main Street."

"You have such childish tastes," Jake said.

"Sophia doesn't allow fried foods at home. Lunch is the only time I can sneak them."

"If Sophia was cooking for me every day, I'd brown-bag it."

"You'd get tired of good food all the time, too."

* * * *

After lunch, Jake dropped Louie at his car. "I want to process a couple of things before we interview the fiancé."

"I have one stop to make, then I'll meet you back here," Louie said, staring down at his cell phone and frowning.

"Something wrong?"

Louie walked away without responding.

Odd, Jake thought.

Chapter 2

Back at the station, Jake typed his notes into his computer. After printing the documents, he placed a copy in the murder book. His head snapped up when someone knocked on his door. Expecting Louie, he instead saw Detective Kirk Brown and had to switch his mind-set.

"Yes, Kirk?"

"I heard you found the missing girl. Is she tied to the others?" Brown asked.

"It seems to be."

"Are you going to form a task force?"

"It's too early for that. Why?"

"I want in, if you do. I knew the first girl, Lizzy."

"Elizabeth Bartholomew?"

"Yes, my youngest sister went to school with her."

"I'll consider it, Kirk, after I weigh the pros and cons. When you go back to your desk, send Romanelli in."

"He's not back from lunch yet."

Jake frowned at Brown. "Thanks."

Something was definitely up with Louie. It wasn't like him to disappear. Jake reached for his cell phone to give him a call, then thought better of it.

I'll give him another twenty minutes before I head out to interview the fiancé alone.

* * * *

Jake reread the file on Nadia Carren. He searched for any information the original case detectives of the Missing Persons department might've overlooked. He found none. The case detectives had done their jobs. When the third woman went missing, that's when they'd made the connection to the first two victims. Elizabeth Bartholomew's file mirrored Nadia's, as did the Baudlion, Roberts, and Greene files. Jake started a spreadsheet. On one side he listed what the women had in common and on the other side their differences. He glanced up when there was another knock on his door.

"I heard you wanted to see me," Louie said, going directly to the coffee machine.

"Where have you been?"

"I had something to take care of," Louie said. "What's up?"

Okay, he doesn't want to talk. He pulls information from everyone else, but rarely offers anything about his life. I'll find out what's up in the car.

"Let's go interview Donny Donahue. See what light he can shed on his fiancée's demise."

"What were you doing?"

"I'm culling facts from all their files to see what they had in common. I started a spreadsheet."

"I'll work on that."

"You want to do it together at my house tonight?" *Say no. I promised Mia I wouldn't work tonight.*

"I can't. I'm on kid duty."

Quirking his brow at the tone of Louie's voice, he said, "Close the door." Jake stood, and watched Louie push his door shut. "Spill."

"There's nothing to spill. Sophia's out tonight."

And you're not happy about that. "She got something hot going on?" Jake joked.

"I don't want to talk about it…really. Let's move on."

"Okay, you do the spreadsheet. Be ready, I want to leave within five minutes to interview Donahue."

"Ten-four."

Jake watched him leave his office, then put a call in to Sophia. "Hey, Sophia, it's Jake."

"This is a surprise. What's up?"

"I haven't spoken to you in a while, thought I'd call to say hello."

"Cut the baloney, we've been friends too long. What has Louie said to you?"

"Nothing, that's why I'm calling. What bug crawled up his ass?"

"Jake, no cursing. If he isn't speaking to you about it, I can't either. Please respect his boundaries."

Well, Christ. What now? "Okay, but—"

"Thanks for being there. We'll call if either one of us needs you."

"No problem." He hung up and stared at his phone as if it had exploded in his hand before he headed to Louie's desk.

* * * *

Jake drove with the window open. Louie blasted the air conditioner, pointing the vents at himself. At Donahue's place of business they found he had left abruptly after receiving a phone call. Jake figured one of the Carrens must've called him. Donny's boss had no idea when he'd return to work.

"The kid's broken up, Lieutenant. He never figured it would end this way."

"Thanks. You got his home address? It would save us some time."

The boss gave it to them, but not without a warning. "You won't get anything from him today, he's a mess."

Jake climbed into the car, waited for Louie to do the same, and entered Donahue's address into his GPS. Lost in his own thoughts, he missed what Louie said.

"What?"

"I said, this case sucks big time. Here they were planning their future—marriage, kids, all the rest of it—and now he's burying the girl."

"Yeah, life sucks."

* * * *

He pulled up in front of a modest yellow house, lined with rosebushes still in bloom. *The last rose of summer,* he thought. They walked to the front door. It opened before Jake could knock.

"You're the police? Mike called from work," Donny said.

"We need to speak to you." Jake held out his badge. Louie did the same.

"I figured. Come in."

As he stepped in, Jake noted the red, puffy eyes, the runny nose and the hunched shoulders—Donny's world had been destroyed. With Nadia only missing there was still hope. Now with the body found, the final chapter had been written.

"Mr. Donahue, we have some questions."

A woman walked into the living room carrying a tray of tea and scones. She placed it on the coffee table then sat down next to Donahue and took his left hand in both of hers. Based on age, he assumed her to be Donahue's mother.

"I'm Lieutenant Carrington and this is Sergeant Romanelli. We're in charge of Nadia's case." Jake continued, "Can you think of anyone who would want to hurt Nadia?"

"No, damn it. She was good…shy. She never hurt anyone," Donahue said.

"I'm sorry to put you through this, Donny, but we need to ask. We have to eliminate anyone who knew the victim."

"The victim's name is Nadia…Nadia Carren," Donny said through clenched teeth.

"Donny, Nadia's ours now, and we won't forget who she is. We'll work until we can give her justice. Understood?"

"Yes," he whispered.

"Did you or Nadia have any problems with friends or anyone at work?"

"No."

"Did either one of you make any new friends, individuals or couples, as the wedding drew near?"

"No. Well, we did meet a new couple at the pre-Cana conference. We went out to dinner with them after one of the sessions. We've been too busy to do it again, what with the wedding plans, and we were trying to hold down expenses. We didn't go out much after that. I don't think Nadia stayed in touch."

"What were their names?" Louie asked.

"Nadia kept track of things like that. The guy's name was Jim. No, Tom. Sorry, I'm not sure."

"Where was the conference held? We can get their names from the priest."

"At St. Pete's church."

"Is there anything else, Donny?"

"No."

"Did any of your buddies joke how you didn't deserve Nadia?"

"Steve told me she was too good for me… No, man…he wouldn't hurt her. You're looking in the wrong direction if that's where you're heading." Donny got up and paced the room.

"We have to investigate everyone who knew her, Donny." Jake turned to the mother. "Mrs. Donahue, do you have anything to add?"

"No. We're heartbroken. Nadia was a lovely young woman. I couldn't wait until she was officially in our family." She left the room, crying.

"One last question, Donny. Where were you on the night of Nadia's disappearance?"

"I wouldn't harm a hair on her head. I love her."

"We need to ask to eliminate you."

He gave them the information. Jake had read the file. Donahue's alibi was verified the first time around. They'd do it a second time—but there wasn't anything there. If the kid killed her, he'd turn in his badge.

"This shattered me and my family. Nadia's parents and sister are devastated. I went right over there when I found out." He lowered his eyes to Jake and asked, "How will we survive?"

"It's never the same, but you do." Jake left it at that.

Outside in the car, Jake sat for a few minutes, lost in thought as he made notes. After a few minutes, Louie glanced up from his pad and started talking. Jake scrubbed his mind and turned back to the conversation.

"Are you all right?"

"Yeah, fine. I'll drop you at the station. I need to make a stop before I return. When I get back I'm going to want to grab the Missing Persons files. I'll review them again tonight."

"I need them to do the spreadsheet," Louie said.

"I'll work from copies. Get Katrina to make copies for both of us."

"If she's busy I'll have a uniform copy them for you."

"Loving the rank, Louie?" Jake grinned.

"You bet."

* * * *

Back at the station, after his errand, Jake opened his email. He was thrilled to see the pictures from the crime scene attached to McKay's email. The speed with which he received them told Jake everyone was getting pressure on the case. Hoping to find something the killer left behind he grabbed a magnifying glass and did a quick inspection of each picture. On his second pass through he studied each one, dissecting them for anything out of place.

Ah, it would have been too easy, he thought when nothing popped. Next, he viewed the pictures Nadia's family supplied when she went missing. Young, beautiful with a hint of shyness in her smile, her shoulder-length, brown-black hair framed big brown doe eyes which accented her olive complexion. At five feet five inches, she weighed one hundred and ten pounds. She'd never see her twenty-first birthday or her wedding day. Would her family be able to picture her past this age? He'd never been able to see his sister past the age of death. Eva would always be fifteen in his eyes.

Nadia's disappearance had caused a media sensation. "Another Bride Missing" read the headline. Almost two months ago, on July sixth, she disappeared, leaving not a single clue. The frustrated Missing Persons detectives interviewed her family, her fiancé, her friends, and her coworkers. Nobody could help them. A quiet girl, Nadia worked hard, and by all accounts was excited about her wedding in September. Her fiancé, Donavan "Donny" Donahue, hadn't taken the news of her disappearance well. He'd swung at the lead detective, moving Donny up to the top of the list of suspects. Nothing panned out when the detectives investigated him.

There weren't any reports of harassment. She didn't do any kind of drugs—she never partied. Basically, she hung out with her fiancé or her girlfriends and religiously went to the gym three times a week after work at a downtown law firm. She disappeared on her way home from the gym on a hot July night. After she left the gym no one saw or heard from her—until this morning, when the kids had discovered her body.

Jake inspected each picture he and the medical examiner had taken, comparing them to the crime scene photographer's. He hoped for one lousy piece of evidence to lead him to the killer and maybe give her family some closure.

Dead Nadia was a shadow of the live version. Decomposition put time of death somewhere around the end of August, he guessed. She wasn't dead for long. Where did he hold her from July until now? The ME's pictures also showed severe trauma to the body. Nadia's last days on this earth were not peaceful. Someone had brutally tortured her. Cause of death couldn't be determined at the scene. He needed the autopsy results. Jake reached for the phone then thought better of it. McKay didn't like to be rushed. When he had the results, he would email or call.

He knew he'd have to tread carefully. This case could push him to the limit. At night, he lay awake in bed and wondered how much more blood and gore he'd be able to take. Each murder snatched a piece of his heart, especially the deaths of young women and children. What or who created these monsters?

Wilkesbury, Connecticut, had crime, but murder cases the last couple of years had decreased. Ten years ago they had twenty-four murders. This year, only ten, but there'd be more before December.

Chapter 3

"I'm not discussing it over the phone." Louie's face turned beet red as he spoke in a loud whisper.

"All I'm saying, Louie, is a lot of wives work and it doesn't affect their families," Sophia shouted back. "Why do you always have to be so pigheaded?"

"You don't have to yell. I can hear you."

"No, you're not hearing me. I'm going to take the job."

He slammed the phone down, caught a couple of the other detectives staring at him. "What, you don't have lives of your own?"

Grabbing the copies the uniform had placed on his desk, he marched into Jake's office without knocking. "Here are the copies you wanted." He tossed them on the desk.

Then he went to Jake's private coffee machine and helped himself to a cup of strong Colombian.

"You used my promotion as an excuse to get good coffee," Jake said.

"We were both promoted, remember? And your point? A better gift you'll never receive. I was watching out for our health. The department sludge will kill you. This way you get a fresh cup each time." Louie tried to smile though his mind kept replaying the conversation with his wife.

"I love it, but it's not the same. Good coffee doesn't go with the job. It was the first thing I had to get used to: black sludge. I thought I'd lost the lining of my stomach my first month on the job," Jake joked.

"I have the original Missing Persons file on Nadia. I also got the list of friends and family from her sister. Let's match them up and see if anyone was missed the first time around." Louie finished as he blew on the hot coffee before sipping it, "Ah, nothing better."

"What's up, Louie? You seem aggravated."

"Nothing, I don't want to talk about it."

"I see…is Sophia okay?"

"Yes, she's okay and freaking independent. Can we move on?"

"Louie, I'm dropping the subject, but two things. One, I'm here if you need me and two, don't take out the fight you had with your wife on me, got it?"

"Yeah, I got it. You understand how you don't want to speak about Eva? That's where I'm at right now. Please back the hell off."

Jake threw his hands up in surrender. "Like I said, Louie, it's not a problem. When you want to talk I'll be here."

Louie trusted no one more than Jake, but he couldn't talk about Sophia getting a job. He was a good provider. There was no reason for his wife to work. And her wanting to work for that sleazeball lawyer didn't make him feel any better. Louie couldn't determine which bothered him more, who Sophia was going to work for or the job. The guy had several sexual harassment suits on file against him. But she had to make up her own mind.

"Louie?"

"I'm sorry, I didn't hear you."

"You need some time off?"

"No, I don't," he snapped, then put his hand up to hold back Jake's comment. "Sorry, I need to put my mind back on the job." *Damn this headache, it won't go away,* he thought, rubbing his forehead.

"Okay, make time tomorrow morning to review the spreadsheets with me. I want to concentrate on what these women had in common besides their appearances."

* * * *

Louie walked out of his office, and not for the first time today Jake wondered what was wrong with him. The top file was Nadia's. He opened it and splayed it on his desk, then did the same to all the others. He knew he would be duplicating Louie's work but he needed to dig in to figure out what motivated this bastard.

Moira Baudlion, the second girl to go missing, disappeared three years ago on July sixth. The only similarity besides their looks was the fact they both were getting married. They weren't getting married in the same church, didn't work at the same place, one exercised at a club, one didn't. They didn't even have the same blood type. He tapped his pencil on his desk. Why these women? Not a single clue left behind to their whereabouts. Why had the killer dumped Nadia's body out in the open where it was guaranteed to be found within hours? Or had he planned for the train to run her over? Who did these women represent to the killer?

Jake wrote these and many more questions in his notebook. He'd review the other files again, with the hope a connection would pop out. But each victim was the same: Dark hair, dark eyes, and engaged to be married. All had different backgrounds, different religions, different interests, different photographers, and different reception halls. Or maybe one or two had the same venues, but not all five. Something niggled in the back of his brain, though he couldn't pull it out. *Let it simmer, eventually it will come forward,* he thought. It always does.

Noise filtered into his office, signaling the change of shift. Packing up the file copies he wanted to review more carefully at home tonight, he pushed them aside and picked up his overdue evaluations. How was he supposed to evaluate Detective Gannon when he had only worked for him for two weeks? This wasn't fair to him or the detective. Jake knew he needed to speak with the captain on this issue.

Joe Green had worked the last case with Jake, impressing him with his dedication and steadiness. He'd do Green's evaluation first, then read his previous evaluations to see if any significant discrepancies showed up. Green's other lieutenant had worked with him for three years and Jake respected him. His opinion would mean something. Was Joe related to the Greene victim? Different spellings, but he'd check before he put him on the case.

He worked for an hour then decided it was time to hit the road. Mia should be at his house in a half hour. If he wanted to be there before her, he'd better get a move on. *Should I cook or take her out?* Deciding on takeout instead, he put a call in to Mia.

"Do you want Italian, Chinese or burgers?" he asked before she could say hello.

"Italian's good. Are we eating in or out?"

"I thought in."

"In is good. Does that mean you're working tonight?"

"Yeah, I have to put some time in on today's case. I hope that's not a problem."

"No, Jake, it's not a problem. I'll bring my computer and work on my book."

He let out the breath he didn't realize he was holding. Navigating a relationship was hard enough—trying to make one work again that had been shut down in a nanosecond before resuming it, took care and thought. A minefield until you got your rhythm back.

"I'll order now and be home in about a half hour."

"I'm here now and starved, hurry."

"Oh, you only want me for the food," he said, laughing.

"Yes."

He disconnected the call, ordered, then retrieved his briefcase and headed out.

* * * *

Once he picked up dinner, Jake headed home. It would have been nice to be alone tonight to work the new case with no interruptions. The last fifteen years he'd been on his own. Sharing space with someone was going to take some getting used to.

"Christ, Jake, pull yourself together," he said aloud, turning into his driveway.

The garage door opened and he glided the car into the first space. He took a few moments before heading inside with the food. The door between the garage and the living room opened. Mia waited there with Brigh at her side. The dog jumped on Jake's legs waiting for him to pet her. Jake leaned into Mia, kissed her as he dropped his hand and petted Brigh before walking to the kitchen.

"Is something wrong?"

"No, why?" He put the food on the counter and his briefcase on the chair.

"You took a long time to come in."

"Christ, Mia, I was decompressing. My mind is on the poor girl we found this morning." He knew he wasn't being fair but having someone come at him the minute he walked in… Days like today he wasn't fit for human interaction.

He took a couple of plates from the cabinet then reached into the utility drawer for knives and forks. Mia pulled open another drawer, took out napkins, and placed them on the table. She still hadn't responded to his comment. Rubbing his temples to ease the headache that had formed on the way home, he turned back to her.

"I'm sorry. I'm not used to having to socialize when I get home."

"Socialize?" He noticed the way she pursed her lips. *Pissed,* he thought. *Am I looking for a fight?*

"Mia, please. I need time to process my day."

"That won't be a problem, Jake, because after I eat, I'm leaving."

Nothing was ever easy. Why had he pushed her? This was one for the shrinks. He and Mia each retained their own places, but mostly she stayed here. The last month had been great, but today he needed his space.

"I don't want you to leave, Mia. I'm sorry I'm making a mess of this. There are times…after I examine a body that I'm not fit for human company. This poor girl was tortured before the bastard killed her. It brings up a lot of buried memories."

"Was it so hard to say, Jake? It will do you good to be alone."

"I don't want you to leave mad."

"I'm not. You forget I'm a psychologist. I understand you need your space tonight. There will be days I'll need mine. Let's leave it at that."

They ate their dinners in silence. What little conversation they had was forced. Crimes like Nadia's murder brought back every memory of Eva's death.

"Mia…" Jake pushed his half-eaten dinner away from him, stood and began to pace. "I understand this is going to sound stupid but…my anger isn't directed at you."

"We'll talk tomorrow."

* * * *

After Mia left, he poured himself some whiskey, then put his feet up on the coffee table. He stared into the unlit fireplace.

"I screwed up big time, Brigh," he said to the dog as she jumped on the couch with him.

So many thoughts and emotions ran through his mind. His heart ached when he thought of Eva. A murder, the loss of a loved one, created ripples in many lives. It had torn the fabric of his universe and nothing was ever the same. His father died young, his mother lost her ability to function, and Jake was left alone to fend for himself. *If it wasn't for Louie and his family, I'd have probably lost it too.*

He understood tonight what the Carrens and Nadia's fiancé were feeling—even when life went on, it would never be quite the same again for them, either.

Downing his drink, he pushed off the couch and went back into the kitchen. He opened his briefcase, took out the files, and spread each one out on the table. Next, he laid out the file photos of Nadia both alive and dead. Side by side he matched the engagement pictures of all five women.

The killer definitely had a type. All dark-haired, dark-eyed beauties, and though their heights varied, each had a certain innocence about them. In each photo the woman appeared demure, as if they were daydreaming, maybe of their wedding days or their new lives. Damn, he was putting too much of Eva into their expressions.

Were they all shy? Donahue said Nadia was. And Christ, what was Louie's problem? It wasn't like Louie not to talk to him when something bothered him. He and Sophia couldn't possibly be having problems. Could they?

Jake resumed reading the files on each girl until he had them memorized. He took notes, wrote down questions for the families and the fiancés. He picked up the lab reports on all the missing women's cars and read what the CSIs had found. It amounted to nothing that would point a finger in any direction. Fingerprints belonged to each woman and their family members. The few odd prints they found were matched up to mechanics. Only two of the women had had work done on their car within two months of their disappearance.

Three hours of work produced nothing new. He put the files away and headed off to bed, with Brigh following. Earlier, his scan of the news stations had annoyed him. WPD had released little information on the case. The reporters had filled in the blanks to suit their own needs instead of reporting the facts. "Lead story, girl tortured and killed, more to come at six." He hated when they used the dead for ratings. No, he didn't need to watch the news again tonight.

Reaching for his cell phone, he wanted to call Mia, but decided against it. He started to dial Louie's number and stopped. Tonight, even when Mia had been here, and now alone, he couldn't share the heartbreak or misery he lived with every minute of every day. Unless a person experienced it, they couldn't fully understand it. Damn, the last thing he wanted to feel before sleep was broody. *Maybe I should have the second drink after all.* Debating whether it was worth getting up for, he decided no. In the end he turned on his side and forced his mind to rest.

Chapter 4

Tired and cranky after tossing and turning all night, he got up and made coffee. He didn't want to eat or go for his run, but Brigh needed to go out, so he summoned up some energy and headed to the sidewalk. After the run he fed the dog, showered, and dressed before heading into the station. Two of the night shift detectives approached him.

"A little early even for you, Jake," Detective Williams said.

Jake lifted his wrist, checked the time, then did a double take. It was only five-thirty in the morning. He grunted to Williams and McMahon, and then continued on to his office. More coffee was what he needed. It was going to be one of those days he'd have to load up on caffeine and sugar to survive. He dropped his briefcase on his desk, grabbed his mug, and programmed his first cup strong. Inhaling the aroma, he hoped the coffee would clear his fuzzy brain. Lack of sleep wasn't anything new to him, though this case might push his limits.

He rang the captain's office, discovered he hadn't arrived yet and left him a voicemail. Stalling—that's what he was doing with the evaluations. He decided to knock them out before he got too deep into the Carren case. When he got to the last one, someone knocked on his door.

"Come in."

"Hey, I heard you got here early. Did Mia kick you out?"

"No, Louie, she didn't kick me out. Mia left early last night at my request." Jake watched Louie's reaction and almost laughed.

"You guys fighting again?"

"No. Last night…damn." He rubbed a hand over his face, pushed up out of his chair and started pacing. "I needed to be alone. I might have hurt her feelings. I didn't use a lot of tact when I told her."

"Why are you intentionally sabotaging your relationship with her?"

"I'm not."

"Yeah, you are. You couldn't get a better woman, Jake."

"This isn't the time or the place. If you want to grab a beer after work, I'll tell you what's going on in my mind."

"I wish I could, but I'm on kid duty again tonight."

"Why don't we do what we need to do here, and around three continue to work the case at the bar?"

"Why don't you come over tonight?"

"I don't want anyone to overhear us. It's private." And maybe Louie would open up about his problem, too. Jake watched as understanding dawned on Louie. "Thanks."

"I have the spreadsheets completed. When do you want to review them?" Louie asked, changing subjects.

"I'm finishing up the last of my evaluations. Once I turn them in, we'll review the files. Does anything stick out at you?"

"No, not on the surface."

"What do you mean not on the surface?"

"You'll see when we go over everything later."

Louie left the office.

* * * *

A final comment typed on the last evaluation had him sighing with relief. The intercom on his desk buzzed, jarring him from his thoughts.

"Make it quick. I have ten minutes before my next meeting." Captain McGuire's voice filled his office. Before he could reply Shamus hung up.

Jake grabbed his coffee and the evaluations then headed to McGuire's office. Shamus sat at his desk, his head buried in paperwork. Captain Shamus McGuire carried his military background in his posture, running his squad the same way. He commanded respect from his men and gave it back. He'd done his time on the streets but could play politics with the best of them. McGuire's square face looked like it had been in a knife fight.

"My wife used my razor," he offered by way of explanation for the cuts on his face.

Jake made a mental note to keep his out of Mia's reach.

"What can I do for you?" McGuire said.

Jake brought McGuire up to date then returned to his office, surprised to find Louie in his chair with his feet up on his desk.

"Comfortable?" At least Louie had the grace to look embarrassed.

"Sorry, needed a quiet space for a few minutes."

Jake pushed Louie's feet off his desk and sat down after Louie vacated the chair. "Before we hit the road again, let's review the spreadsheet."

Jake turned his attention to his email after Louie left his office. He opened it, read it, then printed out the spreadsheet. Louie had come through again. Jake was amazed at the information he'd gathered in such a short time. He'd used the file Missing Persons had put together along with information he dug up on the women.

Twenty-one columns, which included date gone missing, age, hair color, eye color, height, weight, occupation, when each victim's announcement hit the paper, their wedding dates, officiating clergy, photographer, church, if they exercised, what club they used, dwelling (lived alone or with family), blood type, where they were last seen, colleges they attended, nationality, if they had memberships to any organizations, employers, and sports they participated in. The only thing missing, Jake mused, was their daily bowel movement.

"Where did you get all this information? Most of this wasn't in the original files."

"I called the families and asked," Louie said over his cup.

"Tell me what you got from all this."

Louie pulled one of Jake's visitor chairs around the desk and sat next to Jake. "See the announcement dates?"

"Yes."

"Most hit the papers in March and April, only one appeared in February. I…" Louie hesitated.

"Finish your thought." Jake glanced up from the spreadsheet.

"My guess, he's finding them there. The individual announcements carry pictures of the women. I also checked with each family to see if the women had Facebook pages or the same Internet provider. Only two of the girls belonged to Facebook. He's not finding them there."

Jake scratched his head, gazed at the spreadsheet then glanced back at Louie. "Did Missing Persons miss this the first time through?"

"There were different detectives for the first two cases, then Brian Kelly caught the third and fourth ones. He's the one who made the connection, but he retired last year. He pointed me in this direction. I dug deep for the details and gossip. You know it makes my day."

Something still bothered Jake. Why hadn't the first two detectives put this together? He had dealt with corruption in Missing Persons before. Was this the same? Or was it sloppy detecting? Either way, it was a gross injustice. Would Missing Persons' new lieutenant extend him the courtesy of examining the personnel files of the detectives who'd been assigned to the case?

"Let's check the demographics on the circulation of the paper to see how far it reaches."

The research showed the majority of the paper's circulation was within a fifty-mile radius. It didn't narrow down their search at all. The paper also had deliveries as far as Florida and Arizona. Must be for people who moved away and still wanted to see what went on in their hometown. They'd have to eliminate the out-of-towners eventually. No small task, as it would be more than two thousand people. Why the hell did they need to read about people they left behind? Every nerve in his body told him the killer lived right here in Wilkesbury.

"Go to the newspaper and reach out to the editor in chief. See if he can give us a list of their subscribers . We'll do a search against all the names associated with the victims."

"You're an optimist. They won't give us their subscriber list without a warrant or a bribe."

"If we ask nice, he will. If not, promise him we'll contact him directly when we get the next new piece of information on the case, an hour before anyone else receives it. They also own Channel 71."

"A bribe." Louie grinned, rubbing his hands together.

Chapter 5

Three months ago
June 7

The heat built in the car. Even with the windows open, sweat dripped into his eyes. How much longer could she exercise in this freakin' humidity? The damn air conditioning in the car wasn't doing much but overheating the car. *I don't have all damn day. Where is she?* He stared at her picture in the paper for the thousandth time. It didn't do her justice. This time, he'd found her. *Ah, Ciara, after all this time. The hair, the eyes, all perfect—soon, we'll be married.*

His bottle of water had gone warm. *Piss*, he thought, though he still drank it. Motion at the front of the gym caught his eye and had him recapping the water bottle. *Here she is.* He would wait her out. She was always oblivious. *Oh, my Ciara.* He followed her out of the parking lot. He'd been tailing her for weeks now. Next, she would drive home or to the other man's house.

The paper didn't list me as the fiancé. Why?

Her schedule didn't vary. Tonight, she went home. Pulling into a space on the other side of the road from her house he watched to see if she would go out again. Forty-five minutes later the "fiancé" showed up. What a boring existence they led. He would rescue her. After another thirty minutes, he called it quits. *Only one more month to go, then I can claim her as my own.* He wrote the time and activity into his notebook, carefully placing it back in his glove compartment before driving away.

* * * *

Present day
September 2

It was a good walk to the newspaper from the police station, but Louie didn't mind. He needed the air and time to throw around his thoughts and organize them. But they kept returning, not to the poor murdered girl, but the fight he had with Sophia last night. After seventeen years of marriage, they'd fought more this week than ever before. As he stepped out into the street without looking—a horn blasted and shot his mind back to the present.

He walked through the double doors of the newspaper building. A guard at the front door stopped him. After presenting his shield, Louie asked for the editor in chief. He waited in the lobby for a good fifteen minutes before a young woman came to escort him up. It took all his willpower to rein in his annoyance as he followed her to an elevator. On the top floor they walked out into another reception area. A long console desk staffed by two women faced them.

"Go right back," one of the receptionists said.

The hallway ended at large double doors. His companion knocked. Without waiting for an answer, she entered, motioning him in. His first impression of the man—*he's a pompous ass*. The editor's slicked-back deep black hair had obviously been dyed in an attempt to camouflage his age, which Louie placed in the late forties. There was a large cigar burning in an ashtray. The man he assumed was Wilson kept talking into the phone. Without being asked, Louie took a seat to wait out the guy. From what he could grasp of the conversation, it was trivial. Blanking his expression, Louie quietly continued to observe him. Wrinkled white shirt gone dingy, tie loose, stained with some kind of red sauce, all stretched over an extended belly. He pegged him as divorced.

The man hung up his desk phone and asked, "What can I do for you, officer?"

"It's Sergeant Romanelli and you are?"

"Ed Wilson."

Louie nodded. "I'm here to officially request your cooperation in the Carren murder."

"What's in it for me?"

Pompous or not, the guy wasn't stupid. "Justice and the American way."

"Cute. What's in it for me?"

"You didn't ask what information I need."

"We're negotiating, son, the information part comes later." Wilson gave him a toothy smile.

Louie studied the guy. He hated to be called "son" by anyone. It was disrespect disguised as endearment. He figured he was being goaded and ignored it. It took a lot to contain his temper. "I see." Louie sat quietly. Wilson started to fidget. He who flinches first, loses. *Christ, Jake should be here doing this, not me. He's better at handling this kind of negotiation.*

"Sergeant, you want something from me, I want something from you. Let's not waste each other's time."

"Okay, we would like a list of your subscribers."

"Is that all?" The sarcasm in Wilson's voice didn't go unnoticed.

"Yes, and in return I'm willing to give you an update on the case the next time something new turns up, an hour before any other paper or channel gets it. "

Louie watched Wilson process the information. A bevy of emotions ran across his face, probably converting the rating points to dollars.

"I want a two-hour notice before any other channel." Wilson picked up his cigar and started chewing on the end.

"Can't do it. You more than anyone should understand how information leaks. I can guarantee an hour only."

"Two or no deal."

"No deal then. I want you to understand I'll be offering this deal to Gwenn Langley at Channel 5 next. I'm sure with her research skills she'll be able to cull the information I need." Louie got up and turned to leave, and Wilson cleared his throat.

"Sit down, Sergeant. You give up too fast."

"Not giving up. I just don't have time to dick around," Louie said.

He hated negotiating with the likes of Wilson.

"One question."

"What?"

"How do I know I can trust you to follow through with the deal?" Wilson asked.

"Because I'm giving you my word. But understand, it's a one-time offer," Louie said, staring Wilson in the eye.

"One time?"

"Yes, the next time something of importance turns up, you get it first."

"One more question. Why didn't you go to Hayes?" Wilson asked.

Louie considered toning down his answer, but decided to go with the truth. "He's as annoying as a pimple on my ass."

Wilson was still laughing as he steered Louie to his IT room and introduced him to the head of the department, Steve Morgan. Before he walked away he pulled Louie aside.

"I have your word, Sergeant." Wilson held out his hand. Louie took it. "This information is for the department's use only?"

"You have my word, Wilson. It will be locked up every night."

"I look forward to doing business with you."

* * * *

Jake grabbed Louie's spreadsheets. The lead he gave him this morning was good, but the paper had thousands of subscribers. How would they narrow it down in this lifetime? Louie hadn't filled in where each woman intersected with the other. While he waited for him to get back, Jake started matching anything any of them had in common.

For the most part, the job was tedious. Some days Jake wished for a nice rowdy arrest to get his fists bloody. *Cop humor,* he thought as he pushed it from his head. He stood up then reached over his head to stretch out the kinks in his back. Deep in thought, he walked to the coffee machine to brew a cup in the hopes it would clear out the cobwebs. While he watched the fluid drip into his cup, he listened as familiar footsteps approached his office.

"Come in, Louie. You want a cup?"

"Yes."

Jake made Louie a cup as he continued to talk. "Here's what I came up with while you were at the paper. By the way, how'd it go there?"

"Wilson's going to cooperate. He took the bribe," Louie said.

"I expected nothing less," Jake said in an amused tone. "Let's check your spreadsheet before we head out for that beer."

Louie sat down at Jake's conference table in a chair facing the door. He set his cup down.

"Louie, move your ass. That's my seat."

"Christ, you've gotten bossy since your promotion."

"My office, my choice," Jake said, wanting his flank covered.

He handed Louie the legal pad where he'd made his notes. Louie studied the connections. Jake wondered if he'd find any more intercepts. Scribbling in the margins of the notepad, Jake waited Louie out and let his mind wander.

What time is it? He nearly jumped out of his seat. *I haven't called Mia yet today. I should've called her first thing this morning after my attitude last night. Freak, I'm losing it.*

Louie scowled at Jake. "There's a small pattern here, but it doesn't connect to all of them."

Chapter 6

"The photographers move from company to company or freelance for the highest bidder. The videographer Carl Pisani is connected to victims one, two and five and at one time or another he's worked for all the photographers."

"I see that, but no connection to the other two. It'd be interesting to see when he worked for the others."

A check of the time told Jake the downtown traffic would be a nightmare. "It would. You have his contact information?"

"Yes."

"It's your lead, give him a call and make the appointment for ten tomorrow morning."

While Louie was on the phone, Jake entered his conclusions on a new spreadsheet attached to Louie's original one.

"The other connections are ambiguous. With each one only two of the victims connect at any point. Then you take the age difference. Five years is a big separation at that age. It washes away the connections unless the coloring is what matters to the killer," Jake said.

"It has to be their resemblance to one another," Louie said, scratching his head. "It's the only common denominator in all five."

"You're right. If you arrange their engagement pictures in a group side by side and take a quick glance you wouldn't be able to tell the difference." Jake walked to his window. The street below was filled with kids getting out of UConn and the local grammar school. It was a perfect summer day in the beginning of September. Next month the leaves would change color and litter the ground.

Somewhere out there this guy's walking around, mingling with everyone on a daily basis and nobody has a clue he's possibly killed at least five times. When he's caught, they'll say he was a normal guy. Who was this bastard and what set him off?

"Let's head out now, this way you're on time for kid duty."

* * * *

They fought traffic as they headed out of the downtown area. In the bar parking lot Jake paced while waiting for Louie to arrive. He watched Louie pull in and back up three times before he put his car into park and get out. *A man old before his time,* he thought. Jake started walking toward the door.

"Hey, wait up," Louie called.

"I've been waiting. Who taught you how to park?"

"I shut everything off before I get out," Louie said as he caught up.

Jake held back his comment. They'd picked an out-of-the-way bar that wasn't frequented by cops. He wanted to be away from prying eyes. This little Irish pub owned by a man from Dublin gave you the feel of Ireland. He liked it and was familiar with most of the patrons, who had been his parents' friends.

"I stick out like a sore thumb here," Louie complained, referring to his Italian coloring.

A scattering of bar patrons waved when Jake and Louie walked in. Jake took the bar stool farthest from them all. Sean, the bartender and owner, put a beer in front of each of them.

"What's up, Jake?"

"Same old, Sean."

A discreet man, Sean walked to the other side of the bar. *Okay, let's do it.* "This is going to drive you nuts, but I'm not sure my relationship with Mia will run the full course." It was a half-truth. But he needed an opening to approach Louie's problem. He was surprised when Louie didn't jump right in to give his opinion. Jake sat silently while he waited for his response.

"I'm not the person to talk to. You should speak to a professional." Louie put his hand up to silence Jake when he started to speak. "It's not Mia you're having a problem with…it's unresolved issues about Eva. You've never dealt with her death. You always have to prove you're the strongest, the bravest, and it isn't working anymore. Before you totally commit to Mia or to any other woman, you need to address this issue."

To keep quiet, Jake lifted the glass to his mouth to give him time to respond. His intentions to help Louie had backfired on him. Louie's words jabbed at him.

"I don't want to talk to the department shrink."

"I don't blame you. She's off. Why not talk to my priest? He's great, Jake, and he's discreet."

Louie gave him the perfect opening. "Why aren't you speaking to him then?" The surprise on Louie's face was priceless.

"Was this a ploy to get me to open up?" Louie pushed his beer away and stood up.

"Sit down." Jake put his hand on his partner's arm. "No, I need to sort everything out. We've always helped each other, why not this time?"

"Because this is a first, and I can't figure out how to handle it. It's driving me nuts," Louie raised his voice. The other patrons gave them a cursory glance before going back to their drinks..

"Did LJ do something wrong? We can fix it, if he did," Jake asked, concerned.

"No, the kids are great. It's…" Louie slugged back his beer. "Sophia got a job," he blurted out.

With several jokes on his tongue, Jake bit down hard to keep them from popping out. It was obvious his friend was in pain. Louie's agony washed over him. He chose his words with care.

"A lot of women work. Is it interfering at home?"

"I'm a good provider. She doesn't need to work."

"Louie, it probably has nothing to do with you or need. She's probably doing it for herself."

"I knew you wouldn't understand."

"Don't shut me out. The kids are growing up nicely. LJ's a teenager now, Marisa's in middle school and Carmen's starting to come into his own. You both did a great job there. Maybe—just maybe, she needs something to engage her mind now that they're all involved with school and their friends."

"But that's not the whole problem. The problem is who she's working for." *He's mad as hell,* Jake thought. "Who is it?"

"She's working for that deviant…" Jake watched in amazement as Louie's face went from olive to puce. "She's working for that *stronzo* lawyer Richie Malone."

He'd been friends with Louie long enough to understand the Italian word for asshole. And he was correct. Richie Malone was a *stronzo* and more.

"Why him? Didn't you warn her about his sexual harassment cases?"

"Of course I did. When I asked her why him, she said and I quote, 'Because he's the only person who offered me a job, after I've been out of the workforce for seventeen years.' Can you believe it?"

Jake had no answer for Louie. Yeah, the guy was a predator, but Sophia could take care of herself. Louie had made sure of it. Then it dawned on him. Sophia was working nights.

"Why are you watching the kids at night?" Jake asked.

"She's working on a big project, which has a deadline. It requires overtime. I'm telling you, Jake, I don't trust him."

"Well, you need to make an unscheduled visit to the office. Act like it's a truce and bring her dinner. This tells the guy she's your wife and to stay away, or else."

"Good idea. Maybe I'll flash my gun at him," Louie quipped.

"Don't be obvious about it, for God's sake. Pop in at unexpected times to put his guard up."

"Then Sophia will think I don't trust her, which I do. It's the aberrant bastard I don't trust."

"I see your dilemma. Did you explain calmly to Sophia about the charges levied against him by other women?" Jake asked again.

"I tried, but we wound up yelling at each other before I could finish."

"Why don't you let me try?"

"I don't…" Louie buried his face in his hands and groaned. "You know what? Sure. She respects your opinions. Thanks, Jake."

"Not a problem. Thanks for being here when I needed you."

"Freaking relationships," Louie said, as he cocked his head in the bartender's direction and held up two fingers.

* * * *

Their mistake was staying for the second beer. The mayor strutted in, followed by his entire entourage. Jake couldn't stand the lying ass-kisser. Mayor Velky had tried to block Jake's promotion. Unfortunately, Jake still had to deal with the guy.

"It's a little early for drinking, Lieutenant. Sitting down on the job?" The mayor sneered as he walked to Jake with his hand out, like he'd want to touch the bastard. Jake had no choice but to accept it, though when he caught Sean's eye Jake had to fight not to laugh at his expression.

Grinding his teeth together, he held back the first thing that came to his mind. Instead he said, "Mayor, I'd have to ask you the same thing."

Their mutual dislike was palpable. This wasn't his usual joint. How did the mayor end up here?

"What have you got on the murdered girl?"

Asshole! This wasn't the time or the place for that question.

"Not much, sir. We're actually working the case now," Jake nodded at Louie, whom the mayor totally ignored.

"I don't want bullshit. I want answers."

"With all due respect, we've had the case less than twenty-four hours."

"With all due respect, Jake, it's been five years," the mayor shot back.

His anger bubbled over, burned a path up his neck to his face, the heat scorching his skin. "It's been less than thirty hours since this investigation came into my department, before yesterday it was a Missing Persons case."

The mayor ignored Jake and turned to his party. "Make a note, Brent. I need to see the commissioner and the chief to plan our strategy on this case. I don't want or need any bad publicity in an election year."

"I'm sure Miss Carren didn't get murdered to foil your reelection plans," Jake murmured.

"What was that, Lieutenant?"

What the hell. "I said, I'm sure Miss Carren didn't plan to ruin your chances of reelection." He stared the mayor down.

"It's not easy, Lieutenant, to keep this city in a good light. I love Wilkesbury and two years is not enough time to make a difference. A man needs at least four years to accomplish anything."

"I understand your position perfectly, Mayor," Jake said.

He figured the mayor could interpret the comment any way he wanted. *This pain in my ass is going to insinuate himself into my investigation. Velky plans on using the victims as his stepping-stone to another two years. Give me strength.*

"I'm sure we'll be seeing more of each other. Take care, Lieutenant. Sergeant."

Jake watched the mayor walk over to the table his groupies had commandeered. "You hear what he didn't say, Louie?"

"Yeah, he's playing to the press. What else is new?"

"Besides that, he's going to be interfering in our investigation. Let's blow this joint." Jake signaled Sean to settle up their bill.

"Yeah, the stench in here is unbearable," Louie muttered for Jake's ears only.

Sean approached. "The Honorable Mayor," Sean said, his voice overflowing with sarcasm, "settled your bill."

"Christ, Sean. Why did you let him?"

"I had no choice. I can't afford to piss him off. It's bad for business."

On his way out, though it killed him, Jake thanked the mayor for the drink.

Chapter 7

Jake decided to fix a nice dinner as a peace offering to Mia. When she arrived an hour later he set her to making the salad. Together they worked in quiet harmony as Brigh sat at their feet hoping for scraps to either be tossed to her or dropped. The minute they sat down to dinner his cell phone rang. He checked the caller ID, apologized to Mia, stood and walked from the room to take the call.

"Yeah, Cap."

"You ran into the mayor this afternoon?"

Damn it. "We did. Louie was with me." Jake held the phone from his ear as McGuire yelled into it. It was a rare thing for Shamus to raise his voice. What the hell had the mayor said?

"What's wrong?"

"What's wrong? I'll tell you what's wrong, Jake. You're in charge of a high-profile case—and you spend the afternoon drinking in a dive bar. The mayor's throwing it in the commissioner's and the chief's faces. He's asking them how we can let a compromised cop handle such a sensitive case. That's what's wrong."

Jake's barely restrained temper crawled to the surface. He bit it down. *I shouldn't have to explain myself.*

Jake fought to keep his voice even when he responded. "I'm not a compromised cop, Shamus," he said between clenched teeth. He watched Mia inch her way into the living room.

"I understand that, but Velky is trying to use anything he can get to his advantage. Ralph Miller and his brother belong to Velky, always have."

Why is it, when a good cop gets a bad one off the force, the good cop pays for it with his entire career?

"Christ, Miller doesn't belong on the force any more than his brother did."

"Again, I agree. I need you in the chief's office at eight sharp. This is a sensitive case—if possible, I want it to be the end of Velky and Miller once and for all. Got it?"

"Yes." McGuire had thrown his support in Jake's corner. He let out the breath he'd been holding.

"And don't have any more midday meetings at the bar."

* * * *

Mia had listened in on Jake's side of the conversation. It wasn't good. Jake's coloring had gone from fair to lobster red in less than ten seconds. *Well, I guess I'll see him blow.* Even when they broke up, he had contained his temper. Louie always made jokes about Jake's legendary Irish temper but she'd yet to see it in full force. She walked back into the kitchen, picked up their wine glasses, and carried them into the living room.

Jake sat on the sofa hunched over, his head in his hands. When he raised his head his face held a distant expression...or was it surprise? Deep in thought, he probably hadn't heard her walk back in. Mia wanted to wrap her arms around him and make whatever was bothering him go away. But she held back.

"What is it, Jake?"

He stood, paced, and laid it all out for her. *Wound tighter than a caged tiger*, she thought. Mia listened, making mental notes here and there. She watched him down his wine like medicine when he finished speaking.

Silently, she sat, analyzing his report, because it was that, a report. Jake had relayed the facts in a neutral tone, his face at times void of expression. It amazed her how he slipped into his cop persona when needed, his tone and attitude detached from the situation as he spoke.

"You're not going to let them take you off the case, are you?"

"No."

"How are you going to handle the chief tomorrow?"

"I'm going to have to sleep on it. If Velky wants to play dirty, I'll find something to smear his name for the election."

"Call him on it."

"I can't. Technically he's my boss. The captain and the chief can't protect me all the time. They have their own careers to guard. As for the commissioner, his job is a political appointment, which sucks, because he runs the department. Fortunately for me, he was appointed by the last mayor."

Mia studied Jake.

"Sit down next to me." She patted the sofa.

"These cases are important to me because of the victims and their families, Mia. And that son of a bitch is going to use them to get reelected." He plopped down beside her.

"You can't let something you don't have any control over bother you to this extreme. Move forward. Work your case, keeping the victims, not the mayor, out front. If I were you I'd contact a trusted media person and feed them a little. Use them to your advantage.

"After that, I would find someone you trust, not within the department, and talk to them. I can give you names of good doctors who you can work with, both personally and professionally."

She stopped talking to let him process her words. One of the things she liked most about Jake—he'd really listen before he'd reply. He'd consider their opinions and then make his decisions based on all the facts. She thought it his strongest attribute.

"You think I need a psychiatrist?"

Mia searched in her heart for the answer. It was a risk telling him the truth. There was a possibility it could affect their relationship going forward. A chance she had to take.

"You need someone you can trust to talk to. This case brings back personal demons for you. How much more can you take?"

"I don't know," he whispered.

"I don't either. I'm here if you need me, but I understand I'm not the one you can talk to." She took his hand. "I'm not going anywhere."

He leaned his head on her shoulder. She wrapped her arms around him, held him tight, as she rested her head on his. She hoped he'd seriously consider her advice because Jake was stretched to his limit.

"I guess dinner's cold by now. Do you want to go out?" Jake asked. Not exactly the answer Mia wanted.

"No, I'll reheat what's there. When you pick someone to talk to, I'll make sure it's the right person."

"Louie told me the same damn thing today."

Mia's laughter broke the tension in the room.

* * * *

Louie sat in his car outside Sophia's office, debating whether to follow through with Jake's advice. He knew it would piss Sophia off royally when he walked into her office. Seventeen years, and they'd never been this far apart on any subject. It was killing him.

He questioned his judgment as the grease seeped through the takeout bag. Sophia wouldn't eat this shit. Louie put the car in gear, drove down the block, cursed, then turned it around and parked in the same spot again. He was overthinking this as the food got cold. He dialed Jake's cell.

"Louie?"

"I'm sitting outside her office with some fast food, which is going cold. Should I go in?"

"I'm going to pass you to Mia for that question. I don't trust my own judgment right now."

"Louie, what's up?" Mia asked.

He told her everything—his feelings—his frustrations—Jake's advice. It felt good to speak about it. Hopefully, Mia, being a woman, had the right answer. He should've thought of her sooner.

"Don't go in tonight. Make a date with Sophia to bring her dinner. That way she won't feel like you're checking up on her. Don't break her trust, Louie. Once you do, it will be hard to get it back."

Louie thought about Mia's answer for a minute. It coincided with his instincts. He felt his insides relax as the fist of indecision released its hold.

"Thanks, Mia." He hung up, turned his car on and slipped it into gear, then drove straight home. Relieved he hadn't made a fool of himself tonight.

* * * *

Louie walked in his front door and went directly into the living room, toward his easy chair. He dropped down into it.

"What's the matter, Dad?"

"Nothing, LJ, I'm exhausted."

"It's the thing with Mom working, isn't it? You guys are fighting a lot lately."

Out of the mouths of babes, he thought. Louie rubbed his eyes as he searched for the right answer for his oldest son. Fifteen should be an age of carefree thoughts and actions, not his parents' troubles. This was his and Sophia's problem.

"Marriage has its ups and downs, right now your mother and I are dealing with some issues as we try to make her new schedule work. It's nothing."

"We're not stupid, Dad. Even Marisa and Carmen can feel something's up. Why does her working bother you? A lot of my friends' mothers work. It's no big deal."

"Well…it's complicated."

"You're not going to get a divorce over this, are you?"

"Lord, no. Where did that come from?" It hadn't dawned on him what the fighting was doing to the kids.

"I never saw you and Mom fight like this before."

"Things should be getting better soon. I'm maturing." Louie offered his son a smile.

"Funny, Dad." LJ got up, walked to him and patted his back before he walked from the room.

It was easy for children to accept change. I wish I was as flexible. Would Sophia tell me if her boss made a pass after all the idiotic things I've said and done? I certainly hope so. I love her beyond reason. She should understand that after all this time.

Work would distract him from watching the clock. He opened the Nadia Carren file.

* * * *

Sophia walked in around nine. He saw the exhaustion in her face. With a promise to himself not to say anything derogatory, he put his file down, stood, and kissed her hello.

"Long day?"

"Yes."

"Do you want me to fix you something to eat?" He watched her watch him. "What?"

"What's going on, Louie?"

He could respond two ways: one, on the defensive, or two, apologize. It was always a difficult thing for him to admit when he was wrong. But he needed harmony back in his life.

"I'm sorry for being such a jerk lately." He kissed her.

"I was also. Truce?" Nobody understood him like his Sophia. Thank God, she'd forgiven him for now.

"No truce. I surrender. I love you. I'm being ridiculous." He took her into his arms and held her to comfort himself.

"I'm doing this for me, Louie. I needed a self-esteem boost, can you understand that? It's not a reflection on us."

He felt better they were speaking again. But the ache in his stomach hadn't gone away—the exact same pain he always got before something went awry.

Chapter 8

With the morning meeting with the brass hanging over his head, Jake woke early. Shamus understood the bullshit the mayor was pulling, but would the chief or the commissioner also understand? One thing he didn't need during a high-profile investigation was the petty bullshit the Honorable John Velky liked to pull. Velky was a puffed-up, egotistical, useless human being. One of these days he would get what he deserved. Wouldn't it be rich if the mayor turned out to be the killer? The thought struck him as funny. It wasn't possible. The man didn't have any balls.

At seven, he walked directly to the coffee machine in his office. Jake had one hour to prepare for the meeting. The best way, he thought, was to present the facts in the case. Being the better man, he decided to ignore the pettiness of the mayor's actions. Jake pulled out his cellphone and scrolled through his contacts until he reached Gwenn Langley.

Ah, he had fond memories of Gwenn. He hoped Gwenn had fond memories of him. Her help would be crucial to his investigation. He trusted her, even though he knew they'd use each other to achieve their individual goals. She was a reporter he respected. He'd honor his deal with Wilson. After he gave Wilson the information on the next break in the case, he'd deal with Gwenn going forward.

Louie walked into his office whistling. Well, at least someone was in a good mood this morning. "What's up?" Jake asked, as he turned from his computer.

"Me and Sophia are doing better."

"Good." Jake grinned, turning his attention back to his screen.

Right at home, Louie helped himself to a cup of coffee. Jake ignored him as he continued to type up the facts in the case with the hope the commissioner would not try to pull the file from him.

"Why are you typing furiously this early in the morning?"

"I have an eight o'clock meeting with the commissioner, the chief, and the captain."

"When did this come about? And why didn't you tell me? I would've had my report ready to hand in with yours," Louie asked, annoyed.

"You're not invited to the meeting. Shamus called last night. The mayor reported us being in the bar yesterday afternoon. He's trying to wrangle the case from us."

"That bastard! That fat ignoramus…that *stronzo*." Anger spilled from every pore as Louie's temper exploded.

"Calm down. I can handle this. It's a ploy to turn the Carren case over to Miller. I'm not going to let that happen, nor will the captain," Jake reassured Louie.

"Miller couldn't find his way out of a paper bag, plus he doesn't have the rank."

"The mayor's only concern is his own career. I won't have him leaping to the governorship on Nadia's body if I can help it."

"Good luck."

Jake checked his watch and printed out the report before he headed up to the meeting.

* * * *

The elevator creaked as it opened into a wide, spacious area. On this floor there were only four offices: the commissioner's, the chief's, the media liaison's, and the police psychiatrist's. As if having the psychiatrist's office on this floor would encourage the ranks to talk to her. Cops only went there if ordered. He'd never been.

Jake knocked on the last door.

"Come in." He couldn't place the voice.

Well, well, well, the gang's all here. In the center of the room, sitting at a large, dark, wooden desk, the commissioner held court. The captain and the chief were already seated. Jake took the only empty chair, situated between the chief and McGuire. Trapped, he felt the office walls close in around him. Were they flanking him or crucifying him?

Though he projected great height while sitting, the commissioner actually stood at a mere five-ten. His solid girth showcased his two-thousand-dollar suit. Jake noted in cop speak the commissioner's attributes—red/green, one-ninety. Blake was not someone to battle with—his alliance could break or make a cop. Many sought it out, mostly in the wrong way. Kissing his ass didn't get you an alliance. Respect, hard work, and honesty did the trick. Jake didn't fear him, he respected him. Commissioner Blake's position was a political one—an appointment from the former mayor—an honest mayor he would have gone to the wall for.

"Jake, let's get right to this," Blake said.

He decided to give his report standing and pushed from the chair. "Commissioner, the mayor has no right to complain. Louie and I put in more than ten hours each day as homicide detectives. Yesterday alone we were on the job at five-thirty a.m. We took the 'what if' part of the job to O'Donnell's a little after three p. m., which put us on the job for about ten and a half hours. What part of that does the mayor have a problem with?"

"You're angry and you have a right to be. But the man is not only after your job, but mine as well. Let's play this one by the book." He held up his hand when Jake went to interrupt him. "It sucks, but in an election year you have to make sure you're not the poor unfortunate slob the politicians use for their own gain. Consider yourself spoken to—now, update us on your investigation."

He updated the three of them. The chief and Shamus left the commissioner's office first. As Jake reached the door the commissioner called out to him.

"Jake, close the door for a second."

He stood at attention and waited for the other shoe to drop.

"I respect you and your talent. You're a great cop and more importantly, an honest one. You make this department proud—but you've made enemies. I understand it was in the course of your duty. Dirty cops somehow garner loyalty. Watch your back, because someday I can see you sitting in the chief's chair."

Numb, Jake was at a loss for words. In both cases, he wouldn't change how he'd processed the evidence.

"And, Jake, next time pick a place out of town to unwind."

"I thought we did." The commissioner had given him a lot to mull over. Not only about his future, but the reason he now had a target on his back.

* * * *

"So, how'd it go?" Louie asked, following Jake as he passed his desk without slowing down.

"Fine, Louie." Jake didn't want to talk in the bullpen. "I need a few minutes before we head out to interview the people on our list."

Jake closed the door in his face. He needed time to process the real reason this morning's meeting had been called. Neither the chief nor Shamus had said a word. Jake began to type a short email to Shamus but changed his mind. *CYA,* he thought. He called Shamus and asked for a meet.

"Come to my house at eight tonight." The phone went dead in his hand.

Jake called the private number for Gwenn Langley on his cell phone. Cops were nosy by nature. He decided not to take a chance and call on the station's line. Who knew who might be eavesdropping?

"Long time, no hear, Jake," she said in her buttery on-air voice. "I'm on my way out to a story. What's up?"

No-nonsense Gwenn. He loved that. "I need to talk to you. In person."

"When?"

"Whenever you're available today," Jake said. A savvy reporter, Gwenn would catch on to the case he was working and their meeting would be business, not personal.

"Can I call you when I'm done with this story?"

"Yes. I'll make myself available."

She hung up without another word. Jake smiled. Two could play the mayor's game.

He took his files to Louie's desk. "Ready? I want to get in as many interviews as possible today," he said for everyone's benefit. Politics was a dirty game, one he'd learned how to play over the years.

He had to remember, Detective Stack had belonged to Missing Persons. Not one of the detectives from his department ever said a word directly to Jake about his pursuit of Stack or his death last month, but Jake had heard the insults and innuendos. He'd find out who was spreading them…he always did.

He walked to the elevator while Louie rushed behind him, shrugging into his jacket. "What's the hurry? I didn't even finish my coffee."

"I need to get out of here," Jake said.

"Are you going to tell me about it?"

"Not now."

Jake jammed his finger on the down button for the elevator. The doors opened, and several officers stampeded off. Most greeted him but a few ignored him and Louie as they stepped in. Mariano's snub hurt the worst. Jake had considered him a good cop. Mariano's switch didn't bode well for

Jake. The elevator jolted to a stop on the main floor before it proceeded to the basement parking garage. He and Louie got off and walked to his car.

Once in the car he filled Louie in on his morning meeting. "Well, it's nice they're backing you up, but…"

"Yeah, but. Something else is going on. I'm meeting Shamus tonight at his house. Hopefully, I'll get the whole story. In the meantime, let's do our jobs. I have a meet with Gwenn later."

"Seriously? Rethinking your relationship with her?"

Jake groaned. He should've known Louie would drag his and Gwenn's past into this.

"No, leave it be. Gwenn's only concerned with her career."

"You live dangerously."

Only Louie would try to make a drama out of nothing, Jake thought. *I hope the meet pays off.*

* * * *

"First up is Carl Pisani, the videographer. According to your spreadsheet he was supposed to work three out of the five weddings."

Jake handed Louie the file. Louie found the address while he concentrated on the road. As they sat at a light waiting on the car in front of them to turn left, some idiot whipped around them and almost hit the car turning in the opposite direction.

"If I had time I'd give that fool a ticket."

Louie ignored him. "Pisani lives in Watertown. I got a number. You want to call ahead?"

"No, let's surprise him." He turned the car around and headed toward Watertown.

Pisani resided in a crumbling old Victorian house set on a dead-end street. Jake knocked several times before he heard someone approach. Carl Pisani filled the doorway, literally. At probably two-seventy, his wide triple chin showed a few days' growth. Jake couldn't imagine the man in front of him moving around a wedding with any grace. When he smiled his teeth showed a lack of interest in dental hygiene. The guy couldn't be more than forty though his face read sixty. Jake immediately felt uneasy about the man. He badged Pisani. Louie did the same.

"What can I do for the Wilkesbury police?" Pisani said as he leaned on the door.

"May we come in, Mr. Pisani?" Jake asked.

Pisani studied them through his screen door before he opened it wider and pointed to the room on his right. Jake scanned the living room. Clutter on the sofas, tables, and floor. Books, pictures, and newspapers everywhere—the room gave off a musty odor. Pisani pushed papers off the chairs to clear a sitting area. Jake decided to stand and took up a position by the fireplace. Louie stood by the room's entrance.

"Mr. Pisani, I need to verify your places of employment in the last five years."

"Why?"

"Five women have gone missing. One has turned up murdered. You were scheduled to work three out of the five weddings for these women. You're a connection we need to investigate."

"How am I connected? I don't interview these couples for their pictures, the photographers do."

"It's how cases are worked," Jake said, offering nothing more. "You were scheduled to be the videographer for Elizabeth Bartholomew, Moira Baudlion, and Nadia Carren…"

"Jesus, you're trying to tie me to the poor girl you found dead yesterday?"

"We're not trying to tie you to anything. Your name came up in three individual cases. We need to eliminate you and your connection."

"When these couples hire a photographer, the photographer suggests they might want a video of their special day. That's where I come in. I work for the photographer, not the couple. If they say yes, then I show up at the wedding and tape the day. It's the first time I see the couple or interact with them."

"You're not given their names beforehand?" Jake asked.

"I get the dates and names, sure, but I've worked for seven different photographers in the last six years. I freelance. Whoever books first gets me. They notify me to reserve the date and time, and the main photographer has the couple sign my contract for the video portion. After they sign, he faxes the contract to me with the information for the church and the reception venue. That's it. The couples leave a check with the photographer for me, half up front as a deposit and the other half due upon delivery of the wedding video. You'd be surprised how often I get stiffed."

He folded and unfolded his hands over his huge belly while he talked. Jake picked up on the nervous tick. He caught Louie's eye and passed the interview over to him. Jake roamed the room.

"Mr. Pisani, are you sure you don't recognize any of the five women? The other two were Shelly Greene and Jerri Roberts," Louie asked.

"I never said I wasn't acquainted with any of them. I've met Jerri Roberts once or twice. I'm friends with her uncle. He's the one who recommended me to her. Jerri referred me to her photographer."

"What's the uncle's name?"

"Robert B. Roberts, but everyone calls him Bobby." Jake noticed Pisani had started sweating.

"Okay, do you have any contact information for him?" Louie wrote down the name.

Jake continued to prowl the room while Louie questioned Pisani. He picked up books, read the titles, put them down, then picked up notepads Pisani had scribbled on. When Jake got to the table in the corner by a reading lamp, Pisani jumped up, practically ran over to him and took the book he'd picked up. Carl placed it face down on the table. Surprised at Pisani's speed, Jake took a mental snapshot of the other books and notepads on the table.

While he was up Pisani got out his address book and gave Louie Bobby Roberts's address and phone number.

Jake kept his expression blank. "Thanks for your time, Mr. Pisani."

"That's it?" Pisani asked.

"For now. If we have any other questions, we'll contact you. Here's my card if you remember anything else."

Outside in the car, Louie said, "What was on the table?"

"One minute, while I jot down some notes." Jake proceeded to write down titles and websites he spotted on the notepads and book covers. When he finished writing, he turned to Louie.

"The book covers were dicey and bordered on the illegal. The guy's into porn big time." Ripping off the top sheet Jake handed it to Louie. "Check out these titles. I wonder if he ever propositioned any of the victims."

Jake put the car into gear. Next on his list were the photography studios and their owners.

"The first site is child pornography. That sick mother...I'll notify Vice," Louie said with disgust.

"Let's hope he's only into reading about it and not using his cameras. I knew there was something off about this guy from the beginning." *You put one pervert away and another follows,* Jake thought.

Chapter 9

Louie got off the phone with Vice and turned toward Jake. He pinched his nose. "It amazes me when we run into freaking creeps like this one. What do they see in children? I swear if one of these degenerates came anywhere near my kids…" he left his thought hanging.

"Yeah, and I'd help."

"It makes me sick."

"Get the address from the file for the closest photography studio tour location?"

"Glamorous You. After this one I need to eat." If he didn't remind Jake, he'd forget about food when involved in a case. *Me, I need my nourishment.* Louie rubbed his stomach.

"If I hear back from Gwenn I'll need to drop you off and meet with her alone."

"Your funeral. I hear she has quite the temper." Louie grinned.

"Give it a freakin' rest, Louie. It's only business, and I'm committed to Mia."

"It was a joke, where's your sense of humor?"

"I lost it when the mayor decided to stick his nose into my case."

"I thought it was our case," Louie said, sarcasm dripping from his voice.

"You know what I meant," Jake said.

Louie backed off. When Jake got in a mood you didn't push him. Although he'd love to be a fly on the wall at Jake and Gwenn's meeting, he'd have to wait to hear all about it from Jake.

The ace television reporter wouldn't be easy on Jake after the way he left their relationship hanging. It was Gwenn's own fault. She had asked to move in with Jake after only a couple of months of dating. He ran faster than a jackal when confronted with a commitment. That was until

Mia came along. Before her, Jake's usual relationship with a woman ran ninety days or less.

Louie scanned the area as Jake pulled into the parking lot behind the building. A commercial area with a few older homes fighting to remain a neighborhood even as the flavor of it changed. The Glamorous You studio took up the first floor of a two-story, aging brick building. They entered through the back. A loud, large bell attached to the door announced their arrival. The long hallway cluttered with frames and poster boards narrowed the walking space, making it a fire hazard. They pushed their way to the front and had to stop several times to right frames they'd knocked over. At the front of the studio a tall, thin man greeted them.

"Ah, you've arrived."

"You were expecting us?" Jake asked.

"Yes, Carl Pisani thought I might get a visit from you."

"Good, that'll speed things up. You're Kevin Farrell?" Louie asked. The man nodded. "You were scheduled to shoot the weddings of Elizabeth Bartholomew and Shelly Greene. Do you remember these women?"

"How could I not? Their disappearances were unfortunate, but I don't see how it has anything to do with me or my business."

Louie went through the same routine with Farrell as he had with Pisani. Explaining connections and asking questions while Jake prowled the shop. His last question got Farrell's attention.

"Is your wife around?"

"No, she's out today. Why?"

"She was scheduled to work both of the weddings with you, according to information supplied by the families."

"My wife is at every wedding with me. She's my assistant and a damn good photographer in her own right. I won't have you upsetting her. This has to do with the girl who was found yesterday, doesn't it?"

"We're investigating the disappearance of four women. Mr. Farrell, we're going to need to interview your wife. When is she available?"

"I'll have her call you."

Back at the car Louie turned to Jake. "Are you leaning toward one of the photographers?"

"No, this murder is more personal. The date of the disappearances is our only clue to the why of it… it has to do with a wedding on the sixth of July, but what year? Damn, maybe the ME will come up with another piece of evidence off the body."

"We can only hope." Louie rescanned the area around the parking lot as they climbed into Jake's car.

* * * *

On the drive to his next interview Jake listened with half an ear to the radio while the case rolled around inside his head. What he told Louie, he believed wholeheartedly—the only clue, the date—was the key to the case, though he didn't understand why yet or where it would lead them.

The last two interviews, Louie had run with the questions. The next one he'd handle. Preoccupied, he answered his phone when it rang and had to slam on the brakes as the light turned red and a pedestrian dodged in front of the car. The old woman threw him the bird.

"Damn, pay attention!" Louie shouted.

"Jake, it's Tim McKay." He pressed his phone between ear and shoulder while he reached into the back seat for his briefcase.

"Doc, I'm driving, hold on while I pull over. Louie's with me. I'm going to put you on speaker." He pulled to the curb once the light turned green. "Okay, go ahead."

"I'll start with the cause of death. Her throat was slit left to right. She suffered tremendously in the weeks before she died. The killer, I'm going to call him he—tortured her. There were electrical burns that had scarred her bones." *Nadia suffered what no human being should*, Jake thought. How did a man turn into a monster? How was he able to do these things to another human being? He tuned back in to McKay's voice. "Whatever he used, he held it against Nadia's skin until it penetrated the surface."

McKay stopped to clear his throat. Jake waited a few moments before he asked, "You there, Doc?"

"Yes. I'm sorry. This one got to me. She was too young… You can't predict when a case might affect you."

"Not a problem, and thanks for your speed on this."

"I'm not done with the entire autopsy, but I wanted to give you my preliminary findings. This will give you something to work with. Before this horrible act of violence, she was a healthy twenty-year-old in excellent condition. He not only used electrical currents, he sliced her skin on the arms, legs and chest area—"

Jake interrupted McKay. "Were they deep cuts or were they for mutilation only?"

"Each one was deep enough to cause pain but not have her bleed out. Different forms of torture were used to prolong her pain. Some of the wounds are close to a month old. Others are only a week old. I personally don't understand how she lived through most of them. My educated guess right now, she's been dead about a week. I'll be able to pinpoint it more closely when I'm finished posting her. The bad news—he washed the body. There were no fibers anywhere."

Jake processed the information while Louie took notes.

"Nothing under her nails, Doc?"

"No, her nails were scraped and washed. The body was expertly cleaned, no trace evidence left behind. The killer knew something about forensics and police procedures."

"Every schmo has some idea how to do it, with the Internet and television supplying information, even if the details are inaccurate. It's making it damn near impossible to catch them."

"So we want everyone to think." Jake heard the smile in McKay's voice. He smiled back. Forensic shows and others like them were produced for entertainment, not accuracy. Most law enforcement officials didn't correct the inaccuracies on purpose. Why assist the criminals in their endeavors?

"Jake, there were two things on the body. On visual exam it was almost missed because of how swollen the wounds were. The killer carved two words on her left breast. 'I do.'"

"Are you sure of the words?" *I guess the media was right. If they got hold of this information they'd have a field day.*

"Yes, and the last piece of information I have for you is…" Jake was glad McKay couldn't see him, because he rolled his eyes at the dramatic pause.

McKay continued. "A symbol has been burned into the bottom of her left foot. I have my assistant searching the Internet for the origin of it or a definition. I'll call you if we hit on anything."

"I'm going to withhold both pieces of evidence from the general file and public. I'll verify with Shamus, but I'm sure he'll agree. Any guesses on what the symbol means?"

"No, not a clue. It could be Greek, Egyptian, or even German for all I can make out. I'm thinking a bird of some kind. I'll call if anything else turns up. I'm still waiting on the lab for the tox report. And Jake, both the 'I do' and the symbol were ante mortem."

"Christ!" Both injuries would have caused a tremendous amount of pain to the victim. Branded like an animal. What kind of cruel asshole did this to another human being? His stomach turned at the thought.

He hung up with McKay and tried to absorb all the information the doc had supplied. Obviously, Louie was doing the same since he hadn't uttered a word. Who did these women represent to this psycho? Though it was too soon to draw a conclusion, he'd bet the house the killer had an ex-fiancée. Had she died? Had she jilted him? Was she incapacitated by an illness or an accident? Jake was sure the marriage had not taken place as planned. *Aw, hell. As with any piece of evidence, it only raised more questions.*

"What jumps out at you?"

"Probably the same thing you're thinking—a jilted groom," Louie said.

"Yeah." He glanced over at Louie.

"The pain Nadia had to endure." Louie rubbed his chin, furrowing his brow at what Jake was sure was the image McKay had put into their heads.

Jake shifted the car into gear and pulled away from the curb, still deep in thought. Halfway to the next photography studio his cell rang again. He handed it to Louie.

"Check the caller ID for me."

"It's Gwenn Langley."

"Great." He pulled back out of traffic and took the phone from Louie. "Thanks for getting back to me, Gwenn."

"Jake, it's a killer of a day. What have you got?"

"I need a meet. I'm not doing this on the phone. I only need fifteen minutes to a half hour of your time."

"I'm in West Hartford right now. How soon can you get here?"

"Give me a half hour. I have to drop off my partner."

"Say hi to Louie for me. I'll see you in a half hour at The Coffee Café by the mall. Are you familiar with it?"

"Yes." Disconnecting the call, he turned the car around and headed to the station to drop Louie off.

* * * *

It took him forty-five minutes to get to the café. Gwenn wasn't happy. As he walked in the door, she turned her wrist up and pointed to her watch. *This is not a good way to start the meet,* he thought. He glanced at his own watch. The morning gone, he'd have to work tonight to catch up.

"Traffic," was all he said as he sat down.

"All the nuts are out today. It must be a full moon. I got stuck in it a couple of times myself." *She's giving me a break. Why?* Jake shifted, crossing his legs to protect the family jewels. Gwenn was only this nice when she needed something.

"I'm working the body we discovered on the train tracks yesterday," Jake started. "I need to have a media go-to and I want it to be you." He stared at her while she processed his statement. To organize his thoughts, he stood and asked, "Do you want another cup?"

"No, sit back down. Why me?"

He'd expected the question and wondered about it himself. Why her indeed? "You're honest. I like your reporting style, and the story and people are important to you. The information I give you can only be released when I give the go-ahead. I need your word you'll agree to my terms."

"So, it will only be a professional relationship?"

"Yes." *Oh boy, here it comes.*

"I see. I don't have a problem with that, Jake, but after we conclude our business today, I have some questions for you on the personal front." It was her turn to stare him down. Jake shifted in his chair to face her head-on.

"Not a problem. First, we promised the next lead to the local paper in exchange for their subscriber list. I can't back out of the deal Louie made. They've given us their list." He watched her take notes as he spoke. "There's this annoying reporter on their paper who's turning up at all my scenes, even before I do. I need to dig out how he does it."

"You're talking about Hayes, right?" Perceptive—it was one of the reasons he liked her.

"Yes. I have no leads at this time, and in and of itself, that's a lead. I hate the term 'Bride Murders' but it seems to be accurate. At this point, it's the only connection we've found between the victims." Jake stopped to give Gwenn a chance to catch up with him as she wrote.

"Is Hayes linked to the killings?"

Leave it to Gwenn. He answered honestly, "I haven't given it much thought, but I will now."

"Do they have photographers, caterers, florists in common?" She thought like a cop, another thing he liked about her.

"One or two have maybe one or two of those vendors in common, but not all five."

"You're assuming all five are dead?"

"Yes, but it's not for release. I think he practiced on the first ones. For some reason he wanted this one found."

"Practiced how?"

"Nadia's body was too clean. All evidence had been washed away," Jake said.

"What is it you need from me?" Gwenn asked.

"You have a way of digging out more information than I can on these victims and their circle of friends and families, without the constraints of the law. Somewhere, somehow, maybe they connect..."

"But they don't, do they?"

"It's not about the individual women but who they represent. I'd bet on it," Jake said.

"Are you wasting my time?"

"No, Gwenn, it's an end we have to tie off. You can be more thorough. I have another angle I'm going to be working."

"What is it?"

"I can't say…" He held his hand up to hold off her interruption. "I can't say right now. Please trust me. If and when I can, you'll be the first I give the information to."

Jake felt her sharp, intelligent, arctic eyes penetrate his skull. A lesser man would've caved.

"What else is going on, Jake?" Intuitive little witch. Another reason they didn't match. Gwenn, always the curious reporter, didn't hold conversations. She held interviews.

"I have the mayor breathing down my neck on this case. He's trying to use Nadia Carren's murder to discredit me and pave his way to the governor's mansion come next fall."

They sat in silence for a few minutes. Jake pointed to her cup. Gwenn put her hand over hers. He went to the counter and ordered a large, black coffee. After paying the girl at the register he walked back to the table.

"Velky's dirty," Gwenn said.

"Yep he is but try to prove it and you'll be as dead as a doorknob."

"Seriously, Jake, those small-town, small-minded, small-dick politicians don't scare me."

"Wilkesbury is a city of one hundred thousand people. It's not a small town. I forgot who I was speaking with. Be careful. He's a nasty piece of work. And, I could use a little shine to keep Velky in his place."

"You do your job. I'll do mine. Now, on the personal front," she said, with a raised eyebrow.

Crap.

"I thought we were moving along nicely, until you bolted. Why?"

How do I answer her? "You wanted to move in, I wasn't ready. The offer scared me."

"Big bad Jake scared. I don't buy it. What's with this new woman? I hear you're serious."

He reached into his mind for an explanation that wouldn't wound her ego. "I met Mia at Louie's picnic and fell hard. I seemed to have no control over it. It was right after you and I cooled down. I never had any intention of getting serious with anyone, Gwenn. Not you or any other woman.

Mia slammed right into me." *Until she shut me down for a month or two before she came back into my life. Not something Gwenn needs to hear.*

"What makes this one special?"

"Everything. I'm not trying to hurt you. I can't put into words what she does to me. She makes me happy, crazy, and sad, sometimes all at the same time. It's wild."

Her intense blue eyes stared at him for a few minutes before she responded. "She's a lucky woman, Jake. I hope she realizes it. If things don't work out…"

They sat in the coffee shop for another fifteen minutes while Gwenn pummeled him with more questions before she got called to another story. Jake felt good about where they had left things.

"Thanks, Gwenn. I'll be in touch," he said, as she rushed off.

Chapter 10

He stopped in at some tattoo parlors on his way back into town. Jake replayed all of the day's interviews and conversations in his head as he drove back to the station. The photographers and the few tattoo parlor employees he had interviewed hadn't given him anything useful. He wondered if the ME had hit on anything pertaining to the symbol. Maybe he should give Tim a call? A quick check of his watch had him swearing. Where had the afternoon gone? He hoped Gwenn wouldn't do anything stupid—like take on City Hall. A well-protected politician, both locally and nationally, John Velky wasn't a man he'd want to see Gwenn ruin her career over.

On the personal front, he thought, she'd handled his explanation well. As he approached the exit for his house, his cell phone played the tune he'd programmed for Louie: "Nag" by The Halos. Jake smiled when he answered.

"How'd it go with Gwenn?" Louie jumped in.

"Fine, why?"

"Don't give me that bull. How bad did she bust your balls?"

"She didn't. The research department at her station is excellent. She can dig deeper into the victims' lives and families for us."

"Oh," Louie said his tone dripping with disappointment.

"What's the matter?" He understood what was bothering Louie. His friend and partner loved gossip and Jake wasn't feeding him.

"Nothing."

"I have another angle I want us to concentrate on—shit." He'd driven past his street. He made a sharp U-turn, turned left onto his street and pulled into his garage.

"What?" Louie pounced on it.

"Nothing. Anyway, as I was saying, let's dig back six or seven years, maybe even ten years with our research. We need to search for brides who fit the same description as the missing women. We have to locate the wedding that wasn't. Are you following my logic?" Jake asked.

"Yeah, it's a good angle. If he started four or five years ago, then logic follows it happened six years ago or more. What happened if he practiced out of town?"

"We have to narrow the search. We'll start with the Wilkesbury paper first, go back ten years and work forward." The excitement buzzed through him. It was the right direction, he could feel it.

"Are you working on it tonight?" Louie asked.

"Yes. And I'll give McKay a call, instead of waiting until tomorrow to see if his searches turned anything up. And I'll have him send me an email with the design on Nadia's foot. This way I can start my own search. I'll be working from home."

"I'll start with ten years back and work forward—check out all the engagement and wedding announcements," Louie said.

"I'll go with five years back and work forward. If McKay has anything for us I'll ring you back."

Jake hung up with Louie then called the ME's office.

"McKay."

"Tim, I'm sorry to bother you this close to the end of the day. Did anything turn up?" Jake asked.

"Nothing yet, it's a crude picture at best—if the wound was allowed to heal we'd have had a better picture. Now, we have to give it our best guess. I'm thinking the tool used was a branding iron for animals. If it turns out I'm right, it has to be a custom job. I searched all kinds of branding tools on the Internet and didn't see anything like it. It's a quality piece of work. All the edges are even and uniform. I'll check for branding irons next," Tim McKay said.

"That gives me a direction to search. I'll vet out people with knowledge of steel work, maybe a tool and die maker?"

"Could be, but don't forget tattoo parlors also brand people," McKay said.

Sometimes these criminals were so smart they were stupid. There weren't many tool and die companies left around here. There used to be over a hundred in the Wilkesbury area alone, now there were about thirty. Tattoo parlors in town numbered in the high forties. Damn, there seemed to be one on every corner. According to Google there were forty-eight of them in town and the surrounding areas which also needed to be checked out. Tomorrow he could take the tool and die shops and Louie could start on the tattoo parlors.

"Could you email me a picture of it? I'll start a search tonight."

"I haven't left the morgue yet. I'll send it over. Take some down time, Jake. She's not going anywhere."

There'd be no rest for him. His plans for the evening included research on branding. Maybe if he got lucky the design would be a common one. *Right, Jake, and the tooth fairy is real.* He'd ask Mia if she had any thoughts on the subject.

* * * *

Mia answered on the second ring. "Hey, did we make plans tonight?" Such was his day, he couldn't remember. Though he hoped they didn't, he'd miss her.

Her laughter filled his ear. "No, Jake, we didn't. Why?"

"I'm going to order pizza and work. I couldn't remember if we had anything scheduled."

"No, and I could use a night alone to write. Why don't you spend tomorrow night here?"

"I'm going to say yes, but it'll depend on how the case is going."

"Understood, enjoy your pizza. I'll talk to you tomorrow."

A cop's job made relationships hard. So many divorces broke his heart. He learned from others when you found a partner who understood the job, you hit gold. Mia was his pot of gold. She needed her space as much as he needed his.

Jake called in the pizza for delivery. While he waited for dinner to arrive he searched for names and address for the area's tattoo parlors on his computer. He listed them first by their location to his house, then by which ads showed branding services. Bunch of sick people out there, who for whatever reason intentionally burned and mutilated themselves. It had to hurt like a bitch. He shuddered at the thought.

The location of the brand on Nadia—bottom of her left foot, dead center on the arch—had to cause extreme pain. What kind of pleasure could he possibly get from that? Was it her screams? Her tears? Had she begged? Had she passed out from the pain? He hoped so. This creep had cut her, branded her and electrically shocked and burned her.

Pulling his notes from Quantico out of his file, he reviewed the characteristics of a serial killer. He was sure this wasn't the guy's first kill. The other four women were almost certainly dead, but why hadn't their bodies ever turned up? Was he practicing his method? Perfecting it?

Next, he noted phone numbers and addresses of the area tool and die shops before opening his email. He printed three copies of McKay's photo, one for the file, one for Louie and one for himself to show around tomorrow. It would be hard to keep this quiet. He put a call in to Louie.

"Give the brand on the foot to Wilson at the paper, but don't tell him what the ME thinks it is."

"I thought we were keeping this quiet."

"Tomorrow we'll be showing a picture of the brand on her foot all around town. Word will leak. Let's control how it's presented and win a few brownie points with Wilson."

"I see your point. We won't mention the carved 'I do'?"

"Correct, we'll keep it close to the vest. I'll ask Shamus to keep it out of the file for now. It won't go into the murder book until the ME finishes his report. This will give us a couple of extra days to research it."

"I'll see you in the morning," Louie said.

The bell rang as he hung up with Louie. After paying the delivery guy, Jake ate before jumping back on his research. He didn't want grease on his notes. He checked his wall clock and eased out a breath. He had an hour to get across town for the meet with Shamus, more than enough time to get some research in.

Custom branding dies varied in price. All you had to do was pick a range then fax over your design and, voila, in a week to ten days you had your branding iron. Jake made a note of the site and moved on. There were three million, nine hundred thousand results on branding. Sticking with only the first ten sites, he gathered the background information he needed. In his experience, the killer had to have made his own iron. Why advertise what you planned to do? No, this killer was cautious. He'd washed the body and cleaned under her nails. He wouldn't do something stupid like hire a die maker. He packed up all his materials and notes before he headed over to Shamus's house. Curious, he was sure he'd find out the real meaning to this morning's meeting.

* * * *

On his way into the bullpen the next morning, Jake replayed last night's meeting with Shamus. He rapped his knuckles on Louie's desk until Louie looked up. "My office." Jake continued walking to his office. As he reached the door Louie grabbed his arm.

"Got something hot?"

"No, close the door. I want Walsh to think I do."

Louie said nothing.

Jake slipped on his jacket. "I'll be stopping at Rosie's for a coffee before I start on my list, if you want to join me." Louie acknowledged the unspoken message with a slight nod.

Louie would take half the list of the tool and die makers. The tattoo parlors didn't open until ten. *The middle of the day,* Jake thought, *must be nice.* As they walked back into the bullpen, he said to Louie, "Don't forget to call me when you complete your interviews. We'll meet up and start in on the tattoo parlors once they open up."

He stood by Louie's desk as Louie grabbed his jacket off the back of his chair. "Sounds like a plan."

After Louie left the bullpen, Jake took his notepad out of his jacket pocket. Purposely, he stalled, jotted down a few notes on his pad as he waited to see who would ask a question. It didn't take long. Detective Harry Walsh didn't disappoint.

"Hey LT, you have a lead on the case?" Walsh asked.

Walsh has to be Velky's inside guy. It makes sense. Last week, Walsh was having lunch with Miller. Hmmm. How can I use him?

Chapter 11

"No new leads, Harry." Jake rubbed his chin.

"Who are you interviewing?" *Nosy bastard.*

"Family, friends, coworkers, people who knew her at the gym."

"Missing Persons already did all that."

A little miffed. Interesting. "Were you part of the team who investigated the others?"

"No, but if you need any help with the interviews, I'm available," Walsh offered.

"Thanks, I'll keep you in mind." Whistling, Jake left the bullpen.

As he entered Rosie's Diner, Jake greeted a few people at the counter but didn't stop to chat. He spied Louie in the back of the restaurant away from the crowd. Jake slid in the booth chair across from Louie.

The waitress slithered up to the table, order pad in hand. "Getcha something?" she asked, in the Wilkesbury twang.

"I'll have a coffee, black, and an egg sandwich, no cheese." Jake waited for her to walk back to the counter. A quick glance over his shoulder confirmed no one sat behind him. He outlined for Louie what his meeting with the captain had produced.

"Who is the mayor's spy?"

"The mayor must be feeling damn chirpy. He didn't have to plant anyone. Walsh came to us through Missing Persons." Jake smacked his head. *Oh, what a damn fool I've been. It was the mayor who had kept Walsh in place.*

"Ah, the reason his transfer fell through," Louie said.

Jake loved working with Louie. Not too much got by him. The waitress had returned with his coffee and sandwich. He took a bite from the sandwich while he waited for her to walk away again.

"If Velky is this set on getting rid of me or disgracing me, some of it could fall on you. I don't want you in the crosshairs. I'm thinking I'll give you a back seat on this investigation."

"Bullshit!" Several customers turned their way.

"Lower your voice, Louie."

"Anyone who knows us understands we're not only tight on the job but outside of it, too. I'm not stepping back. You're going to need me more than ever. You have to have someone you trust by your side."

Jake knew Louie wouldn't step back, even when given the chance. "Standing by me could be career suicide."

"I don't care."

Emotion swirled through him, choked him up. He cleared his throat. "Let's move forward then. I'll take my interviews. Call me when you're done with yours." Jake dropped a ten-dollar bill on the table and got up.

He walked out of the restaurant, then climbed into his car. Sat with the engine running to give the appearance he was taking notes. The next customer to walk out of the restaurant was a die-hard Velky stooge. Jake had thought he spotted the tail yesterday. It was no coincidence Velky had showed up at the bar. It was time to play a little game. He called Louie and directed him to an abandoned warehouse down the road. They would corner the bastard. It was illegal to follow a cop around while he performed his duty. Maybe he'd arrest him, then leak it to the papers, dropping Velky's name along the way. Gwenn would have a field day with the info.

Keeping the phone to his ear, Jake took off when Louie exited the dinner. He wasn't disappointed; Kawecki, a former WPD cop, followed him. Half a mile later, Jake took the turn into the parking lot of the abandoned millworks company. He pulled in between two outlying buildings and waited. Kawecki sped into the alley and had to slam on his brakes before he rear-ended Jake's city-issued car. A moment later, Louie pulled in behind Kawecki, successfully trapping him between them.

Jake drew his gun as he approached Kawecki. Not a stupid man, Kawecki raised his hands over his head. Jake stood at the front bumper while Louie opened the door.

"Hey, I'm unarmed!" Kawecki yelled.

"Get out of the car and keep your hands up," Jake said.

Kawecki slowly got out of the car, started to turn to face Louie. "Turn toward me," Jake called.

Louie patted him down, pulled a gun from Kawecki's ankle holster. "Unarmed, are you? You can put your hands down now," Jake said as he stared Kawecki in the eyes before lowering his gun. Jake let silence fill the air. Kawecki filled it.

"Why did you pull a gun on me?"

"Not the right question," Jake said.

"What do you want?" Sweat poured off Kawecki's face.

Jake gave Louie the go-ahead to search the car.

"I haven't figured out yet, Kawecki, if you're stupid or arrogant." Jake pursed his lips, cocked his head. "That's a lot of equipment you've got there, and a concealed weapon to boot."

"I'm doing my job and I'm licensed to carry," Kawecki whined.

"It's illegal to tail an officer of the law while he performs his duty. Any former cop ought to understand the law. I can lock you up here and now. If I do, I'll make sure the paperwork gets lost after announcing to the other inmates you were once a cop. What do you think will happen to you on the inside?"

Louie let out a low whistle. "I don't want to be in your shoes," Louie said.

"I want a straight answer, Stan. Why are you following us?" Jake asked.

"Velky doesn't trust you. I'm to follow you and report back to him. He wants to stay ahead of the investigation."

"You go back and tell your boss the next time, not only will I throw his stooge in jail, I'll come after him for ordering someone to break the law in the name of politics. And I'll make sure there is a reporter with me when I do it. Got all that, Stan?"

"Yes."

"Got the tape?" Jake asked.

"Yep," Louie replied.

"Good. Give Mr. Kawecki a receipt for the evidence."

"You can't take my tape. That's illegal. Where's your warrant?"

"My warrant? You tailed an officer and interfered with the performance of his duty. Come on, are you really going to try and fight me on this, Stan?" Jake stared Stan down. Kawecki flinched.

After a long moment of silence, Kawecki said, "No."

"Tell your boss he better not have me tailed again."

Louie got into his car and backed out of the alley, then returned after Kawecki drove away.

"Were you tailed?"

"I didn't see anyone. I took a couple of extra turns to be sure."

"Okay, let's get back to work."

"Jake, how are you going to handle this?"

"I'll call Shamus on the way to my interviews. He and the chief can figure out what to do about the honorable mayor. I don't have time to dick around."

* * * *

Tools Today Manufacturing Inc., a tool and die company in business for over fifty years according to their website, was Jake's first stop. A heavy oily smell smacked him like a brick. Machine oil on top of the loud noise first thing in the morning had his egg sandwich doing flips. The battle was on: who would win—the sandwich or his stomach?

The current owner's age surprised him. Luke Jacobs couldn't be more than forty. More like thirty-five, if he had to guess. Tall, slim with brown hair and brown eyes, dressed in jeans and a nice shirt, his appearance set Jacobs off from his uniformed employees. Jacobs had a firm handshake and a quick smile.

Jake's research had provided general information on the current owner, not the statistics. Luke Jacobs took over the helm about five years ago. Now he mostly pushed paper and filled in where needed. A master tool and die maker himself, according to the bio on the website, Jacobs had worked his way up in the company like his father before him.

Luke led him into a second-floor office, shutting the door behind them. It offered some quiet, though not much. Maybe after years on the job the workers didn't hear the noise or smell the oil.

"What can we do for the Wilkesbury Police today?"

Jake pulled the picture of Nadia's foot from his briefcase and presented it to Jacobs. Luke studied it.

"What you're looking at is a branding mark on a human foot." Jake didn't tell him whose foot it was.

"I see. It had to hurt like a bitch."

"I'm sure. Could one of your tool or die makers create such a branding iron?"

"Yes."

"Could you?"

Luke lifted his eyes to meet Jake's. Jake saw realization dawn on him. "Yes, I could, but for what purpose? Branding yourself is mutilation. I don't understand why a person would do it in the first place. What department are you with again?"

"Homicide."

Jacobs dropped the picture on his desk as if it had caught on fire. "You're investigating the Bride Murders?"

"I'm investigating Nadia Carren's murder."

"We don't make brands here, Lieutenant."

"Could an employee create this on their own time?"

"I'd like to say no, but in reality, I suppose so."

He got no tingle, no aha moment. It wasn't Luke. Jake ran through his questions anyway. When he had exhausted them all, he had Jacobs's employees brought in one at a time.

"Mr. Carson, can you tell me your whereabouts on the night of July sixth between seven p. m. and midnight?"

"It's Ray. I can't. I probably was at some bar or another partying." Carson continually pushed his greasy hair off his forehead as he spoke.

"Are you married?"

"No, never been. My longest relationship was in high school. I dated this girl for three months."

"I'll need you to contact me with the information for the date we discussed. The more detailed the better."

Jake introduced himself to another machinist.

"Arnie Velky." Velky wiped his hands on a towel hanging from his belt and extended a greasy paw to Jake.

When the name sank in, Jake's pen hovered in midair. He lifted his eyes from his notebook to scrutinize the man in front of him. Velky's uniform was immaculate, with only a square-shaped necklace to mark him as an individual.

"Any relation to John Velky?"

"Brother." Velky grimaced.

Rosie's egg sandwich swished in Jake's stomach. *Dammit, what were the odds?* Despite his discomfort, Jake noted Velky's sour tone. *Interesting.*

"What's your position here?"

"I'm the floor supervisor."

"Do you like your work?"

"Yes, it's an honest day's work for an honest day's pay," Arnie said, defensively.

"Are you married?"

"No."

Like pulling teeth, Jake thought. "Have you ever been engaged, or married?"

"Yes to engaged, no to being married. Why?"

"It's a question we're asking everyone. When were you engaged?"

"Crap." Arnie scratched his belly. "A few years ago."

"How long ago and why did you break it off?"

"I'd say six or seven years ago, you lose track. My fiancée decided she didn't like the idea of a shopworker for a husband," Arnie said.

Timing's right, Jake mused. But he didn't get a tingle on this one. Still, Arnie Velky fit the standard serial killer profile. Jake would have to meet with the shrink and have it tailored to fit his crime scenes. He still had several other companies to visit and people to interview before homing in on a suspect.

Jake returned to Jacobs.

"Thanks again."

"Not a problem, Lieutenant."

"Oh, one more question. Arnie Velky, is he a good employee?"

"The best, that's why I promoted him to supervisor two years ago."

"Why didn't he get married?"

"You'd need to ask him. Why?"

"I'm curious. Is he a good die maker?"

"The best. He's meticulous with an eye to details."

"How about Carson?"

"You've met him…" Jacobs left it hanging and crunched his shoulders.

"Yeah, I have. Thanks."

Once inside his car, Jake wrote down his impressions of all the interviews. How different could two brothers be? Arnie seemed like a nice guy, hardworking, and yet his brother, the mayor, was a snake. He drove to the other companies and interviewed ten tool and die makers before lunch. Three individuals stood out. He made notes to add them to his list for further study, then dialed Louie's cell.

"Where are you?"

"I'm on Thomaston Avenue around the DMV," Louie said.

"Do you want to grab lunch and compare notes?"

"I still have about twelve companies to interview today."

"I have about eight left myself, not to mention the tattoo parlors, but I'm starved," Jake said.

"Okay, where do you want to meet?"

"You pick it. I met an interesting person today."

Louie picked a place. Jake hung up, leaving him hanging when he tried to guess. There was no better entertainment than leaving Louie guessing. True to form, Louie pounced on Jake as he climbed from his car minutes later.

"Give. Who'd you meet?"

"Christ, Louie. Give a guy a chance to get out of his car." Jake grinned.

"Cut the bull," Louie said.

"The mayor's brother happens to be a tool and die maker. Not only a worker, he's also a supervisor with superior skills, according to his boss."

"Wouldn't it be poetic justice if the killer turned out to be the mayor's brother?" Louie asked as he smirked at the thought.

"I liked the guy. He's hardworking. And here's the clincher," Jake paused for effect. "He hates his brother."

"Seriously?"

"Yep, he didn't come right out and say it, but his tone spoke volumes. How about you? You hit on any candidates?"

"Yeah, I got a couple who rang some bells. Let's go in and talk. I need to eat," Louie said.

They ordered their lunches, then Louie filled him in on his interviews between greasy bites of pastrami.

"I have this guy, Scott Pencer, who I didn't care for. He's been engaged three times and each time the girl broke off the engagement. Scott has a real bad attitude toward women. Then there was his coworker, Mikey Stalls. The God's-gift-to-women type, he made my skin crawl. His fiancée recently dumped him. The reason being, and I quote, "because he couldn't keep it in his pants.' The slimeball bragged about it."

"Sounds like a piece of work," Jake affirmed.

"My second stop netted me three more candidates," Louie said, wiping the grease off his chin with a bunch of napkins.

He eyed his friend, as Louie habitually wiped his mouth after each bite even before he started chewing. "What stood out?"

"They fit the standard profile. Each had a broken engagement. Each is considered a master in his field. Let me tell you, they do produce beautiful work. Not only did they brag about their work, their bosses did, too. And a few seemed socially repugnant. Most were loners, came in, did the job, and left. No interaction with the other employees."

"Hmmm, most of mine were social. They couldn't wait to show off their work and how they were liked by all the other employees."

"How about Arnie Velky?"

"The same, even the guys Velky supervises respected him." He finished off his coffee. "Let's hit the road. We'll meet up later and compare notes. The tattoo parlors are going to have to wait until tomorrow."

Jake found most of the tool and die shops worked until six or seven, and none had a third shift. It was probably cheaper to offer overtime when necessary than to run another shift of employees with benefits. He rubbed his temples as the headache built from the noise levels in some shops, accompanied by the sickening oil smells that hung heavy in the air in others. Yet, he found others where the noise and smells were hardly noticeable. The temperature had dropped to forty-five degrees as he headed to the station. Jake didn't care. Though not as fastidious as Louie, he rolled down all his windows to air out his clothes.

Exhausted, he walked through the bullpen to his office. Jake noticed the night shift had already clocked in. Louie's desk was empty. The digital clock in his office read 6:30. Damn, it had been a long day and he still had his incident reports to process, as well as update Shamus. But first, he wanted an update from Louie. He dug his cell phone out of his pocket.

"Come up with any other suspects?"

"At this point nobody rings my bell but some gave me a twinge," Louie said.

"Same here, except one who didn't hit me right. We'll discuss it when you get back; come to my office. I'm going to file my reports then run the ones that fit the profile from home tonight. Where are you?"

"I'm pulling into the garage as we speak. I can't stay long, because Sophia's working late again tonight. I don't like leaving LJ there to watch the other two. They always wind up in an argument."

"See you in five." Jake hung up, went back to his reports, and reviewed the daily caseload for his department. It had been a busy day all around; two homicides, one suicide, and a vehicular accident resulting in the death of a woman. He made notes on his copies of the reports to question the case detectives in the morning. Louie walked in.

"I have to tell you. I'm glad I'm not a shopworker. I couldn't do the job."

"Why don't you leave your report until the morning? Go take care of your kids."

"Naw, I can get it done in fifteen and then it won't be on my mind all night. Oh, I forgot to tell you. I did have one who put my hackles up. I'll run him tonight, see what shakes out."

Chapter 12

Jake walked from his garage into the foyer, approaching the kitchen. The heavenly smell of sautéed garlic assaulted his olfactory senses. He stopped in the entrance way and observed Mia as she stood with her back to him at the stove, stirring something in a shallow pan. Brigh sat at her feet as she waited for a handout. The scene stuck him as homey. She preferred his cooking to her own or takeout, as did he. Mia's cooking skills left a lot to be desired. It was a surprise to see her here after how they had left things last night. He stood motionless as she danced around the kitchen with the grace of a tiger. Turning, she flashed him a wide smile. It blew the day's stress away.

Brigh walked to him and sat at his feet. After giving Brigh a little attention, he turned and wrapped his arms around Mia as he started nibbling on her lips. It wasn't enough. It never was. Pulling her closer, he explored. Each day he needed her in his life more and more. God, he hoped she stuck around this time. Never before had he given a woman a second chance. But with Mia, he was afraid he'd give her as many as she needed.

He felt her draw back. "If you don't let go of me dinner will burn."

"Who needs dinner?" He tightened his arms around her.

"Ah, I rarely cook. I thought I'd entice you to the table."

"Oh, you have. How about right here, right now?" He picked her up and placed her on the table.

"This is too wicked, Jake."

"Dessert first." Chortling, he snuggled his lips to her neck.

With her head thrown back it gave him easy access. He feasted as he worked his way down her neck. Water hissing and bubbling over caught their attention. He jumped up and almost tripped over Brigh.

"Shit, don't move," he ordered as he rushed to the stove. Grabbing the handles, he removed the pan from the burner.

"Bastard," he cursed as the stinging pain shocked his brain into action. He ran his hand under cold water to ease the pain. Mia started off the table to help. "No, don't move. I'm fine. Brigh, sit."

He shut off the stove and came back to her. "Now, where were we?"

"Let me see your hand."

"It's fine. Instead of looking, why don't you concentrate on the feel of it?"

"A tough guy, huh?" She smiled.

"You bet." He lifted her off the table and carried her to the bedroom.

Unceremoniously, he dropped her on the bed before turning toward the closet to put his guns away in the safe. When he returned to the bed, the lust in her eyes brought his blood to the boiling point.

"Brigh, go to the living room." He shut the door after scooting the dog out of the room.

"How'd I get so lucky to have you?"

"You haven't had me yet." She giggled.

"A comedian, huh?"

"Let me show you how funny I am."

She wiggled her brows. He laughed as he folded her into in his arms. While his mouth traversed her lips, his passion flamed from smolder to a five-alarm fire of desire as he snugged her to his body. A perfect fit. It rocked him to his toes when it hit him—she was all he'd ever need. Deep within his heart, the last lock opened as he realized it was, and always would be, Mia.

Jake took his time exploring her body. It seemed like years since they'd been together, though it was only days. Somehow this woman had come to be a vital part of his everyday existence—as necessary as the air he breathed.

* * * *

An hour and a half later, they stirred, satisfied and starving. Jake called for a pizza. While devouring the quick meal, Mia asked about his case. Not only did she approach the case from a psychological point of view, she brought her writing experience to the table. It surprised him how helpful she'd been.

"So, you spent your whole day interviewing tool and die professionals. What useful information did you glean?" She picked at the cheese on her third slice, twirled it on her fork.

"The design on the brand could've been created for this murder and maybe the others." Jake grabbed his fourth slice. He didn't tell her about the carving on Nadia's breast.

"He didn't brand her anywhere else?"

Ignoring her question, Jake continued to eat. Mia raised an eyebrow and waited him out. "There was something else on the body, which I can't discuss at this time. We're holding it back," he said.

"Why, what's the significance of the item?"

Jake scratched his head. "I'm not sure. Anything I'm thinking right now would be an educated guess."

"I'll come back to that. Who did you net in your interviews?"

Jake had discovered talking it out with Mia helped bring his day back into focus, sometimes shedding new light on things he missed. It added a new dimension to their relationship, brought back memories of his father talking out his cases with his mother before Eva's death... *Best not to go there.*

"Both Louie and I have a couple of people who need to be checked out, though I didn't get any big ping on my end. Louie says he got one. I did net the mayor's brother. Who happens not only to be a tool and die maker, he's a supervisor, which means in a company as small as the one Velky works in, he might have some leeway to come and go as he pleases after-hours."

"Is he as big of a prick as his brother?"

Jake's eyes followed Mia's hands as they lifted the wineglass to her lips. "What...you can't possibly be ready again?"

"Ah, a challenge?" He was not only ready—he was deciding on where to take her next.

"Seriously, Jake? Concentrate and answer my question," Mia said, exasperated.

"You're no fun." He frowned.

"That's not what you said a little while ago." She winked. "Now, tell me about the brother."

Tough Irishwoman, he thought, *with a one-track mind.* "Okay. A personable guy, he's been with his current employer since high school, worked his way up to supervisor. And the men under his supervision like him well enough. He's highly skilled, according to his boss, the owner."

"Okay, but is he considered the black sheep of the family?"

"An interesting question," Jake said and considered it. Mia never felt the need to fill every silence. Her question gave him another angle.

"I didn't think about it until you brought it up. He's an average guy. Average height, average looks, in a job most people don't want or can't do with all the math that's involved in it."

"Is he married?"

"No, he fits profile there. He was once engaged, though the owner didn't have any information on it. And if he did he would've given it to me."

"What did this man have to say about his brother?"

"Nothing really. He acknowledged the mayor was his brother, though he didn't offer the information up front." Jake watched Mia make notes while he spoke.

"Hmmm, he's not living in his brother's so-called glory. Did he seem jealous of him?"

"No, but definitely not a fan." Jake said, making notes of his own. *Maybe my first impressions were off. She brought up some interesting points about Arnie Velky.*

Mia questioned him on all the other interviews. She dug out some interesting points on the other people, too, who had caught his eye. Her perspective and pointed questions gave him other areas to research for all the individuals who made his list.

"Jake, you can open any standard book on profiling at this point to get a profile. Once the clues start to come in, I can give you more detail, but here's my take on him. Your killer is between twenty-five and fifty, but I'd lean toward the early thirties. He's organized, wants attention for his kill, and most times is pushed to the background, or is a pillar of the community. He's a charismatic person. When caught, people will say, 'he was such a nice guy. He always lent a helping hand.' He set up the scene like a stage. It shouts 'look at me.' The washed body tells me he understands police procedure and evidence and might be a cop. He wants to prove he's smarter than you. I'd say this isn't his first kill."

"Why?"

"He had to develop his style and brand. His rigging of the scene was his stage, and the cleaning of the body demonstrated his cleverness. I'm afraid this is the beginning of his quest."

He got up from the sofa in the living room where they'd eaten. After clearing away the pizza dishes and the empty wineglasses, he thought the sofa would offer a comfortable spot to accept her challenge. Sneaking up behind her, he pinned Mia down before she could react.

Laughing, she said, "My own fault."

* * * *

First thing Friday morning, Jake fielded a call from Nadia's mother
Each word oozed misery.

"Mrs. Carren, I don't have anything new for you," he said. "The
investigation is active and ongoing." He gave her the standard answer.

"I thought with the foot…" She faltered. "With what he did to her
foot… you had more to go on." Jake listened to her cry into the other
end of the phone.

"It's a lead. A solid lead we're investigating. I'm sorry I don't have
anything more for you."

Families of the victims needed answers, and sometimes there weren't
any. For Nadia and her parents' sake he hoped he'd find them. Their grief
drenched him and if he let it, it would drag out his demons. Some cops he
had worked with didn't feel the anguish. It was nothing but a job to them.
Jake had promised himself years ago if he got to that point he'd quit. He
hung up from his call to see Louie standing at his door.

"Morning." Louie tilted his head to the phone. "The fiancé?"

"No, the mother."

"Ah. I got a couple of hits on three of my guys. You get anything on yours?"

"I didn't get a chance to run them at all last night," Jake said, grinning.

"Zip it. I don't want to hear about it. With Sophia working late hours
I'm not getting any."

"Poor baby. Back to murder—my search is running now. Close the
door." Once Louie did, Jake continued. "Mia gave me some psychological
insights on this type of killer. She came at it from a different angle—it
has me reconsidering people who I might've pushed aside because of their
connections." He hoped Louie read between the lines.

"I see. What time are we interviewing the tattoo parlor employees?"

Good, he understood. "They open at ten. Give me an hour or two to
finish these runs. I'll come out and get you when they're done."

* * * *

After an intense study of his readouts, Jake found four of his candidates
had criminal records. Two had sealed juvenile records. Of the two, one
happened to be the mayor's brother, Arnie. He'd need cause before he could
get a warrant to open the juvie records. He didn't have one yet. Dialing
his cell phone instead of his desk phone, he reached his friend Detective

Damien Dunn from the Criminal Investigation Division (CID). Damien had specialized training in computer forensics.

"Hey," Damien answered.

"Hey, back at you. Don't use my name, okay?"

"Yeah, where are you?"

"Downstairs."

"Cool. What do you need?"

"How hard is it to unseal a juvie record? I don't mean with a warrant. In today's times, could I find it on the Internet?"

"You might, if a state worker had been careless, and you knew what you were looking for."

"Want to come over tonight for a beer?" Jake offered.

"Does the offer include pizza?"

Shit, pizza three nights in a row. "Sure."

"I'll be there around seven."

"See you at seven and thanks."

"No problem."

Jake grabbed his jacket. He turned off his lights as he headed into the bullpen. Harry Walsh stopped him.

"How'd it go yesterday with your interviews?"

"Good, Harry. Thanks for asking."

"Heading out?" *Brilliant,* Jake thought.

"Yeah, see you later."

Walsh pressed. "Get anything from yesterday's interviews?"

"Nothing solid." It was time to turn the focus on him. "Fill me in as we walk on the case you caught yesterday—the vehicular accident."

Walsh had no choice. Harry started to fill Jake in—something he should've done yesterday. He'd let it slide, not only on Walsh, but on the other detectives too. He needed to catch up and stay on top of things. He didn't want to give the mayor any little excuse to bust his ass. Jake timed his pace to coincide with the end of Walsh's verbal report in front of Louie's desk.

"Thanks, Harry. Make sure I have the written report on my desk by the end of your shift today." He dismissed Walsh by turning away from him to face Louie. Jake said, "Ready?"

"Will do, Lieutenant," Walsh said, moving slowly back to his own desk.

Jake barely moved his head, signaling to Louie not to make a comment. Louie stood, grabbed his jacket, and walked toward the elevator with Jake. As the doors opened Jake noted it was filled to capacity.

"Let's walk," Jake said, turning toward the stairwell.

"Harry can't be…"

Jake interrupted Louie as they started walking down the stairs. "Harry was updating me on the case he pulled yesterday. Something he had failed to do in a timely manner." Jake had stopped short. Pointed his index finger up the stairwell, he stared at Louie to make sure he got his message.

"Since I'm now a sergeant, you can delegate those pesky details to me."

"Soon, I will." They started walking down the stairs again.

* * * *

"It's a pisser when you can't even discuss work at work," Louie complained.

"It's what Velky's reduced us to. He loves drama."

"So, what did you tell Walsh?"

"Things are progressing, though we don't have any solid leads at this time. I wonder how long it will be before I'm called to the chief's office again to discuss our lack of progress." Jake smirked. "Okay, let's get back to police work for a change. What's the first name on the list?"

"Kool Ink," Louie said.

Jake pulled up in front of the building. He studied the outside of the parlor. A dark film covered the windows. It kept out both the sun and curiosity seekers. One of the windows displayed several types of designs a person could choose from if they were brave enough to scar their bodies. On the door a sign flashed Tattoos, Branding, and Body Piercing. *Lovely, legal mutilation.* He knew fellow officers who had fifty percent of their bodies covered in ink, if not more. *To each his own.*

A bell sounded overhead as they pushed their way into the darkened store. A young woman with tattoos up and down both arms greeted them.

"And what can I do for the cops today?" she asked as she took a drag on a cigarette.

A young woman who didn't need to look at his badge—one who could spot a cop at fifty yards. Her life, written on her face, didn't tell of a fairy-tale existence. On closer study, Jake noticed her left eyebrow sported three tiny gold rings, her nose sparkled with a tiny diamond, and her tongue, not to be outdone, was pierced with a gold ball. Her jet-black hair was severely cut and spiked. Wrinkles fanned out at the corners of her eyes. Jake shuddered at the thought of having such sensitive body parts pierced and wondered where else she'd been marred. On closer inspection, this tough young woman was older than he'd first thought. She'd been around the bend and survived it. The black lipstick against her white skin made her look ghoulish.

"A problem with cops?" Jake asked.

"None whatsoever. What do you need?"

He and Louie placed their shields on the counter. "I need information on branding. Can you do a search on it?" Jake asked.

"Yes. Do you have a warrant for my customer list?"

"No, I didn't ask for your customer list, miss."

"It's Karen. If you don't want the list, what do you want?"

"Information."

"Such as?"

"How is the branding done? Who does it? And do your customers choose from a selection of irons you have or do they supply their own?"

"I do the branding, as does the owner, Kyle. We have a selection of brands over there in the corner you can choose from. If none are to your liking, we can special order. We have a book of a hundred brands or so. I've never had anyone bring in their own."

"Can I look through your brand book?"

"Sure, I'll get it."

Jake watched her walk to the back of the store. Louie had already moved to the corner to inspect the brands on display. When Karen came back with the book, Jake started thumbing through it.

"Is there a particular design you're searching for, officer?"

"It's lieutenant, Lieutenant Carrington. Yes, there is." He pulled out the design the ME had sent him last night.

"Ouch, that's a sensitive part of the foot. Why would someone put it on the foot where it couldn't be seen?" she asked.

"My thoughts exactly."

"Wait, are you investigating the Bride Murders?"

Jake schooled his face until it was void of emotions before answering. "We're investigating Nadia Carren's death. Are you acquainted with her?"

"No, only what I read in the papers. The killer do this to her?"

He made a decision, answered without breaking eye contact. "Yes."

"I've never seen a design even close to this one before or had any special orders to make a brand similar to it."

"Do you recognize the shape?" Jake asked.

"Hmm, could be a bird. An egret or a white heron, or it could be a crane, with the long legs. Does that help?"

"Yes. If you can research the mold with your distributors, I'd appreciate it," Jake said, handing her his card.

"Sure. Will it help catch the bastard?"

"I hope so."

She took his card. "Most people don't treat us with respect because of our piercings and tattoos. For some reason they fear us," she said.

"I figure it's a personal choice, though one I don't understand. Thanks for your help, Karen."

The rest of their interviews went much the same way, some offering help, others treating them as if they had the plague. Jake noted the clerks who smelled of marijuana in case he needed to go back and badger them on other issues. Karen was the most forthcoming. A few made Jake's person-of-interest list for their blatant disregard of the law. Others made the list for their disrespect for women. One such conversation stood out in Jake's mind. It pushed the owner of Black Ink to the top of the suspect list.

"You have a problem with branding?" Nick Tedessco had asked.

"Mr. Tedessco—"

"It's Nick."

"Nick, I don't have a problem with anything. Branding, piercing, and tattooing are personal choices. What I have a problem with is a person being branded against their will."

"I only brand people over eighteen years of age with their written consent," he said defensively.

Right, and I'll eat my gun if that's true. "We're not here to bust your chops about who did or didn't give their consent."

Jake didn't break eye contact with Nick as he pulled the picture out of his case and handed it to Tedessco. "What I am interested in is this brand. Have you seen anything like it?"

Jake had to give the guy credit. Tedessco studied it, even pulled out a magnifying glass to view all the details. "No, and I don't have any brands even close to this. The brands are in the corner. Check them out." Tedessco pointed to the front of the store.

Louie walked to the display counter while Jake continued to question Nick.

"Do you take special orders for brands?"

"I do. A guy wants to brand his woman with a special mark, I'm all for it."

"You think women should be branded like animals?"

"I didn't say that. Don't put words into my mouth," Tedessco hissed.

"What are you saying?" Jake asked, quirking his brow.

"All I'm saying is a man has a right to mark his property. If the woman is willing, why not brand her?"

"So, you consider women property?"

"Damn right. No one has the right to go near my woman."

Disbelief left Jake speechless for a second or two. How backward in today's times to think like that. No more than thirty, Nick was a short, squat man with a belly starting to bulge, his black hair thinning enough to show more scalp than hair. *What woman would put up with a guy like Tedessco?* Jake hid his disgust. Only an extremely damaged one would do it, he figured. Even then, the last thing he'd want would be a submissive woman. Personally, he liked them strong and intelligent. It made life much more interesting.

Not happy with the answer, he asked the question another way. "Nick, did anyone order a brand like this or similar to this one?"

"No, I haven't had any special orders in some time."

As he started for the door, Jake stopped and asked over his shoulder. "Are you married?"

"Was, twice. I divorced both bitches after a year or two. Why?"

"Call me curious," Jake said.

Chapter 13

"Did you notice the prison ink on his fingers and neck?" Louie asked.

"Yeah, I did. We'll run him when we get back to the station. I'll bet there'll be a few domestics on his record. Asshole thinks women should be branded." Jake fumed at the stupidity of it.

"Man, if I was a woman I'd slice his throat as he slept," Louie said.

"I was thinking lower."

Louie started to laugh but something caught in his throat and had him choking instead.

"He'd certainly deserve it," Jake continued. "We need to dig a little deeper into Mr. Nick Tedessco. You up for a little side trip?"

"Sure, where are we going?"

"To the morgue."

"Ah, a vacation paradise," Louie said.

* * * *

While Louie joked with Jake, Sophia checked her temper. Called into her boss's office on the pretext of taking a letter, she sat in the chair in front of his desk. He came around it and leaned over her. The idiot was trying to look down her neckline.

"Sophia, that dress hugs all your curves. It looks great on you."

"Mr. Malone—"

"I told you, Sophia"—she shivered with disgust when he said her name with a caress—"call me Richie."

"I prefer Mr. Malone. And I also prefer you refrain from making personal comments about me."

She needed this job if she was going to help Frankie, but she wasn't going to put up with Malone's crap. Lord, after the way she'd fought Louie on this, ignored all his warnings about the man, she couldn't go home and tell him Malone was harassing her. Louie would kill him. *Should I talk to Jake? No, maybe I'll speak with Mia. If only Mia would forgive me and answer one of my calls.* She hadn't meant to cause a fight between Jake and Mia. She still couldn't understand why Mia broke it off with Jake. It was an innocent question she asked. Why Jake kept the incident a secret, she had no idea. Mia's temper was way over the top. Deep in her thoughts, she didn't hear Malone's response.

"Excuse me?" she said.

"I don't understand why you're taking offense to a compliment."

"'Nice dress is a compliment. A description of how it fits my body is not." She used the same tone she used on her children when they did something wrong.

"Sorry to insult you," Malone said, his annoyance obvious. "We're working late again tonight on the Krueger case I have coming up next week. I need to be prepared for court."

The hair on the back of Sophia's neck stood on end. She didn't want to work tonight. Lately, Malone had been standing a little too close or had put his hand on her arm or back while he spoke to her, intimate gestures she didn't invite or appreciate. Something about Malone's expression forced her stomach upward into her throat, the bile burning as she tried to swallow. Tonight, Louie would be tied up with his case.

"I'm sorry, Mr. Malone, I'm not available tonight."

"I'm sorry, too. No work, no job." He leered at her, making her skin crawl.

Sophia stared him down. Malone looked away first, though he didn't retract his threat. If she quit she'd never live it down. Darn Louie for being right. He'd told her she didn't understand what she was getting herself into. She had ignored all his warnings and for what? For Frankie. He needed her. But how far was she willing to go to help her godson?

I must continue for Frankie's sake. If only his mother and father would help him out, I wouldn't need to be here. Not even Louie would help the poor kid. She didn't understand. Family was family.

"I have three children at home, I can't work any later than seven," she stated. At lunchtime tomorrow, she'd shop for a different type of outfit to wear to work. A smile tugged at the corner of her lips. Yep, she'd dress like the Amish. See how Malone liked that.

"What about your husband? Why can't he watch them?"

"He's working." She offered him no other explanation. Malone's grin didn't go unnoticed. The creep knew he had won.

She went back to her desk to call Louie. Her pride would get her into trouble someday.

* * * *

Their steps echoed on the white-tiled floors as they approached the morgue theater where Doc McKay was working on yet another victim. Louie and Jake threw gowns over their street clothes before entering the room. Louie pulled the loops of the mask up over his ears as did Jake.

"Ah," McKay said, holding an organ in his hand.

Louie's lunch flipped back and forth, then up and down. He dropped his mask and popped an antacid into his mouth to try to calm the waves. Even after all these years, he got squeamish in the morgue. It never seemed to bother Jake, though Louie knew better—most times it was a facade.

"Care to venture a guess?" McKay smiled.

"No, not really," Louie said as he swallowed hard.

Jake leaned over the dish, rubbed his chin. "A liver?"

"You win, Jake. Now, what can I do for you boys today?"

"I have something for you on the brand that I need to show you. Plus...I need to ask you a favor," Jake said.

"All right. Tell me first, then ask your favor."

"One of the tattoo parlor employees recognized it as either an egret or a crane."

"Interesting."

"We're also going to be checking it out. If we come up with anything I'll share it with you."

"Same here; now what is the favor?"

"Everything we share with you, especially on the brand, you keep to yourself and don't discuss with anyone."

"I haven't spoken with anyone except my assistant, Gerard. I'll remind him to keep it quiet."

"Thanks. The second part of the favor is the carved 'I do.' Did you tell anyone else about your findings?"

"Just the four of us."

"Four?" Jake asked.

"Four. You, Louie, me, and Gerard."

"Okay, I've shared it with my captain and no one else. I am not releasing the carving or mentioning it in any of my reports. Shamus agrees with me. We're only sharing the branding. The shape has to be shared with people we question or officers I pick to help in the investigation. It makes sense, since Louie and I are showing the picture around at the tool and die shops and tattoo parlors."

"Okay, I'll scrub the carving from my records here. I'll keep it on my home computer."

"Thanks, Doc."

"Jake, you didn't have to come here in person to ask the favor."

"Call me crazy, but I'm getting paranoid with people right now. One of our persons of interest"—Louie watched Jake hold up two fingers on each hand to imitate quotes—"is a prominent citizen."

"You don't say. Care to share?"

"I can't, it might get sticky and you'd want to be as far away from it as possible. I hope you understand, Doc."

"You've got my curiosity up, but I get it."

Louie's cell phone rang, playing "True Love," the Elvis Presley version of the Cole Porter song. He tilted his head toward the door and walked from the room.

"Sophia."

"Louie, I'm sorry to do this again to you. Malone gave me an ultimatum. I have to work late tonight. I'll be home by seven-thirty." The tight, clipped words spilled out like a waterfall and each screamed aggravation to him, even stress. Was it something caused by Malone? Maybe he'd go down there and break the bastard in two.

"Is everything okay?"

"Yes. I'm frustrated to have to work late again."

Louie stared at the white walls in the hallway. He knew and loved every one of Sophia's nuances—something was off.

"Sophia?"

"Everything's fine, Louie, I'm having a crappy day."

Crappy? She must be over-the-moon upset, he thought. Sophia considered "crappy" cursing and rarely used the word. If the bastard had touched her...

"You sure?"

"Yes."

"We'll talk later." Louie hung up and then smacked the wall.

He didn't hear Jake walk up behind him until Jake touched his shoulder. It jolted him back from his dark thoughts.

"Christ, you're jumpy, everything okay?" Jake asked.

"I'm not sure." Turning to Jake, Louie said, "Sophia used the word 'crappy.'"

"Is she hurt?"

"It's something to do with the creep she works for. She lied to me," Louie said, shocked. His wife had lied to him.

"Louie, maybe you're not used to Sophia dealing with the stress of an outside job. It could be as simple as that."

"I hope you're right, but something was off in her voice. Maybe I'll call her back and offer to bring her dinner. She wouldn't have anything with her because she wasn't planning on working tonight."

"Good idea. Now, are you interested in, let's say, a little thing like murder?"

"Don't bust my balls, Jake. I'm not in the mood," Louie snapped.

"The doc scrubbed his records. He trusts his assistant Gerard completely, and I also spoke with Gerard. We should be good on the carving. Some of the tox screens have come back. Nadia had a mix of drugs in her body. Most notable was the drug Restoril. It's used for insomnia and it requires a prescription. The other drug in her system was Ecstasy."

"I'll do a search on dealers."

"It's another string to pull once we can narrow down the field of suspects. When we do, we'll get a warrant for their medical records and prescribed drugs. The Ecstasy will be harder to track down," Jake said.

"I'll contact Carey in Vice and ask him who's currently dealing it. And if we need to we'll pull them all in and see if they sold to any of our persons of interest," Louie said.

"While you talk to Max, I'll start the search on egrets and cranes."

* * * *

Back at the station, Jake headed to his office, Louie to his desk. Halfway to his office Detective Walsh caught up with him. *How predictable.* Before Jake turned to Walsh he wiped the smile off his face. *Christ, this guy doesn't have a discreet bone in his body.*

"Did you finish your report?" Jake asked before Walsh could start questioning him. Overseeing a department cut into his case time. It was a necessary evil if he wanted his team to solve cases.

"Yes, it's on your desk. Quick rundown, the kid said the woman stepped out from between two parked cars. He didn't have enough time to stop. Wit said he flew down the street. I'm waiting on the CSI for the exact speed. I have to tell you, his skid marks were fifty feet if they were an inch."

"Sounds like speed. Was the woman in the crosswalk?"

"No."

"How old is the kid?" Jake asked.

"He's sixteen, not a good thing to put on your record at any age. I feel bad for him."

"Was there anyone in the car with him?"

"Yeah, his older sister."

"How old is she?"

"Twenty. She was teaching him how to deal with traffic. He was driving with a learner's permit."

Jake considered all the possibilities. He felt bad for both the kids, but a woman died yesterday because of their negligence. "Have you interviewed their parents?"

"Me and Van Dyke are scheduled to interview them at five tonight."

"Keep me informed," Jake said, turning from Walsh to dismiss him.

"LT…"

"Yes?" Jake turned back.

"Nothing."

Walsh's thoughts warred in his expression. *About time he caught on,* Jake thought.

Once he settled his butt in the chair, Jake got down to some serious computer work. He rubbed his forehead to relieve the pressure from the forming headache. Damn, his search turned up fifteen types of long-legged or variations on the birds, especially the cranes. If he had to pick—and he did—he'd pick the Japanese crane. It was a popular item lately among brides. Origami Japanese cranes were now used as symbols at weddings. They were a monogamous bird, not only representing longevity and a harmonious marriage, but also representing financial success. *What a wedding planner could sell to the unsuspecting couples—anything for a buck today.*

Egrets had symbolism for many people and many cultures. It represented the spiritual world. The Egyptian heron, or egret, represented light. A double-headed one represented prosperity. For the Chinese they represented strength, purity, patience, and long life. Good symbols, he thought, for marriage.

In other nations, the birds represented anything from wisdom, communication with the gods to good judgment. *You can make anything into anything,* he mused. The Japanese crane was the only one mentioned in relationship to marriage. Jake continued his research on the Japanese crane until his mind shouted *enough.*

A knot in the small of his back forced him to stand and stretch. As he worked the kinks out he gazed out his window. The day blew by him. After five, the streets were jammed with cars, and pedestrians as they rushed here and there after a long day at work or school. He had another hour of paperwork before he could even consider leaving the building. Detective Dunn would be stopping over at seven. *I hope Mia will understand about this. Damn, something else I'll have to make up to her.* He'd put her as his number one on his phone. As he pressed it he had to chuckle. The Seinfeld episode about who's first on your speed dial popped into his head.

"Mia, where are you?" he asked.

"Something wrong, Jake?"

"No. You didn't leave your house yet, did you?"

"No, why?"

"I have a meet at seven. Instead of my house I'll come to your place after my meeting. It will probably be around nine if that's not too late?"

"Not a problem, I'll see you at nine."

He sat back in his chair. Yep, he was a lucky guy. Mia got the job and the hours. Well, most times she understood, considering they hadn't talked about the future or what each expected from the other. A knock at his door pulled him from his thoughts. Louie stood in the doorway with his file bag draped over his shoulder.

"Leaving?"

"Yeah, I'm bringing Sophia dinner."

"You called first, right?"

"I did. She seemed pleased I thought of it, which confirms my suspicions something is wrong."

"Don't jump to conclusions, Louie."

"I'm not."

"Want me to check in on the kids on my way home?"

"No, LJ's fifteen now. Sophia reminded me we have to show him we trust him even if it scares the *merda* out of me."

Once Louie left, Jake finished up his paperwork. He headed out at six-fifteen. Halfway home he remembered to call in the pizza. He ordered one with everything on it, including anchovies, for Damien, and a small veggie for him to compensate for all the cheese ones he'd eaten this week.

* * * *

He fed Brigh and then he tossed a couple of paper plates and napkins on the table for the pizza. Jake reviewed his notes before Damien arrived. On one side, he listed all the persons of interest who warranted another look. Normally he wouldn't have included Velky. It was his connection to the mayor which put him on the list. Damn, he even liked the guy, for Christ's sake. The bell sounded. When he opened the door, Damien stood poised to ring the bell again. The pizza delivery guy stood off to his left.

"I have perfect timing." Damien grinned.

"You do. Why don't you grab the pizzas while I pay the guy?"

"Can do." Damien took the boxes and waltzed by Jake on his way to the kitchen.

Jake joined him at the table. Sprinkling parmesan cheese onto his slice, he watched Damien shovel in the food. By the time he finished his first slice, Damien had half of his pizza gone. The amount of food this beanpole consumed always amazed him. Lanky, Damien wore his brown hair short on the sides and long on top, which constantly fell over his glasses into his eyes. He walked hunched over, reminding Jake of an actual beanstalk. On occasion, Jake had even called him it to his face.

With his mouth full, Damien asked, "So who do you want me to run?"

"You're not going to like it. And I'll understand if you say no. And please don't tell anyone else I asked. Okay?" Jake ran the back of his hand over his mouth. "It could mean our jobs if we're caught."

"I'm insulted, Jake. Me getting caught, come on." Damien eyed him through his large tortoiseshell glasses, a cocky grin playing at the corners of his mouth. "You want me to run the chief or the mayor?" He wiggled his brows.

"It's not a laughing matter." Jake tried to hide his grin. "I want you to unlock a juvie record on the mayor's brother and three other suspects that gave me a tingle. I don't have probable cause right now to request a warrant." Jake watched his request sink in.

"Is he the sick bastard who's killing these women?"

"I don't have any evidence pointing at him, but he fits the profile right now, as do the others." Jake got up from the table and paced back and forth. He decided to trust Damien and take him into his confidence. "The mayor can't stand me. Velky's making this personal. You need to understand he's watching me closely and hoping I trip up. He even has his own men in my department spying on me."

"Why?"

"He wants my badge. You remember Captain Miller?"

"Ralph Miller's brother?"

"Yep, I'm the cop who took him down. He was Velky's inside man back when he was campaigning for mayor."

"I hate freakin' politics." As Damien lowered his head in disgust, his hair tumbled over his forehead. Damien pushed it back. A minute later it was in his eyes again. Jake wondered how many times a day Damien had to perform the task.

"Me too. You can see how this might have a negative effect on your career."

"I'm a big boy. I can't stand the honorable mayor. He cut so much money from our budget it's ridiculous. We lost two good officers. I'm in." Damien stuck out his hand.

Jake reached out, took Damien's outstretched hand, gripped it firmly, and hoped he wasn't ending this bright young detective's career. Or his own.

Chapter 14

With Damien in Jake's study to search the juvie files on Arnie Velky and the others, Jake took some much-needed thinking time. Brigh sat next to him on the couch. Absently he rubbed his hands over her back. Though he thought it was probably a waste of time searching Velky's record, Jake understood it had to be done. Would the mayor get wind of it? Jake was at the point of not caring. He wasn't about to let Velky use the dead woman as a stepping-stone. From the study he heard a lot of cursing. Confident Damien would get into the sealed files, Jake put his feet up on the coffee table and grabbed the remote. He had recorded the six o'clock news. Fast-forwarding to Gwenn's segment, he pushed the Play button. He knew she would do a bang-up job of reporting the facts. Too bad she brought her pushy and possessive nature into her personal life. She'd been a tiger in bed, and he had fond memories of their two months together. Shaking his head, he turned his attention back to the screen. True to her words, she put a little shine on him and Louie while updating the case for her viewers. Her ending comment had Jake silently thanking her.

"I also wanted to mention the team that's working on the Carren case. It consists of professional homicide detectives who care about the victim as well as closing the case. Lieutenant Carrington and Sergeant Romanelli always put the victim first. This is Gwenn Langley signing off, for now."

He shut off the television and thought about Gwenn's report. It was sure to piss off the mayor. It would also reassure Nadia Carren's family she remained the center of the investigation. He'd deal with the fallout from the report tomorrow.

"Jake," Damien yelled excitedly from the other room. Jake jumped off the couch and ran into the office.

"What'd you find?"

"Check it out. It's Arnold Velky's juvie record." Jake leaned in over Damien's shoulder. A low whistle blew through his lips.

"Animal cruelty charges fit the standard profile."

When you fished, you sometimes caught a big one. But how was he going to get this into evidence? He didn't have authorization to unseal this document. Jake went back into the kitchen while ideas jumped around in his head. He grabbed his file.

Damien followed him. "You can have it come in as an anonymous tip."

"That would be too obvious. Who knew you were coming here tonight?"

"Just us."

"Good. If they trace this back to my computer, it will only fall on me." Jake scratched his head. How could he introduce this information into the file without a warrant? He'd be asked where it came from. Maybe it was best to hold it back.

"Jake, isn't the reporter on Channel 5 your friend?"

"We used to date, why?"

"First, you use her to leak the information. Then you would have no choice. You'd be obligated to verify the information."

"It would be a good idea, Damien, except the mayor's aware Gwenn and I dated awhile back. What's the second thing?"

"Crap, it won't work then. The second thing… can you introduce me to her? She's hot."

Jake cocked his head and smiled at Damien. "Sure, next time she's in town."

He thumped his hand to his heart and grinned. "Thanks, I appreciate it. Is Arnie Velky your only suspect?"

"No—as I said before, he wasn't even being considered until his juvie record showed up. Now his job and the information in the sealed file moves him up the list." Jake paced around his kitchen. "Christ, I didn't get any vibes from the guy. Did you run the others yet?"

"No. I'll do that now." Whistling, Damien left the room.

He'd have to give it some thought before he proceeded. The other potential suspects on his list created more of an initial buzz than Velky. Each had an adult criminal record. Jake walked down the hall to his office.

"My other potentials fit the profile with their continued criminal backgrounds and attitudes toward women in general. Only one has a juvie record. Can you run him next? And please keep this under your hat."

"Not a problem, Jake. This is like walking on a minefield."

"Good description. Did you print out the information?"

"Yeah, I figured you didn't want it saved to your hard drive. Here's a thumb drive with the info, plus the printout."

"Good thinking."

Damien ran the other potential suspect with the juvie record. The charges levied against Nick Tedessco were breaking and entering. Those charges earned him two years as a guest of the state when he was fourteen. How much did the animal cruelty charge against Velky weigh in here? He'd bounce these results off Mia tonight. See her take on them.

After he completed the runs, Damien hung around for another hour sucking down beers. Jake enjoyed his company. Though he didn't want to rush him after the big favor he'd done, he'd promised Mia he would be at her house by nine. Jake checked his watch.

Damien looked at his, too. "Shit, eight thirty. Is your clock right?"

"Yeah, why?"

"I promised my girlfriend I wouldn't be any later than eight. I'll be on her shit list for sure." Damien rolled his eyes as he stood to leave.

Jake held out his hand. "Thanks for everything. I mean it. If you ever need anything…" Jake left it hanging.

"Will do. Enjoy your weekend, Jake."

* * * *

Jake headed to his garage with Brigh in tow the minute Damien left. On the way to Mia's he pondered the information on Velky. Even with this new information his instincts stayed quiet, no excitement, no anything. *Am I protecting him because I hate his brother, and I'm missing something major?*

Now, the guy in the tattoo parlor, Nick Tedessco, gave him a real ping. His views on women alone put him near the top of the list. He parked by Mia's door. He made a note to dig deeper into Tedessco's life, either here tonight or first thing in the morning. The guy had Jake's skin crawling. He wasn't sure if it was the comments about branding a woman or his whole attitude toward life.

Jake rang the bell. Mia opened the door. Brigh jumped up to greet her. "You didn't have to ring. I left the door open for you."

"Mia, I told you before to keep it locked at all times, especially since we never caught whoever was leaving you those dead animals."

"I'm fine, Jake. You worry too much. Besides, I haven't had any deliveries in a while. Come in." She opened the door wider and knelt down to pet Brigh.

"I bet you didn't even look through the peephole. I thought NY101 taught you to keep the door locked." He threw her words at her.

"Okay, I'll be more cautious in the future. Did you eat?"

"Yeah, I had pizza for the third night in a row. If I don't see another pizza for a week I'll be a happy guy." He leaned in, nipped her bottom lip.

She pushed out of his arms and said, "Oh, let me lock up before I get another lecture from my cop boyfriend." She laughed, locking the door. Jake tugged her to him.

Together they walked into her living room. Jake plopped himself on the snow-white sofa, tossing aside a pile of red pillows. Brigh rested her chin on his lap. All of a sudden he felt tired right down to the bone. The stress from the mayor complicated his job, sensitive investigation or not. Now he had the brother to contend with. Mia knelt beside him on the couch and massaged his shoulders.

"Tough day?" Mia asked.

"Yes. The mayor's brother shot to the top of my list of suspects. Except I can't use the information I have on him because I obtained it illegally." He turned to her when she stopped rubbing his shoulders. "Please don't stop."

"Okay. When did this come about?" She moved her fingers to the base of his neck and had him moaning in pleasure.

"You found the spot. My meet tonight was with an electronics expert. I asked him to hack into Arnie's sealed juvie record to eliminate him from the mix. Instead, I hit the jackpot. He fits the profile, right down to killing and maiming small animals as a child," Jake said.

"Be honest here, Jake. Is he a person of interest because of his connection to the mayor?"

"Hell no, he's an okay guy, nothing like his brother."

"This is political suicide," Mia said, pointing out the obvious.

"Tell me about it." Jake rubbed his hand over his forehead. "Arnie is either a slick adversary or he's exactly what he purports to be, a hard-working tool and die maker, nothing more."

"Which one are you leaning toward?"

"I no longer trust my instincts on this one."

"Can anyone else dig into him without pointing a finger back at you?" Mia asked.

"I have another one with a juvie. It's for B&E only. The others have adult records. I'd like to run them tonight if that's okay with you? I can try to use the other records to get a warrant for Velky's file. But it's thin."

"Go up. I'll make us drinks and join you in a few," Mia said.

Jake walked into Mia's office, sat in her chair, and turned on her computer. He enjoyed the efficiency and the setup of the room, along with the fashionable touches Mia had added to personalize it. Blue curtains framed a wide window. It would flood the room in light during the day. The blue-gray silk wallpaper deflected glare from the overhead lights. Knickknacks filled the top shelf of the bookcase.

After signing into the WPD system, he started his run on Nicholas Tedessco. The guy had three domestics against him, all with restraining orders. One as recent as July of this year—his current girlfriend had filed one of the complaints. His ex-wives were the other complainants. It seemed old Nick couldn't control his temper, which, in Jake's opinion, took him out of the mix. Tedessco wasn't a planner, more of a hothead. Jake made notes of the current addresses for all three women, adding them to his growing interview list. Mia walked in with the drinks.

"Sorry to put you out of your office," Jake said as he took his drink from her.

"Not a problem, anything interesting?"

"A wife beater," Jake said.

"Lovely company you keep."

"Yep. What's new?"

"I spoke with my mother today." *This couldn't be good.* He waited her out. "She asked us to join them next weekend."

"Join them where?" Jake didn't like the turn in the conversation.

"In the City," Mia said.

Something was up. It wasn't like Mia to be coy. "Why?"

"Well..."

"Mia?" Jake coaxed.

"They want to meet you."

"Interesting." Not really, but what else could he say?

"That's it? Interesting."

"What do you want me to say, Mia? Of course, I'll meet your parents. But why do we have to spend the whole weekend there? Why can't it be dinner only?"

"It's their way of locking me in for an overnight visit." Jake took a sip of his drink, Mia rushed on. "Don't worry. I'll make it clear to my mother that we'll be staying at my condo."

"Did you tell them we'd bring Brigh along?"

"I thought you'd ask Louie to watch him."

If he wasn't mistaken, the idea of this visit made Mia more nervous than him. It was probably how she left things the last time she visited. She and her father did not see eye to eye on anything, especially her living in Connecticut. A thought blew through him. "You don't want me to meet them, or them to meet me. Which is it?"

"I don't get along with my father. He puts every man I date through a process. It's infuriating and ridiculous at my age to have to go through it or to defend my choices. My mother will embarrass you and tell you to your face you're not good enough for me. Now how do you feel about the visit?"

"The same. I didn't want to go in the first place, but if it's important to you, then it's important to me. I'm tough, I'll suffer through it." A smile played at his lips. Opening his arms, he drew her onto his lap as he snuggled her to his chest, then kissed the top of her head.

"Thank you."

"I have to add this, though. It all depends on the case. If something breaks, I'll need to stay here and deal with it."

Boy, I certainly hope something breaks. A whole weekend with Mia's people could be a nightmare.

"I understand. I'll preface it when I respond to my mother. Why the long face?"

"Thinking about you meeting my mother—oh, what a lovely evening it will be: you, me, and her eating strained food while she argues with her noisy neighbors," Jake said.

"It can't be that bad."

"Wait and see." Jake rolled his eyes.

"I'll leave you to your work. I'll be editing my book in the bedroom. Don't be too late." Pushing off his lap, she threw him a coquettish look over her shoulder. Brigh followed her from the room.

Jake heard the promise and decided tomorrow was soon enough to analyze the files he'd printed. He got up and followed her into the bedroom. Brigh had made herself comfortable on his side of the bed.

"So, I'm not getting any editing done, huh?" Following the movement of her hands as she placed her printed-out manuscript on the nightstand, he sat beside her and stroked her thigh.

"I love a woman who understands subtleties."

"Subtleties? Hmm." She peered over her reading glasses at him with that impish expression he loved. His blood raced through his veins as it left a trail of heat. *So much for working tonight.* He was consumed by everything Mia. Work forgotten.

"Put Brigh in the kitchen first," she said, interrupting his actions.

* * * *

Louie pulled up to the front entrance of the law firm where Sophia worked. He took a few minutes to put his emotions in check before he confronted her sleazebag boss. Taking a deep breath, he reminded himself he was there only to deliver her dinner, not to start a fight. More than anything, he wanted her safe and happy again. There was one thing he knew without a doubt; Sophia had not been happy since she took this stupid job. Despite her stubbornness and pride, or because of it, he loved every inch of her.

The anger that had consumed him for the past few weeks rose to the surface, because he understood firsthand that Richard Malone, Esquire, was the world's biggest loser. Last year he was accused of sexual harassment by two different women. One accused him of attempted rape. Malone beat all the charges because the women refused to pursue them. Instead they settled out of court for an undisclosed amount of money. It devastated Jake when he heard the news. They settled for money, instead of putting the guy behind bars where he belonged. Damn it. It left Malone out there to harass more women.

Louie blew his breath into his hands to check it. *I definitely need a mint.* Popping one into his mouth as he climbed from the car, he grabbed the takeout order he had picked up at the Fish House. Sophia would be surprised with the elaborate dinner. Laughing, he realized only an Italian would equate food to love. It brought a smile to his face because he knew, deep down, Sophia would understand the gesture.

The front door wasn't locked and in this neighborhood, after six, it was a dangerous mistake. Even more concerned for her safety, he walked in quietly, finding Sophia and Malone in a large conference room. Louie's gaze landed on Sophia's face. She was tense as the bastard Malone sat there throwing out orders to her at the speed of a car in a NASCAR race. She couldn't possibly keep up.

"Ahem." He loved the way Malone jumped when he realized someone else was in the room.

"Officer Romanelli, I didn't hear you come in." *Of course the bastard remembers me. Was this the reason he hired Sophia in the first place?*

"It's Sergeant Romanelli now, Malone."

Turning to his wife, Louie held up the bags of food. The annoyed expression on Sophia's face had Louie's heart burning, his stomach churning. It not only said, "I'm glad you're here," it also said, "I'm tired, and I want out of this place." How could he bring up the subject tonight to give her the option of quitting without her feeling like a failure or a fool? It had to be her idea to quit or he'd never hear the end of it.

"Why don't you two eat in here? I've got things to do," Malone said.

Sophia spoke up before Louie could. "Thanks, no need. We'll take it into the kitchen."

Louie followed her out of the room. Over his shoulder Louie caught Malone staring at Sophia's ass. The bastard shrugged and put his hands in his pockets. It took all of Louie's willpower not to smash Malone's face in.

In the kitchen Sophia spun around, pointing a finger at Louie. "Not one word, Louie."

"What? I didn't say anything." He'd forgotten how hard it was to keep his thoughts from Sophia.

"You're thinking out loud." Sophia lowered her voice. "The man's an idiot. A total lowlife, Louie, though he hasn't done anything to me. Please don't say a word to him."

"The choice to work is yours. I'm not interfering." Louie put his hands up in surrender. "I want you to understand, if you decide to quit it's no reflection on you." He grabbed his wife's hands, massaged them in his. "I love you, *amante*. I'm behind you one hundred percent with whatever you decide."

Sophia's emotions played out on her face. He leaned into her, nestled his head in her hair, and whispered, "Please don't put yourself in danger. I'll kill him if he touches a hair on your head."

Sophia tried to push him away; he held on. "Tell me the stress I hear in your voice isn't work related." Louie pushed back this time to stare into her mahogany eyes.

Her non-answer was his answer. She dropped her head. He lifted her chin up until their eyes met. Louie kissed her and enjoyed that he could still surprise her. He was sure she thought a fight was coming.

Though he wore a smile, the hard edge to his voice could cut glass. "You're not the only one who can read a person."

Sophia pursed her lips which told him she was close to losing it. He understood he needed to back off. Though he'd make sure they continued this conversation at home, right now he needed to back down.

"We'll talk at home tonight?"

"Yes. You're not leaving, are you?"

"No, I brought enough for two."

They ate their dinners in silence. After a half hour Louie got up to leave.

"I'm only a phone call away, Sophia." He gazed down when she grabbed his hand and squeezed. "What time are you getting off?"

"Why?"

"Because I'll be back to drive you to your car—"

"Not necessary. I'll drive her." Years of training kept him from jumping out of his skin. Louie hadn't heard Malone's approach.

"No, I will, Malone. It's six thirty. I'll be back in forty-five minutes."

"Suit yourself," Malone said, on his way out of the kitchen. How much had Malone heard? When Louie left the kitchen, it took every ounce of control he had not to make a comment and start a fight with the dickhead. He hoped Sophia appreciated his restraint.

He kissed Sophia good-bye then walked to his car. Sitting there for a few minutes, he made a decision. Louie pulled around the block and parked halfway up the street. If Sophia needed him he would be right there. Taking his phone out of his pocket, he called LJ.

"It's Dad. How are things going there?"

"Good, why?"

"I'm going to be another hour or so. You can reach me on my cell. If I don't answer, call Uncle Jake."

"Dad, I'm fifteen. Nothing's going to happen. Chill out."

"Such an old man. I'm serious, LJ, call if you need me."

"I will."

Satisfied he couldn't do anymore, Louie settled into his seat and listened. He'd slipped a listening device into her pocket. On his way out he whispered in her ear to let her know it was there. He gave her kudos for keeping it on. He adjusted the earpiece and flipped the recorder on to record all conversations. It would be his backup in case he needed to cover his ass when he took out Malone.

Chapter 15

Forty-five minutes later Sophia joined Louie in his car. Her exhaustion whipped at him. All he wanted to do was pull her into his arms and hold her. How had this job gotten out of hand? She handed him back the listening device.

"Why don't you keep it?"

"I don't need it, Louie. I understand you don't like the man, but he hasn't done anything wrong."

"Yet," he emphasized. "Listen, it has an on and off button. You're in control. You turn it on when you want me to listen in. It's a small precaution for when you're working late."

He handed it back to her. She placed it in her purse then put her head back on the headrest and closed her eyes.

"What's bothering you, *amante*?" Using his favorite pet name for her in Italian, he hoped it would penetrate her heart.

"I never expected to work such long hours. I feel guilty about leaving you and the children to fend for yourselves."

He took his time answering her, choosing his words carefully. "We miss you. I don't understand why you want this, but if it gets to be too much or you decide you don't like the job…"

"I understand, *miele*, but I'm not at that point yet—though if these hours keep up I might quit."

The defeated tone of her voice broke his heart. When she called him honey in Italian, she owned his heart. He couldn't resist her or her wishes.

Dear God, let the stronzo *keep giving her these hours. This way we can both get out of this with some grace.*

"Nothing to say to that, Louie?"

"I want what you want. You have my full support with whatever you decide." *Grow a pair and tell her what you really feel.* "Sophia…" *Be selfish, go ahead.* "I want our life back the way it was."

"Lately, I've had the same wish, then I get mad at myself for being a quitter."

"You're anything but."

She patted his cheek. "I want to last at least another month."

"Why?"

"I can't tell you. It's a secret."

Louie didn't answer right away. He gave her words a lot of thought. When he spoke, it was with care. He didn't want to insult her or push her away. "Sophia, I don't care what you're saving for. It has to be something for me or one of the children, but the only thing we need is you. Do you understand what I'm saying? If it's something for yourself, let me buy it for you. It would make me feel good."

"Please be patient with me for a little while longer. If the creep makes a pass I'll tell you. For now, I'm keeping my job."

Louie banged his hand on the wheel. Anything he had to say right now would sound morose and insulting. He'd keep his mouth shut. Sophia reached out and rubbed his shoulder. The silence filled the car until it deafened them both. Louie pulled into the ramp garage and hunted up Sophia's car.

"It's on the next level."

He nodded, not trusting his temper.

"Louie, I'm not trying to hurt you. I wish you'd understand that. This job is for me, not you, not the children. Me. My self-esteem hasn't been good lately and I can't explain why. I had to do something for me. Please don't be mad."

He pulled up to her car, threw the gear shift into Park. Sulking, he hadn't looked at her all the way to the garage. Pivoting in his seat, he took her face in his hands. "I'm not mad at you. I'm worried for your safety."

Sophia leaned into him, gently kissed him. Louie ran his hand over her hair. "Let's go home. I'll follow you."

He watched her get out of his car then into her own. He couldn't live without her. She was his every breath. She had to feel it. She blinked her lights twice; Louie backed up a little to let her pull ahead of him then he followed her home. He never saw Malone in the shadows.

* * * *

Awakened by his ringing phone, Jake reached over Mia to answer it. Somehow during the night, they had exchanged sides.

"Yeah," he answered ungraciously.

"Jake, I need you at the station right away," Captain McGuire said.

Checking his watch, he swore. It was only five thirty. "What's up, Cap?"

"We'll talk at the station."

"Do you want me to pick up Louie?"

"No, I only need you."

"I'm in Woodbury. It will take me half an hour to get there."

"No problem. I'll see you then."

What the hell was going on? Why only him and not Louie? It had to be the damn mayor again.

Mia stirred beside him. "Who was that?"

"My captain."

"What did he want?"

"Me, at the station, now."

"Why?" Mia rubbed sleep from her eyes.

"I don't know, something's up! Shamus isn't talking. If I can, I'll fill you in later. Just go back to sleep, Mia." Jake threw the covers off himself, as his thoughts jumped all over the place. *Why the urgency?*

Annoyed with Shamus, Jake climbed out of bed without another word. He took a quick shower. When he came out, Mia was sitting up. Jake dressed without speaking. Once done, he walked over to the bed. Leaning down, he bent to give her a kiss, but she pulled back.

"What?"

"What? You snap at me then walk out in the middle of a conversation and you think that's all right? I don't think so, Jake. Call me later."

What bug crawled up everyone's ass this morning? Mia scooted down under the covers and turned her back to him. He opened his mouth to apologize. Forget it. He turned and left.

What was her problem anyway? She was close enough to the phone to have heard the conversation. He didn't need two hundred questions first thing in the morning. This was the reason he'd previously avoided relationships. They were minefields waiting to explode.

* * * *

On the drive to the station he raked his mind for a clue. He gave up when he pulled into the underground garage at the station. The captain's call had his mind in overdrive.

I guess I'll find out shortly.

The elevator doors opened. Relieved to find the car empty, he walked in then pressed the button for the third floor for the captain's office. The last thing he needed this morning was trivial conversation.

McGuire's door opened immediately when he knocked. And not by McGuire. *Not good. What the hell was the chief doing here?* "Good morning," he said.

"Come in, Jake." McGuire motioned.

"Chief." Jake looked from Chief Doolittle to his captain.

"Sit down." The chief pointed to one of the visitor chairs.

"What's the mayor up to now?" Jake ventured a guess.

"Nothing. This has nothing to do with him."

McGuire handed Jake a pair of gloves. Once he put them on, Shamus handed him an envelope. Jake examined it. His name was on the front of the envelope in cut-and-pasted letters.

"Who delivered it?"

"One of the homeless. We've got him in interview room four. I thought you might want to speak with him," Shamus said.

"I do. Did he say anything?"

"Only that the nice man gave him a ten-dollar bill to deliver this here," Doolittle said.

"Hmm."

With a sinking stomach, Jake opened the envelope and took out a letter addressed to him. Scanning it first then reading it carefully, he tried to analyze the content and nuances. Crude blocks of print from various publications were pasted together, forming sentences to create the message.

Lieutenant **Carrington**,

I understand since you found the body, you feel you'll be **able to solve this case.** I'm impressed how fast you and your team arrived on the scene. I'm not **laughing at you yet, but will be soon.** If you do not **solve this case** within two weeks, **I will abduct another woman** and her life will be in **your hands**. The **clock is ticking**. TICK-**TOCK**!

By the way, you **missed talking** to me the other day. **I'm closer** than you think.

Yours truly,
The Groom

"He's taunting me. Two weeks. He's not giving us enough time," Jake said, frustrated, running his hands through his hair. Standing, he started to pace McGuire's office.

"No matter what happens or who dies, it's not on you, Jake. Understand you have no control over what this nut does."

"No, I don't. But in the meantime, another girl dies if I can't find him."

"Jake, you're a good cop. We'll work it like any other case. Tell me what you need and you'll have it," the chief said.

Jake stepped to the window, his back to the room. He stared out at nothing in particular. His mind ran in all directions. This was worse than he'd anticipated. A problem from the mayor would've been better. Reining in his thoughts, he turned back to McGuire and Doolittle.

"Has the letter been authenticated? You're sure it's not some prank?"

"We're not. Are you willing to ignore the warning?"

"No."

"Neither are we. We'll work it as a valid threat and pray it's not," Chief Doolittle said.

"What this does is divide our attention from the original case if it's not legitimate."

"I understand, though we have no choice," McGuire said.

"Damn it! I'll need extra hands looking through the engagement and wedding announcements to find women who match the deceased. I have two officers in mind. Louie and I will continue to interview the tool and die makers along with the tattoo parlors. Then I'm going to need to return to the shops I've already interviewed to see who I missed. He's breaking his pattern here if he takes another woman so soon," Jake said.

"You've figured out the brand. You've figured out where he's picking the women. I think you're on the right track. Keep running with that thread. I'll head a team and explore other avenues. Maybe we'll meet in the middle."

"I better go wake up Louie."

"Before you go, Jake, I have a question. Shamus said Velky has a mole in your department?"

"I'm aware, it's Detective Harry Walsh. He's one of the transfers from Missing Persons. I wouldn't be surprised if he's dirty."

"Do you have proof?"

"No, that's why I'm quietly investigating him. Please, I don't want to put his name in front of IA till I'm sure. He's definitely Velky's man."

"Okay, we'll spoon-feed Velky with useless information. Now about the letter… I don't want it released to the press. I'm not feeding this creep's ego," Chief Doolittle said.

"I agree for now," Jake said. "We should have an alternative plan in case the information finds its way into the media."

"You're thinking the killer might send it?"

"Yes. Before this morning, I would have said no. He's changing his MO if he's taking another woman before the year is up. Plus, there was a reason he wanted Carren's body found. We have to figure out why." Jake stopped there to gather his thoughts, then continued. "We should notify each bride whose announcement has been published within the last six months who fits the description."

"That'll cause a citywide panic! Why six months why not go back a year?" Doolittle asked.

"No, it might save someone's life. Carren's announcement was published in February, and she was abducted in July. This guy's a planner. We might even have to go further back after our initial search."

"It's time to put together a small task force. I want you to handpick the men and women you want on it. I want to find this one alive," McGuire said.

"Me too."

"Do you have anything else, Mike?"

"No, Shamus. Jake, email the list of people you want and I'll have them reassigned to you."

"Thanks, Chief."

* * * *

Wasted time is what it was, he thought. He'd interviewed the homeless man who had delivered the letter. The only thing 'John Smith' could concentrate on was how he was going to spend his money. Frustrated, copy of the letter in hand, Jake released him and headed back to his office. He reread it several times. First, he would have to verify it came from the killer. How the hell would he do that?

Pulling out his duty roster, he reviewed the names of each detective and officer assigned to his department. Then a thought struck him. Shamus hadn't said he had to stay within the confines of his department. Besides the two officers reviewing the announcements, he would need one to research the Internet announcements and a couple of detectives for door-to-door interviews in the neighborhoods of all the missing women. The task was daunting. How could they save the next victim? He opened his second drawer and retrieved a yellow legal pad. Names of detectives and officers he'd like to work with made the top of list. Next, he listed their special talents and outlined the guidelines for each member of the task force and their duties beside their names. Vacations, sick days or personal days would be canceled until the case was solved. No exceptions. Each member needed to understand what they were giving up before they signed on. It was a preliminary sketch of the operations, later he'd update it.

Jake reached for his phone then changed his mind. He grabbed his keys and phone. He would wake Louie up in person. First, he'd go home to change before heading back to Mia's to deliver his apology in person.

As he approached her home, the open garage door stopped his heart. A quick scan of the area as he parked signaled the all clear. Mia's car still in the first bay concerned him. Why would she leave the door open? Jake walked into the house. Brigh stood by the door, shaking. Jake called out Mia's name. No answer.

"Some watchdog you are," he said to Brigh. Concern turned to worry in a New York minute. With nerves on edge and his stomach jumping, he drew his gun as he ran through the house checking every room.

His heart echoing in his ears, he found her right where he left her, under the covers. *This means I left the damn garage door open and put her at risk. Christ Jesus, I'm losing it.* Jake took a deep breath, hoping to slow his pounding heart before he stepped further into the bedroom. Calmer, he walked over to the bed, sat down beside her, and then pulled the cover back gently.

"Mia, are you awake?"

"I am now."

He smiled. She wasn't a morning person. "I'm sorry about before."

She wiped her eyes before looking at him. "I don't understand why you were mad."

"I was upset, not mad. I thought the mayor was playing games again. And I needed time to try to figure out what could warrant pulling me in at five thirty in the morning. I was pissed, but not at you."

"So, I was a handy target?" She rubbed her eyes with her fists.

"Yes."

"What was it?"

"Worse than the mayor." He looked directly into her eyes. "It was a note to me from the killer." She shot straight up into a sitting position, exposing her breasts as the covers pooled around her waist. His thoughts shot in all directions. *Rein them in, you fool.*

Following his gaze, she pulled the covers up and clutched them at her breasts. "Jake, that's not good. What are you going to do?"

"I'm going to work the case, Mia. It's all I can do."

"Tell me word for word what the note said."

He did. She sat quietly while he recited from memory each word. He didn't like her expression. They sat in silence for a few minutes more after he'd finished reading aloud, and he realized this was the real reason he'd stopped here first. He knew Mia's mind. She was thinking and analyzing each phrase before she spoke.

"Jake, this disturbs me on many levels. Here's my quick take. He's escalating, and I'm sure I'm not telling you something you hadn't determined already. More, he's making it a contest between the two of you, which scares me. He has something to prove, not only to you, but to the world. I'd bet the house on it. You didn't miss him yesterday. You probably engaged him in conversation and he figured you'd be a worthy opponent. I would let Louie and the other team members continue with interviewing other shops and parlors. You personally need to review everyone you spoke to within the last two days, then start a profile on them, digging deep into each of their lives. Once you do that, then and only then do you go back and reinterview them."

Jake took in everything she said, then played it over and over in his mind. He'd spoken to a lot of people yesterday. He'd need to rethink it. No one he spoke with yesterday but Velky jumped out in his mind.

"Why should I wait?"

"Because if you rush right out to speak with them now, the killer gets what he wants—your full attention," Mia said.

"Won't my attention cause him to make a mistake?"

"No, it could make him more cautious. Running out and announcing his plans tells him he's the one in control. Not saying a word will piss him off and force his next move."

"God, Mia, he does control everything." Frustrated, he got up from the bed, roaming around the room like a caged animal.

"No, Jake, you do. That's why he's challenging you. You got too close yesterday or the day before and you got him running scared. Use his fear against him and he'll make a mistake. Come back here and sit down."

"I can't. I stopped in to apologize to you. I'm on my way to pick up Louie. I need to get started assembling my team for the task force I told you about."

"I'm editing today. If you send me an email with your interview notes I can start a profile for you." She looked at him, saw the doubt. "It's between us."

"I'll get them to you. I don't want to leave a trail. No emails." *Here comes the hard part. Will she fight me on this?* "One other thing… I don't want you staying at my place while this killer is out there. If he puts us together it might put you in danger. And I wouldn't be able to do my job or think if any harm came to you."

He sat down on the bed and rubbed his thumb over her lips.

"I'm good at taking care of myself, Jake. Don't waste your time worrying about me."

"I can't help it. I love you." He leaned down, placed a chaste kiss on her lips.

"I love you back. On the nights you can't make it here, I'll need to see you, for my own peace of mind. Please, no arguments."

He didn't want to fight. It wasn't the time or the place. He was short on time. The argument would wait until later. He called Louie and made arrangements to pick him up in a half hour. It seemed like he had put in a full day already and it was only eight.

"I can't give you a time when I'll stop by. This type of case grabs me and doesn't let go."

"I'll be here. If I decide to stay at your house, I'll give you enough notice to be there."

"Let's compromise." He grinned without mirth.

"How?" She narrowed her eyes at him. Lord forgive him, it turned him on. He rubbed his fingers over her silky arms.

"I'll send a messenger service with copies if I can't make it. When I get back here tonight we can discuss them."

"It would be much easier on you if I met you at your house."

"No, I'll come here. I'm serious. Worrying about you will be a distraction I can't afford. What do you say?" He took her in his arms, kissed her passionately. Pulling away, he searched her brilliant blue eyes for her answer. "I need you safe. Please understand, Mia, nothing else is as important as your safety." Jake knew he had her when she sighed.

"Okay. When will you bring them over?"

"I have to contact the people I want on the team and interview them. Then introduce them to each other. It will take a good five or six hours. What will you do in the meantime?"

"I'll work on my book all day today. Wait, maybe I can meet you for lunch and get an early start on them."

"No, I'll send them over." He kissed her on the tip of her nose. Before leaving to pick up Louie he rechecked all the windows and doors at her condo and made sure this time he closed the garage.

Chapter 16

"What's the bastard up to?" Louie said after Jake brought him up to date on the drive to the station.

"Something not good. This is all about his ego."

"I can head one of the teams. It'll take some of the pressure off you."

Jake stayed silent, slipping a glance now and then at him while keeping an eye on the road. He respected Louie's opinion. His partner always approached a case from a different angle, shedding light where others didn't venture.

"Have you gone back over your notes yet?"

"No."

"I thought you said you only got a buzz from one of them. Is he the guy?"

"No, I don't think so. He would be too obvious. When we get to the station, I'll type up my notes. You do the same. Then we'll exchange them. I want to see if anything sticks out at you. Something I might've missed."

"What could we have missed?"

Jake concentrated on driving. Something in the back of his head niggled at him, something beyond his consciousness. It fought to come forward but failed. Was it doubt or had he missed something big in the last two days? Would another woman die because he didn't, or couldn't, see what was right in front of his eyes?

"It's not your fault."

"I understand it's not, but it doesn't save the women, does it?" Jake pulled into the garage at the station. "How are things going with Sophia?" he asked, to change the subject.

They got out of the car and walked to the elevator before Louie answered him. Jake watched as Louie pounded the Up button like it was an unruly suspect.

"I think the bastard is making passes at her." Louie ran his hand through his hair. Jake recognized Louie's habitual gesture of frustration.

"Did she say something?"

"No, that's the problem. She doesn't talk. She's always upset, working late hours, too tired when she gets home to do anything. Last night I brought her dinner and she seemed relieved. He snuck up on us in the break room. I mean, I never heard him approach, Jake. He could've been eavesdropping through our entire conversation or for a few minutes."

"I'm not surprised he would eavesdrop. I'll speak with Sophia if you want. You only have to say the word."

"No, she wouldn't talk to you about it. Maybe she would have with Mia, but now she's too embarrassed to call her."

The elevator arrived. Jake stepped in first, pressed the button for the second floor. "Why don't I have Mia give her a call and clear the air? This way we're both removed from the situation."

"I hope it works," Louie said. "I want my wife back and happy."

At the second floor the doors opened and together they stepped out.

"Louie, reserve a conference room for noon. I'll invite Shamus and Doolittle. After you do that, come into my office and we'll go over the people I picked for the team. You can fill me in on the ones you think are a good fit before I interview them. I've picked detectives and officers whose specialties run from the CID, Homicide, Vice and Illegals."

"Why Vice and Illegals?"

"Illegals because of the drugs found in Carren's body, and Vice because he'll come in handy. This type of predator needs to hook up with a woman throughout the year to relieve tension or prove his manhood."

"Now you sound like Mia." Louie smiled.

"She does rub off on you." He grinned back. "Seriously, Louie, she has some great insights into the creeps we deal with each day. I've been bouncing things off her and it helps."

At the bullpen they parted ways. Jake went directly to his office, Louie to his desk. He put in calls to both McGuire and Doolittle then turned his attention to the files he'd had Katrina, the squad secretary, pull.

Damien's file was on top. He didn't need to read it. On the legal notepad in front of him Jake listed Damien's name and attributes. The next file he opened belonged to Joe Green, a detective he had recently worked with on the Stack case. No relation to the Greene victim. Green had proved himself on Stack's case, he'd use him on the team. For Vice, Jake picked Max Carey. Max was a decorated detective who had a problem with authority figures, though he knew the streets, his drugs and who was the latest dealer of choice. When something went down on the streets, Max had first-hand knowledge. *I can rein him in if it becomes necessary.*

Next, he reviewed the caseloads of all his detectives in the homicide department. There were a few who were free, though he didn't want them anywhere near this case. Burke's caseload was light. Kraus, Burke's partner, could continue to work their cases alone. Jake put Burke's name on the list.

Kirk Brown had asked to be considered for the task force, if Jake formed one, but due to his personal connection to one of the victims, it would be dicey. This should have immediately disqualified Kirk, but Jake understood his need to work the case. Brown was a solid cop. Jake kept him on the list, though he'd watch him. As he sat there debating whether Brown should be on or off the team, Louie walked in.

Jake turned his notepad toward Louie when he sat. He watched Louie study each name before he looked up. "Why the question mark next to Brown's name?"

"He knew one of the victims."

Louie continued to read. "Doesn't Carey have a reputation for not being a team player?"

"No. He has a reputation for being difficult with his current supervisor. Max is familiar with the streets. His expertise is what we need right now."

"Your call," Louie said, shrugging.

While Jake continued to review the personnel files of the other detectives, Louie made notes next to the ones already on the list. "What have you come up with?"

"You're breaking up teams. Why?"

"I still need detectives I trust who have experience in homicide working the other cases. I don't want to pull the whole team off a current case."

"Kraus isn't going to handle this well. He's going to get pissy."

"It can't be helped. I can't spread this department thin. I need experienced officers to cover the other cases."

"How are you making the announcement?"

"I'll do it Monday morning. Today, I'm only informing the team members I've chosen."

"Word will get back to everyone, Jake. It will cause problems."

"I can't help it. Most aren't on the roster for the weekend." Louie's expression had Jake cocking his head.

"I picked the best damn team available. I don't want another woman to die on our watch. If any of them have a problem with that, they can transfer out of homicide. Only the victims matter here."

"You're preaching to the choir. You have to tread carefully, if you want the department to continue to be a team," Louie said.

"I do. And the ones who have been in homicide and have worked alongside me all these years understand what counts in the end." *Damn, Louie's right.* Jake's stomach curdled at the thought of having to deal with bruised egos.

After two hours, Jake was satisfied he had the right team. Louie's warning continued to play in his head. He decided to make the calls and stop trouble before it started. "I'm going to call Kraus and explain why he's not on the team. The others will continue to work their actives. There shouldn't be any problems. Happy, Louie?"

"Yes."

"Good, I live to make you happy. I'm also going to call Kirk Brown and dig deeper into his association with victim number one, Elizabeth Bartholomew, before I assign him to the team," Jake said, as the knot in his belly unwound. Louie stood as they finished up. "Do me a favor and set up a board with the pictures of all the victims. I'll set up what evidence we want to share. Shamus and the chief are on board with holding back some of it. I'll see you in a little over an hour in the conference room," Jake said.

After Louie left his office, Jake checked his watch then started calling his detectives. First up was Kirk Brown. It sounded like he woke him up. Jake explained the reason for his Saturday call.

"I need you to be honest with me, Kirk. How close were you to Elizabeth Bartholomew?"

"Give me a second." Jake heard him speak to someone in the background before he came back on the line.

"Okay, I'm back. She was friends with my sister. I would see her when I went over to my parents'."

"Bartholomew..." Jake ruffled through the paperwork on his desk. "She was only twenty-six when she disappeared. How long had your sister been friends with her?"

"My sister's six years younger than me. Lizzy and Karen went to school together. They hung out with the same crowd. They even attended the same college."

"Kirk, I have to ask the next question." Kirk answered before he could continue.

"No, I never slept with her. She was too young for me."

With some guys it wouldn't matter, but Kirk was a stand-up guy and he trusted him.

"I'll need your word—if at any time you feel you're too close to the victims, you'll step away."

"You have it, Jake."

"I mean it, if we have a suspect. I can't take a chance you'll lose it or act inappropriately"

"I'll want to, but I won't."

Jake let out his breath. He explained to Kirk about the no-time-off policy. He had no conflicts.

"Great, welcome to the team. Be in conference room one at noon."

Jake checked his watch, ten twenty-five. *Shit, where had the time gone?* Next up was Gunner Kraus. He wasn't looking forward to the confrontation but placed the call anyway. Kraus sounded harried when he answered.

"Gunner, it's Jake. Do you have a minute?"

"Not really, but what's up?" Gunner shouted to a kid in the background. Jake pulled the phone from his ear.

"I'm forming a task force on the Carren murder. I need to break up some of the teams. I'm going to have you work your and Burke's caseload. I'm putting Al on the team."

"Why him and not me?" Jake heard the insult in Gunner's voice.

"What are you doing right now?"

"I'm watching the kids. Sally had to work today. What's that got to do with anything?"

Jake exhaled and took Gunner's lead-in. Kraus had given him the perfect excuse. "Because there'll be no time off, including vacation, personal or sick time while the task force is in play, and the hours required are not negotiable. Burke won't have to rearrange his schedule."

"Who else did you pick?"

He didn't need this bullshit today, but Louie was right. Kraus wouldn't stop until he had his answers. Jake gave Kraus the list of names on the team and why he picked them. He thought the call had gotten disconnected when the line went quiet.

"I would consider Brian Kelly even though he's retired. Use him as a consultant. He worked the Missing Persons case on two of the victims."

Relieved, Kraus had stopped busting his ass, Jake questioned his logic. "Why?"

"The guy still lives the case. It's all he talks about when you run into him."

"I'll think about it and see if we can use him. And thanks, Gunner."

"If you need more hands, Jake, I'm available. It'll give me a reason to hire a babysitter."

Jake pushed his chair away from his desk then stood. He rubbed out the kinks in the small of his back. He walked out of his office. For the next proposed team members, he would need to see their supervisors before he could add them to the team. He needed two uniforms, but lately four of them had impressed him.

Stella "Estee" Fisher was his first choice. The other three would depend on their availability. Tara Jones, Carl Burrows, and Liam Sherman had showed character under pressure when he worked with them. Burrows would be his second choice. Jake liked his reaction on the Orlando murder case. A seasoned officer with quick reflexes who worked in unison with Louie to disable the chase car, he had allowed Jake to get the witness and her children into a safe house before the Feds took over.

Yeah, he wanted Burrows on the team. He scanned the area as he walked past the bullpen. Few desks were occupied, though Jake spotted Burke and decided now would be the time to speak with him, before Kraus did. Burke signed on before Jake could even finish outlining the rules. The job was all Burke had. Thrice divorced, he had no one at home who'd complain. They shot the bull for a few minutes before Jake continued on to the first floor to speak with the duty sergeant about Fisher and Burrows.

As he entered a voice made him look to his right. "Jake, you ugly bastard, what are you doing in my neck of the woods?"

Laughing, Jake said, "Why, to see you, you handsome devil."

Handsome wouldn't be a term anyone would use to describe Sergeant Luis Santora. A three-inch scar ran down the right side of his cheek to his mouth, courtesy of a drugged-up suspect who was now serving a ten-year sentence for assault with a deadly. The animal deserved a life sentence for attempted murder of a police officer. Santora was lucky he still had his eye.

The sergeant grinned. "Seriously, what are you doing here on a Saturday?"

"I need to talk to you in private."

"Sounds ominous," Santora said while walking down the hall with Jake. "In here."

They walked into an empty office. Jake closed the door then turned to Santora. "I'm working the Carren murder and the chief decided a task force was needed."

"I'll ask again, Jake, what do you need from me?" Santora replied.

"I need two uniforms. I want Stella Fisher and Carl Burrows." Jake watched Santora process his request.

"Naturally, you want my two best officers." Santora scratched his head. "I'll need to look at the schedule before I give you an answer."

"Good enough," Jake said, extending his hand. Santora gripped it hard. "You have any leads on this one?"

"A few, but not nearly enough," Jake said as he released Santora's hand.

As he stepped on the elevator to head back to his office he encountered Sergeant Miller. Miller still hadn't gotten over their last encounter, when he'd tried to bring Jake up on charges.

"Miller," Jake said.

"Bite me," Miller said as he pushed off the elevator and took the stairs.

Jake smiled inwardly. *All's right with the world, Miller still hates me.* He pressed the button for his floor, relieved to be alone for a few minutes to gather his thoughts. The peace didn't last long. As he stepped off the elevator on the second floor, Jake noticed activity in the bullpen. A suspect or maybe a witness was loudly recounting a series of events to Detective Walsh. Jake continued walking to his office and almost collided with Louie at his door.

"Jeez, Jake, you almost spilled my coffee."

"How rude of me to think I could walk into my office without encountering someone."

Louie ignored Jake's comment. "You get Fisher and Burrows?"

"Not yet. After Santora checks his roster he'll give me a call."

"I have all the victims' photographs set up on the board. I got an easel in case you needed it."

"Good thinking. We have another half hour before everyone assembles. I need some time alone to outline the presentation. Can you head off anyone coming my way?"

Alone for the first time today, Jake started typing up his thoughts as he outlined them for his presentation. Next, he worked on the assignments. Time passed quickly. He checked his watch. *Shit, time's run out.* He took two minutes to review his notes. Satisfied, he downloaded the files to a flash drive and cleared his screen. Nothing would be stored on his computer. He grabbed his files and printouts then headed to the conference room.

Chapter 17

Most of the team had taken their seats by the time Jake walked into the room, though some were standing and chatting. Captain McGuire and Chief Doolittle were the only two who hadn't arrived yet. Jake noticed Louie had set up the bullpen's coffee machine in the back of the room. He turned to Louie and grinned. *You couldn't have a meeting with cops without serving coffee. I could use an IV of the stuff today.* Jake stepped toward the machine to pour a cup for himself. Without looking over his shoulder he knew the chief and/or the captain had walked into the room. All chatter had stopped.

With the sludge in his cup, Jake turned. "Cap, Chief."

"Is everyone here, Jake?" Chief Doolittle asked.

"Everyone but the two uniforms… I'm waiting on Santora to see who he can spare."

"Good enough. Let's get started then," Captain McGuire said, nodding to the board where the victims' photos were displayed.

Jake had purposely used the board and actual photos of the victims instead of a PowerPoint presentation. He felt it presented a starker picture with a bigger impact. According to the expressions on everyone's faces in the room, he was right.

"I'm going to start with victim number one, Elizabeth Bartholomew, even though the first four women are listed as missing—I'm assuming each of these women is a victim of this killer, which the papers have labeled the Bride Murders. I want to make this clear right here and now. At no time, in private or in public, do you refer to them as such. When asked, you refer to the victim by name. Nadia Carren. She is the only victim of this killer at this time. Understood?"

Jake scanned the room, waited until he received a nod from everyone. "I also want it understood no member of this team will issue statements of any kind to the press. Captain McGuire will be choosing a media liaison to deal with them directly.

"The uniforms, once named, will be recanvassing the neighborhood of each victim. They will be assigned to and report to Sergeant Romanelli, who will then coordinate their schedules. Each detective will reinterview family members, coworkers, and friends of the victims. Detective Brown will be researching the local papers for women who fits the description along with the assigned uniforms. Once he finds any who match the description, he'll be doing a safety check on each of them. Kirk, assess the volume; if there are too many for three people to handle, I'll assign more uniforms to help you.

"This pertains to everyone in the room. If I'm not available, report to Sergeant Romanelli. If anyone gets even a minute tingle, I want to hear about it. We'll meet back here every morning to review the previous day's interviews. Folks, there's a young woman's life hanging in the balance. The killer has given us only two weeks to solve this horrendous crime and save our unknown victim's life. Got it?"

Jake continued to outline assignments and noticed Joe Green's raised hand. Jake pointed to him and Green stood.

"Jake, for those of us from the different departments, wouldn't it be wise to pair us up with a homicide detective to begin with?"

"Everyone, this is Detective Joe Green, a new addition to Homicide from Missing Persons. Joe, I think you'll find the methods you used in Missing Persons are very similar to Homicide. Any more questions?" Jake looked around the room. "Okay, let's hit the streets. I don't want another woman's picture on this board if we can help it."

Green stayed back. Jake also noticed the chief and his captain remained at the back of the room. "Yes, Joe?"

"I didn't mean any disrespect, LT."

"None taken. I wouldn't have picked you, Joe, if I didn't think you'd be a valuable member of this team."

Green said, "Thanks. Are we supposed to work this any different than our other investigations?"

"Yes, we are by using a team, but it's steady police work that's going to solve this case, like any other."

"Thanks for your patience."

"Joe, I want my detectives to ask questions if they're not sure. It's the only way we'll all work well together." After dismissing Green, Jake walked over to Shamus and Doolittle. The meeting had taken a little over two hours and Jake was beat. The case had too many areas of interest and they'd only begun to dig below the surface.

"If you need more men, give me a call," Chief Doolittle said.

Jake waited for Doolittle to leave then turned to Shamus.

"Are you good with my picks, Shamus?"

"I'm familiar with most of them, but I'd like to see everyone's files anyway. Who did you have in mind for the media liaison?"

"I haven't decided yet. I wanted your input on who'd work best with the team."

"I'll appoint someone."

Shamus left, leaving Jake alone with the pictures of the five women. Nadia's picture took center stage. He heard someone clearing their throat and turned. "Yes, Louie?"

"You want me to work with Green?"

"No, he'll be fine on his own."

"Okay." Louie turned to leave.

"Louie, what are our chances of finding the next one alive?"

"I haven't a clue."

"Me either," Jake said absently. "How are you going to make this work with Sophia working late?"

Louie ran his hand through his hair. "I haven't had a chance to discuss it with her. I was planning on taking some time before I get too deep into it today."

"I'll try to make exceptions for you, but they can't be too obvious."

"I don't want you to make an exception for me. It would cause resentment. Plus, this might be the thing I was looking for. It's my career, which should freakin' come before the job she got on a whim."

"I'd find a different way to present it to her, if you want to keep your balls," Jake said.

"Yeah, I get it, but…"

"Bring your interview files from yesterday and Thursday to my office. I want to review the ones you thought needed a deeper look. While I'm doing that, I want you to review mine. I don't believe we missed this guy. It's a ploy to throw us off his trail." Jake held his copy of the killer's note in his hand. "Too bad he didn't say where I supposedly missed him. It could be either the tattoo parlors or the damn die shops—too many choices."

"I'll be in after I instruct the duty officer to move the coffee machine back to the bullpen."

Jake turned toward the board again. Each woman's face tugged at his heart. *They had their whole lives before them when this sick bastard cut their futures short. The game's on, and I will win. Failure is not an option.* Jake walked back to his office with his files tucked under his arm.

In his office he programmed a strong cup of joe. Coffee dripped noisily into his cup as he tried to put himself in the killer's head. Though he was using Mia's profile of the killer, he understood eventually he'd need to bring in the police shrink for an official profile. *Damn.* They had butted heads at one of his crime scenes in the past and the woman hadn't forgiven him. Dr. Julie Maxwell, a statuesque blonde with classic good looks, was cold and uncaring.

Though she was the Wilkesbury Police Department's resident psychiatrist, she was not full time nor was she a police officer. Maxwell only consulted for the department; her main career and interest remained with her private practice. He got the impression she was using the department as a stepping-stone to better things. He wished there were other psychiatrists on staff he could use, but no, he had to use her. He dialed Maxwell's number and left her a message when her voicemail picked up.

He crossed out the call on his to do list and grabbed his interview folders and started rereading them before he had to hand them over to Louie. He rubbed his throbbing forehead. Two files stood out each time—Arnie Velky's and Nick Tedessco's. *Could my feelings toward the mayor be clouding my judgment? Arnie didn't set off any alarms with me, though my instinct's been wrong before. Now, Tedessco, he rang my bells.* But hotheads didn't fit Mia's profile MO.

It took patience to torture a person. Tedessco had a quick and violent temper. This killer planned. It took time to construct a plan to kidnap and torture a person and dispose of a body. It involved a certain pathology, a love of pain—not to one's self but to others. Did Tedessco have the brains to plan this out? He did own and operate his own business, which gave him control over his time. Jake would have to look more closely at Tedessco's record before he dismissed him completely.

The intercom buzzed and tugged him from his thoughts. Jake depressed the key and said a little harshly, "Yes."

"Sorry to bother you, Lieutenant, but Dr. Maxwell is on the line for you," Katrina, the squad secretary, informed him.

"It's no bother. Put her through please." *Here we go,* he thought.

"Doc, thanks for getting back to me."

"Lieutenant, when do you want to meet?"

Why was she being friendly? What's up with that? It wasn't Maxwell's style to be agreeable. "I would like to meet this afternoon if you have the time."

"I'm available around four."

Jake took the phone from his ear and stared. Who was this person on the other end of the line? He noted the time: two forty-five. It gave him an hour to put together what he wanted her to see. He put the phone back to his ear and said, "Four's good. I'll see you here."

"Oh, I thought we'd meet in my office." *And the dance begins.*

"No, we'll meet in my office. All the files are here. I'll see you at four." Jake didn't give her a chance to argue. *It's my dance, so I lead.* He hung up.

He'd won the first round, but she had to have a personal agenda. Jake needed to figure out what it was before their meet. He sensed more than heard Louie at his door.

"All set?"

"Yep. Who were you talking to?"

"Louie, most people who eavesdrop do it more discreetly."

"Oh, well," Louie said, shrugging. "Give, who was it?"

"Dr. Maxwell."

"Shit, Jake, do we have to work with her? Why can't you use Mia?"

The good doctor had treated Louie like a peon on the last scene. Louie still hadn't forgiven her.

"It's what it is, Louie. She's the official consultant. We use her until she's replaced."

Louie took a seat across from Jake. "Here are my files."

Jake took them. He moved around several files before picking up a few. He handed his notes to Louie. "Two people stick out for me from my interviews. I'm not going to tell which ones until you give me your impressions of each."

"I had four who didn't ring right with me. Do you want me to work in here or at my desk?"

"Here's good, in case either of us has questions."

"Well, in that case…" Louie got up and helped himself to a cup.

"Are you going to offer me some of my own coffee?"

"Oh sure, you want some?" Louie grinned.

Jake picked up Louie's first file. He read through all of them once, then went back through them again, this time taking notes. He had to agree with Louie. There were four interviews where the interviewees fit the profile: Jack Burns, Scott Pencer, Mikey Stalls, and Kyle Simmons. Two of them had juvie records, all four had adult records. Jake pulled the juvie files first.

The warrants on Kyle Simmons's and Scott Pencer's juvie records gave Jake some insights, but no smoking guns. Kyle Simmons was a sociable guy according to Louie's notes. Kyle had been at his job as a toolmaker for the past eighteen years. He had the skill set to create the brand. Never married, but was engaged once. He told Louie he'd love to be married, but all the women he met were bitches and he wasn't settling.

Simmons's view on women put him on the list. Simmons also had a juvie record, though the charges were minor in comparison to some of the others. He'd been caught shoplifting at the local mall at the age of fifteen. Simmons got off with community service. Jake put a checkmark next to his name for a follow-up interview.

Scott Pencer, a tool and die maker, had been on the job for seven years. His juvie record was serious. He was also the youngest on the list of persons of interest. Pencer had pleaded no contest to date rape and spent a year in juvie. He still claimed, to this day, it was consensual sex until her parents walked in on them. The court must've agreed. It gave Pencer a reduced sentence.

Louie also commented on Pencer's personal hygiene—dirty blond hair, greasy fingernails, a day's growth on his face. Pencer had struck Louie as a stoner. Jake figured Louie's impressions were correct. The guy was engaged three times. What kind of women would date a man like him, let alone marry him? Pencer also got a checkmark next to his name.

Jake Burns: married twice, he admitted to hating women in general. He was the oldest on the list at forty-two, but still fit the profile on the high end. His second wife had called the police on him, claiming he hit her. They'd been in the middle of a nasty divorce and a bitter custody battle. He originally had custody of his children because of the ex's drug problems. She pressed charges. He spent time in jail and lost custody of his children. He also stayed on the list, another checkmark.

Next up, Mikey Stalls, a swell guy, who was stupid enough to brag to Louie that his fiancée broke their engagement because he couldn't keep it in his pants. Louie had put his bragging down to Mikey's Napoleon complex. The man didn't stand more than five feet three inches tall. He was also the right age and had the skill set like the rest. Stalls was an unkempt individual, but most people he had met today were.

Jake found out a good tool and die maker was worth his weight in gold, according to the owners of different shops. It also surprised him how much math was involved in their jobs. It proved they weren't stupid men, another checkmark in the serial killer category. Did women look at a man like Pencer for his earning potential? Did these men disclose their records when they dated? What caused the broken engagements or ended their marriages?

"How're you doing over there, Louie?"

"I finished with two a while ago and I'm studying the third one. And I read through the rest of the interviews. We should reinterview this guy Luke Jacobs, the owner of the first shop you visited."

"Why?"

"If we stick to the profile, we're looking for a successful person who blends well, he'd fit right in. Jacobs worked in the shop for years before his father passed him the reins. And he offered the information on how Velky was left at the altar...kind of like throwing you a bone."

"Good catch. I knew I kept you around for something," Jake said, joking.

"No one else stood out, though the killer's letter said you didn't interview him."

"Yeah it did; it's a ploy to throw us off his trail." Louie threw him a questioning look. "Hear me out. It was easy to single me out after Gwenn's report the other night. What if you or I got too close and he's using the letter as a smoke screen? The only thing I'm going to take as the truth from his letter is the fact we only have two weeks left before he grabs another woman."

"I agree. We still have some tattoo parlor employees to interview on Monday. Jake, have you considered it might be a jilted bride."

"I played with the idea but it doesn't hold together for me." Jake checked his watch. *Shit, the good doctor will be here in fifteen minutes.* He hadn't realized how much time had gone by.

"Why?"

"I don't have the time to get into it now. We'll discuss it after my meeting with Dr. Maxwell."

Louie started to open his mouth. Jake waved him off with a slight movement of his hand. Dr. Maxwell stood in his doorway. Early.

"Dr. Maxwell, please come in. We'll be finished here in a minute. You remember Sergeant Romanelli."

"Yes, Sergeant, it's nice to see you again."

Jake spoke before Louie could greet Maxwell. "Louie, can you do me a favor? Touch base with your team. Have the officer on duty make copies of our notes." He was offering Louie an out.

"I'm going to make the appointments with the other persons of interest for tomorrow unless you need me in this meeting. I'll inform them we want to meet in private and not where they work."

"I got this covered, thanks." Louie could barely tolerate Maxwell, so Jake gave him a pass. Louie left the office. "Please sit down, Doctor."

"How much time do you need?"

"I'm not sure, why?" Maxwell still hadn't sat down.

"I normally provide my answering service with a time frame so I won't be disturbed while I'm in a meeting. This way they'll only interrupt in case of an emergency."

"I want to run through the case and give you our impressions of the six men who caught our eyes. I'll need a written profile from you, but for today a verbal one will do. I'd say we'll be about an hour, two at the most."

"Fine, close enough. Excuse me while I call in."

Jake never took his eyes off her as she walked to his window. She spoke quietly into her phone. He had to admit she was a fine-looking woman with a haughty way about her. His best guess, she stood five-ten with long blond hair highlighted by her pale blue eyes and fair skin. Some would call her a classic beauty. He called her a snob.

"I'm ready."

Maxwell put her phone away in her huge purse then sat in his visitor's chair, crossing her impressive legs. *Oh yeah, this woman knows what she looks like and uses it to her advantage.* Except it wasn't working on him. He purposely held eye contact with her, never lowering his eyes to her well-displayed cleavage or her long, shapely legs, though he saw it all. She had dressed casually for their meeting in a button-down blouse in the same color as her eyes. She had left the top three buttons open to expose the tops of her breasts. Maxwell paired the blouse with a hip hugging black skirt. Yep, he took it all in and had no interest whatsoever.

"I was surprised you had the time today," he said.

"My schedule is light on the weekends. I only take emergency calls."

"Thanks for letting me know."

The officer on duty knocked as he entered. "Here are the copies, Lieutenant." He dropped the folders on Jake's desk.

"Thanks, Erik."

Jake reiterated the obvious to Maxwell. "Sergeant Romanelli and I are partners. If I'm not available, he'll answer your questions." Jake waited for Maxwell's acknowledgment before continuing.

"We had copies made of the crime scene and the interviews of the six men who top our list and fit our profile—"

Maxwell cut him off. "Where did you get your profile?" *Ah, tricky area.*

"I took an FBI course last year at Quantico on serial killers and profiling. In the file I've included my initial profile for your review. It's standard serial-killer stuff, until we learn more. Please feel free to add or subtract from it."

"One course doesn't make a profiler."

Jake stayed quiet and waited until Maxwell picked up the file and started reading it. She didn't discount the profile immediately, but he knew she would. She studied the crime scene photos first before she picked up the files on the six men. Maxwell took her time and read through each one before she answered him.

"This is a thorough profile, Lieutenant, for a novice." Jake couldn't hide his surprise.

"I've been in homicide quite a while, Doctor. Most murderers fall into established categories."

She ignored his comment and continued, "Each of these men fit it perfectly. You'll want to make sure you don't miss anyone because they don't fit your profile, though maybe it's the reason he sent you the note. You or the sergeant might have missed him the first time around."

"We're going to be working in close quarters, Doctor, please call me Jake," he said to give himself a minute.

"I will add to it, but I'll need the rest of the weekend to work it up. Is there any evidence you want me to review?"

"I need you to work up the profile based on the crime scene photos first. Once we have your profile, we can go from there." He couldn't say why he'd held back the rest of the evidence. "The entire team is under strict orders not to speak with the press. Any releases will come through me to the media liaison. If a member of the team is caught giving a statement, they'll be off the team and reprimanded. Everything I share with you is in confidence. Understood?"

"Naturally. I'll take care of the profile. Will you be available Monday night?"

He'd expected an argument. She continued to throw him off-balance. Jake brought up his calendar on his computer. "What time Monday?"

"I finish my rounds at seven. Is seven thirty good?"

"I'll have to call you on Monday. I've already scheduled some interviews. When I have an idea of when they'll be done, I'll give you a call. Is that workable for you?"

"Yes, I'll expect your call. If you're available, do you want to make it a dinner meeting?" Jake raised an eyebrow. She rushed on. "It's my normal dinner hour, Lieut…I mean, Jake."

"That's fine, Doctor, unless you'd like me to order something for here?"

"This would be the last place I'd like to eat," she snipped.

"We'll touch base on Monday to see if the time still works for both of us. I'll be in the field most of the day. I'll give you my cell number." He wrote it down then handed it to her. He took hers, entered it into his phone, and watched her do the same.

"I'll call you when I've completed the profile."

She stood, extended her hand. Jake stood, took her hand in his, and noted her strong grip. It didn't get past him she'd never invited him to call her by her first name. The doctor had stood on protocol. He started to count to ten after she left his office and smiled when Louie walked in on eight.

"Well?"

"Well what?"

"Did she pick apart Mia's profile?"

"She liked my profile. I didn't tell her Mia did it."

"How's Mia going to handle that?"

"Louie, it's not a big deal." Seeing Louie's expression, Jake added, "I didn't want my chops busted by Maxwell for not calling her into this sooner."

"What were her opinions on the case and the direction we're heading in?"

"I only shared the crime scene photos and our interview notes with her. She warned me not to ignore people who don't fit our profile. It's good advice."

"It is. Why didn't you share everything?"

"Something's off. This might sound crazy—but she was too agreeable. It was out of character. I could almost hear her salivating. Cases like this can make or break careers."

"You think she's in it for the notoriety."

"I hope not, but it's an impression I got. I did stress no member of this team is allowed to speak with the press. We'll see if she follows the rules."

* * * *

At the bar in his living room, he wondered how his letter had been received. *Is Carrington up to the challenge? Did I wipe all my fingerprints? Are they right now coming for me?* Sweat trickled down his face as each question raced through his mind. Doubt had plagued him all night after he handed over the letter to the bum. *Why did I send a letter? Damn, what a mistake. Now they'll come back and reinterview me. What the hell was I thinking?*

For the first time in a long time, doubt and a nameless fear made him feel alive. *The chase is on. Will the bumbling Wilkesbury Police Department catch me? No, they won't. I'm smarter than they are. Damn it, I'm tired. I must find Ciara soon.* He sipped his beer and contemplated his next move with both Carrington and Ciara. *How much longer can I survive without you, darling? I'm exhausted.* A vast, dark, empty hole engulfed him. Time, minute by minute, ate away at his heart and mind. He'd not had a reprieve from it for years.

He threw his beer bottle across the room. As the bottle shattered against the wall, he let out a toe-curling scream. "Why the hell did you leave me, Ciara?"

He had been paying her parents' next-door neighbors in Florida for the last five years. They had called to tell him Ciara was visiting her parents this week. Right away he booked the next flight out, only to arrive fifty minutes too late. His flight got delayed in Atlanta. He cursed his bad luck at not being able to get a nonstop flight on such short notice. He held his hands shoulders' width apart. *God, I got so close to holding her again.* The images of her brought a half smile to his face. How would she feel about the special ceremony he had planned for them when they came together again? This time, her promise would be upheld...her vows spoken...the ceremony completed. They'd mate and start their family. Words danced before his tear-filled eyes. Before he hopped a plane again, he'd verify she was still there.

"Now and forever, until death do us part, Ciara."

Chapter 18

On his second stop, Jake hit the mother lode with Bill Samuels, the owner of Dark Ink. Samuels, a beefy five-foot-ten-inch man with hands the size of hams, liked to talk, and, funny thing, Jake liked to listen. The place looked like the other tattoo parlors except with a lot more grime. Why anyone would trust the needles in this place was beyond him.

As Jake approached the counter he reached for his badge. The clerk said, "Not necessary. I was wondering if you guys would get around to me."

"And you would be?"

"I'm the owner here. Bill Samuels." He reached a hand out to Jake. He took it, then dropped it while Samuels continued talking. A listless handshake said a lot about a guy. "I ran into Nick Tedessco last night at the bar. He told me you were around asking about branding."

"What else did Mr. Tedessco say?" Jake casually leaned a hip against the glass counter.

"He said you were going to hassle him because of his record. Are you?" Bill was seated behind the counter on a stool. He placed his elbows on top of it and rested his chin on his chubby hands.

"Am I what?"

"Going to hassle him?"

"If he warrants it. How about you? Do you have a record?" Jake pegged him as an attention seeker from the get-go. You couldn't discount the people who wanted to insert themselves into your investigation for one reason or another. *What was Samuels's reason*, he wondered.

"Naw, I'm clean. Run me if you need to, you'll see."

"I will."

Jake asked him the same questions he'd asked everyone else. Mostly he got the same answers until Bill slipped up.

"You got any other pictures to show? Did the guy actually hack her up?"

"Where did you get your information?"

"I watch true-crime shows. The killers always hack up the women."

"And you enjoy how the killers cut them up?"

"God, no, I was only pointing out what happens on television."

"I'm not allowed to comment on ongoing cases, Bill. You have your ear to the street, right?" Jake spoke low, in a confidential tone. He played to Bill's ego.

"Yeah, I do. People come in for tattoos, they get nervous. They talk up a storm."

"Have you heard anything about this victim?" Jake didn't want to lead him, though he thought Samuels might have something here. Or was he only another nut who wanted his fifteen minutes of fame?

"Man, everyone's talking about her. Someone last night said she was mutilated. What did he do to her?"

The guy's eyes glazed over as he moistened his lips. It sickened Jake. Morbid curiosity, that's all Nadia was to this guy. Balling his fists at his sides, a smile plastered on his face, he asked his next question.

"Who told you that? Did they give you a lot of details, Bill?"

"The guy I shot the breeze with on the barstool next to me said she was branded. Is that true?"

The hair on the back of Jake's neck stood on end. "What'd the guy look like, Bill?"

"He was an average Joe."

"You see him at the bar before last night? Is he a regular? How tall was he?"

"Man, why all the questions?" Bill's face lit up as if it was New York City on New Year's Eve. "Hey, she was mutilated, wasn't she?"

"No. I'm interested in all idiots who spread rumors. You ever see the guy before?" Jake reined himself in, schooled his face and voice.

"There's something familiar about him but I couldn't put my finger on it."

"What did he look like?"

"I can't tell you how tall he was because he was seated when I got to the bar. He had small shoulders—about this wide." Samuels held his hands out about twenty inches apart.

"That's good. What color hair and eyes did he have?" He didn't write anything down. Jake didn't want to show Bill his excitement or put too much credence in his answers.

"Brown hair, I'm not sure of the eye color." Samuels scratched his head as he looked off in the distance. "He wore glasses."

"What kind of glasses?" Jake pressed.

"Glasses, glasses, I didn't study the damn guy. I'm not into men."

"Were they wire frames, black frames, square, round or oblong?"

Samuels rubbed his scruffy chin. Jake wanted to hit the man over the head to jar his memory but remained aloof.

"Brown, I'd have to say brown. I remember they didn't fit him right. He kept pushing them up his nose."

"Will you work with a police artist?" This idiot wanted his fifteen minutes of fame. If it helped his case he'd give it to him.

"Is he the guy who killed the bride?"

"No, as I told you before, I'm interested because he's spreading rumors." Jake kept his voice bored, his face blank.

"I see. Yeah, I'll work with your artist. If I see the guy at the bar again, do you want me to call you?" This guy was either involved or stupid. Either way it would be interesting.

"Yes, but don't be obvious about it."

Jake turned to leave, then nonchalantly he turned back to Bill. "One last question. What's the name of the bar?"

"Hard Rider. I'm there every night."

"Are you married?"

"That's two questions." Samuels smiled.

"Excuse me?"

"You said you had one last question and then you asked two. I'm teasing you."

Jake never took his eyes off of Samuels as he waited for him to answer the question. "Yeah, I'm married. Why?"

"Your wife doesn't mind you hanging out at the bar every night?"

"Naw, she hates me, but that's marriage for ya." He flashed Jake a toothy grin.

It took all kinds, he thought. Jake thanked Bill Samuels before he left the shop. Quite the character and personable, he fit the profile perfectly. Outside in his car, Jake made notes from his interview. Samuels could be jerking his chain, though it didn't make sense for him to do it. *If the killer has pitted himself against me personally, did he intentionally seek out Samuels, figuring out I'd have to interview him eventually? Or is Samuels challenging me? It's food for thought.*

Still sitting out in front of Dark Ink, Jake placed a call to Louie. "Any luck on your end?" he asked, before giving Louie a chance to even say hello.

"I'm picking away at the list."

"Anything pop out?"

"No, how about you? Did you find something?"

"We might've caught a break. Are you with Green right now?"

"Yeah, why?"

"Leave him the car and have him continue on with the list. I'll pick you up. Where are you?"

"I'm in the west end canvassing Nadia's neighbors. I'll be on Joycraft Avenue."

"I'll be there in ten minutes to pick you up."

Jake finished writing up his notes before heading to the west end of town to get Louie. The bar would be their first stop. Could he possibly be lucky enough to get a visual on the killer? It would all depend on the bar and if they had their surveillance cameras on during business hours. He was familiar with Hard Rider. Biker bar, pick-up joint, its customers were rough, most with an axe to grind. Jake was friendly with the owner, Timothy Fahey, who had cooperated with him on other investigations. Jake even liked to hang there on occasion. No one ever bothered him. The alcohol was cheap and strong and the conversation limited. After a hard day on the job it eased his heavy heart. As he pulled up, he eyed Louie standing on the street corner in front of his police-issued car talking to Detective Green. Jake pulled alongside and lowered his passenger-side window.

"Slumming, guys?" Jake said, looking over the tops of his sunglasses.

"LT, you hit on something?" Green said.

"Not yet. Keep up the interviews." Jake checked his watch. "We'll meet back at the station in two hours and discuss what you discover, if anything."

Joe Green nodded to Jake as Louie climbed into Jake's passenger seat. Before Louie could buckle his seat belt, Jake pulled away from the curb.

"What's got your panties in a twist?" Louie asked.

Jake filled Louie in on his interview and his impressions of Samuels.

"Hmmm. Is he for real?"

"I'm hoping he is, but I'm not ruling out anyone who could help us solve this. I find it suspicious the alleged guy at the bar singled Samuels out. If he was the killer, how did he know we hadn't interviewed Samuels yet?"

"Good point."

"Yeah, but… something in the killer's life has changed recently, which now has him upping the game. You asked, Louie, why this body, why now? I'm sure we'll find some recent event or circumstance that altered his life."

"Jake, I hate to bring this up. Do you think it's a cop?"

"Christ Jesus! I hope not. The question remains, though, how'd he figure out we hadn't gotten around to interviewing Samuels yet?"

"Are we going to backtrack and ask the other owners if they were approached?"

"Not us, but I'll have the junior detectives do that. It could be a ruse to get us to waste our time with busywork."

"I'll check to see who reviewed the murder book. Don't look at me that way. Someone is shadowing us and is familiar with the questions we're asking. It's bothering me," Louie said.

"Go ahead. It has to be crossed off the list anyway."

Jake pulled into the parking lot of Hard Rider. At six o'clock on a Saturday night there would be a few leftovers from the afternoon crowd before it got jammed around ten with the normal evening crowd. The lot had three cars and a half-dozen bikes lined up on the left. On the way in Jake admired a full-dressed hog. Someone had spent some serious bucks on this baby. It was beautiful.

"Hey, stay away from my bike," someone called out over his shoulder.

Jake pulled his jacket back to expose his shield and gun and turned to address the speaker. "I'm only admiring it. You got a problem with that?"

Eyeing his badge, the guy looked up at Jake. "I don't like anyone handling it, cop or not."

"Do I look like I'm handling it?" Five feet nine inches, beer gut hanging over the belt, balding on top, the guy didn't present the Easy Rider image of the movies. This one shouted out office worker, not rebel.

"Then we don't have a problem." The biker shrugged.

"No, we don't."

Jake could have busted the guy's chops for drinking and driving, but he wasn't in the mood. *Asshat.* He and Louie continued to walk toward the door. Jake walked in first. The bar patrons turned in unison to check out the newcomers. A couple turned back to the bar, but the seasoned ones eyed them. A few discreetly pocketed items, probably in the hopes it wasn't a bust. Jake scanned the entire room.

From behind the bar, Tim Fahey, the owner, shouted out, "Hey, Jake, Louie."

Louie returned the greeting, but neither walked further into the bar. An intimidation move he had learned over the years. Sometimes, he didn't even have to act to catch a suspect. They'd give themselves away with their nervous tics. Tonight, Jake was hoping to spy Samuels's drinking buddy. As he and Louie bellied up to the bar, Tim thrust a big, beefy hand across the counter, grabbing Jake's hand, then Louie's. *The man's a bear,* Jake thought, at six two, Tim's two-hundred-forty-pound girth kept most of his clientele in order. There were some, after a few drinks, who decided to try their luck and throw a punch or two at Tim when he ousted them. Fahey always won.

"What can I get you?"

"Nothing right now. You have someone who can handle the bar while we speak in private?"

"Helen, come man the bar," Tim yelled to the lone waitress. Turning back to Jake he said, "Come into my office."

Tim motioned for them to follow him. Once inside, Jake closed the door and walked over to the window. He observed the back parking lot. Only two cars occupied it. He turned back to Tim.

"Do have your surveillance on during operating hours?"

"Yeah, we do. Why?"

"I need last night's tapes. I don't have a warrant, Tim. It's not going to be a problem is it?"

"It depends on what you're going to do with them."

"The only thing I care about right now is one guy who was talking to a person of interest in the Carren murder investigation."

"That killer bastard hangs out here?"

"Not sure, I'm only asking, that's all. I'm trying to figure out if he's a regular or not. I need to get a visual and hopefully an ID."

Tim turned from his desk and opened his floor safe. Reaching in, he dug out several tapes. After checking the dates, he handed Jake the one for the night in question. Next, he went to a closet and popped out the one currently recording before popping another one into the machine.

"Two tapes?"

"Yeah, I use them until they're full. Last night started on the one marked Thursday and this one marked Friday is the rest of the night. Am I going to get them back?"

"I'll make you a copy if there's something on it we need. If not, I'll return the originals."

* * * *

Jake drove to his house, not the station. Brigh lifted her head as he walked in, then chose to ignore him. He wanted to view the tapes in private. Before putting them into the video machine they both grabbed a beer. Louie sat down on the couch. Jake kicked back in the chair with the ottoman. He turned the volume all the way down. It seemed surreal with no sound. They watched the ritual of mating clearly expressed in body language. Other patrons preened, strutted their stuff in a display of strength.

Ten minutes into the second tape, Jake saw Samuels take a seat at the bar. To his right a twentysomething woman flirted with the guy on her right. On Samuels's left, sitting on the bar stool, a man with Coke-bottle eyeglasses and a slight hunch toyed with his drink. Bill was right. The guy did have small shoulders. A New York Yankees baseball cap perched on his head partially shaded his face. Samuels, the idiot, hadn't mentioned the thick glasses the suspect wore. Bill ordered a beer and nursed it for fifteen minutes. When Samuels ordered his next drink the guy to his left started talking to him. Jake froze the screen as he and Louie moved closer to the television to study the man Jake suspected was their killer.

Years of doing the job had taught them to take nothing for granted. The man's height would be difficult to judge until he stood up, so he concentrated on the details of the face. A square jawline, high, defined cheekbones. His brown eyes appeared huge due to the magnification of the glasses. Brown shoulder-length hair hid his ears. Age seemed right. Jake pegged him around thirty to thirty-five years old. If asked to describe the man, the first word that came to his mind was average. Average build, average looks and, Jake guessed, average height.

"Is this his face, or a disguise?" Jake asked.

"I'd say theatrical implants, around the cheekbones."

"Why?"

"They're too uniform on both sides. It's perfectly symmetrical," Louie said, pointing with his beer can.

Jake agreed. "I can't say I interviewed him yesterday or today. In that getup he could be anyone. It makes him generic. Let's keep watching, maybe we'll at least get his height," Louie said as he walked to the couch and sat.

Jake pressed the play button and watched the scene unfold in front of him. Five minutes later, he stopped the video again.

"What's up?"

"Look at his neck. What kind of necklace is that?"

"Hard to tell, but it's not a religious one. Whatever it is, it's big. It looks like silver with multicolored stones on either side of it. Not sure of the shape. Maybe Thomas can play with the video back at the station and enhance it. The shape almost reminds me of a family crest. Doesn't it?" Louie said, pushing off the couch to get closer to the television. "What kind of person would wear a family crest?"

"Not sure. I've only seen them in pictures. Let's get an enhanced print of the necklace and show it to all the jewelers in town," Jake said, smiling. "We just caught our first huge break. It's the killer's first mistake. Though it's unremarkable, I'll also want a print of his face to be handed out to the team. I understand when we find him he won't look anything like the picture."

"Neither one of us recognized him. The necklace isn't significant. What are you seeing that I'm not?"

"His hands scream shop worker to me. Look closer at the design on the necklace. It's not common, though I'm positive I've seen it before. Right now, I can't place where. When we catch up to him we'll find tonight's disguise in his closet if we're lucky."

The square-shaped necklace nudged at him. Where had he seen it? Jake thought it looked like an eagle, but hell, he could be seeing what he wanted at this point. The colored stones made it unique. The necklace also had a raised design on each side of the gem. He and Louie watched the film until the suspect left. Samuels stood behind his chair talking to Tedessco, who had shown up five minutes before the man left. The suspect stood, exchanged words with Bill and Tedessco, and left the bar. Jake used Bill Samuels's height to gauge his drinking buddy's height. He'd put the guy at approximately five ten or five eleven.

"Why would this suspect play games like this? Is the killer annoyed we didn't publicize his letter? The mention of the mutilation to Samuels is what got my radar clicking," Jake said.

"Samuels could be the killer, putting words into the other guy's mouth. Can Dunn filter out the bar noise and give us a clean copy of the conversation between him and Samuels?" Louie asked.

"I plan on asking. Let's hope he can perform miracles."

Jake and Louie drove to the station in silence. They'd watched the video once with the sound turned off and then again with sound. With no sound it looked like the unknown man had started the conversation. With the volume up, Samuels's bar voice echoed through Jake's speakers. Bill Samuels must have had a few drinks before he hit the bar. His speech was slurred as he spoke at an extremely loud volume over the noisy crowd. If he hadn't had a purpose and wasn't looking for this scene, Jake would have put the volume down to a normal level. The thing was, the bar wasn't crowded and the band was on break. Bill Samuels's volume seemed forced, not by necessity but by choice.

If his purpose for telling Jake about this encounter had been to shed light on a different suspect, he'd failed. The tape put Samuels near the top of the list along with his companion. Were they partners? Jake didn't buy the theory his killer worked with another. All the evidence pointed to a single killer. Did he use peons to collect the victims? Could it simply be a chance meeting of like minds which eventually led to murder? Nothing on the tape showed they had any familiarity with each other. Nor did the bartender treat the unknown as a regular customer. Louie broke into his train of thought.

"This puts Samuels in a new light. From what I heard on the video he brought up the murder first, not the new guy," Louie said.

"I agree. We move him up. I'm going to delegate the other shops to the other detectives while we concentrate on the ones we've already interviewed."

Jake pulled into the station's garage. Louie went straight to his desk in the bullpen, Jake to his office. First thing, he unlocked his desk, pulled out the murder book and updated it with the latest information. Procedure required it. But what he put in it and what he didn't would be up to Shamus. He called Damien Dunn next. After hanging up with Damien, Jake felt better. Dunn didn't see a problem with editing out the background noise on the video. The conversation between Samuels and his new friend would determine which direction the investigation would head.

Am I putting too much into this?

The mayor's unwarranted pressure had put doubt in Jake's mind. It was something new for him. He'd never admit it aloud, but the slap and the IA investigation had shaken his confidence. Never had his career been on the line before. And he didn't want it there again. He forced his focus back on the case—nothing but the case; it was difficult, but it held precedence over his career. Nadia deserved no less.

He pressed the intercom button on his phone. "Green, get in here."

Green rushed into his office. "What's up, LT?"

"Take this photo up to Joel Bennett and ask him four questions. One, is this a disguise and two, if it is, can he remove the glasses and give us a better look at the guy's face, especially his eyes? Third, can he show him with short hair? And does he think the subject enhanced his cheeks and jawline?"

"I'm on it. Is this a new suspect?"

"Yes." Jake trusted Green not to spread rumors but added. "Green, that's between us, got it?"

"I do."

Alone, Jake turned his chair to the window and put his faith in Bennett's talents. If anyone could get him the guy's face, he would. After five years, could it be this simple? Why had the killer decided to engage him after all this time?

What the hell changed? What pushed up the killer's timeline? Or has he been killing all along, somewhere else?

He'd assigned Burke to search CODIS files for like crimes. After he gave Al his instructions, he'd throw Kraus a bone and utilize his downtime. Maybe mend a bridge while he was at it for putting Kraus's partner, Burke, on the task force instead of him. Jake would have him search the papers for any unusual events or deaths connected to his main suspects. He turned back to his desk and sent out an email from his personal account to both Burke and Kraus detailing their search parameters.

He grabbed his cell phone and hit speed dial. Before Mia, he would have worked the case into the wee hours with nothing else on his mind. But commitment demanded courtesy.

"Hello." She sounded groggy.

"Hi, were you sleeping?"

"No, editing. How'd it go today?"

"I'm still at it. I'll probably be another hour. Do you still want me to come over?" Yawning, he knew he wasn't up to the drive.

"Yes, if you're up to it."

No, I'm not up to it. Who am I kidding? Nothing else would be accomplished tonight, though a drink and some alone time would be great.

"Did you get the files I sent?"

"Yes, I made some notes for you. Why don't we have lunch tomorrow? You can review them and update me?"

"Thanks, I'll be heading home in an hour. I'll call when I get in."

After he hung up with Mia, Jake opened his emails. The first one came from Green. He reported nothing new from his interviews with Nadia's neighbors. Brown's email listed several women with their attached engagement photos. To date, they were all alive and kicking. He noted Brown was only up to the March announcements in the Wilkesbury paper and still needed to do the same in the Hartford and Danbury papers. Jake reread Brown's email. He tried to dig out a vague thought forming at the back of his head. Why wasn't Brown researching the smaller papers and the free papers each town seemed to have these days? Jake sent Brown his ideas on those papers. He scanned a copy of the printout of the necklace and attached it to an email he composed to all the jewelers in town. Maybe he'd get lucky and someone in town had sold it. If not, he'd send it to the surrounding towns' jewelers before researching it on the Internet. He hit the Send key then shut down his computer before he headed out. He'd answer the rest of the emails once he settled in at home and had a meal.

* * * *

He paced his kitchen. Would Carrington take the bait? Why was there nothing on the news today about the letter? *I watched the homeless bastard go into the station house this morning. Why are they holding it back? I even put my neck out there last night and spoke to that idiot Samuels. Will Samuels tell them about me?* Are Carrington and his team smart enough to follow through on the information?

Nerves jiggled inside him. He decided to go down into his workroom. In the basement he walked to the wall of cabinets. Inside he had collected hair samples of not only his victims, but the bumbling idiot he planned on framing for the crimes.

His lips curled.

"I can see the headlines now. The high and mighty bastard will lose his shine after he's arrested. Mother won't think so highly of him then, the witch."

On the wall, next to the last cabinet, hung pictures of Ciara and all the imposters in wedding dresses. None compared to her in beauty or intelligence. He wondered if he'd have killed sometime in the future even if he and Ciara had married—a question with no answer. Looking back now, he could see how antsy she'd been. What had he done to scare her away?

"Even if we had married, you wouldn't have stayed around for long. Would you, Ciara?" he asked the picture.

He grabbed the knife off the counter and slashed her picture as he started to cry. He collapsed onto the basement's concrete floor as his emotions overtook him. Time passed as the cold seeped into his bones. He swiped at his tears as he stood. With a gentle touch, he removed her picture. From the drawer in front of him he pulled out another picture of Ciara and hung it on the wall.

"Ah, my beauty. Someday soon." The dream restored, he stood for another couple of minutes as he admired her before he turned toward his calendar.

"Shit, I hate Sundays. Dinner at the queen's tomorrow, along with my ass-kisser brother, his wife and their perfect children. 'Are you dating yet?' 'When are you going to move forward?' 'How long do you plan on mooning over Ciara?'" *Ah, yes. They don't tire of their questions. I wish I could tell them all it's none of their damn business.*

A delicious thought ran through his head. Maybe he should kill all of them next, instead of the woman he'd picked out today.

Chapter 19

Louie washed the supper dishes while the kids continued to bend Sophia's ear with their chatter. This past month he'd missed this the most, and he could see she did, too. More than anything he missed bouncing his cases off her. She always gave him a fresh view of them. It helped him see the bigger picture. One by one the kids left the kitchen.

The last dish washed and dried, he put it into the cabinet and turned to his wife. "Would you like a cup of coffee?"

"Why all the special treatment?"

"I can't fix you a cup of coffee?" he asked, annoyed. She raised her eyebrows at him. Oh, how he hated when she did that.

"Louie, you fixed dinner, washed the dishes, and now you want to make me a cup of coffee. What gives?"

"Nothing. I missed you."

"And?"

"Christ, see if I fix you dinner again." He threw down the dish towel and stormed from the room mumbling, "Can't a guy be nice to his wife anymore?"

She followed him into the living room. "You're always nice. Are you trying to guilt me?"

"Shit!"

"Louie, no cursing, you're not at the station."

"I'm not trying to guilt you, as you put it. I'm trying to be nice because I understand you're tired. Why are you making such a big deal out of it?"

She took a seat across from him. Louie couldn't figure out what he had done wrong. All he had hoped for was a peaceful evening with his wife after all the damn bickering. Now it looked like she was ready to pick a fight. An excruciatingly loud silence filled the room.

When she spoke after a few minutes, he wasn't prepared for her answer. "I'm sorry. You did nothing wrong, Louie. Watching you tonight made me realize that you and the children don't need me—"

He cut off her next words. "What do you mean we don't need you? Of course we need you. And for the love of Pete, I'm trying my best to understand your reasons. We've all been forced to adjust to the new schedule. The kids are adjusting a little easier than me. No one understands better than me how our life around here has changed, and with it, our responsibilities have also shifted." Pushing out of his chair, Louie knelt in front of her. It was his turn to grovel. "I can't live without you, *tesoro.*" His treasure. He used Italian because he knew she loved it.

A single tear fell from her eye. He thumbed it away. "I… I watched the kids ask you questions they normally ask me and it hurt. I never meant to disrupt our household. To be honest, I was feeling no one needed me anymore."

"*Amante,* you didn't upset the household. I did. I'm such a jerk. We'll figure it out, if you want to keep working." *God,* he hoped she didn't.

"I meant what I said in the parking garage. Give me one more month and then I'm going to quit."

"Why are you going to work one more second for that cretin?"

"I can't explain it. Not right now, Louie. Please understand."

All righty then, she's made up her mind and there was no way in heaven or hell a person could change it. I can be patient for one more month if Malone behaves. If not…

"I'm going to continue to bring you dinner if you work late. Nothing's changed in relationship to my opinion of him. *Ti amo.*"

"I love you back."

Forced to stand once his knees locked, he pushed off them. Sophia jumped up to help him. Christ, he was getting old. Standing, he looked down into her eyes and took her chin in his hand and placed a kiss on her lips. At least for now, it seemed they had agreed to a compromise. Louie hoped he could keep his end of it.

"I did need to talk to you. Jake's formed a task force because the killer has given us two weeks to catch him. If we don't, he's going to take another woman."

"I'm sorry. This puts a lot of pressure on you two."

"Not only us, but our families. All team members' vacation, sick time, and personal time has been canceled until further notice." Louie watched as understanding hit Sophia.

"What do we do when I have to work late?"

Shit! Shit! Shit! Wrong question, Sophia. How do I handle this? He went with his gut.

"LJ is old enough to watch the other children. We need to show him we trust him. It will only be for a couple of hours at a time and not every night I hope." A subtle hint, but obviously one she didn't get.

Concern washed over her face. "He is old enough, but he's never had this kind of responsibility before. Marisa and Carmen can be a handful at the best of times."

"I've left him in charge a couple of times over the past few weeks and he's handled them. What choice do we have? I can't back out of this case."

"I'm not asking you to."

She turned her back on him and walked across the room. She stopped at the window and looked out. He came up behind her and wrapped his arms around her waist. "We taught him well, Sophia. Besides, we're only a phone call away if he needs us." Her cell phone vibrated in her pocket. "Do you need to get that?"

"No. I'm not answering it tonight. This evening is for us," she said.

Louie frowned over her shoulder and wondered who she'd be ignoring this late. If he needed to, he could always check the bill later for the phone number.

* * * *

Papers everywhere greeted Jake when he woke Sunday morning. Last night, a thought had flitted through his mind. The idea never fully developed, though he'd recognized the importance of his failure to grasp it. God, he hated when that happened. Maybe if he thought of something else the puzzle piece might present itself again. He made a full pot of coffee, grabbed a mug of it, and sat on the floor. As he studied the papers, he reached up onto the table and pulled down his notepad. For some reason, he couldn't explain why, he had grouped the players into pairs instead of individuals.

He jotted down info on each pair and listed their connections to the missing women and Nadia. His cell phone rang. It interrupted his thought process.

"Yo."

"Lieutenant, it's Brown."

"What'd you find?" Cases like this one did away with social etiquette.

"You asked me to search for a major event we could connect to any of the suspects. I found one, but the connection isn't to a suspect."

"Who does it connect to, Kirk?"

"Neil McMichaels."

"Son of a bitch!" He never even considered the railroad safety inspector a viable suspect. For one thing he was on the high side of the profile at forty-five years old. Was he losing it?

"Yeah."

"What happened?"

"Are you home?"

"Yes. What do you have?" Annoyed, Jake couldn't understand why Brown was stalling.

"I'll scan it to your email. This way you can see what I see."

Patience was a virtue he didn't possess, though he heard something in Brown's voice, he agreed to wait for the email and didn't push Brown for more information. Jake got up off the floor and walked to his office.

"It's on its way. McMichaels lost his younger sister six years ago in a hit-and-run accident. Neil was considerably older than her, like fifteen years older. The police assumed it was a drunk driver. But here's the thing. They never caught the person. Did you get the picture?"

As his email opened Jake let out a low whistle as he viewed his screen. "Yes."

"Danielle McMichaels was twenty-two at the time of the accident—the same age as Nadia. Neil McMichaels was her only living relative. I sent you another picture."

Danielle McMichaels and Nadia Carren could be identical twins. The other picture showed the injuries Danielle had incurred at the time of death. Jake next read the police report Brown had also emailed him. McMichaels almost got arrested after he hounded the detectives who handled the case, or in McMichaels's opinion, mishandled the case.

"Does the file have a picture of Neil?"

"Yes."

"Send it over."

An idea pushed forward. He printed out the photo. Jake ran into the kitchen and pulled out the printouts he had ordered yesterday of the man at the bar on Friday night. Though they were grainy like McMichaels's photo, it gave Jake what he needed. The two men were similar in coloring but McMichaels's build was a bit wider. Good enough for him to pull McMichaels in for an interview. On his notepad, he wrote down a question. *Does McMichaels wear colored contact lenses?*

"Are you at the station?"

"Yep."

"Kirk, grab a uniform and a car, pick up McMichaels right away. I'll meet you at the station after I get a warrant to search his house." Jake started to hang up, changed his mind. "If he asks, tell him some information came into our hands and we need to investigate it to eliminate him. And we appreciate his cooperation. Got that, Kirk?"

"Yeah, LT."

The minute he hung up Jake dialed a cell number he'd memorized years ago. Normally, Judge Eisenberg was his best shot for warrants with little evidence, but today was Sunday. He wouldn't be well received. With fingers crossed Jake called his second choice, Judge Warner, instead and waited for him to answer.

"This better be good at this ungodly hour," Warner barked into Jake's ear.

Shit, what time is it? He looked down at his wrist to see the time. Jake cursed his stupidity. *Who but me called a judge at five thirty on a Sunday morning? No one. Please let him think this is as important as I do. I'm already on his shit list.*

"It's Lieutenant Carrington, Judge."

"Get to the point, Jake."

"I have a strong lead on the Carren case. The girl who—"

"I'm familiar with the case, continue."

"I received information this morning about the railroad safety inspector. I need to move fast."

"What have you got?"

"Not a lot…"

"You woke me up with not a lot of evidence. Might I remind you, it's Sunday."

"I'm sorry, Judge." Christ, he hated to grovel. "The man lost his sister six years ago and Carren was the spitting image of her. The case was never solved. He also had access to the train tracks. I'm checking now to see if McMichaels wears glasses."

"Why the glasses?"

"I have a witness who was approached at a bar and the guy discussed the mutilation in the case. He wore thick glasses. The video from the bar puts the man and McMichaels around the same build. Also, McMichaels had accused the police department of deliberately screwing up his sister's case. He filed a formal complaint months after her murder."

"It's not enough to search his house," Judge Warner said.

"He found the body, Your Honor. Had the opportunity to dump the body and had control of the scene before calling it in. The whole scene was staged. His sister is a dead ringer for the victim. A letter was delivered to the precinct yesterday morning, challenging me to solve this case in two weeks or the killer would take another woman. I have the mayor breathing down my neck to solve this one quickly. McMichaels had opportunity, means, and motive."

Jake hoped the mention of the mayor would push Warner into Jake's corner. Warner hated the mayor more than he did, which raised his respect for Warner. Silence. Though he was champing at the bit, Jake waited the judge out.

"It's all circumstantial."

"It is."

More silence. Jake paced his kitchen. He stopped in front of the coffeepot and filled his cup for the third time this morning. What he wanted to do was reach into the phone and pull the warrant from Warner. Years of dealing with the judge had taught him to control his impatience.

"Jake, do me a favor and call another judge next time. You better find something."

He let out the breath he'd been holding. "Thank you."

"Don't thank me. You put both our asses on the line for Velky to shoot at."

Jake hung up and dialed Louie next. Annoyed when the call went to Louie's voicemail, Jake hung up without leaving a message.

Forty-five minutes later his phone beeped in his hand. Opening the text message, he almost let out a hoot. He loved technology. Warner had come through with the warrant. Jake forwarded the warrant to Brown, instructing him to leave a copy of it on Jake's desk. He wanted it in hand when he interviewed McMichaels. He scooped all the papers off the floor and table and placed them in his briefcase and headed out. First stop, Louie's.

Jake tried Louie's phone one more time before he banged on his front door. The whole team was on call. It wasn't like Louie to turn his phone off at any time.

With Louie's key in hand, Jake banged on the front door again as he put the key in the lock. Falling forward as Louie pulled the door open, he raised his hands as Louie pointed his service revolver at him.

"Hey, take it easy." Louie didn't lower his weapon.

"I ought to shoot you on principle for banging on the door this early on a Sunday morning. What's your problem, Jake?"

"Why aren't you answering your phone?"

"My phone?"

"Snap out of it, Louie. We've got a solid lead on Carren's killer. Get dressed. I'll be in the car waiting."

"What have you got?" Louie asked fifteen minutes later when he climbed into the car.

Jake filled him in as he drove over to McMichaels's apartment.

"Son of gun, he wasn't even a blip on my radar."

"Or mine."

Jake pulled up in front of McMichaels's apartment house on Wilson Street. The gray, square, brick building loomed in the dawn. Dark shadows cast over the front door gave the entrance a sinister and uninviting appearance. According to Lanoue, who he pulled from his bed this morning to research McMichaels, McMichaels made almost a hundred thousand dollars a year. Why would he live in this neighborhood and building? The area skirted the line between decent neighborhood and the "hood." Jake made a note to check McMichaels's off-duty hours activities. What was his form of vice—gambling or drugs? He certainly wasn't spending his money on housing. He made a note to search real estate records for McMichaels, his sister and his parents. If Neil McMichaels was the killer, he wasn't killing them here.

As they reached the top step a loud noise inside the door had them drawing their guns. They went through the door, Jake to the right, Louie to the left. A man lay on the floor at the bottom of the interior staircase in a pool of vomit and blood. Louie gagged on the stench. Jake bent down and spoke quietly to the man.

"What happened?"

"I fell down the stairs."

A likely story, Jake thought. "Someone push you?"

"No, man. Get it out of my face. I don't need no cop. I didn't do nothing wrong."

Jake pulled a pair of gloves from his pocket and examined the cut on the man's forehead. "It looks like you'll need a couple of stitches. What's your name?"

"I don't want no doctors, got it?"

Jake shone his flashlight into the guy's eyes. His pupils didn't dilate. "Name and what you're on?"

"I'm not hurting no one. Why don't you leave me alone?"

Jake pinned him with his best cop expression.

"Jamal."

"I called for the meat wagon. It should be here shortly," Louie said from behind him.

Jake turned back to the man. "The EMTs will check you out, Jamal. If you're fine, you get a free pass tonight. Understand?" Jamal nodded. Jake turned to Louie.

"I'm going up. Wait with Jamal. If they clear him, meet me upstairs."

Jake climbed the stairs, gun still in hand, as he surveyed the second floor. McMichaels's apartment was 2D, the corner unit, which gave him a full view of the front of the building and street. Jake knocked. No answer. From his pocket he pulled out his lock set. Once he had the door open, he stood inside the small foyer and listened. The water running through a pipe to the ice maker echoed through the hall. The sound of ice cubes dropping into their tray boomed like cannons in the field. He cocked his head as he listened.

He searched each room and closet. Satisfied he was alone, Jake walked back to the cluttered, postage-stamp living room. The sofa, chair, coffee table and forty-two-inch television set barely fit in it. Nevertheless, McMichaels had the coffee table piled high with papers. The kitchen was a little bump off the room on the right. Jake followed the short hallway, which led him to the bathroom and one bedroom. All done in the "I'm a bachelor, I don't care" motif. Nothing matched. Each room looked thrown together.

The man he met at the tracks on the day the body was found was meticulously groomed and clothed. His office at the rail station was immaculate. How did hoarding fit into his personality? He had piles of shit everywhere. Newspapers, magazines, empty boxes, clothing, you name it. Jake checked to make sure his gloves were on snugly before touching anything, then put on a second pair to ensure protection. Not only to preserve the evidence; he feared he'd catch something. At forty-five, McMichaels fit the profile Mia had given him. But again, his instincts disagreed. The killer, when found, would be on the young side of the profile, around twenty-five to thirty-five. He decided to start the search in the living room.

"What a freaking mess," Louie said as he came into the apartment.

"This apartment is like the television show about hoarders. How can a person stand it?"

"Beats me. I'll take the bedroom," Louie said.

Jake kept working. McMichaels had several recent newspapers with Nadia's picture, all laid out on the coffee table along with several papers which were months old and didn't relate to the recent murder. Once he finished in the living room, Jake moved to the kitchen. When finished he walked back to the bedroom as Louie was coming out.

"I didn't find anything. Did you?"

"No. Call Brown and have him recheck the real estate records to see if McMichaels owns any other property in town. And have him run McMichaels's financials. Tell him to text anything he gets to my phone."

"Will do. Anything else, my mighty lieutenant, while you're barking orders?"

"Ah, an attempt at humor—it's too early and too lame, Louie. Get to it."

Louie stepped to the front of the apartment to get a signal on his phone, while Jake scanned the bedroom. Something about the room bothered him and he couldn't put his finger on it. Louie came back in the room.

"I already searched it. What are you looking for?"

"The dimensions are off. Did you toss the bed?"

"I did. You going to waste our time rechecking my work?"

"This is a corner unit. Where's the window?"

"It's buried in the closet."

Jake opened the closet door, pushed some clothes out of the way, and looked out the window. Next, he walked over to the dresser. He pushed it away from the wall to look behind it. Nothing. He scanned the room again.

"Are you going to share exactly what you're looking for? Because it has to be something twisted."

"His sister looks too much like the victims to be a coincidence. He made such a stink about the investigation, and how badly it was handled, yet there's not one picture of her here. It doesn't jibe."

"Maybe it's too painful."

Jake ignored Louie's reference to his sister Eva and continued tossing the room. "Give me a hand here."

On the count of three, they flipped the mattress, then the box spring. Nothing attached to either. Ready to walk away, Jake spied a slit in the box spring. Reaching in, he dug around until he hit on something and pulled it out.

"Well, here's his private stash." Jake held a package of marijuana, though it wasn't large enough to collar McMichaels for dealing.

"Big deal, he gets high."

"When did you get all nonchalant about drugs?"

"I'm not. And I'd kill my kids if I found it on them. McMichaels is forty-five years old, Jake. Who cares, if this is his worst crime? We need to stay focused."

"Let's turn over the couch in the living room."

Together they tossed the chair, the sofa, and the tables and found nothing more than evidence McMichaels was a lousy housekeeper. It didn't make sense to Jake. McMichaels's uniform had been immaculate, his hair styled, and he'd seemed disgusted with the filth surrounding the crime scene. And not one picture of his sister. *Okay, maybe not odd, it took me six years before I put up pictures of Eva.*

Louie had already checked the bathroom, but Jake wanted a look.

"What now?" Louie said.

"What did the bathroom look like?"

"Not as messy as the rest of the house, but I still wouldn't shower here," Louie said.

"This place doesn't hit me. There are no work uniforms. Did you find anything? His appearance the other day was pristine. It doesn't fit with this environment. Have Brown call when he's finished checking the real estate records. McMichaels doesn't live here."

* * * *

Jake grabbed a slice of pizza from a box in the bullpen. He ate without tasting it. When Louie finished his slice, they walked down the hall to interview McMichaels. Jake released the uniform on the door. He and Louie entered the room. Aggravated he hadn't found anything at McMichaels's apartment, Jake's foul mood didn't improve. But years of training had taught him to compartmentalize his personal feelings while interrogating a suspect.

"What the hell's going on here?" McMichaels demanded.

"Let me explain how this process works, Neil. I ask the questions. You answer them. Got it?" Jake nailed him with a look until Neil agreed. "Good. Now let's get started." He listed the five dates for McMichaels. "Where were you on those dates?"

"Does this have anything to do with the body I found?"

"Don't play stupid with me." Jake got in McMichaels's face.

Louie pulled Jake back. "Neil, the lieutenant isn't playing games here. We need your whereabouts on those dates."

"I want a lawyer. I'm not saying another word until he gets here."

"You have something to hide?" Jake baited.

"No, but I more than anyone understand how inefficient this department is. And I'm not going to be your scapegoat."

"That's right, your sister's case." Jake watched his comment land on McMichaels.

"You leave my sister out of this. Danielle was a gentle soul who hurt no one. And the cops did nothing. You'll never understand what I went through when she died. How it ripped me apart. I was responsible for her.

It was my job to protect her." Neil rested his head in his hands. Jake felt for him, but he couldn't let personal feelings interfere with a case.

He knew he should push, but looking at McMichaels, he didn't have it in him, nor did he want the evidence or interview tainted. He changed tactics. "I'm sorry about your sister, Neil. When this case is closed, I'll look into it."

"It won't matter. She'll still be dead."

"Yes."

"Don't try to empathize with me. No one understands what I'm feeling."

"My sister was raped and murdered when she and I were in our teens. Her suspect was caught, tried and now is serving a life sentence. Did it bring her back? No, but it gave us some closure. The bastard is up for parole."

Studying Jake, McMichaels broke the silence. "I still want a lawyer."

"Let the record show Mr. McMichaels will be contacting his lawyer and this interview will continue when his attorney arrives." Jake pushed away from the table and stood. "There'll be an officer outside the door if you need anything." He left McMichaels to stew alone in the room while they all waited for the attorney.

"Can I talk to you in your office?"

"Sure." Jake knew what was on Louie's mind, but sometimes you had to go in a different direction.

Once inside, Jake said, "What's on your mind?"

"Why did you back off? We could've ended this today."

"No, we couldn't."

"He's not you, Jake."

"I understand, but the guy was pacing the room when we came in. Did you notice how hard he was breathing?"

"So?"

"There's no way he carried a body from a car to the curb let alone to the tracks."

"People find strength when they need it."

"Some do. Not seeing it with this guy. We're still going to go through the motions and interview him when the lawyer gets here." Louie nodded. "Before we go back in, I want to follow up with Brown. You continue with your list. Close the door on your way out."

Jake hit the intercom to summon Brown to his office. When he didn't get a reply, he dialed his phone.

"Brown here."

"Kirk, it's Jake. What did you get on McMichaels?"

"The search was still running when I left to get some breakfast. I'll be back in about ten. Is that good?"

"Yeah, I'll see you then."

Jake went to the coffee machine sitting on his credenza. After he made a selection, waited, and then took the cup to his window. He ran the evidence and the players through his mind. Ten thirty on a Sunday morning didn't generate a lot of traffic in town. Then it hit him. He punched in Brown's cell number.

"Where did you pick up McMichaels?" Jake asked before Brown could say hello.

"At his house."

"Where exactly is his house?"

"Carawoods Avenue. Why?"

"Damn it, we searched his apartment on Wilson Street. The address you gave me this morning. What's on Carawoods?"

"It's still listed in his parents' name, but that's actually where he lives, according to his railroad personnel records."

"Son of a bitch! Why didn't you call me back with this information, Kirk?"

An awkward silence followed.

"I'm sorry, LT, I didn't think."

Jake knew there was a time to criticize and a time to encourage. Brown had been up most of the night following through on leads. Exhaustion along with bad communication created dangerous situations in cases like this one. Jake took a deep breath.

"I understand you've been up all night and I appreciate your efforts, Kirk—"

Kirk interrupted him. "But there's no room for failure here."

"When you get back, call Judge Warner and get a warrant for the house on Carawoods while I'm in the interview with McMichaels."

"Okay, and I'm sorry."

Jake hung up. He turned his attention back to Neil McMichaels. Why would someone keep two places? Neither answer he came up with sat well with him. If McMichaels was married Jake would understand if he had another place for trysts. But McMichaels wasn't married. Was it drugs or drug distribution? But outside of the small bag of pot they hadn't found anything else.

"What are you up to, Neil?" He didn't realize he'd spoken his thoughts aloud.

"Ahem." Jake looked up to find Brown standing in his doorway.

"I have the warrant for you. Judge Warner sure is grumpy." *You don't know the half of it,* Jake thought.

"He can be, when he has to duplicate his work." Brown cringed. To throw him a bone, Jake added. "I'm still on his shit list from a case I had to use him on three months ago."

"Really?"

"Yeah." *Okay, crisis averted.* "What else do you have for me?"

"I've sent you eleven women who are still alive and kicking who match the victim's profile. I also eliminated Kyle Simmons, Mike Stalls, and Ray Carson. All their alibis check out. I'll be running Jack Burns, Scott Pencer, and Luke Jacobs next. Is there anyone else you want me to run?"

"No, I want you to take a couple of hours of downtime. You've been at this too long. Pass some of the grunt work on to Burke when he gets in."

Brown started to say something but was interrupted by a knock at Jake's door.

"McMichaels's lawyer's here."

"I'll be right out," Jake said.

"I'm serious, Kirk. Don't come back until you've had a minimum of five hours' sleep."

"Okay, I'll see you later. LT, I'm sor—"

"I said forget it. You did good work on this. Now go get some rest."

Chapter 20

A half hour later, Jake stopped at Louie's desk, tapped on it, then kept walking. Louie hurriedly hung up his phone, then shrugged into his jacket.

"What's the damn rush?" Louie asked.

"I'm ready to get started." Jake updated him on the real estate search.

"I'm pissed Brown didn't contact us. Damn it."

"He understands he screwed up. It won't happen again." Jake didn't elaborate.

At the door to interview room three, they put on their game faces and entered.

Shit!

He hoped Louie would be able to keep his personal feelings to himself. Jake sat down. With his back to the far wall, Louie took up the position behind McMichaels and Richard Malone.

"Counselor."

"My client and I have been kept waiting for over half an hour. Why?"

Jake ignored Malone and took care of the housekeeping chores. He recorded all pertinent information on tape as he watched Malone's annoyed expression.

"With your attorney here, Mr. McMichaels, I'm going to reread you the Miranda Act. Do you also acknowledge it has already been read to you?"

"Yes, I..." Malone put his hand on McMichaels's arm.

"Good." Jake proceeded to reread the information into the record. "Okay, let's get started."

"Once again, why were we kept waiting?"

"Here's the deal, counselor. As we were waiting for you to arrive, new information came into our hands. Information we had to investigate before we reconvened with your client."

"Why was he denied counsel to begin with?" Malone asked.

"Mr. McMichaels, at any time were you denied your right to counsel?" Jake cocked his brow at McMichaels.

"I'll answer for my client."

"No, you won't. You can direct your client to answer or not answer a question. Are you ready to stop wasting our time, Counselor?"

"No, I wasn't denied anything except my freedom."

"Mr. McMichaels, you were free to leave at any time. You chose to stay. You're here to answer a few questions about the Carren murder."

"I didn't murder anyone. I didn't even know the girl," McMichaels said.

"Why do you keep an apartment and a house?"

"I had the apartment for years. When my parents died, I realized it wasn't a great neighborhood to raise my sister in. I moved into my parents' house. I didn't want Danielle's life disrupted any more than it had already been. I figured when she got older we'd sell it and split the profits, or she could continue to live in it until she got married."

"It doesn't explain why you still kept the apartment," Jake pressed.

"I wanted privacy. I wasn't going to bring a date home with Danielle in the house. The apartment was for me time."

"That's where you got high?"

"I...I..." Malone put his hand on McMichaels's arm again as he leaned in and whispered in his ear.

"My client takes the Fifth. What's your point in this line of questioning, Jake?"

"It's Lieutenant, Counselor."

"Okeydokey, Lieutenant." It sounded like a curse coming from Malone's lips. "Where are you going here?"

"Mr. McMichaels, I understand your sister died six years ago, is that correct?" Jake changed up the questions. He watched his question land as if he'd thrown a fist into McMichaels's gut.

"Yes, she did. What's her death got to do with anything?"

Jake pulled out a picture of Danielle, placed it in front of McMichaels. Neil ran his index finger over Danielle's forehead. Next, Jake pulled out Nadia's picture and placed it alongside Danielle's. The shock on McMichaels's face threw him. Jake pitied him.

"They could be twins," McMichaels whispered, looking up.

"Yes, they could. You didn't see the resemblance in the newspapers in your apartment? Nadia Carren's picture's been front-page news now for over a week."

"I didn't read the stories after the first day. What sick bastard takes a life, a young life?"

"That's what I'm going to find out, Neil, and if it's you, I'll nail you to the wall."

"It's not me," he said, without anger.

"When we searched your apartment this morning we found some marijuana."

Shock registered on McMichaels's face along with indignation. Malone whispered in his client's ear. He pushed the lawyer away. "How dare you invade my privacy? And for your information, I have glaucoma. Marijuana is a known treatment for it."

"Everyone in your age group has glaucoma, it seems. We didn't invade your privacy. We had a warrant. And we have a warrant for your home, which is being executed as we speak."

McMichaels turned to Malone. "Can they do that? Go in there without reason?"

"What's your probable cause? I'd like to see a copy of both warrants."

Malone reached out his hand to Jake. He had copies in his file. But to bust Malone's chops and to unnerve McMichaels, Jake slowly pulled them out, then got up and headed out the door. He whispered to the uniform and handed him the copies.

"The officer is making copies for you now."

Jake sat back down, folded his hands and waited for the uniform to return. After several minutes of crossing, uncrossing, and recrossing his legs, McMichaels put his feet flat on the floor and leaned forward.

"Are you doing this to me because I found the body?"

"No. When we investigate a crime like this we look for triggers. The timing of your sister's death coincides with the time period the first woman disappeared. And you must admit, Danielle and Nadia are almost identical."

"I see that, but I still don't understand why you're picking on me."

"I'm not picking on you. I'm going where the evidence leads me." Jake left it at that. McMichaels and Jake studied each other, one assessing the other.

After a brief pause, Jake said, "You were engaged to be married?"

"When my parents died…" Malone banged on the table. He leaned into McMichaels and whispered furiously into his ear.

"Okay, Lieutenant… I want—"

The uniform knocked on the door, interrupting Malone and his argument. Jake got up, opened the door, and took the papers back from the officer. He stalled. Shuffled them around then placed them on the table to make a matched set. Slowly, he put a set back into his folder and handed the other set to Malone. Attorney Malone snapped the warrants from his hand and read them. Richie's patience was clearly running thin.

"I don't understand how you got these warrants. Everything in them is based on circumstantial evidence."

"I'm sure Judge Warner will be glad to explain it to you, Counselor. Can we move on?" Malone remained stone-faced. "Good. Mr. McMichaels, please answer my previous question. Were you engaged to be married?"

"Yes."

"Why didn't you marry?"

"My parents died within months of each other and left me as guardian for my sister. Louise didn't want to take on the responsibility of caring for Danielle, especially since they didn't get along."

"Why didn't they get along?"

"Christ, I don't know, they're women!" He threw his hands up in the air. Jake hid his smile. "Where's Louise now? I also need her last name."

"Last I heard she was Louise Bennington. She married three or four times, each time trading up."

"Piss you off, does it?"

"No, it makes me thankful. I dodged a bullet there."

Jake's phone rang. Checking the number, he stood up and left the room before answering.

"What have you got, Al?"

"A bunch of knives in his basement show traces of blood. The lab guys took them away. They promised to put a rush on them," Burke said.

"Excellent. What kind of knives?"

"You're asking me? I guess they could be used for anything, fishing, hunting, or shop work."

"Were there large of amounts of blood anywhere?" Jake asked.

"Nope, only the traces we found on the knives."

"Good work." Jake hung up. *How to play him?* After a few minutes of thought, he walked back into the room.

"Neil, what do you use the knives in your basement for?" Jake caught Louie's frown but chose to ignore it. He'd hear about it later, he was sure.

"Knives?" Neil scratched his head. "You mean the fishing knives?"

"You use them to fish? My detectives found traces of blood on them."

"I use them to cut up the fish once I catch them. Since when did fishing become a crime?" McMichaels scoffed.

"It's not, as long as that's all you used them for."

"Christ, I wouldn't want to live in your head, Lieutenant." Sometimes, Jake didn't want to be inside of it either. "If this is how you think of people and their innocent hobbies."

Jake concluded he wasn't going to get anything further from McMichaels today and dismissed him along with Malone. He needed the knives processed before he would continue questioning Neil. Gathering his files, Jake stood and turned to leave the room.

"I should have been informed about the knives," Louie said through his teeth, outside the room.

"Louie, for God's sake, you watched me take the call. I wanted you in there in case McMichaels said anything. What gives?"

"You made me look like a peon in front of Malone." *Damn, Louie's overreacting. Why?*

"I did not. This is the usual way we handle an interview. I didn't do anything different today," Jake said, an edge creeping into his voice.

"This *stronzo,* he's got me turned around," Louie said, his fingers pinched together as he waved them at Jake. "Of all the freaking lawyers in this town and he hires Malone." Louie always cursed in Italian when he was angry. Jake let his hissy fit play out before he got back on point.

"We don't get to pick the suspects' lawyers. It might work in our favor. Malone's incompetent. Besides, if we do arrest McMichaels, you'll have to excuse yourself from the case, Louie."

"Damn it. What else can interfere with the investigation?"

* * * *

At his desk, Louie placed a call to Sophia. "Hey, what's going on?"

"The kids are hanging out. Are you going to be able to spend any time here today?"

"I'm hoping to in about two or three hours. What's that?"

"My cell phone, hold on."

Louie waited for what seemed like hours before she returned to him. "Who was that?"

"Malone, he wants me to work today."

"That stupid, slimy bastard only left here seconds ago. He's the lawyer for one of the suspects. I hope you told him no."

Movement in front of the door caught his eye. Malone stood there with a shit-eating grin on his face. Louie threw down the phone and vaulted over his desk as he went for Malone. Before he was able to reach him, someone pulled him back.

"Let go."

"Control yourself," Jake whispered for Louie's ear only, as he narrowed his eyes at Malone. "What's your business here, Malone?"

"I wanted to make it quite clear when you receive the test results on the knives, I'm to be copied on the outcome."

Under his breath, Jake said to Armand, who had assisted in holding Louie back, "Lanoue, don't let go of him. Louie, get ahold of yourself."

Jake walked over to Malone and quietly spoke into Malone's ear. What he had to say wasn't intended for anyone else. "What game are you playing? I suggest you rethink it for your own safety."

"Are you threatening me, Lieutenant?" Malone asked as he quirked his brow. *The asswipe's got a screw loose,* Jake thought.

"Nope," Jake said, staring Malone down until he walked away.

To Louie, he said, "In my office, now." Louie walked in behind him and slammed the door.

"Jake, I—" Jake stopped Louie from continuing. It bothered him Malone had wandered into that part of the building.

"Don't. You almost screwed up this investigation for personal reasons." Jake understood his friend and his mood.

"Jake—"

Jake put a finger to his own lips, motioning Louie to shut up. He pulled his phone from his pocket and called Damien. It went to voicemail. Jake left a message.

"Let's go, grab your jacket." Louie looked at him like he was nuts.

Jake didn't speak until they were a block away from the station.

"What started it?"

"I called Sophia. She told me Malone had called seconds after I did. He demanded she work today. Movement at the entrance to the bullpen caught my eye. When I looked up, that *stronzo*'s standing there grinning at me. I lost it."

"The man's baiting you, Louie. You've got to get a grip on your emotions or he'll get you kicked off the force or worse."

"He's up to something, Jake, and I'm not going to allow him to hurt my wife. I'll try to rein it in."

"Did you finish your call with Sophia?"

"No."

"I suggest you call her back and fill her in on Malone's actions."

* * * *

"Sophia?" Louie said when the line connected. Jake stepped away, but not far enough away where he couldn't eavesdrop.

"What happened?"

"A few minutes after I get out of an interview with him and his client, he calls you. You don't find that crazy? He called you to come into the office because I'm working."

"Oh, don't be ridiculous."

"Ridiculous? Well, the bastard was standing right by my desk while I was on the phone with you. He had a big fat smirk on his face. What do you make of that?"

"First, Louie, lose that tone of voice with me. Second, for your thick-headed information, I told him I couldn't work today."

"And what did he say?"

"Same thing he said the last time. Only this time I told him fine. He can take his job."

Hallelujah! "You quit?"

"No. He apologized and said he understood my husband was working and he'd bring the work to the house—"

"Christ Almighty, you didn't give him our address, did you?"

"I'm serious, Louie, stop swearing. I didn't have to give it to him. He has it in my employment records."

Something needs to be done about Malone. I don't understand why Sophia's being so pigheaded.

"Louie?"

"Yeah?"

"I told him not to bring anything to my home. I made it clear. Please relax."

Easier said than done—all I need is one hour alone in a room with the guy... "I'll see you when I see you."

"Don't hang up."

"Why?"

"Because you're too mad. Reason this out: even if he comes to the door, I'm not letting him in. I'll call you. Do you understand me?"

"Yes. I swear, Sophia, he comes near you or the kids, I won't be—"

"Enough."

* * * *

Jake heard enough of the conversation to get the gist of it. Louie had to work from home today if he was going to accomplish anything. He'd send him home when he got off the phone. Or would he? If he was home, wouldn't Sophia be available to go into work?

Damned if I do, damned if I don't. There was never an easy solution. And they didn't have time for distractions.

Resigned, he'd have to talk to Louie once he got off the phone. Afraid Louie would slam the phone to the ground and walk away, Jake waited impatiently for the call to end. Louie hung up but kept looking at his phone.

They headed back to the station, but Jake stopped short, put a hand on Louie's arm. "We need to talk upstairs. Let's go in."

In the hallway on the second floor, Jake spied Malone before Louie did. He grabbed Malone by the back of the collar and slammed him against the wall. Louie walked to the other side of him.

"Louie, go to my office."

"No."

Jake scorched him a look. Without another word, Louie walked away. Jake shoved Malone a little harder into the wall after Louie was gone.

"Where's your client?"

"He left."

"What are you still doing here?"

"I was waiting to talk to you," Malone huffed.

"Richie, don't give me that line of bullshit. I can throw your ass in jail right this minute for eavesdropping on police conversation. This is a restricted area, as you're aware. I'll give you one chance to explain why you've been hanging out outside my bullpen."

"Lieutenant, you need help?" a uniform offered.

"No, I'm all set, Ralph, thanks." Jake kneed Malone, who lost his balance. Jake grabbed Malone by the neck to stop his fall. "I asked you a question."

"I was trying to find out what you had on my client."

Jake didn't trust him, not for one second. "You'll find out what we have on your client in discovery, after we levy charges. In the meantime, if I catch you here again without an invitation, I'll consider you illegally spying on my officers and will have you brought up on charges. Understood?"

"Yes."

"Good. I'm issuing you a written warning, for the record," Jake said.

Jake gave one final shove before releasing him. Malone pushed off the wall and shot his cuffs in a show of bravery.

"Touch me again, and you'll be the one up on charges."

Jake noticed Officer Ralph Kettletown standing off to the side. "Ralph, did I touch the suspect?"

"No, sir."

"See, Richie, it will be your word against mine. You're out of the camera's view." Jake pointed down the hall. "Whose word will the judge take after reviewing your past arrests?" Jake tilted his head toward his officer who waited a few feet away. "Escort him out, Ralph." Then he walked away without another word.

At the door to his office he watched Louie pace with an untouched cup of coffee in his right hand.

"Louie."

"Don't start in on me. The bastard deserves an ass-kicking. And I'm going to be the one who gives it to him," Louie said.

Jake closed his door.

"Calm down. And take a damn seat, your pacing's driving me nuts."

"I swear..." Resigned, Louie plopped into the chair.

"Shut up and listen to me. You can't go around talking like this, especially here. Everything's recorded. It's a good thing Kettletown was blocking the cameras. Christ, Velky would have both our badges if he got a load of that. If anything happens to Malone, it'll come back and bite you on the ass and then me."

"That's all this is about, you?"

Louie pushed up and out of the chair as he pointed a finger in Jake's face. Anyone else tried that stunt and he'd have broken it without a second thought. Taking a deep breath, he grabbed Louie's finger and applied the right amount of pressure, until he was sure he had Louie's full attention.

"No. It's about keeping Sophia safe from predators like Malone. You need to tuck it away for now. Velky will grab any bit of information to use against you down the line. Or incite another encounter."

"It's my wife!"

"Lower your voice. You're both my family. I agree something needs to be done, but don't advertise it. He'll hang himself soon enough. He's escalating," Jake said.

Jake let his comment sink into Louie's thick skull. Sophia and Louie had been the only ones there for him through all the trauma. Jake considered Sophia his sister and would protect her to the death. When he saw Louie absorb it, he continued. "I don't like her working for him either, but damn, you need to back off for the sake of your marriage and your career."

"I get crazy when anything threatens my family."

"Understood. Let's get back to McMichaels. Check in with the CSI team."

When Louie left his office, Jake got up and closed his door. As he walked to the window he debated whether he should give Sophia a call. He did understand Louie's predicament. Malone was a time bomb. It seems he'd picked Sophia for the explosion. With both his and Louie's history with the guy, they dare not touch him. It would mean their careers. If Malone touched Sophia, he'd... Jake didn't finish his thought. Instead he dialed the phone.

"Hello."

"It's Jake."

"Yes." Oh, how he hated Sophia's tone. The long, drawn-out yes in a questioning voice—she knew why he was calling. "Jake?"

"Seconds ago, I had to calm Louie down after another encounter with Malone. I want you to understand Malone is baiting him on purpose. It's payback for us arresting him last year. Sophia, make sure you're taking the threats seriously."

"I am. For God's sake, I'm not stupid."

"I never said you were. Though at times, you can be naïve. Why in the name of heaven are you still working for him?"

"I'm not naïve. There's something off with Malone. I told Louie it won't be an issue. In another month I'm going to quit."

"Why wait?"

"I'm not telling you or him. This is private, Jake. Please respect that."

Christ Jesus, the woman could be stubborn. "Do you need money?"

Her laughter filled his ear. "Thanks, but I'm not taking your money. I'll have what I need in another month. You both need to be patient. Thanks for the offer, but no thanks."

"What good is money, if you're not around to spend it? Is putting yourself at risk worth it?"

"It's something I have to do alone."

"What about Louie?"

"He wouldn't help if he knew what the money was for. Drop it, Jake."

Disheartened, Jake looked out his window. He felt Louie's pain. When Sophia got this way there was no changing her mind.

Brown knocked on his door as he hung up with Sophia. "What's up, Kirk?"

"I've eliminated some of our suspects. I thought you'd want to know."

"I do. Grab a cup of coffee while I review your list." Kirk started to walk out. "No, use my machine and sit in here in case I have any questions."

Jake ran his finger down the list and stopped at one name.

"Why Burns?"

"He was where he said he was."

"Who verified his alibi?"

"The week Nadia disappeared, he had his kids the whole week. I talked to his fifteen-year-old daughter. Who said, and I quote, 'I remember the week from hell. He didn't leave the house once. I never got to see my boyfriend,' unquote." Brown smiled.

"How can she be positive about the date?"

"She checked her calendar."

"Her calendar?" Jake questioned.

"Yeah, it's the only way she can keep track of where she is sleeping. Her words, not mine. Plus, her boyfriend broke up with her the week after because he didn't get to see her."

"You got a lot of history from her."

"I did. In fact, I couldn't shut her up. She was eating up the drama."

"Hmm."

Kirk had eliminated Stalls, Burns, Simmons, and Carson. "Let's move on. Where do you stand on Tedessco and Pencer?"

"They're next on my list. Do you want me to have someone else check Velky and Jacobs?"

"No. I'll personally check out Velky. I don't want to put anyone else in the mayor's crosshairs. I'll handle Jacobs too. I did some checking into him, and he's also politically connected."

"Glad I'm not you for this one," Kirk stated before leaving his office.

Jake wished it wasn't him for this one, too. They were down to five viable suspects: McMichaels, Pencer, Tedessco, Jacobs, and Velky. How the hell was he supposed to update the commissioner, the chief and the mayor at the same time? Why hadn't the chief asked for a meeting first before putting Jake in front of the other two? Damn freaking politics. It was time to speak with Shamus.

Chapter 21

Jake left Shamus a voice message. He continued to work on suspects' backgrounds while he waited for a return call. He still felt Tedessco was a viable suspect, but the guy didn't seem to have the patience to plan out this type of kill. Peeling layers off a person took time, but it was time well spent. Tedessco's finances said a lot about him. His largest bills outside of supplies for the tattoo shop included the liquor store and his bar bill. He spent sixty dollars a week in the liquor store and one hundred dollars at the bar. Jake hoped the bar bill also included food, otherwise this guy had a real problem. Years of working as a cop had taught Jake to pay cash for most things. He didn't want his habits documented. Maybe a little paranoid, but what he did was his own business. He liked the trail Tedessco left. The trouble was, it confirmed Jake's suspicions. Tedessco was a hothead and a coward, nothing more. He picked on women. Tedessco skirted the line with his activities. Jake was positive he'd see Tedessco sometime down the road. He put his file aside, marked it "Cleared."

Next, he took Jacobs. Luke Jacobs had taken over as head of the tool and die shop five years ago when his father retired. Married for ten years with two children, one of each gender, his wife was a stay-at-home mom and the kids were in private school. The financial burden had to add pressure to one's life. Jacobs held memberships in the local country club and Shriners. Attended church regularly with the family and contributed to it in a generous way. His financials fit that of a well-to-do businessman, nothing excessive. None of his bills were late nor did his financials show any bad habits like liquor or drugs. There were no large withdrawals of cash from his bank accounts.

If Jacobs moved up the list at some point, Jake would pull the financials for his business in case he was skimming. But there was no vibe here, and skimming wouldn't make him a serial killer, only a crook. Frustrated, Jake ran a hand through his hair. If Luke Jacobs was the guy, he'd eat his hat. Though, after the fact, a lot of people said serial killers were nice guys and they hadn't had a clue.

He marked the file "Cleared" before moving on to Scott Pencer. Jake scanned the information. Scott was a piece of work. He reviewed Louie's preliminary notes. Engaged three times, not one stuck. All three times the girls broke it off. Louie noted a derogatory attitude toward women in general. Had it pushed him over the edge? Outside his juvie record, Pencer had had some minor scrapes with the law as an adult. An arrest for pot but no time served, a few parking tickets, and an arrest with a group of others in a bar brawl. Nothing said serial killer.

Louie's file included everything, even notes from Pencer's boss about his annual evaluations. If push came to shove, he'd get a warrant to see the actual evaluations. Louie noted Pencer's poor work ethic and a combative personality, but his boss had still given him a three percent raise last year, same as everyone else. Jake figured it was a union raise across the board. At various times in Pencer's life he'd had his own apartment or lived with someone else, but now he resided with his mother. All of which matched the profile. Jake kept him on the list. The more he thought about it, the more he thought they should speak with Pencer's ex-fiancées. It was midday, his team should be awake by this time on a Sunday. Three fiancées. Pencer was either a fool or a romantic to keep trying. Jake dialed the first woman on the list and leaned back in his chair.

"Hello?"

"Ms. Joanne Kennedy, please."

"Who's calling?"

"It's Lieutenant Carrington from the WPD."

"Give me your badge number and I'll call you back."

Cautious. He wondered why. After giving it to her, he waited for the return call. It didn't take long.

"Sorry, Lieutenant, you can't be too careful these days."

"Ms. Kennedy, can I ask if you've had trouble before?"

"I have, though I don't want to get into it."

"Did it have anything to do with Scott Pencer?"

"Why?" Her voice shot up an octave.

"He's a person of interest in a case I'm working on."

"What department do you work for again, Lieutenant?"

"Homicide." Jake left it hanging out.

"Who'd he kill?"

"I didn't say he killed anyone. Is he capable of killing, in your opinion?"

"Yes."

Interesting. "Can I ask why, Ms. Kennedy?"

"It's Joanne. Scott's crazy, with a mean temper. It's one of the reasons I broke it off with him."

"What were the other reasons?" Jake made notes as he listened.

"Besides his low opinion of women in general, the bastard hit me. I don't put up with a guy who thinks getting physical means using his fists. He begged for forgiveness, emphasized he'd never do it again. But once was too much."

"I agree, Ms.—Joanne. Anything else—weird habits, actions or thoughts you care to share with me?" He felt her hesitation through the phone. "Joanne, it would be a big help, and it would be confidential."

"You can't say it came from me."

"I'm also interviewing his other former fiancées."

"Others? How many did he have?"

"He's been engaged three times."

"Is he married?"

How did I lose control of this interview? "Joanne, the answer's no, and no more questions. Please, what were you going to tell me?"

"This is embarrassing." Her voice dropped in volume. "He liked bondage. I didn't. I tried it a few times with him but didn't like not being in control. It pissed him off."

"I understand this was difficult to say, Joanne. Thanks for telling me. Anything else?"

"No."

He thanked her for her time and information. Next, he called Phyllis Santos. She had nothing new to add to his profile on Pencer. Rereading his notes, he formulated his questions for the last fiancée. Iris Levy had been engaged to Pencer last year. She'd be more helpful about Pencer's recent behavior patterns. After placing the call and greeting her, Jake jumped right in.

"Ms. Levy, as I stated, I'm calling to ask about Scott Pencer. Can you tell me why you broke off your engagement?"

"He got weird."

"How so?"

"Well…we… How do I say this?"

"Was it the bondage?"

"My God, who told you?" Her voice squeaked in his ear. He pulled the phone away to keep from going deaf.

"I spoke with his former fiancées. Was this the reason you broke it off with him?"

"I didn't mind the bondage at first," she whispered. "Then he started to get into it too much. Scott started to whip me and wouldn't stop when I asked or begged. The more I begged, the more he got into it. After one brutally painful night, I decided to call off the engagement. That's the night he tied me up and brought a friend in to join us. After he untied me, I left and didn't go back."

"Why didn't you file a rape charge?"

"I was living with the guy, for Pete's sake. No one would've taken me seriously, not even the cops. And I didn't want to embarrass my family."

Jake strained to hear her. She spoke in hushed tones. He was angry another bastard had walked because of the stigma society placed on a woman for being brutalized. The attitudes were changing, but not fast enough.

"Iris, you realize what he did wasn't your fault? How long ago did this happen?"

"I do now, after a lot of therapy. It was last year."

"Who was the other guy?" Silence filled Jake's ears. "Iris?"

"I never met him before, but he might've worked with Scott. It's the impression I got when they were talking when they thought I was sleeping."

"Would you recognize him, if you saw him again?"

"Yes. He's in my nightmares."

"The statute of limitations hasn't run out yet. You should press charges against them. They should pay for victimizing you."

"Please, Lieutenant, don't. I don't want any trouble. It's taken me this entire year to even start to date again. I've met a wonderful man who cherishes me. I never told him about Scott. He's pretty straightforward and might walk away."

"If he did he wouldn't be worth it."

"It's easy for you to say as a man. You don't understand what it feels like to be helpless."

Jake lowered his voice. She would have to strain to hear him. "You're right. But there are different degrees of helplessness, Iris." *Should I?* "My sister was brutally attacked and killed in high school. I felt extremely helpless. I even changed my career path to feel in control." *Why the hell am I telling her this?* "The choice is yours, and I understand your decision. But he's out there doing it to other women."

"I'm sorry, Lieutenant, for you, for your sister, for the other women, but I can't."

Jake sat there, stunned and angry. Iris Levy had slammed the phone in his ear. He wanted to tell her Pencer got away with what he did because she, along with other women, had refused to press charges. Creeps like Pencer needed to be taken off the streets. Why would a thirtysomething-year-old man choose to live with his mother? It had to cramp his kinky lifestyle. Plus, he made decent money. The further he dug into Pencer's financials, the more convinced he became Pencer had a drug problem. He dialed Louie's extension.

"Yo!"

"Very professional way to answer your phone, Louie."

"I knew it was you, chill out." Someone must have put a bag of ice on him in the last two hours.

"Why are you happy?"

"Malone showed up at the house. Sophia was smart enough to engage the security cameras to document it. And she didn't open the door. She sent me the video. Want to watch?"

"You bet." He headed out to Louie's desk.

Malone appeared agitated, evidenced not only by his words, but by his actions. It was clear he was extremely pissed off. He banged on Louie's door for over ten minutes. Sophia had called Louie and he had sent over a patrol car. They watched as Malone marched to his own car on the tape, slammed his door, and sped away while the patrol officer watched.

"That was stupid on his part." Jake grinned.

"It sure was."

Jake got the drift. "Not right away, Louie."

"I'm not stupid."

"He's up to something. Malone had to see your security. Please stay smart, that's all I'm saying."

"I will."

"What's Scott Pencer's boss's number? I'm sure it's there but I couldn't find it in the file. Something's not right there." Jake jotted down the number Louie read off.

"This is the work number. Want me to find the home one?"

"Yeah." Jake headed back to his office. "When you get off the line give me a call, I'll be in my office."

While Louie searched out the home number for Pencer's boss, Kenneth Graves, Jake continued to read through Pencer's file. A man who loved detail, Louie hadn't missed much, but every nerve in Jake's body told him there should be more. Any man with his record with women should have an official complaint lodged against him somewhere. The question was, where? Maybe it was in his work record. He'd been at three different companies in ten years. Had he changed jobs for money, or had he been forced out? The call with Iris Levy still bothered him. He understood the humiliation and pain the women must've felt, but how could they leave him out there to do it again? The phone on his desk rang. Louie's extension popped up. He took down the number Louie gave him.

Jake pressed in Graves's number. In the background, a television blasted as a man screamed his response. "What?"

"Mr. Graves?"

"I'm not buying what you're selling." The line went dead.

Jake pulled the phone from his ear. It was the second time today someone had hung up on him and he wasn't happy. He hit redial and spoke before Graves could.

"This is Lieutenant Carrington from the WPD. Please don't hang up again."

"Jeez, how was I supposed to know?" he screamed into the phone.

"Could you turn down the volume on your television before you blow out my eardrums?"

"Sorry. Wait while I find the remote. The damn Yankees are losing again."

"Shit, they're playing the Red Sox, aren't they?"

"Sure are; got it." The volume of the TV reduced dramatically, much to Jake's relief. "You're a cop?"

"Yes, do you need to verify my badge number?"

"I spoke with a Sergeant Roman or somebody with a similar name already. What do you need?"

"Sergeant Romanelli's also working the case. I have some follow-up questions on Scott Pencer."

"Shoot. For crying out loud, Judge struck out again. He gave it all away at the Home Run Derby."

Jake felt his pain. The team was blowing a chance to clinch a spot in the playoffs. Well, at least they were a given for the wild card if they didn't lose any more games. Crime was easier to understand than his Yankees. Shaking his head, Jake asked, "What kind of employee is Scott Pencer?"

"I don't want to be sued. I'll have to check with our lawyers to see if I'm stomping on the guy's frigging rights. Damn new privacy laws. Can I ask why you're interested in him?"

"Mr. Graves…"

"It's Kenny."

"Okay, Kenny, can we shoot the breeze off the record? If I need anything more or need to put it on the record I'll be happy to get a warrant and talk to your lawyer." Jake hoped he read between the lines.

A hard scratching noise blared over the phone. *The guy must have been rubbing his chin,* Jake mused. After a considerable silence Graves started talking. Jake couldn't shut him up.

"I don't like the guy. Let's make it clear he's a real scumbag. At the company picnics he goes after wives or girlfriends. Even started a few fights. He's one of the reasons we don't have holiday parties anymore. The last one we had to call the cops—"

Jake interrupted him. "When was that?"

"A few years ago, maybe three or four."

"Was he arrested?"

"Yes, the cops arrested Scott and Matt Crane."

"Was it here in Wilkesbury?"

"Yeah, the party was held at the Wilkesbury Country Club, why?"

"No reason. Outside of him being a dirtbag, how were his performance evaluations?" Jake figured this would ingratiate him to Graves.

"Pencer's a lazy worker. He meets his quota every day, nothing more, nothing less, and his work is acceptable, not outstanding. He never offers to help when we're pushed with orders. He's got this idea in his head he's the best tool and die maker around. His work is good, but not the top. I wish he sucked at it. It would give me a reason to fire him. You never answered me. What did he do?"

"As I said, I'm following through on Sergeant Romanelli's visit. Anything else you can offer me off the record?"

"I probably shouldn't say this… never mind."

"Kenny, anything you can share would be helpful. Did the sergeant explain what case we're investigating?" Jake held up his hand and brought his finger to his lips to silence Louie as he walked into his office.

"It's hearsay, Lieutenant, you get my drift?"

"I do."

"Well, this other idiot who works for me, Mikey Stalls, came in bragging one Monday morning how Pencer had tied up his fiancée and the two of them had a go at her all weekend. True or false, you'll have to determine the validity of it. For the girl's sake, I hope it's not true."

Steam raced through Jake's veins as it burned a path to his brain. The first chance he got, he'd put both Pencer and Stalls in jail, even if he had to trump up the charges. Those two animals didn't belong on the street. No wonder Iris Levy was afraid.

"If you ask me, Lieutenant, one of these days Pencer's going to kill someone. Or get killed."

Jake agreed. Hopefully it would be Pencer, not some innocent person. He shouldn't entertain thoughts of torturous deaths for his suspects, but after years of doing this job there were days he got fed up with the likes of Pencer. Jake thanked Graves for his time. He turned toward Louie as he hung up then filled him in on the conversation with Graves.

"It's narrowed down to McMichaels, Pencer, and Velky."

"After speaking with Iris Levy and Graves, I'm adding Mikey Stalls. Don't forget, I'm still working on Velky's records and contacts. Why don't you take Pencer and Stalls and run the next layer while I concentrate on the mayor's brother—" Jake's desk phone rang, interrupting his train of thought. "Yes?"

"It's Shamus. Come to my office." The captain hung up without waiting for a reply. What the heck was he doing here on a Sunday?

"Louie, follow through on those files. I'll be in the captain's office."

"What's up?"

"I left him a message to update him."

Jake pushed his chair away from the desk and stood. Second-guessing the captain was impossible. He picked up his file notes on the case. In the last two hours the bullpen had come to life. Sunday was usually worse than a Saturday night. Brown hailed him. Jake pointed up to the ceiling to the captain's office. He took the stairs to the third floor. As he approached, Jake noted the closed door. Knocking, he waited.

"Come in."

He walked into an ambush. There sat the mayor with his hands folded over his large belly, his lips pressed into a razor-thin line. In the corner by the window stood Chief Doolittle, and this time there was no commissioner. Shamus sat at his desk.

"Gentlemen." He'd assume the offensive.

"Why the hell are you investigating my brother? You arrogant bastard, you've gone too far this time," spewed the red-faced mayor, veins protruding in his forehead.

If he wasn't careful the guy would have a stroke, Jake thought, and was amazed at his own calm. It was a way-over-the-top reaction to a simple inquiry. *What's he not sharing?* Arnie Velky hadn't seemed to like his brother at all. His brother didn't seem to feel the same. Could he use the information against the mayor? Jake opened his mouth to speak but Shamus cut him off.

"John, calm down. I asked Jake in here to update all of us. He's not gunning for any one person yet. And to be fair to him, if Jake had skipped over your brother, who he came across in the normal duties of his investigation, he'd be accused of favoritism, especially in an election year. You want it out there you and your family are being given special treatment?"

Shamus was good. There was still steam coming from the mayor's ears, but at least he wasn't boring his gaze into Jake any longer. Jake chose to wait them out.

"Well, I don't have all damn day, update us," Velky said.

"We're eliminating suspects as we go and still have other die shops and tattoo parlors to visit. We've only been on this for a few short days and have covered quite a bit of ground."

"Why haven't you eliminated my brother yet?"

Right back where we started, I see. "I didn't want anyone else to investigate your brother and invade his privacy. I understand it's a delicate matter. You understand as I do, the media will grab what they can and run with it, whether it's true or not. This way I can control the information we put out there."

A subtle warning to you, John, to keep your mouth shut. Jake watched as the mayor processed the information.

"Thank you for your discretion." Mayor John Velky cleared his throat as he pushed from the chair and left the office without another word.

Jake relaxed for the first time since entering the room. The chief had yet to speak.

"Okay, Jake, give us the real update," Shamus said.

Jake did.

"And where did you get this information on Velky's juvie record? I didn't see a request for a warrant." The chief spoke for the first time.

"I came across it in my search of criminal activities for all persons of interest. I didn't dig deeper because, as you said, I'd need a warrant." The chief eyed him. Jake didn't flinch.

"That might hold up if you're questioned."

Jake opened his mouth to speak.

"No, don't ruin it. I want no knowledge of it in case I'm questioned. If it does lean toward Arnie Velky, you better be sure of your evidence because you'll be in for the fight of your life."

"I understand, Chief."

"Good. We've taken up enough of your time for today. I'll let you get back to it."

Jake walked into the bullpen and went straight to Kirk Brown's desk. "What's up?"

"The manager at the Gas-N-Pump called. His company recirculates their surveillance tapes every thirty days. For some reason his July tape never got recorded over. It's a good thing I recanvassed him."

"Excellent," Jake said, amused at Kirk's self-praise.

"Long story short, this guy decides to play the tape after all the noise on the news about Nadia, and lo and behold it shows Nadia getting gas after the gym. The tape is time stamped," Kirk said.

"Good work. Go pick up the original tape. This adds to her timeline. I wonder if she stopped anywhere else? Before you go, put in calls to all the mom-and-pop stores in the area. See if they have their surveillance tapes. Also check again with all the fast-food joints on the strip. Retrace Missing Persons' route and make sure they didn't miss anything."

Turning from Brown's desk, Jake walked right into Louie. "Jeez, give me some space."

"Brown got a lead?" Louie asked.

He didn't understand how Louie did it, whether he heard or sniffed out leads, but it always spooked Jake. "Eavesdropping again?" he said while continuing to walk to his office.

"No, Brown's been pacing back and forth since before you went into the captain's office. What's he got?" Louie asked, as he followed Jake into his office and shut the door behind him. "I saw the mayor leave Shamus's office. What's up with that?"

"Boy, you're filled with questions today, aren't you?"

"That's me, Mr. Inquisitive," Louie said.

Jake updated Louie.

"I eliminated Stalls while you were in the office," Louie said. "He worked late on the night Nadia disappeared. The reason he remembers it, he was running late for a date. The girl busted his ass all night long and because of it, he didn't get laid. That's a direct quote, by the way. His boss verified he was on the job for the night in question.."

"Okay, move on to Pencer while I keep digging on Velky."

* * * *

Sophia paced her living room as she tried to figure out what she was going to do about work or if she still had a job. All she needed was three or four more weeks to have enough money to check Frankie into Serenity

Hills, then she could quit the job and life would go back to normal. Was it too much to ask? She couldn't believe Malone had come to the house. Louie had been right...

"Mom, what's wrong?" Sophia jumped. She hadn't heard her oldest son sneak up on her. "Nothing, LJ."

"It has to do with the guy who showed up at the door before, doesn't it?"

"Yes."

"Did you call Dad?"

"Yes, he's taking care of it. Don't worry."

"I'm worried about you. Isn't he the man you work for?"

Ah, you think the kids aren't listening, but nothing gets past them. "Yes." The less said the better.

"The guy's a psycho," LJ said.

"Yes."

"Why are you still working for him?"

For children, life was black or white, right or wrong. She wished. "LJ, this is between your father and me. Please go to your room or watch some TV. I want to be alone right now."

He stared at her like she had three heads. When had he become his father? The cross, concerned look on her son's face had her smiling. "I'm fine, LJ, go."

"You're not, not since your boss arrived here. Mom, please watch yourself with him." *Yep, a carbon copy of his father.*

It would come to a head tonight. She'd brace for Louie's reaction. There was nothing else she could do. Louie wasn't going to let this latest incident go. Oh, how she dreaded the confrontation. Why had she told Louie? Or better yet, why hadn't she let Malone in? Louie had put too much doubt in her mind. He purposely scared her. She'd handled it on her own. Tired of being treated like a helpless female, Sophia lined up her arguments. The more she thought about it, the tenser she became. Then it dawned on her why she hadn't let Malone into her home. *Marisa. I don't want him around my daughter. Oh my God, Louie's right.*

If she told Louie her reason for working, it would be a bigger fight. Poor Frankie had been abandoned by his whole family, including Louie. He had an addiction, and until someone took the reins and put him in rehab, Frankie wouldn't get well. Or he'd die. And didn't he say he was ready? It was the only reason she'd agreed to help him. *How would Victoria feel if she knew I helped her kid?* And Louie would never have been the wiser if she worked for anyone else. Why, of all the jobs in the city, did she wind up with Malone? After sending out fifty resumes, he'd been the only one who responded and offered her a job. He'd even offered her a great salary. It's not like she didn't apply elsewhere. She applied at food stores, the mall, restaurants, and other law firms.

Her cell phone in her pocket started ringing. Looking down, she pressed Talk. "Frankie, how are you doing?"

"Auntie, did you get the money?"

His voice was scratchy, high-pitched, and a bit weak. He didn't sound good. "No. I told you I needed two months to pull it together. Won't they let you sign into rehab with my signature and a promise to pay?"

"Auntie, I can't stay out here much longer. The streets will eat me up. It's bad."

The desperation in his voice tore at her heart. Even though he had stolen from his parents and grandparents, she still had a soft spot for her godchild. "I'm sorry, Frankie. I don't have it yet."

"How much do you got?"

"Not enough." She couldn't say why, but she didn't want to give him a dollar amount. Something in his voice set off alarms.

"Why don't you give it to me? I'll see if they'll take a down payment."

"No, when I have it all, we'll go to the place together."

"What the hell good are you?" he shouted into the phone.

"Frankie…" she realized he'd hung up. She rubbed her head to ease the pain as tears fell down her face.

When had her easy life gotten this complicated?

Chapter 22

Louie dug deeper into Scott Pencer's life. His financials were nothing outstanding, though he spent his money on some kinky things like porn videos, sex toys, and restraints, to name a few. Bondage videos, one item even looked like a snuff film. He dialed Vice.

"Vice, Ford speaking."

"Hey, Ed, it's Louie Romanelli from Homicide."

"What's up, Romanelli?"

"I have a name of a film here I want to check out. I think it's a snuff film. Would you be able to verify if it is?"

"I'll try, give me the title."

"It's called *Are You Ready for the End.*"

"Let me do some research and I'll call you back. What's your extension?"

"5455."

Louie hung up and continued to examine Pencer's financials. Tomorrow he'd recanvass Pencer's coworkers and pull out more information. Jake was right. There had to be some way to get Mikey Stalls charged with something, too. The number of deviants he'd had to deal with over the years had increased. Was something in the water, or were all those fanatics right to blame the increase in violent behavior on video games loaded with sex and brutality? He didn't have an answer, he only knew his job got tougher every day.

He thought back to the conversation with Sophia. She wanted to fight. Well, he'd give her a fight. Malone had stepped over the line when he had showed up at the house. His house, damn it. Never mind Sophia put herself in danger, which was unacceptable, but their daughter had been in the house. If Malone got within one inch of Marisa or his other children, the gloves would come off.

"What are you mumbling about?" Jake asked.

Jumping, he said, "Nothing. What do you want?" Hell, he was losing it. He hadn't heard Jake approach his desk.

"How's it going with Pencer?"

"I got Vice checking out a porn movie," Louie said.

"You'll be their new hero. Why?"

"It sounds like a snuff film."

"How'd you discover it?" Jake asked.

"It's on Pencer's financials. The title caught my eye."

"I got something on Velky. It might not be anything, but it seems weird compared to his other expenses. Six months ago, Velky flew to Arizona, then flew home twelve hours later. He's not a traveler. The guy doesn't even take vacations," Jake said.

"What do you make of it?"

"He had to have met with someone. He did the turnaround trip on the same day. It's as if he didn't want anyone to know he'd been gone. His company shuts down every year for two weeks in the summer and two weeks at Christmastime. It's strange he doesn't go anywhere," Jake said as he pondered that.

"Some people have families and don't like to travel. It's nothing in and of itself, Jake."

"He doesn't have a family. I mean, he's not married. His family is his mother and his brother."

"Maybe he's the caregiver for his mother," Louie said.

"He's not, I checked. She lives on her own. In fact, she moved into a condo and my guy took over the family home. The guy's financials are healthy. He's a saver, though he spends a lot at the lumberyard. Outside of his home expenses, he doesn't spend much on any one thing. I want to take a ride by his house to check out all the improvements."

"What about him got you thinking?" Louie asked.

"I'm thinking over the last five years he's spent a lot of money at hardware stores and lumberyards," Jake said.

"You'll have to research it on your own. I'm heading home, remember?"

"I do. How are you going to handle it?"

"I'm not sure."

"Stay calm."

"I'll try. But my daughter was in the house."

"I understand." Jake grabbed his arm. "Stay cool. Once you lose it, Sophia will shut down."

Louie picked up his files. "If you need me call, but give me an hour with Sophia."

"Call me after you talk with her."

Unable to speak, he understood Jake had his back. If only he could find the right words before he walked in his front door.

* * * *

Jake watched Louie leave the bullpen before heading into his office. Poor guy had his hands full. Personally, he'd like to break Malone's neck. If he even came close to Marisa... Hell, they didn't need this kind of distraction while they worked this case. He also needed a break. He almost couldn't remember what Mia looked like. He decided to call it a night. He stuffed his files in his briefcase and stopped in the bullpen on his way out.

"Kirk, I'll be working from home this afternoon. If anything comes up, no matter how insignificant, call me on my cell."

"All right, LT."

Jake walked to the elevator, pushed the button, and waited. The doors opened and Ford from Vice started to walk out.

"Jake."

"Looking for Louie?"

"Yeah."

"He's working from home. What do you have?"

"He was right. It's a snuff film. I'll need the information on the suspect."

"Come into my office." *Damn, I should have taken the stairs.*

Jake let go of the elevator door he'd been holding back. He wouldn't be able to get out of the station anytime soon. Ford followed. Once in his office, he offered him coffee. Like a vulture after prey Ford swooped down, grabbed a cup, and programmed the machine.

"Thanks, this stuff's like gold."

Jake thought the same thing. "Fill me in."

"It's a German film, produced earlier in the year. I notified the FBI. It's on their list and they're working with the German government to try to identify the woman in it. The website your suspect bought it from is no longer active."

"We won't be able to trace the owners of the website?"

"I didn't say that, Jake. I got their IP address and traced it to two other sites. I watched the video. It's freaking sick. The woman was killed. I don't understand sick bastards who find this entertaining or erotic. You can see the terror in the girl's eyes. You can watch the life drain from them. They kept the cameras rolling until they filmed over. Is this related to the Bride Murders?"

"Ford, please don't refer to them that way. It is related to the Carren case. One of our suspects bought this particular movie on his credit card."

"It was stupid on his part to leave an evidence trail."

"Probably thought he'd never get caught, and he wouldn't have if his name hadn't come up in the investigation. I don't have any solid evidence against him, but we're building it piece by piece."

Detective Ford handed Jake copies of all his research including the FBI's response, then left. Jake stuck it in his file and decided to do a quick search on Velky's financials again before he left the building. Originally, nothing like the snuff film popped out, but he hadn't been looking for it. An hour later he stretched to work out the kinks in his neck. Nothing—the guy didn't spend any money on entertainment. It was all about his house. Why? What did he do, remodel every year? The excessive amounts of money spent at the lumberyard still bothered him. No one was that obsessive about their home. It was time for a drive-by.

With Velky's financials and Pencer's snuff info added to the folder, Jake ventured out again. This time he took the stairs. He dialed Mia's number.

"Hello, stranger," she answered.

"Sorry. How's it going?"

"I'm getting a lot of research done for my next book."

"Ah, there's an advantage to not having me around."

"I'd rather you be here." *Progress,* he thought, much better than the first time around.

"I'll pick up food and come over. What do you want to eat?"

"I'm getting cabin fever, can't we go to yours?"

"I told you, I don't want you at the house. The guy could be watching me."

"Don't be ridiculous, Jake, I'm a big girl. Plus, I've got the state of the art security system. No one's going to get through it."

Through clenched teeth he said, "Mia, I'm not asking. You saw the crime-scene photos, what don't you get?" he asked, his voice harsher than he intended. Having an argument wasn't how he'd planned to spend his night. He'd had visions of blowing off a little steam, in a good way. If she wanted to be stubborn he'd cancel the date. "Mia, I'd never survive if you wound up in one of those pictures."

He hated when she remained silent—but he waited.

"That's low. What has this killer done to get under your skin?" Her tone of voice clued him to a change of mood.

"The killer is accelerating. He's got too much personal information on you and me. It's unacceptable. If I don't act fast he'll target anyone close to me. He might get desperate enough to go after you even though your height and age differs from past victims."

"I'll take extra precautions."

He wanted to scream but fought for control. "Famous last words. I'd rather err on the side of caution. Please, until this case is over, I don't want you anywhere near my place. When we go out we'll stay close to your house or Hartford or maybe even Danbury. It's closer to your house than Hartford."

"I'll agree because I don't want to fight, but do note, when you get here we're going to discuss this."

"Noted—I'll see you in an hour."

It was a small victory. Now all he had to do was convince her going forward. He'd been so busy arguing with Mia he didn't realize he was close to home. He had to pay better attention. She could drive him crazy. This blew his plans to hang close to home and the crime scene. He hit the garage door opener on the visor and pulled into his garage. He got out of the car and walked up the stairs to his living room without putting on a light. Brigh barked and jumped up on his leg.

After calming her down he walked to the window by the front door and eased the curtain back to look out. Was he being crazy? Since he had left McMichaels's place today, he'd had the weird feeling someone was watching him. After a quick scan nothing unusual popped out. *There was an old saying cops liked to use in jest*, Jake thought. *You never saw the bullet that took you down.* Jake had learned years ago to listen to his instincts. And they were buzzing. He rarely turned the security cameras on when he left the house, usually only engaging the alarm system. But now seemed like the right time to activate them in case the killer got up close and personal. After programming the system, he stripped as he headed toward the shower.

The hot water rained down on his head and back as it helped ease the tension from his body. Truth be told, he could use about eight hours of sleep instead of dinner, but a promise was a promise. He stepped out of the shower and dried off. As he started to shave an alarm sounded. After cutting his chin as he jumped ten feet, he realized it was the camera alarms he had engaged a few minutes ago. With the towel wrapped around his waist, he walked back into his office to check the monitor.

LJ? Jake opened the front door and let him in. "What's up, LJ?"

"Sorry to bother you, Uncle Jake, but things aren't good at home. Mom and Dad are at it again and I couldn't stand to be there."

Shit. Louie didn't listen to me. "What are they going on about?"

"That creep Mom works for and why Mom won't quit."

"How long have they been fighting?"

"About a month now."

Jake smiled for the first time today. "No, I meant today."

"Since Dad got home."

Jake realized he was still wearing a towel. "Wait here while I get my phone."

"You're going to tell them I'm here?"

"I'm going to ask your father what his problem is first. Then I'm going to tell him you're here."

Jake then realized an in person visit would have more impact on Louie.

"I'm heading out, LJ, and I don't want you here alone. This guy we're after is targeting me. It's not safe, otherwise I'd let you stay."

"Can't I come with you?"

"No, I'm taking Mia out to dinner."

"And you don't want a third party along. I get it." LJ fisted his hand, held it up to Jake. Jake bumped it as he tried not to laugh. LJ's mind was probably running the gamut of what he and Mia would be doing tonight. *Ah, to be fifteen again.*

"I'll drive you home once I get dressed."

"No need. I'll walk."

"I insist. Did you tell your parents you were going out?"

"No."

Louie and Sophia needed to understand what their fighting was doing to the children. With the sunshine comes the pain. What song was that? Boy, he was tired if he'd stooped to quoting songs.

After dressing, Jake reset the cameras and the alarm before he and LJ headed out. At Louie's front door, Jake knocked.

"You don't have to knock, I live here," LJ said.

"I'm knocking on purpose. I heard them as we got out of the car. This is to stop them for a minute."

"Oh…"

Louie opened the door. "What the hell?"

"Nice greeting. I have a date, so can we make this quick? LJ, go in and straight up to your room," Jake ordered.

"When did you lea—" Louie asked, as he watched LJ rush by him.

Jake cut him off. "Go, LJ." Once LJ headed upstairs, Jake walked further into the room. "Listen. He came to my house to get away from the fighting. Your kids aren't used to it. You both need to take a step back. You got the children worried and I heard you out on the street." He turned toward Sophia and continued. "I don't understand why this job is important to you, but is it worth all this tension and what it's doing to the kids?"

Both Sophia and Louie started talking at once. Jake raised his hand. "Please."

"It's none of your business, Jake," Louie and Sophia said in unison.

"You're my business. Why don't you both reevaluate what's going on here and who it affects?"

"It's a family matter."

That hurt. Jake said, "I thought I was family."

"*Porca miseria*! You are! This is between my wife and I and no one else, not even the kids," Louie said, throwing his hands in the air.

"Louie, the cursing," Sophia said automatically, turning back to Jake. "You are family, but like we told the children, this is between Louie and me and not you or them."

Louie was famous for swearing in Italian when he got mad. *Porca miseria* meant dammit in Italian. To Sophia it was cursing. "I'm leaving now. All I'm saying is take a break and talk to them and put them at ease." Jake couldn't keep the edge from his voice.

"Jake…"

He kept walking.

* * * *

Call him crazy… his nerve endings danced as he drove away. He pulled onto the highway in the opposite direction from Mia's place. As he merged into traffic he watched the entrance ramp behind to see if there were headlights. His was the only car to use the ramp. At the next exit Jake pulled off, crossed over the highway and got back on in the right direction. Still, he couldn't shake the feeling. He marked it down to exhaustion and used the drive time to run the case through his head. By the time he reached Mia's nothing popped out.

He pulled up in front of Mia's house, wondering again why someone would attach themselves to another human being for a lifetime. He hated to admit it. Louie and Sophia's fighting had tilted his world. He understood LJ's fear and discomfort. To Jake, they were the perfect couple. They never fought—well, until recently. They had almost given him hope long-term commitments could work. Now what? Maybe Mia's fear of commitment in the beginning was right. Why was he pushing her to commit? When she opened the door, all his doubts dissipated. *I love this woman. It's normal for couples to have fights. Why am I making such a big deal about Louie and Sophia?* He leaned in to kiss her and she pulled back.

"What's the matter?"

"We need to discuss your need to protect me."

"Mia…"

"Jake, I'm not stupid. I understand your concern, but we can't stop living our lives because of some criminal. If it makes you feel better to drive out here all the time, fine. But who's to say he won't at some point follow you here?"

"I took precautions before I came here in case I was being followed. Please, it's not a permanent change—it's just until this case is solved."

"What about your next case, and the one after that, Jake?"

She had a way of making him feel like a fool. Jake ran his fingers through his hair, ready to pull it out. He was sure the dictionary defined *stubborn* in one word—Mia! *She's got me. I don't have an answer for her.* He couldn't come up with a logical explanation.

"Well, Jake?"

"I'm thinking," he said, annoyed. Her unexpected laughter threw him a curve. "What's so funny?"

"The expression on your face is priceless. You're trying your darnedest to find an answer. There'll always be cases, and some might even target you personally. Come inside and lock the door."

Mia closed the door behind him, turned, and walked down the hallway. He called after her, "I'm not going to rehash our conversation. Please answer me this. If I wasn't a cop, would you be busting my chops about protecting you? I don't know a guy alive who, when he's in love, wouldn't go out of his way to protect his woman."

"Well played. But I'd kick him to the curb, too." She smiled.

"I see. So, the crisis is averted?"

"No crisis. It was a reminder to you I'm not changing my life to suit your suspects."

In the kitchen he plopped down in a chair, never breaking eye contact with her. He decided to change the subject. "I'm starved. Where do you want to eat?"

Mia's stare started to unnerve him. He hoped she understood he wasn't giving up. His gut swirled at her nonchalant attitude.

"Is the Old Rooster good with you?"

"Yes."

"One last thing, Jake, to put your mind at ease, I have guns and I am trained on how to use them. I always have one on me. I have a permit to carry a concealed weapon."

"Just an FYI, Mia," he said putting an emphasis on her name. "It doesn't make me feel good, because if you're ever overpowered your own weapon could be used against you. The reason many gun owners are hurt or die each year is the piece of steel in their hands gives them a false confidence, making them feel invincible. Being trained is one thing, shooting at a man is a completely different animal. Why don't you take Brigh until this is over?"

"No, Brigh would shake to death if an intruder came in. And I don't feel invincible, but I've made up my mind ages ago I'd let no one take my weapon away from me. Why don't you and I engage in a little hand-to-hand?"

Famous last words—he hoped to God they wouldn't be hers. "I might take you up on that. It would be great foreplay." He joked but wasn't the least bit amused. "Are you ready for dinner?"

"Yes, let me get my jacket and purse."

* * * *

Were they fighting? His view through the binoculars didn't give him a clue about what. Boy, he wished he was a fly on the wall. He put down the binoculars and picked up his notepad. He didn't want to turn on the overhead light or put on the flashlight to draw attention to himself. He wrote in the dark. Item one: make sure to pick up a listening device for next time. Earlier, he had tried to clone the lieutenant's phone. And decided to read up on it again to see what he did wrong. Maybe it would be easier to clone the woman's phone instead of a policeman's unit.

The lieutenant thought he was smarter than me with his highway antics. But I'm smarter. The woman didn't just come into my sights. He wondered why she hadn't been at his house all week. Jake's last two cases and their notoriety on the news is what caught my attention.

The man had great taste in women, though I like them with black hair myself. This one's a little too old and taller than I like, but hot nevertheless. Item two: night goggles. If I were the lieutenant I'd keep my woman close, instead of letting her stay out here all by her lonesome self. What was he thinking? He wondered if Carrington knew exactly who he was dating. The woman was seriously loaded. Like Forbes loaded. More baffling was why the hell was she dating Carrington? Though he wasn't in dire straits either; money found money, he supposed. It was about time he upped the game. What should he send this time—their financial reports or a lock of her hair or better yet another letter? Or should he send the next victim's finger? The bastard would have to acknowledge him with his next gift. Jake Carrington could have saved them both a lot of trouble if he'd only published the letter.

Deep in his heart he understood if Ciara was reading the Wilkesbury news, wherever she'd planted herself, she would recognize him and his work. After years of searching and not connecting with her, he understood their time was drawing near.

Chapter 23

After dinner he figured all was forgiven because Mia was affectionate. It made for an enjoyable evening. In the morning he went straight to the station after being summoned by the captain. It sounded urgent, which was why he didn't bother to head home first and change his clothes. He'd change at lunchtime. Once he parked in the garage he bypassed his office and headed straight up to Shamus's office on the third floor.

"He's with the commissioner. He asked me to send you in when you arrived," Shamus's admin said as Jake passed her.

Damn, something big had to be breaking on the case. Jake changed direction and headed to Blake's office. Briskly he knocked and waited for the invite. Once it was received he took a deep breath before entering the office. He was stunned when he scanned the room—the commissioner, the chief, and his captain. No mayor.

"Morning," he managed.

"Have a seat, Jake. We received another communication from the killer."

"Was it addressed to me again?"

"No, it was addressed to me," the commissioner said.

"Ah."

"Not curious, Jake?"

"I am, but you'll share the why when you're ready, sir." Jake sat at attention.

"It's a lock of black hair, silky in texture. The note states it's Mia Andrews's."

His blood froze from head to toe. He was unable to move a muscle as all eyes observed him. He racked his brain as he tried to figure out where the killer could've gotten hold of Mia's hair. He grabbed his phone and hit speed dial. When she answered, he jumped right into it.

"Are you okay?"

"Yes, why?"

"No one's with you?"

"No, Jake. What's up?"

"We received a sample of black hair this morning and the killer is claiming it's yours. Have you had a haircut in the last two weeks?"

"Yes."

"Where?"

"Relax, it wasn't here. I get it cut in the City."

For the first time since he entered the commissioner's office the waves in his stomach subsided. "Okay. I'll call you back in a few minutes." He hung up without waiting for her answer. It didn't matter it might not be her hair. The killer had made it personal.

"It's not hers?" the commissioner asked.

"She gets her hair done in New York City. I can't see the killer going down there for a few strands."

"We discussed this before you got here, Jake. The three of us feel he has a personal vendetta against you—" Jake cut him off.

"I don't think so, sir—"

The commissioner continued, "Jake, don't interrupt me. Hear me out. The reason the mayor's not here is twofold. One, you and the mayor went at it on the last case and we must acknowledge it could be his brother. Two, you and Miller went at it on the last case, too. It could be one of his brothers. We're not going to discount Miller's family."

The commissioner's words sank into his head. Jake mulled over the possibilities. God, he hated the Miller brothers. Both dirty cops. Sergeant Ralph Miller lost a promotion due to Jake's investigation on a brutality case. Ralph's brother, the captain at the time, encouraged the rank and file by ignoring cops who used force. The captain lost his job and pension. Neither took responsibility for their actions. No, according to them it was all Jake's fault he dug up evidence when the case landed in his lap. They felt he hadn't protected the blue wall. Damn, he wished both Millers had been fired at the time.

"There's also a third possibility. He threw this at us to throw us off his scent. I'm going with the third one, myself. Your captain feels the Miller family has it out for you. What are your feelings on the subject?"

The question hung out there as he took a minute to gather his thoughts, Jake contemplated his choices. "May I see the hair sample and the note?"

The commissioner handed Jake the plastic see-through evidence bags containing the items. Same as before, the killer used print from different publications to form his words. The sample didn't feel like Mia's hair texture, Jake noted, as his stomach muscles began to relax more.

If you don't move faster, I'll give you a reason to.
Yours truly,
The Groom

"I'd like to ask for protection for Mia."

"It's already done. I spoke with the Woodbury Police Department. They're going to put Officer Dave Guerrera in charge of the detail. I understand you're acquainted with him."

"Yeah, Dave and I go way back."

"Then that's settled."

"Commissioner, I'd like to ask another favor." Jake waited. When the commissioner nodded, Jake continued. "I'd like a detail at my house. I activated the cameras on my security system. I can have my company feed them directly to the station for monitoring during the duration of this case. I'm going to ask Mia to go to the city and stay with her parents. But I'm sure she won't go. I'll keep her at my house instead of involving the Woodbury PD."

"It's a bit extreme, Jake."

"She lives in the sticks. I'd never be able to get to her in time if something happened."

It poured out of him. His nerves scolded his skin as if they were a pot of boiling oil as he fought to control the heat surging toward his fists to expel it. If he hadn't already been sitting, he'd have thrown his body into the chair. He scanned the room, made eye contact with each of them and noted their sympathy, though he could have recited the next words to come out of the commissioner's mouth.

"Jake, you understand we're under budget constraints. If you keep Ms. Andrews in Woodbury, it would solve several problems. It frees you up to perform your duty without splitting your attention."

"Perform my duty." He shot out of his chair. Leaned over the commissioner's desk and got in his face. "Would this be your reaction if it were your wife or daughters?"

Shamus cleared his throat as he placed a hand on Jake's shoulder to push him back in his seat. Jake turned around ready to swing, then he realized who had placed a hand on his shoulder. He sat back down and dropped his head into his hands.

"No one is telling you we won't protect Ms. Andrews. We think it's wise she stays put for now. If the threat escalates we'll move her to a safe house," McGuire said.

"Not good enough. I need to speak with the shrink again. I want to understand why the killer has chosen this path. I think you all misread the note. This is a screw-you to the department for not printing his letter and giving him his due. I will not allow him to use Mia as a pawn in his fight."

"I understand you're upset which is why I'm going to overlook your insubordination. Take a look at this and give me a call when you want to meet back here to discuss it," Commissioner Blake said.

Blake looked around the room and dismissed them all. As they left, Shamus said good-bye to the chief, who had not uttered one word in the meeting. When Doolittle walked away, Shamus turned to him.

"In my office, Jake."

"Cap, you have to—"

"In my office."

Inside Shamus's office Jake paced while his captain took a seat. "For God's sake, sit down. It's too early in the morning for all this bullshit." Shamus ran a hand over his mouth.

Jake sat and waited. Shamus buzzed his admin on the intercom. "Sheila, can you get me and the lieutenant a cup of coffee?"

"Yes sir."

The request surprised him. The captain rarely asked his admin to run errands. He drummed his fingers on his legs and waited.

"I agree with you. If it were their wives or daughters, action would be taken, and swiftly. You and Ms. Andrews are only dating. But it doesn't make the danger to her any less real. Give it an hour, and I'll speak to the commissioner."

Overcome with emotion, Jake couldn't find the words to thank him. Shamus continued. "I already dispatched a detail to your and Louie's homes. I thought it prudent after hearing about yesterday's incident."

His captain somehow knew everything that went on in his department. "I'd like to explain."

"There's no need. I find Malone as dangerous as the killer we're hunting. I also spoke with Louie last night. Do you have any idea why his wife is continuing to work for that madman?"

"None whatsoever. I tried to pull it out of her yesterday. I even offered the money for whatever she was saving for." Jake exhaled, as he released the fright of almost losing Sophia. "But she refused it."

"Does she have a gambling problem?"

For the first time since he came to work this morning, Jake laughed. "No, Sophia won't even buy a lottery ticket. She tells Louie all the time it's a waste of money."

"Are you sure?"

Wow, he's serious. "Do you have some information you'd like to share which points to a gambling problem?"

"I'm going to do some research. That's between you and me, Jake."

"You're going to investigate Sophia?" Appalled, he stared into Shamus's hard eyes.

"I'm going to see if she's in trouble."

"That's investigating, Shamus," Jake said, in disbelief. "I wish you hadn't told me."

"I understand you're friends, but you're also his lieutenant. Don't forget it."

The last thing he needed when he left Shamus's office was for Louie to corner him.

"What's going on?" Louie tilted his head toward Shamus's office.

"I have to fill you in. The killer contacted us again."

"Why didn't you call me?"

"I was commanded to make an appearance at five thirty this morning. I didn't want to interrupt your beauty sleep." Jake's attempt at humor failed miserably.

"Are we partners or aren't we?"

"Yes, we are. I am also your boss. My boss's boss requested my presence in his office; any questions?" Jake quirked a brow.

"No." *Exactly what I don't need is Louie in a pissy mood all day.*

He updated Louie on the latest details. After Louie left his office, he put a call in to the shrink.

"Dr. Maxwell, it's Jake Carrington."

"Good morning. What can I do for you?"

"The killer contacted us again."

"Us or you, Jake?"

"Us, the police, but yes, it was directed at me. Can we meet earlier than planned today?"

"It's seven thirty now, how about nine?"

"Great, I'll see you here. Afterward, I have a meeting scheduled with my team, I'd like you to attend."

"I'll make some calls and rearrange my day." She hung up.

What had changed? Maxwell wasn't jerking him around as she normally did. Maybe she was getting with the program. He could only hope. Too many people had been busting his balls lately and it didn't sit well with him.

The next hour and a half he spent putting together his notes for Dr. Maxwell as well as his notes on what he wanted to share with the task force. Each had minor differences and information. If there was a leak, Jake wanted to know where it'd come from. He hadn't realized how much time had passed. A knock on his door told him it was showtime.

"Lieutenant."

"Come in, Doctor."

Jake showed her a copy of the new letter and a picture of the hair sample. Maxwell's eyes grew large as she read the letter. Not in disgust, if he was reading her right, but in delight. His hackles rose. *What's her problem?*

"Your opinion?" he asked, a little too harshly.

The doctor raised her eyes and studied him. Not flinching, he studied her back.

"He's escalating, and the tone has changed. He's more dangerous. You annoyed him when you didn't make his first letter public. I understand your logic, but I don't agree with it. If he is going to take another woman, all women with black hair should be on the lookout and take extra precautions."

"We have decided to keep this letter quiet, too. Only a handful of people have been informed of its existence."

"There's a saying, Jake. If more than one person knows a secret it is no longer a secret. All I'm saying is if you don't release it, two things will happen. First, he'll target Ms. Andrews—"

"Dr. Andrews," Jake interrupted. Something in her tone angered him. It activated his protective nature. Mia would laugh at him, though he didn't find it funny.

"She's a psychologist, right?" Jake didn't bother to answer. "Anyway, Dr. Andrews will continue to be in his sights. Second, if he does take another woman—and I'm sure he will—the media will crucify the department and you for not warning the public."

"It's a chance we're willing to take."

"Is Ms.—Dr. Andrews willing to take it?"

"It's a departmental decision, not mine or hers."

"Let's hope you catch him before he takes her or another woman."

"Any other insights, Doc?" Jake couldn't keep the annoyance out of his voice.

"I'd say he's starting to get to you, too."

"No, he's not. I get annoyed with all the suspects I chase. Please don't assume you know me."

"All right."

Maxwell pushed out of her chair. As Jake stood he reached out his hand to her. "Thank you. The meeting will convene in fifteen minutes in the conference room at the back of the bullpen." From the first moment he'd met Maxwell something hadn't clicked with him. Even now he had no warm feeling toward her. He'd never seen a woman colder than her. Maxwell showed no compassion to victims or survivors.

Jake spent those minutes lining up his strategies. He'd be walking a thin line in the meeting with Maxwell there. For reasons only his brain could explain, he held back information from her. It would be difficult to speak with the whole team while skirting the evidence. With his control groups in place Jake gathered up his files and notes and headed toward the conference room at exactly ten. He noted the empty desks along the way. The team must be assembled already for the meeting. Someone behind him called out. Turning, he recognized Carey from Vice.

"Max."

"Jake, how much of my time are you going to take?"

"I'll need an hour. Why, you got a hot one?"

"In more ways than one." Detective Max Carey grinned.

At the door to the conference room, he scanned the group. At first glance, it appeared to be a motley crew. Most were like-minded in the job, but not in the way they dressed. He'd have thought Dr. Maxwell would stick out in this crowd, not Burke. Burke, with his stained shirt stretched over his Jupiter-sized belly, along with Detective Carey's gangster-grunge look, stood out the most. Kirk Brown sat in the far corner and ducked his head down when Jake pointed to his watch. Jake understood why the young detective was back before his required five hours off duty was up. Something to address after the meeting. He continued to scan the room. He noted Lanoue and Green. The only people missing were the captain and the chief; he wasn't sure if the commissioner planned on attending. Stalling, Jake walked over to the coffeepot someone had set up and took a cup of what he knew would resemble sludge. Warning his taste buds, he took a sip and almost choking on the thick substance, he put it aside. At the door stood his captain and the chief.

"These are our viable suspects." Jake pointed to the board. Lanoue's hand shot up. "Yes, Armand."

"Shouldn't we continue to interview the rest of the shops and parlors?"

"Yes—right now we have no solid evidence, only circumstantial. We'll continue to follow all the leads, which are pointing to the killer as a shop worker."

"I thought you said you had five suspects, Jake?" Dr. Maxwell spoke without raising her hand.

"We've narrowed down the field to these four: Pencer, Stalls, McMichaels, and Tedessco. The fifth suspect comes in at ten percent on the probability list. The other four rate over seventy-five percent. We'll concentrate on them first."

"When you eliminate someone, how can you be sure you're right?"

"Evidence, alibis, and instinct go into eliminating a person, Doctor. In most cases, we move them down the list until we get the killer. Now, let's move on."

Jake gave her no room for more questions. Highlighting the reasons why each of these four were on the list, Jake gave out assignments. Half the team's priority would be to dig deeper into the suspects' lives, the other half to continue to push on for more suspects.

"My experience tells me the killer is not joking when he says he'll take another woman. We have less than two weeks to stop him before he kills again. I don't want another young woman's picture on this board, do you?" Jake used the pointer to highlight each of the missing women before resting it on Nadia. He scanned the room. Satisfied, he moved on to the assignments.

"Green, you and Lanoue keep digging and interview everyone Pencer ever said a word to. I want to know him better than his mother. Burke, stay on the photographers and the videographers—I don't think there's anything there, but let's not drop the ball on them. Brown, you continue your research on McMichaels and Tedessco."

"Who will you be pursuing, Lieutenant?" Dr. Maxwell pushed.

She's like a dog with a bone. "I'll be overseeing and organizing the information as it comes in. I will also be in the field interviewing shop owners. Does it meet with your approval, Doc?"

"I was curious."

Maxwell scribbled notes throughout the briefing. *Let it go, Jake.*

"Okay, you have your assignments. Let's get to it. I want all of you, especially the ones in the field, to check in every two hours with Kirk, even if you have nothing. Oh, and watch your backs out there. It's a hunch, but make sure no one is following you around. Dismissed."

McGuire and Louie hung back. It didn't surprise him when Dr. Maxwell did too. "Something I can do for you, Doctor?"

"I didn't mean to overstep your command. I was curious how an investigation like this ran and what your role was in it. You held back a suspect from your team. Why?"

The woman wasn't stupid. "At this time, Doc, those four men up there are the only plausible suspects. Do you have another one to add?" Jake's eyebrow shot into his hairline.

"No."

"Thanks for sitting in on this today. Doc, if you'll excuse us."

Her eyes widened in shock at being dismissed. Call him small. It lightened his mood. Some people rubbed you the wrong way.

"I'll be talking to you soon."

Jake watched as she strutted out.

"I'd tread carefully there." Shamus lifted his coffee cup and pointed to Maxwell.

"She's off."

"Why was she questioning you and your decisions?"

"I have an idea." Jake grinned without mirth.

He updated Shamus and Louie on what he had learned before the meeting about the good doctor and why he was withholding information from her.

"I see." Shamus scratched his head. "There's no accounting for taste, is there?"

"No, there isn't."

Shamus left. Louie started collecting the notes and files left around the room.

"Who's tailing her?" Louie smirked when Jake tossed him a look. "Birds of a feather and all that, it's what I would've done."

"You're not wrong. Carey will report back soon."

"How'd you come by the information?"

"Not telling. I'm exercising my Fifth Amendment rights." Jake grinned wickedly at Louie.

"You're a real ass sometimes."

"It's all part of my charm."

Together they walked out of the conference room and headed to their desks. Halfway there, Jake's phone rang. He checked the display and smiled.

"Go," he answered.

"You're right on the money," Carey said.

"Thanks, Max. Can you stay on them for while? I need as much info as possible."

"You bet. It will do my heart good to be part of whatever brings him down. I can't stand the scumbag." Carey hung up.

"Is it what you thought?" Louie asked.

"Yep," Jake said.

Chapter 24

Jake's phone rang again. He noted not one but two calls coming in. Al Burke's number appeared first. The second number belonged to Gwenn Langley. Gwenn would have to wait.

"What's up, Al? I'm putting you on speaker. Louie's here."

"I'm on Watertown Avenue by the stadium. There's a late-model green Ford Focus that's been following me around all day. You want to send an unmarked car to box him in?"

"Joe Green is en route now." Jake glanced toward the door. Louie held up five fingers. "He'll be there in approximately five minutes. Did you get a license plate?"

"Only a partial, it's XQE 1. That's Xavier, Quincy, Edwards and the number one. I didn't get the last two numbers."

"Why didn't you report it sooner?"

"I wanted to be sure."

"You should've followed procedure and reported it sooner. It's best not to wait on cases like this, Al."

"Okay, I'll get back to you. Green's pulling in behind the man. Oh, shit, he made us…" Al must have dropped his phone on the seat without disconnecting because Jake heard a soft thud, then the sound of Green detailing the chase to dispatch through his car radio. "Detective Burke, I'm in pursuit." Burke continued his play-by-play. "I'm getting on Route 8 heading south passing the I-84 interchange. My current speed is ninety and the suspect is pulling away from me. Notify the state police to assist in the pursuit," Burke shouted.

Jake listened in, his phone glued to his ear. The portable radio in his office relayed the same info. Louie was also focused on the radio. "Damn, we might have him today. We're getting close," Louie said.

"We'll see. If he's outrunning a cop car, he has to have some serious horsepower under the hood."

Burke's voice boomed over the radio, "The state police have now picked up the chase. I'm heading back to the station."

Jake disconnected his phone then clicked his portal to signal dispatch. "Lieutenant Carrington requests Detective Green to click over to a secure channel immediately."

Jake fumed as he waited for Green to click over. He started right in on Green when he acknowledged his presence. "What the hell went wrong?"

"We had him boxed in when he must have spotted us. The suspect executed a U-turn in front of a loaded school bus. I had to back off," Green defended.

"Were you able to get a license plate at least?"

"The last two numbers were covered. Duct tape would be my best guess."

Jake's cell phone rang. The display showed Gwenn Langley's number. "I have to take this call. Joe, head back to the station."

Switching to his cell phone, he caught the call before Gwenn hung up.

"Hello, sweetheart." Jake took the phone from his ear to check the caller ID again.

"What's up?" he asked briskly.

"Are we on for dinner tonight?"

Gwenn had to be with someone. It was the only explanation he could come up with. "I'll give you a call in a couple of hours. I've got something running hot right now. Can you make it then?"

"I'll wait for your call. How's Sports Town for the meet?"

Gwenn always called Bristol Sports Town because it was home base to ESPN. He processed his paperwork from the meeting while he waited for Green and Burke to return and sent Louie off to research the partial license plate to try to get a name. Hopefully, it turned out to be one of his major suspects, because he had a crowded field. A headache started to form. He ran his fingers through his hair and stopped at the top of his head where the pain throbbed. He massaged his scalp to ease the tension. An experienced cop, Burke spotted the tail easy enough. Why would someone follow him? *Me or Louie I'd understand.* Burke wasn't chasing a smoking gun—or was he? A thought struck Jake between the eyes. He raced to the communications room.

"Thomas, bring up the surveillance of the station. Let's say around eleven to one o'clock."

Clive Thomas greeted him as his fingers started keying in the proper code. Pointing to the monitor in the corner, he said, "Take a seat over there. I'll send the feed to the computer."

"Thanks."

As Clive put the screen in motion, Jake watched. "Clive, can I go back and forward with the tape? And is this the only camera with eyes on the station?"

"Use your mouse, hover over a pic or face and press down the button and hold it. It will freeze the frame. We've got three cameras with eyes on the station. You might get a hit on each one. What I can do if there are more than one is send them to one computer screen or set them on different screens; what's your pleasure?"

"One for now, if anything pops out we'll take it to a larger screen. Would your face recognition program be able to identity a face if it appears more than once?"

"If I program it to do it, it will."

Jake went back to watching the videos. About a half hour into it a familiar face popped up—the man from the bar in the exact same getup. He hovered his cursor over the face and enlarged it before he froze the screen to study the man.

"Thomas, this guy here, can you match his face to this week's tape and see if he pops up again? I'll also want to see if he's a match to the video I turned in earlier from the Hard Rider bar."

"It's going to take some time to set it up and get you the information."

"How long do you think before you have something for me?"

"Roughly about four hours to run it against a week's worth of tapes."

"Here's my cell number. Call me the minute you have something." He had no doubt it'd be a match; though it didn't give him the suspect's name, it might help build a case against him when he was caught. "Thanks, Clive, I'll talk to you later."

The minute Jake walked back into the bullpen Louie nailed him. "What was the rush?"

"Come into my office." Louie followed.

"So…"

"The suspect made another mistake by following Burke. He had to be watching the station. I ran up to communications, watched some videos and found our suspect from the bar."

"What's he driving?"

"Don't have the make or model yet, he was on foot. Thomas is running a facial recognition program now. When he knows, he'll call. He has my cell number, but if he calls here you take the call. I need to meet up with Gwenn. I promised I'd be no more than a couple of hours and it's getting to the time. She's got something hot." Jake tugged his cell phone from his pocket.

"I hope it's not the hots for you. Remember you're taken." Louie cracked himself up.

Jake tossed a wide grin over his shoulder as he snatched up his jacket and keys. He figured it would keep Louie guessing for hours. He let Gwenn know he was on his way.

* * * *

It was a warm, sunny day. Jake took a chair at the outside terrace bar at Reilly's Bar and Grill to wait for Gwenn. A few patrons sipped their beers or chomped on the pretzels and nuts the bartender had put out. Jake wondered how many germs lived in the community bowl. He sipped his beer while he enjoyed the sun beating down on his back. Again, he ran the evidence and facts from the case through his head. Each time he hoped something fell into place or popped out. Gwenn rushed up to the bar minutes later. A beauty, the sweetheart of the six o'clock news who was always camera-ready, she had every head in the place turned toward her as she passed. If she noticed, she didn't let on. She ignored them all, as beautiful woman do who are used to the attention, and came straight to him.

"Sorry I'm late. Water for me," she said to the bartender.

Jake nursed his beer. "I haven't been here long. What's up?"

"Can we get a table inside? I need to eat."

"Sure." With regret, he picked up his beer and Gwenn's water as he left the sunshine behind. In the dank bar, he followed her to the farthest booth. He took the side with his back to the wall. It gave him a view of the whole room and terrace.

"Last night I was having dinner with a date at Bonaterra's and you'll never guess who walked into the joint all snuggled up and cozy with a tall, scrumptious blonde who was not his wife?"

"Wilkesbury's honorable mayor?"

"You're no fun, Jake. When did you find out?"

"I've had my suspicions for a while. I'd see her out to lunch with Velky, or at city hall. I couldn't figure out why she'd be there. You have a name?"

"I'm working on it. Do you?"

"The police shrink." He raised his glass in salute.

"No way," she said, laughing. "Is he using her to gain information on the case?"

"Not sure, though her questions lead me to believe he is. It doesn't matter, I've been limiting what I give to her. She sat in on my update today with the team. I held back a lot of information I didn't want the mayor to have."

"This gets more interesting each time I speak to you. I want the story when this is finished. Do you need anything from me in the meantime?"

Gwenn could dig deeper than he could without his legal restraints. "If you can give me deeper backgrounds on these three people, everything, even minor stuff, I'd appreciate it. And the last one, Gwenn, I can't stress it enough I don't want his name out there. I need you to do the research personally." He pushed a file across the scarred table to her.

Gwenn opened it immediately. She ran her finger down the page landing on one name before she glanced up at Jake. "You do your job, I'll do mine. And for this, what do I get?"

"You might want to start with his juvie record." Jake curled his lip. He'd get the info out there one way or another and cover his ass as well.

"I will. Again, what do I get for my troubles?"

"You'll get an exclusive once I've arrested the suspect. If I can, I'll even give you a heads-up so you can be there with a camera for the perp walk before any of your competitors are informed a suspect's been arrested."

She reached out her hand. "Deal."

Jake took it.

He sat for a few minutes after Gwenn left and nursed his beer, using the time to organize his thoughts. The three names he'd given Gwenn were his real suspects. The others were smoke screens for the mole in his department. When he got back he'd give Walsh busy work to keep him out of his hair. He'd assign him the Stalls file to thoroughly research. His phone buzzed as he started to drive down the street. He pulled back to the curb to answer the phone.

"Lieutenant, it's Thomas. I got your guy outside the station every day this week. Do you want to pick up the pictures or should I email them to you?"

"Sergeant Romanelli will pick up the pictures, no one else. But also send the file to this email address." He gave him his personal email. "And thanks, Thomas."

Jake took his foot off the brake and maneuvered his way back into traffic. According to all he'd read, most serial killers disintegrated over time. Was this one losing control? Were these mistakes or was the suspect playing them? Why now? What could he gain by putting himself forward? He turned these questions and more over in his head on the drive back to the station. What he needed was the rendering from Joel Bennett, the police artist. Time wasn't a commodity he had a lot of. He needed this yesterday. Jake pressed the number five on his cell phone to speed-dial Bennett and bypass the switchboard.

"Joel, what do you have for me?"

"I'm almost there, Lieutenant. Either the witness doesn't have a good memory or he's stalling."

"What's your take on him?"

"He's enjoying this too much. I sent him down to the cafeteria for coffee. I'll have the best I'm going to get after our next session."

"This is urgent..." Jake started to push, stopped, and rubbed his tired eyes.

"I understand, but if I lean too hard on him he'll start making things up to get out of here."

"Sorry, I'm taking my frustrations out on you. Call me when you have a face."

After disconnecting his call, he turned his thoughts back to Mayor Velky. How could he use this information against John Velky? And what should he do about Dr. Maxwell? If Velky had kept his nose out of this case, Jake wouldn't even be considering the issue. It wasn't his business if a man cheated on his wife. But this mudslinger deserved everything he slung back at him.

He pulled his car down a side street a block from the station and worked his way up and down each street until he reached the garage. With his luck the bastard was following him now. He didn't see anyone. Jake gave up and pulled into the garage to plan his next move.

Louie almost spilled his coffee when Jake snuck up behind him.

"Jumping Jesus, you're going to give me a heart attack someday. Why don't you make some noise when you walk up behind someone?"

"Because I love watching you jump. What have you got for me?" Jake said, as he hung his jacket on the back of his chair. "Do you mind if I have a cup, too?"

"Sure, go ahead." Louie waved.

"Thanks. Shoot."

"I have a thousand possibilities with the first four combinations if we stick with the color green, if Burke's right about the make and model."

Jake thought. "He normally is. Have any of the car colors been changed?"

"I didn't get that far."

A smile washed over Jake's face as he sat with his coffee. He pressed the intercom button and summoned Walsh. Yes, this would be better than having him dig into Stalls's background. Harry rushed into his office a minute later.

"Yeah, LT."

"Walsh, Louie's going to give you the thousand names he's come up with in his license plate search related to the case. I need you to vet the ones that weren't green when they came off the assembly line."

Walsh groaned.

"Problem, Harry?"

"No, sir. You sure you don't want me on something more important?"

"This is important, Harry. The car was following Burke as he interviewed people about the case today." Yep, he could see Walsh's mind calculating this tidbit of information.

"Okay." He took the paper from Louie and left the office.

"Now for you, Louie, I want you to run the names against the people involved in the case or related to each victim."

"I know how to do my job, LT," Louie mimed Walsh. "I could've eliminated the color in one step."

"It's busy work." At least for a while it would keep Walsh out of his hair. "What are you still doing here? I've got work to do." He turned on his computer.

"What did Gwenn want?"

"A date for the prom." He chuckled.

"Give." Unamused, Louie stared him down.

"To tell me something we already knew."

Jake turned back to his computer screen after Louie left his office. The first name he typed into his search engine was Julie Maxwell. Most of the stories about her he'd gotten from her personal jacket. What he hadn't known was she'd been arrested in her college days. Not much in the article. It was probably a disorderly conduct or a pot charge. Next, he searched her work record. The computer listed four jobs. Her personnel record had listed two: Maxwell had worked for the Boston PD as an assistant psychiatrist and as a company psychologist at Trends, Inc. This file listed two other police departments in New England. Why hadn't she listed them on her application? *She must have been fired,* he thought. Whatever it was would be easy to verify. He noted the departments and their contact information. How had Personnel missed these—or had they? Jake had found them with a basic Google search. Jake went through the switchboard and was placed on hold for a few minutes before the operator connected him with the chief of police. He identified himself.

"Chief, I understand Dr. Julie Maxwell worked for your department."

"She did. I'll only give you the dates. I have no other comments, Lieutenant."

"Even if it's off the record?"

"Yes, even off the record. I don't know you from Adam."

Jake couldn't pull any more information from the man. After thanking the chief for nothing, he pulled up the local newspapers for each area and matched dates to Maxwell's employment record. Maxwell had brought a suit against the Castleton, New Hampshire police department for sexual harassment, which was later dropped and settled out of court for an undisclosed amount of money. The original article stated Dr. Maxwell had had a personal relationship with the then-chief. When she wasn't promoted from part-time assistant to head of the department, she sued the department. She denied it was brought in retaliation for being passed over. The last article noted the chief was forced to retire and wound up divorcing his wife of forty years. The doc was a home-wrecker. Why hide it? No one cared today about such things. Jake placed the next call, this time to the town of Littleton, Vermont.

"Ah, I remember the doc, the knockout from Boston. With her looks and brains, I couldn't figure out why she was here. We're considered a city, but nothing compared to her hometown."

"She didn't like it there?"

"At first, I'd have to say no, then she hooked up with our mayor. After that, she stopped trying to change the department."

Playing dumb, Jake asked, "She started to work for the mayor's office?"

Laughter echoed through the phone. "I guess you could say that. She wasn't employed by him. She was dating him."

Jake saw a pattern forming here. Maxwell always targeted the highest person in the chain.

And this time around it was Wilkesbury's mayor. What would it cost the city when she was finished with Velky?

"Why'd she leave your department?"

"Because the mayor's wife's a tough woman, if you get my drift."

"I do. Did it cost your town anything?"

"Nope, Mrs. Landry dug up some dirt on the good doctor. She left with her tail between her legs."

Jake smiled. "Thanks, Chief."

"Anytime."

Should he warn the mayor? Nah, he had enough to deal with without outing the mayor's sex life. Maxwell was another story. Her agreeableness this morning was out of character. Was it to gain information for the mayor? But for what purpose? On second thought, it would be best if Gwenn publicized the affair—two birds, one stone.

Jake turned back to his computer and continued digging into Pencer's life. An hour later he concluded Pencer was a rapist, but not his killer. All his alibis checked out. Even so, once Louie and Vice finished their research, Scott Pencer would be put away for a long time. How anyone got off on snuff films flummoxed him. The world was filled with sick, deranged people. People he had to deal with on a daily basis. It was scum like Pencer who often had him questioning why he did what he did. You put one away and ten more crawled out of the woodwork. Really, was he making a difference? These black thoughts were rare, but when they blew through him it made him question his life choices. The biggest choice he still questioned pertained to his sister Eva. What-ifs are killers in and of themselves. To his dying day he would always wonder, if he'd given Eva a ride to her friend's house on that fateful day, if she'd be alive today. Nothing was ever the same after her murder. Not only did he lose his sister, he lost his family. Louie's words about a family matter had stung Jake more than he realized at the time. No matter how close he felt to Louie and his family, it wasn't his family. Understanding drove a stake through his heart.

I'm alone in this world.

It hit hard; until that moment, he hadn't realized how much Louie's comment had shattered his heart. He cocked his head to the side and turned his thoughts to his mother and decided to stop in and visit with her at the nursing home after work. Common sense didn't play into his guilt. He shook off the mood the best he could. It was cases like this one that dredged up the memories. The trick was not to fall into despair—easier said than done, he mulled, turning his attention back to the other suspects.

* * * *

He couldn't control the dark mood after leaving his mother's room at the nursing home. It baffled him how with each visit he hoped she'd step into the now and accept the past. Optimism, it sprung eternal. His cell phone vibrated in his pocket. Jake pulled the phone from his pocket. He recognized Mia's home number. He swiped the Answer arrow.

Before he could say a word, Mia's voice filled his ear. Her terror sent his heart racing. "There's someone in my condo please come...hurry," she whispered in his ear.

"Mia, are you hurt?" Training kicked in, as it warred against his emotions. Jake tried to stay calm, talk her through it, but his stomach lurched.

"Not hurt, I have a gun," she whispered into his ear.

"Did you call 911?"

"Yes, I have a gun." Jake recognized the shock in her voice as she repeated herself.

"Mia, honey, don't confront the intruder. Do you hear sirens yet?" His heart pounded against his rib cage as he made a U-turn and raced toward Woodbury. He hit the steering wheel with his left hand. He was freaking twenty minutes from her.

"No."

"Where are you?" He threw his questions at her, trying to make her focus. God, he'd never get there in time if the suspect was still inside. He floored the gas pedal. He attached the siren to his roof and ran hot. If anything happened to her...he couldn't let his mind go there.

"I'm in my bedroom."

"Lock your door and go into the bathroom and lock the door. I'll be there soon." he said as he counted down the miles. He prayed hard he'd get there in time to save her.

"The doors are locked, I checked them."

"What tipped you off someone was inside?" he repeated, sweat trickling down his back.

"Something broke downstairs."

"Is your unit secure?" he asked again.

"My alarm's on, and my doors are locked. Jake, hurry, please. I don't want to shoot a man, not sure I even can."

"It's a man, are you sure?"

"No."

"Stay on the line with me and don't go downstairs. I'm going to call the Woodbury Police to see how far out they are. Don't hang up. Understand?"

"I hear sirens."

"How close, Mia?" He kept using her name to hold her attention, to center her.

"I can't tell...they're getting louder."

Mia's voice, thick with fear, squeezed his heart, choked off his breath. It rocked him to the core. He'd never seen her afraid of anything before... except for the incident in Hartford... Dammit, he saw flashing lights in his rearview mirror. There was no way in hell he was stopping to explain the situation. The idiot in pursuit should recognize a cop car. He pushed the gas pedal to the floor, navigated the curves on Route 70 as he headed down the long hill. He didn't want to overshoot her driveway or hit a deer. At this speed he'd kill himself, then what good would he be to her?

"Mia, stay on the phone even when the police get there. I'm eight minutes away."

"I'm at the window, I see them now. I'm going to go downstairs to let them in."

"No, wait until they're at the door. Have you heard anything else?"

"No."

Her voice sounded distant and weak. He heard her sniffle into the phone. Tears would undo him. For the second time in his life he might be too late when it mattered most. Five more minutes before he'd reach her. His heart beat ticking as if a bomb as each mile he inched closer to her location.

"The police are at the door. I'm heading down."

The silence throbbed in his ears until he couldn't take it anymore. "Mia…" He didn't even hear her breathing. "Mia!" he screamed into the phone.

"I'm here," she whispered. "I'm checking each room as I pass."

"Good, stay alert. How are you doing?"

"I'm nervous."

"To be expected. Stop talking and pay attention."

"Then stop asking questions." Her snarky tone lifted some of the weight off his heart.

"Honey, inform the police right away you have a gun before you open the door, and un-cock it, okay?"

Mia gasped into the phone.

"What is it?"

"The front door is locked and the alarm's still on. I'm not crazy, I locked it myself before I went to my office." Minutes ticked by. Jake swore it was an hour before she spoke again. "It's your friend Dave."

He listened in as Dave and his officers questioned Mia. At times he missed a word or two but he got the gist of it.

"Jake?" Dave must have taken Mia's phone.

"Yes, I'm on my way, Dave."

"We have the first floor secured."

"How'd they get in?"

"Not sure, we're working on it. The large vase in her living room is broken to pieces."

"It was my Ming," he heard Mia say in the background. Lord, she loved the vase more than any other of her possessions. The last time he stayed over she had told him the story of how she'd acquired it on one of her trips to China.

"Dave, she has a loaded gun…"

"I've taken it from her. I'm going to put her in a cruiser until the entire place has been cleared."

Jake pulled into her parking lot followed by the flashing lights. As he pulled up to Mia's door and jumped out, the cop tailing him jumped out with his gun pointed at him. *What's his freakin' problem?* Jake put his hands in the air as he turned toward Mia's door. He wished Dave would come out and remedy the situation.

"I'm a Wilkesbury detective," Jake said, lowering his hand to pull out his badge.

"Keep your hands up and don't make a move."

Dave walked over, assessed the situation. He gave Jake a toothy grin. "Ease up, Will. This is his girlfriend's condo."

Will kept his gun trained on Jake for another minute. Jake stared him down. "Do you need me here, Dave?" Will asked.

"No." Jake watched as Dave spoke to his uniform.

"What the hell's a matter with him? He had to see the license plate."

"He's new."

"He pulled his damn gun on me."

"Next time, pull over," Dave said.

"Where's Mia?"

"Inside, follow me. She didn't see anything, Jake. She only heard the vase break."

Dave led him into the condo. Mia stood by her couch talking to an officer. Her black hair emphasized her translucent skin giving her a ghostly appearance. Her midnight blue eyes zeroed in on him.

"I've no doubt someone was here," Dave Guerrera said to them. Dave watched Mia closely as he spoke. Jake did the same thing to supposed victims when circumstances couldn't explain an incident. "You don't have pets and something this big doesn't fall over without help."

"But—but how'd they get in? My alarm was on, the door locked," Mia said, as her legs started to tremble.

"Shit!" Jake rushed forward, scooping her up in his arms before she hit the floor.

With Mia in his arms Jake sat on the couch. She needed a doctor. "I'm freezing," Mia said as she snuggled into him. "What happened?"

"You passed out." Jake gently rubbed his hands over her hair, not sure if he was comforting her or himself.

"I can't stay here," her voice quivered as she pushed off his lap. He fastened his arms around her, kept her locked to him. She'd never understand the misery he experienced as she pleaded for help and he was too far away.

"No, you'll stay with me, okay? This way I can get to you faster if you need me." *Will wonders never cease? She's not going to fight me on this.* "I'm also going to assign an officer to my home."

"I don't need a babysitter."

"She's not a babysitter. Officer Fisher is a highly decorated officer who will be there if you need her. I trust her with my life."

"How long?"

"Until we catch him."

Mia still seemed spacey to him. After her first attempt she made no move to get off his lap. "I'll go upstairs and pack some stuff for you." He lifted her off his lap and placed her on the sofa. She grabbed his arm as he tried to stand up.

"It might be interesting to see what you pack, Jake, but I can handle it."

Though she was starting to sound normal, her complexion was still blanched. He searched her eyes as he took her hand. Still clammy, and her jerky movements had him concerned.

"Let me speak with Dave before we go up."

Jake walked over to the front door, where Dave was speaking to one of his officers. "She still seems to be in shock. I'm going to take her to the hospital."

"Do you want an ambulance?"

"No, we're good." He extended his hand to Dave. "Thank you for the quick response."

"It's all part of the service." Dave grinned as he took his hand.

Jake walked back into the living room. "Mia, honey, can you hear me?"

"I'm not deaf, Jake."

He offered her his hand. He tugged her up and she fell into his arms. "I'm going to take you to the hospital to get checked out."

The fact she wasn't fighting him told him she hadn't come all the way back yet. "Let's grab your things."

Jake held on to her arm as he walked up the stairs by her side. He kicked the door closed as he wrapped his arms around her and snugged her to his body as he ran his hands up and down her back. Her expression killed him. Fear had darkened her eyes to a midnight blue. A dazed, faraway look he'd seen on many victims' faces throughout the years danced on hers. He thought he'd lost her. Did he dare tell her the thought of her in danger almost drove him to break every law on the books to get to her? The drive to get here had been the longest of his life.

"Shit."

Mia trembled uncontrollably in his arms. He scooped her up and walked over to her bed. He whipped the covers down and placed her gently on the bed then pulled the covers over her.

"I'm still cold."

Her forehead was ice-cold and clammy to the touch. Her pulse raced under his fingers. She was in shock. A search of her closet turned up more blankets. He covered her, then walked over to the door to call down to Dave. Mia let out a bloodcurdling scream. Jake ran back to the bed, gathered her into his arms, and rocked her.

"Don't leave me here alone, Jake."

"I'm not leaving you, Mia. I'm only stepping outside the door to talk to Dave. I want him to call an ambulance for you."

"I don't need one. I'm fine. See." She tried to push his arms away.

Jake held on tighter. "Now's not the time to be a brave little soldier."

The snarl she tossed him warmed his heart. *And she's back,* he thought. He wasn't sure what had snapped her out of it, but he was glad she'd found her way back.

"I have two words for you, Jake..." She pulled out of his arms, sat back against the headboard.

"Come on, be the lady you are. You don't want to shock Dave, do you?" He grinned.

"Thanks, Dave," Mia said when he poked his head around Jake.

"You're welcome. Jake, can I see you outside for a moment?"

"Whatever you're going to tell him you can tell me, too."

Pale to begin with, Mia had gone transparent earlier. At least now she was only chalk white. Jake took her wrist and rested his fingers on her pulse. It beat steady. He turned to listen to Dave.

"It was a professional job," Dave said. "We're not positive, though the state trooper feels he walked in the front door."

"That's impossible. It was locked and the alarm was on."

Okay, maybe she wasn't all the way back. "Let him finish," Jake said.

"I heard you unlock the door when you opened it to let me in. The state guy said the suspect had to have had access to your condo before today."

It hung out there, all three of them thinking of the what-ifs. Jake's stomach rolled like the sea in a hurricane. If he felt this way, what was going through Mia's mind? He slid his hand down her arm and took her hand in his. Jake rubbed his thumb over the back of hers to soothe her.

"Have you had anyone working here lately?" Dave continued.

"No."

"Service people, house cleaners, anyone?"

"No service people, yes on cleaning. My cleaning lady's been with me for over five years. The only other people who've been inside are Jake and my friend Piper. My edits are kicking my ass, I haven't had time to socialize recently."

"I'll need to talk to all of them. When you travel who waters your plants?"

"My friend, Piper, has helped me out the last few times. She has a key and the code."

Jake gave Guerrera a meaningful glance. It killed him to sit back and let Dave investigate. What choice did he have? It wasn't his town or jurisdiction.

"It's not any of them. It's your killer, isn't it, Jake?" She turned to him. "That's how he got my hair?"

"It's not yours. I'm positive. His sample was coarse, yours is silky. The lab's testing it anyway to be sure." He turned toward Dave. "You need to keep this to yourself, Dave. The killer I'm chasing is targeting me with letters. This morning he sent me another one with a hair sample, claiming it was Mia's."

"Is it?"

"As I said, I'm ninety-nine percent sure it isn't, though the lab hasn't gotten back to me. The chief put a rush on it. I'm hoping by tomorrow to have something."

"If it is hers, you both are going to have to deal with the idea he might've been here while you were sleeping, Mia."

"That's not possible. I'm a light sleeper. I would have heard something."

"Did you hear him today before he broke the vase?"

"No."

"There are no prints, no hair fibers, and no evidence. Whoever broke your vase did it on purpose. He entered your home while you were here and awake, Mia, and left without leaving a trace. It was a warning. We're not even sure of his place of entry. It's as if he's a ghost."

Jake understood Dave's warning. This was no ordinary burglar. Not one of his suspects seemed to have the smarts to disarm a system remotely. It was a new angle to investigate. As soon as he could leave Mia's side, he'd put Louie on it.

"Mia, have you had your car serviced recently?" Jake asked.

"I took it to a garage in town last week. They always service my car."

"I'll check it out," Dave said.

"They've been servicing my car for years. Why would they break in now?"

"Do you leave all your keys on the keychain when you leave your car for service?" Jake asked.

"Yes."

Both he and Dave grunted.

"Mia, never leave your house key or your garage door opener with anyone. It's easy to clone or make copies. Plus, they have your address. Personnel in these places come and go faster than a cheetah can run the fifty-yard dash. You never know who's working on your car. From now on promise me you'll take your house key with you," Jake said.

"I promise."

Someone knocked on the bedroom door. Dave opened it to one of his officers. "The ambulance is here."

"I don't need it," Mia said, a little too forcibly.

"Dave, can you send the EMT up?"

"I don't need them. I'm serious, Jake."

"I want a trained medical person to tell me that. They'll check your vitals and then we'll be on our way. Please?" He lowered his forehead to hers, hoping his plea hadn't fallen on deaf ears.

"Since you said please—okay." She grinned at him as she lowered her head to the pillow.

A knock on the door announced the EMT. Jake didn't leave her side while the woman checked Mia out. He answered all her questions, explained Mia's symptoms, noting how fast she had recovered.

"You're good to go." The EMT announced as she turned to Jake. "It helped you kept her warm. That's probably what brought her around so fast."

Jake winked at Mia. She rewarded him with a full-wattage smile. The EMT left. He reached out a hand to help Mia off the bed. Pulling her into his arms, he whispered in her ear.

"The fear in your voice did me in. I knew I couldn't get here fast enough to help you. Then when I did arrive I found you in shock. It broke me, Mia. I love you more than life."

"I love you." He felt her arms tighten around his waist. They stood there for a few minutes, wrapped around each other, both afraid to let go.

Chapter 25

Jake maneuvered through traffic on the way home. He gave Louie a call to update him. A few times he glanced at Mia. Quiet, she listened in on his conversation. He couldn't afford to hold anything back even though he wanted to protect her.

"I want you to order protection for your house. If both you and Sophia are working, I want an officer in your house. Understand?"

"I do, but it's you he's after, not me."

"It's not the time to be stubborn, Louie. Order the protection. And I want you to go back over each suspect and see who had the knowledge to pull off something like this."

"Slow down, I can't write as fast as you bark orders," Louie said.

"I have Mia's permission to send our own CSIs to process her condo."

"Jake, the state and Dave are good at their jobs, why duplicate their work?"

"Because he went after Mia—I swear, when I catch this bastard I'll…" Mia reached over and put a finger over Jake's mouth.

"Not on the phone," Mia whispered as she removed her finger.

"Now you understand how I feel," Louie quipped.

He ignored Louie's comment. Jake took Mia's hand and lifted it to his lips. He needed the connection. His adrenaline hadn't returned to normal levels. Her pleas continued to echo in his head. What would he have done if he'd lost her to that sick bastard?

"Can you line up Stella for me?"

"I'll take care of everything."

Jake disconnected the call. The next traffic light turned red without warning. He slammed his foot down hard on the brake. Tires squealed as the car went from sixty to zero in under a second. Damn, he wasn't paying attention to the speed limit. It wouldn't do to get a ticket in another town. He stopped, turned toward her as he placed his hand at the base of her neck and massaged. "Why did you stop me?"

"If this creep can clone my alarm, I bet he'd be able to clone your phone."

"My phone has superior security to prevent such a thing. You're awfully calm."

"I'm not. Once we get to your house I want to work with you to get this guy."

"No. I need you as far away from my case as possible." Jake noted her set jaw. "It's become personal for you, but I'm trained for this. You're not. Let me do my job. If I need your help, I'll ask, honestly." He held up his right hand. "Mia, today could've been the man who's been leaving you the dead animals. If it is, he's escalating. Or it could be my killer. We don't have enough information yet to point fingers."

The light turned green. Someone behind him honked their horn. Mia hadn't responded. Five miles down the road Jake found a parking lot on the bike trail. He pulled in and parked.

"Want to talk about it?" he asked as he checked his rearview mirror. A queasy gut kept his nerves on edge.

"What's to talk about? I want to help. You don't want me to, simple."

Jake knew it wasn't simple. It meant Mia would make an end run around him. The last thing he needed in the middle of this case was someone splitting his attention between her and the killer.

"Nothing's simple. What I want is to keep you safe and alive. Is it too much to ask? I will use your help when it's in your field of expertise. Chasing down criminals is my job, not yours. I can't do my job if I'm worried about you every minute. I'm asking...no, I'm pleading with you, Mia, please don't put yourself in harm's way."

"Are we going to my parents' this coming weekend?" Blindsided, he lost his train of thought at the change of subject. Women in general baffled him, but no one more than Mia.

"Someone broke into your home—probably my killer—and you're asking if we're still on to go to your parents' this Saturday?" Mia pinned him with her baby blues. How should he answer her? "I'll answer your question after you answer mine. Will you promise me you won't do anything that puts you in the killer's path?"

"I promise. What about Saturday night? I have to give my mother an answer or she'll haunt me until I do."

"I can't this weekend. You understand why? I promise as soon as this case is over we'll spend the weekend down there." It was out of his mouth before he could he could stop it.

"A whole weekend? You're a glutton for punishment. I wouldn't even commit to such a thing, but I'm going to hold you to it."

"I figured."

Not for one minute did he doubt she'd hold him to it. What did it say about him he'd rather chase down a killer than spend time with her parents? Jake pulled back out into traffic as he continued on to his house at a slower pace. He wanted to give Louie plenty of time to set up the protection for her before they arrived.

The street was clear of any strange cars as Jake approached his house. Only Louie's car and one other occupied the space at the curb. Jake assumed it belonged to Officer Stella Fisher. He hit the garage door button on his visor and drove in. He hit the button to close the door and the one to open his trunk. At the rear of the car, he reached into the trunk and grabbed Mia's suitcase before he proceeded to her side of the car. He gave her a hand, gripping it tightly as he helped her out. Call him crazy, even under all the stress he couldn't help admiring her long legs as her skirt inched up her thighs. There would certainly be some benefits to having her stay with him for a while. Jake cleared his throat and held the suitcase in front of him to avoid any embarrassment as he walked behind her into his living room. Animals sensed when something was wrong. Brigh went straight to Mia instead of him. Jake acknowledged both Fisher and Louie before proceeding to the master bedroom. He dumped her suitcase on the bed, then spun around and reached for his gun when a hand landed on his shoulder.

"Christ, don't sneak up like that." *Helluva day*, he thought, as his stomach danced in his throat.

"Don't like it, do you?" Louie laughed. "Payback's a bitch. I want to update you. You can determine how much you tell Mia. Stalls has been eliminated as a suspect. His alibis check out. The kid's a scumbag, but not a killer. And Tedessco has also been cleared. We're down to two: McMichaels and Velky."

"Have you researched their electronics backgrounds?"

"I've got Green running them now. I figured you wanted me personally to update Fisher and check out your house." Jake gripped Louie's arm and squeezed. Louie continued. "I had Damien sweep the house for bugs and he's now on his way to Mia's to do the same."

Louie always had his back. It was one of the constants in his life.

"I also had my house swept."

"Good. Did you find anything there or here?"

"Nope. Damien said he'd come back every day and sweep to make sure."

"That's nice of him but he doesn't have to do that."

"He said he did. A killer this well versed in electronics could access the property after it's been swept. He said not to worry. It will be on his own time."

"Make sure he stays on the clock when he does it. I don't want anything questioned when we catch this guy and go to trial. I think we gave them enough time for them to get acquainted. Let's head back into the living room."

Both women turned to face them as they walked into the room. Mia was seated on the couch and Officer Stella Fisher was seated in a chair to her right. Louie took the other chair as Jake sat down on the sofa next to Mia.

"Are you all set, Stella?" Jake asked.

"Yes, I'll be spending the nights until the killer's caught."

"You need time off. Who will relieve you?"

"I have Tara Jones coming to cover while I sleep."

Jake had worked with Tara before and liked her style. "Okay." Jake turned to Louie. "Who's covering the front and back of the house?"

Across the street from his house was a wooded area. It went back for miles and would be easy for a person to set up surveillance. The backyard butted against his neighbor's yard. The house to his right was vacant. It offered too many opportunities for this suspect to come at them. The only good thing was there weren't a lot of civilians in the line of fire.

"I have Sherman on the day shift out front, and Officer Kelly on the back of the house. The night shift is Burrows, who's out front, and Officer Tooley, who's out back."

"I trust Sherman and Burrows. I'm not familiar with Tooley and Kelly. Get me their personnel records. I want to check them out."

"I've worked with the two of them before. They're solid cops. It's the reason I picked them."

If Louie said they were okay, then who was he to argue? But he still wanted to review the files. Jake ran through what he needed to accomplish first. "Did you contact my security company and Mia's?"

"Yes, I'll have a list of any new clients within the last six months."

"Call them back and make it a year."

"You and Mia weren't dating a year ago, and we only caught the case this month."

"Louie, it seems too personal. This didn't pop into this guy's head today. Mia and I go back to April. How much turnover do they have with their staff?"

"Your company said not a lot, Mia's a little more."

"Ask what they consider a lot. I'll work from here for the rest of the day. Call me the minute you have anything on the security companies. Dave's also running it from his end. Did you get anywhere with the garage Mia used to service her car?"

"Brown's working that. I'll check with Green and Brown when I get back."

"Who did you pick for your house?"

"I handpicked them, don't worry."

"Who?" Jake stared Louie down. Mia and Stella watched Jake like hawks eyeing a field mouse.

"I got Berkley and Williams during the day and Brogan and Ross at night."

"Who's in the house with you?"

"I can protect my own damn family!"

"I'm sure you can, but I want you to have the manpower to be certain. Did Sophia go back to work today?"

"Yes, damn it. I'll pick officers when I get to the station. When I do I'll email you their names."

"Any questions, ladies?" Jake turned back to them.

"It seems like overkill, Jake," Mia said.

"The man was in your house, Mia. You had no clue until he purposely broke the vase."

Not caring how harsh his words sounded, Jake wanted her to understand the killer could've taken or killed her anytime during the episode. A twinge of regret stroked his heart when fear flooded back into her eyes. She shuddered against him. Jake draped his arm around her and tugged her close to his body. He needed the connection as much as she did.

"I...I want to lie down for a while." Mia pushed off the couch.

"Give me a minute." Jake stood and did a circuit around his house. He rechecked every window and door. With those secured, he pulled down the attic staircase in the hallway and climbed up with his flashlight in front of him. Satisfied everything was in order, he descended the steps and gave Mia the go-ahead to lie down. Louie left for the station after Jake completed his rounds.

In the living room, Stella stopped pacing when Jake walked back in. "Are you expecting the suspect to come here, with all this firepower?"

"I do. I'll need you to be alert. You don't have to stay here at night, I'll be here."

"I'll say the same thing to you that you said to Louie. It's prudent to have two people here to protect her."

He hated his own words being tossed back at him, but Stella did it with a smile. She was one of the few officers with the balls to speak back to him. It was the reason he liked her.

"Duly noted. Why don't you rest up while I work in the office?"

"I'm good. I'll be in here if you need me. On second thought, why don't I walk around the perimeter and stretch out my legs while you're here."

"Aren't Sherman and Kelly out there now?"

"Yes, but they're in cars. I'll walk it." She left.

Jake walked to the window to follow her movements. The radio on his belt crackled to life.

"Yeah, Sherman."

"What's she doing?"

"Exercising. Keep the channel clear."

* * * *

Louie entered Jake's office and made a beeline to the coffee machine. After brewing a cup, he took it to Jake's desk and sat as he riffled through the files and paperwork on top of the desk. He separated them into piles before reading each one.

"Bucking for lieutenant, Sarge?"

"Funny. If any of the guys need Jake, he'll be working out of his house this afternoon. He'll be available on his cell phone. Got anything new for me?"

"Yes, two out of the three graduated from technical schools, both in electronics."

"Seriously, how'd we miss that?"

"We hadn't gotten to their high school years yet. I made it a priority today."

"Who are they?"

"McMichaels and Pencer."

Not who I was expecting. "Thanks. Do me a favor. Call Jake's cell and update him. I'm going to check another angle."

When Green left the office, Louie picked up the desk phone and pushed in Damien's cell number. He hoped Dunn got reception in Woodbury. On the fourth ring Damien picked up.

"Yo."

"Damien, how hard would it be to search a computer for evidence of someone taking online courses?"

"It's on my agenda. The boss man has already asked. But it depends on the computer and the security. Why?"

"I want to do a run on someone else, but I'll check in with Jake first to make sure it's not the same person before I give you his name."

"I'll call when I'm finished here."

"Find anything?" Louie asked.

"You bet. The guy's good but not as good as me. Mia's system was cloned. If we find this guy I bet we could match up his electronic signature to this."

"Electronic signature? You're kidding, right?"

"Nope. I'm surprised the state guys didn't dismantle this. I'm bringing back all the parts. Maybe he left a standard print for us," Damien said.

"We could hope. I'll see you when you get back here."

Louie disconnected then pressed in Sophia's cell number. It went directly to voicemail. He hung up without leaving a message and decided to try her office number.

"Law offices."

"It's me."

"Hi."

"Everything okay?"

"Yes, you're still coming for dinner, right?"

"Are you working late again?"

"Yes." Louie had figured on that. Malone was small enough to punish her for yesterday.

"Okay, what do you want to eat?"

"Anything's good."

"See ya." It was three p.m., a little early for dinner. Sophia's voice had been stretched. He called the meal in for four thirty before heading back to his desk to start his searches. After he entered the criteria, he dialed home.

"LJ, did the officer arrive?"

"Yeah, what's going on, Dad? Does it have anything to do with the creep Mom's working for?"

"No. I'll explain when I get home. Your mother's working late again. Can you heat up last night's spaghetti for your brother and sister for dinner?"

"Yeah."

"Okay, put Officer Huntington on the phone."

He gave Huntington the third degree, then told Green he was heading out for his dinner break. As he pulled into the parking lot of Maria's Ristorante his phone buzzed. Nine-one-one in large text followed by Sophia's number sent ice picks through his veins.

* * * *

All day long her nerves jabbed at her spine. The only reason she continued to work for Malone was his apology and the bonus he offered her to complete her work on the case. The bonus would give her enough money to pay for Frankie's rehab and quit the job sooner than planned. She only had to work five more days, and then she could say good-bye to this idiot.

So far Malone had behaved, except for the incident on Sunday, but every now and then she'd catch him watching her. It kept her off-kilter. She felt like a mouse in the snake's cage. She fingered the pepper spray in her pocket. False courage, Louie had called it. He preferred she carry a weapon. Even though she was an ace shot, she wasn't comfortable around firearms anymore. Since she'd had the kids she'd let her permit expire.

Her back erect, she pushed her chair back a little from the conference room table to stretch her legs. *One more week, then I'll quit. If this jerk invades my space one more time today, I'll set Louie on him. Idiot. But really, I'm the idiot to add this kind of drama to my life. Frankie's parents should be the ones helping him out.* A chair scraping the floor focused her attention to her left.

Malone pushed away from the conference table and walked behind her. The hair on the back of her neck stood up. She pushed further away from the table. Standing, she drew up, squared her shoulders, and put her best "you're in trouble now" expression on her face as she backed away from him. It normally stopped the kids in their tracks. Arctic air raced over her as her stomach lurched toward her throat. Malone's expression, the hatred shooting from his eyes, reminded her of a coyote ready to attack a predator who tried to take his meal.

"If you'll excuse me, I need to use the restroom." She turned to leave. He grabbed her arm with a tight grip and swung her back to face him. "Let go of me, Mr. Malone."

"Mr. Malone? How many times have I told you to call me Richie? Many, many times, if I recall correctly. But no…it's always Mr. Malone to you, like that's going to keep me in my place. I bet you use the same tone on your husband and kids when you want them to behave. Well, Miss Untouchable, you messed with the wrong man when you called the cops. There are consequences to your actions."

Though his voice filled her head, it was his tone sending up warning flags. The man was mad.

"I'm not good enough to be in your home?" he continued. "Or is it you didn't want me around your ripe little daughter? Which is it, Sophia?" It sickened her how his voice caressed her name.

She backed up as she tried to pull her arm free. It was a mistake. She knew it the minute her back slammed into the wall. Trapped. His six-foot frame towered over her. He'd blocked her in-between the credenza and the bookcase. How had she not seen this coming?

Oh God, why did I choose this time to ignore Louie?

With his free hand, he groped her. Sophia threw her left fist at his face while twisting and turning away. But she couldn't loosen his grip. As she turned her head and body to the left she spotted the brass statue on the credenza. Instinct kicked in and she grabbed the heavy object and swung it with all her might at Malone's head. It connected on his right temple with a loud thump. Blood spurted everywhere, drenching her as his eyes rolled back in his head. Malone dragged his hand down her front, ripping her blouse as he collapsed on the floor. She froze at the sight of his still body. Sophia cried as she reached into her pocket for her phone. She pressed 1 on her speed dial and started screaming into the phone when Louie picked up.

* * * *

Louie threw the light on top of his roof as he hit the sirens. Elvis started singing on the radio. "On my way, what's the matter?"

"I killed him, Louie...hurry...please... Oh God, I killed him."

"Sophia, calm down, tell me what happened." Louie shifted into cop mode, talking to Sophia like he would any victim. "Sophia, try to stop crying and tell me exactly what happened."

"I killed him. He attacked me and I...I hit him. There's blood everywhere."

"Did you check for a pulse?"

"No. I..."

"Sophia, call 911 now and report a sexual assault in progress, not murder. I'm going to call Jake. I'm putting you on hold while I do." Placing her on hold, he called Jake, explained the situation and all he knew. Jake told him he'd meet him at the scene. He switched the line back to Sophia. "Are you there, honey?'

"Ye...yes."

"I'll be there in a few minutes. Jake's also on his way. If he gets there first, let him in. Don't touch anything, do you hear me?"

"Yes. I killed him, Louie."

Louie forced himself to stay calm. "Don't hang up. And don't tell anyone you killed him. Tell whoever arrives first that he attacked you.

I'll stay on the phone until the police or Jake arrives. Sophia, I'm serious. You defended yourself, understand?"

"Yes. Hurry, Louie."

* * * *

Jake rushed in the front door, his gun drawn, Officer Fisher behind him. Mia had insisted on coming with them but Jake made her wait in the car. As they cleared a room they proceeded down the hall to the next. When he got to the conference room, he heard a man moan, and a woman crying. Jake forked his fingers to his eyes and pointed to the door. He entered the room on the right and high. Stella went low and left.

"Shit," Jake cursed, after assessing the scene.

Louie stood over Malone with his gun drawn and pointed directly at the man's heart. Malone, on the verge of consciousness and covered in blood, continued to moan, but he was alive, to Jake's relief. Sophia had done a job on him. He found her huddled in the corner, crying. Jake sent Stella across the room to help Sophia.

"Louie, stand down. I'll take over now." Jake's stomach twisted into knots when Louie failed to acknowledge his order. He hoped Louie wouldn't do anything stupid.

"Not going to happen, Jake. He put his hands on my wife. Did you see her blouse? I suggest you and Stella leave the room for a few minutes."

The cold calmness in Louie's voice sent Jake's heart racing. *Dear God, please make him put it down.* "Louie, don't make me have to shoot you." Jake's shirt clung to his back. "I. Said. Put. Your. Weapon. Down. Now. Sergeant."

Louie turned toward Jake at a snail's pace, his gun still aimed at Malone's chest. Anger shot darts from his eyes, his face red as a beet as they stared each other down. Sweat seeped out of every cell of his body, but Jake held his ground. "Now, Sergeant."

He hoped the use of Louie's rank would bring him back to reality.

"If this was Mia, what would you do?"

"I would have shot him before anyone arrived," Jake answered. They eyed each other for what seemed like hours. Every clenched muscle loosened when Louie holstered his gun.

"Officer Fisher, when we arrived on scene, we found an unconscious man and Detective Romanelli attending to his wife. Correct?"

Lord, he certainly hoped she agreed. In the stillness of the room, her silence spoke volumes. Jake swung his head in Stella's direction. Stella continued to care for Sophia. "Stella?"

"I saw the same thing, Lieutenant. Mrs. Romanelli appears to be in shock and needs a medic. I'll call for backup and a wagon."

"Thank you, Stella," both Jake and Louie said in unison.

"You weren't really going to shoot me, were you?"

"I think I might have."

"Great, *you think*. That's not reassuring." Louie stared at him. Jake laughed at his expression. "You would've, wouldn't you?"

"How is he?" Jake pointed to Malone with his gun, ignoring Louie's question because he wasn't sure either.

"The bastard will live and, if I have my way, for a long tedious lifetime behind bars."

Malone chose that moment to wake up. "I'm going to sue the department. He almost shot me."

"Malone, if I were you, I wouldn't go down there. You tried to molest a woman, one who worked for you. With your record, no one's going to believe you. And this time there will be no out-of-court settlement," Jake said.

Jake directed the EMTs to Sophia first, then Malone. The guy's dazed expression hadn't pulled any sympathy from Jake. Too bad Sophia hadn't hit him harder and whacked his brain from deviant to normal. Jake started to question one of the CSIs. He wanted a report on how they found the scene. He wanted to make sure nothing pointed to Sophia or Louie as the aggressor.

"The statue…"

"Jake, step away," McGuire said as he walked into the room, his tone brooking no argument.

"Cap—"

"You're not working this case. You're to concentrate on the Carren case."

"But, Cap—"

"You're too close to this."

"Cap, you can't give this to anyone else. What if they have a vendetta against the sergeant? This is delicate."

"I'm aware of that. It's the reason I'm going to be handling the investigation."

"You, Shamus?"

"Are you questioning my skills, Lieutenant?"

"No, sir."

"Louie, go over to your wife. Officer Fisher, please take both the sergeant and Mrs. Romanelli into the office next door."

"What do you want me to do?" Jake asked.

"I want you to wait here until I interview Sophia and Louie. I then need to interview you and Officer Fisher."

"I can be of service here, Captain." He spotted Mia standing in the doorway behind Shamus. *The woman never listened.*

"No, you can't, Jake. The department is under tight scrutiny right now."

Jake knew Shamus was right, but his heart told him to stay and clear both Louie and Sophia. His life was out of control. Spaulding up for parole again, then Mia being threatened, now this. Maybe after he caught the Carren killer, he'd take Mia away for a few days. Lord, they'd both need it after all that's happened.

"Yes, sir."

Jake walked over to Mia. "Are you ready to leave?" Mia asked.

"No."

* * * *

Inside the office next to the conference room, Louie led Sophia to the couch by the window. Officer Fisher gave them some space, though not enough for him to coach Sophia.

"Are you okay?" Louie asked.

"I'm shaken. He cornered me…"

"Sergeant, I'm sorry. You can't speak to her before she gives her account of the event to the captain."

Louie opened his mouth to answer as the captain walked into the room. Officer Fisher snapped to attention and took up a position by the door.

"Louie, I'll allow you to stay while I question Sophia, but you must remain quiet throughout the interview. Understand?"

"Yes, sir."

The interview took a half hour. Louie understood the captain could've been harder on Sophia, pressed her for more information. But when he finished questioning her, Louie tried to see what he'd written down. He'd worked for Shamus now for five years and would have to trust him and his judgment. Damn, he hated not to have control, especially when it was his wife.

"Thank you, Sergeant and Mrs. Romanelli," Louie hugged her hard to his chest as he prayed everything would work out.

* * * *

Louie loosened his necktie to ease the headache forming at the base of his neck. *Please let McGuire close the case quickly.* The captain, in true military style, would investigate the incident fully and within the guidelines of the department and with no favoritism. McGuire had known them for years and had been a guest at their house. How could he not clear her? Nerves stung as they raced up his spine and settled at the base of his neck. Louie couldn't believe he was praying for Malone to live. It was a good sign he had regained consciousness before being taken to the hospital. Glad Sophia didn't take Malone's life: it was not something he wanted Sophia to have to live with the rest of hers. Deep inside him, it ate away at his heart, his sense of decency when he'd taken a life. It robbed him of a piece of his humanity. Even in the line of duty, or self-defense, taking a life was not easy. Nor should it be.

McGuire stood. Louie pulled Sophia to her feet. "Captain, can I ask what your preliminary findings are?"

"No, Louie, I'm still investigating. I'll keep you informed once the crime scene has been processed and my reports are written. Take your wife home and reassure her everything will be fine." McGuire turned away from them.

Officer Fisher left the room. Shamus turned back to Louie and lowered his voice to a whisper. "It seems to be a clear-cut case of self-defense." McGuire walked out of the room without another word. Louie exhaled for the first time since finding his wife standing over an unconscious Malone.

Sophia folded herself into him as she started speaking into his chest. "I'm sorry, Louie. I should have listened to you."

"Shush. We'll talk at home. I'm sorry, too. I understood your need for independence, but I felt threatened." He hoped his admission would soothe her.

Laughing and crying, she said, "You are an ass sometimes."

Shocked to hear her curse, it did his heart good to hear the sound of her laughter. He kissed the top of her head. "I am. Let's go home and drink a big glass of my father's wine."

"Let's drink two."

* * * *

Half an hour later, after settling Mia in at his house, Jake walked into McGuire's office.

"Will you fill me in on the Romanelli case?"

"In my opinion it was self-defense. I wish she had filed a complaint about his harassment. What will support it, though it's not nearly enough, is him showing up at their house yesterday. I put a rush on forensics, then I'll be able to close the case. Louie can expect a lawsuit once Malone's recovered. Now, fill me in on what went down in Woodbury today."

To detach himself from the story, Jake gave a detailed report to McGuire like he would on any other case.

"What are your thoughts on the suspect targeting Mia?"

"We must be getting too close and he wants to divert my attention."

"Agreed, but will he follow through if he feels threatened?"

"He will."

"Okay, I'll let you get back to it."

Jake turned to leave McGuire's office. "One more thing, Jake. Louie should've followed procedure and called 911 immediately, not you."

"Technically, he did. He had Sophia call 911 and then he notified his supervisor."

"Hopefully it holds up in IA."

"IA? Why would IA be involved?"

"Jake, the incident involves a department member's spouse."

"Christ. Can you request Rinaldi?"

"No, IA will assign an officer."

"You should—"

"Jake, it's better for Louie this way."

* * * *

The ride back to the house was excruciatingly quiet. Louie knew how to handle a victim, but how did he treat his traumatized wife? *God, give us the strength to get through this,* he prayed. He put his signal on and turned onto his street as he pressed the garage door opener on his visor. In the garage he turned off the car and stared straight ahead at the wall. Sophia did the same. *It's crazy,* he thought, then pulled her into his arms and kissed her on the head.

"We'll get through this, *amante.*"

"Oh, Louie. Promise me after I tell you the reason I went to work for him in the first place you won't explode."

"I promise," he said, automatically.

"No, I mean you've got to swear on our kids you'll hold your temper."

He pushed her back but held on to her by the shoulders and stared into her eyes. "I promise, Sophia. I love you. You don't understand what it did to me when I thought I'd lose you. I promise with all my heart not to get mad." Grinning, he added, "But you know me better than anyone. I'll apologize now if I do."

"Fair enough. One more thing. I don't want to do this in front of the kids. Okay?"

"I agree. They don't need to be told what happened. We'll tell them there was an incident at work and you'll no longer be working for the scumbag."

"But not in those exact words." His heart wanted to sing when she smiled for the first time since he'd arrived at her office.

"Why don't we call in a pizza? Are you up for it?"

"Yes."

"You sure? You still seem a bit shaky."

"I'm fine. Call it in."

Louie called the pizza parlor closest to them who delivered. He wasn't hungry, but he knew it was important for the kids that things seemed as normal as possible with dinner this late.

During dinner the children were unusually quiet. Louie figured they knew something was up the way kids did with that sixth sense. LJ confirmed it at the end of the meal, after much forced conversation.

"What's wrong besides what you told us?"

"We told you everything, LJ."

Damn, the kid was staring him down. "I'm not a kid, Dad. If you don't want to tell Marisa or Carmen," LJ said as he pointed to his brother and sister, "we can talk after dinner."

"Hey, we're not kids either," Marisa and Carmen chimed in.

"You're all kids to us. We've already explained everything there is to explain, LJ. The rest is between your mother and me."

LJ studied them, then pushed away from the table and mumbled under his breath as he headed up the stairs to his room. Relieved when the other two followed, Louie turned to Sophia.

"Well, that went well."

Sophia threw her head back and laughed. Louie got up from the table and walked to her. Tilted her chin up and kissed her on the lips. "I love hearing you laugh. You haven't done enough of it lately."

"Neither of us have. Where do you want to talk, in here or the living room?"

"I thought upstairs."

"No."

"No?"

"Louie, for a cop you can be gullible at times. The kids eavesdrop all the time. Especially when we talk upstairs—the walls are thin."

Scratching his head, he thought about it. "Why don't we go for a ride?"

"The living room is fine. Leave the dishes. I'll do them later."

Oh boy, I don't think I'm ready for this.

"I'd like to set some guidelines before we talk."

"Christ, are you leaving me?" He was ready to beg, scream, plead…

"You're such a nut. Of course I'm not leaving you. But I won't be able to talk if you blow up at me or laugh at me. I've been through a lot. Those are my two rules for this conversation. Agreed?"

Lord, she's serious. How the hell am I supposed to control my anger? "Agreed."

"Why don't I start talking?"

He searched her eyes for a clue. *What could be so bad she'd think I'd blow up at her?*

"I was excited when you set up the family vacation to celebrate your parents' fiftieth anniversary. I thought what a wonderful time it would be with all your siblings and their families along with ours to celebrate the occasion. Then…"

She stopped, took a deep breath.

"Go on," Louie said.

She rubbed her fingers across her temple as she continued. "I'll admit here and now, I'm a fool, but sometimes vanity gets the better of me. I went to lunch with Theresa, Carmela, and Joyce right after we made plans to discuss the logistics of the trip. Remember?"

"Yes but what do my sister and sisters-in-law have to do with you working?" Louie tilted his head, rubbed the stubble on his chin. Where was she going with this?

"Well, it was a beautiful summer day. Theresa had this body-hugging dress which set off her well-toned arms and small waist. Carmela, always the goddess, wore her long curly hair flowing down her back, as she stood tall in flaming red dress with these high strappy sandals that had her reaching the sky. And God, I don't even want to tell you about Joyce and her sky-blue sundress that made her eyes even bluer and her long wavy blond hair blonder. It was intimidating. And then there was me. The misfit at the table—"

"Sophia…"

"Don't interrupt, Louie. This is hard enough to get out. I'm short. I've got a full figure. And most times I'm fine with it, but sometimes, well, all the time it's matronly." She held up her hand to stop him again. "I have to say it. I felt dumpy, short, and fat after visiting with them. I started to worry how much fatter I'd be on the beach with these horrible thighs." She pounded her fists on her thighs. "I've hated them since I gained the weight during pregnancy. Even after I lost the baby weight my hips and thighs never got back into shape. The meetings to plan the trip no longer brought me any joy. They brought on anxiety. The more I thought about it, the more misgivings I had about the trip and myself. I decided I didn't want to take any of the house money and blow our budget. And I knew if I told you what I wanted to do you'd object."

"You're damn right, I would've. You were going to have surgery without telling me? My God, you're beautiful exactly the way you are, honey. I'm the luckiest man alive—"

"Louie, I wasn't doing this for you. I was doing it for me."

Dumbfounded, he stared at his beautiful Sophia. She was a natural beauty. Her olive complexion and deep brown eyes always seduced him with a glance. And those full pouty lips, along with her body, curvy in all the right places. She fit in his arms perfectly. He had to hunch over when he danced with her. It had been their joke for years. But height had never been a problem. This couldn't be the reason she'd put herself in danger. There had to be something else here, he decided. He wouldn't push her but he hoped she'd get to it soon. He'd try to be patient.

"Did I say or do anything stupid to have you thinking this way?"

"No! God no."

"Then why?"

"I told you. When someone looks in the mirror they see themselves differently than others do. Each flaw is magnified. For seventeen years, Louie, I've been your wife, the kids' mother—no one thinks of me as Sophia. I'm only your wife and their mother. All my friends work outside the house. I wanted to prove I was more and earn some cash to get the surgery to correct the flaws."

"The flaws? There are none. And you're not only a wife and mother. You're my best friend, and lover, and the sexiest woman alive."

Joy danced in his heart when she smiled.

"See, it's all those things I forgot. I can't explain how I felt. It feels stupid now, after what happened but…" With her hands palms up, she shrugged.

He took a moment, searched for the right words. "I don't want you to have the surgery, but if it's important to you, I'll try to support you, if you go for it. Promise me you'll consider your decision before you do." He stood up, pulled her from the chair. "Come upstairs with me for a minute." She cocked a brow at him. "Please."

He walked behind her up the stairs and admired the view. How could she think she wasn't perfect? He closed the bedroom door and wrapped his arms around her as he steered her to the full-length mirror.

"I want you to see what I see."

"Louie, please don't."

"Shush. I have my own voluptuous Sophia, more beautiful than Sophia Loren." He took a handful of her hair in his hands and breathed in her shampoo. "Full, wild hair that washes over me when we make love, it's as soft as a cloud. It caresses a face God designed himself."

"The children will hear."

"I'm not speaking very loud. Your big brown eyes can tell me you love me one minute and are mad at me the next—and then they're seducing me. It's those eyes I noticed first."

"You noticed my breasts first."

"True, I stand corrected." He dropped her hair, ran his hands up and down each arm before stopping at her shoulders. He started to massage them. "Then I noticed your sensuous lips which, if I recall correctly, were pouting."

"I don't pout."

"You do and it's darn cute." As he unbuttoned her blouse, she grabbed his hand.

"What are you doing?"

"I'm going to make love to my beautiful wife, lover, and friend."

"Louie, it's not even ten o'clock and the kids are awake."

A smirk crossed his lips. "We'll have to be quiet, won't we? Now stop interrupting me." He pushed her hands away as his fingers continued to unbutton the blouse, then slipped it off her shoulders. "I love that bra, the way it nestles your breasts together. Three children and they're as firm as the day I met you."

Pleased when she leaned into him, he kissed the top of her head, worked his way down her neck, trailing kisses to her breasts. His hands worked the zipper on her skirt and tugged it down over her hips. She stood there in her bra, panties, thigh highs, and heels. Lord, he hoped he lasted. He walked in front of her and rested his hands on her hips while nibbling on her bottom lip. Moments like this he loved, when they were the only two people who existed. Sophia reached to push the mirror up and away from them. He straightened the mirror and walked behind her again.

"There's no reason to stand in front of the mirror. Let's head for the bed," Sophia said.

"No. I want you to see the beautiful woman before me. I love you, only you." He continued his exploration of her body until she stood there naked.

"See what I see, *amante*," he said, running his hands up and down her arms. "I love every inch of your body, mind and soul. It's not only a body that makes a woman beautiful. It's everything combined." He turned her to him, tilted her chin up and kissed her gently. "Mine, all mine," he said against her mouth.

"You have too many clothes on. Why is that?"

"Let me remedy that." Shucking his clothes, he picked her up and carried her to the bed, where he laid her down and jumped in after her.

* * * *

Hours later, he lay there with his wife in his arms. "Sophia, are you going to tell me the real reason you were working for Malone?"

She tried to pull out of his arms. He tightened them and brought her closer to him.

"I promised not to get mad, remember."

"Are you sure you can honor it? Please let me go. I need to do this standing."

He let her go and sat up. Sophia pulled on her robe as she paced to the window.

"I'm sure Victoria and Big Frankie have their reasons for not supporting their son. But I'll never understand a parent throwing away a child—"

"Sophia, don't tell me—"

"Let me get this out, Louie. Frankie's my godchild. Right now, he's in desperate need of treatment to handle his addiction. He came to me asking for money for it—"

"Oh, for Christ's freakin' sake, Sophia, tell me you haven't been supporting his habit."

"I certainly have not. I told him I'd get the money, but I'd go with him to the rehab center and sign him in. The other night when you thought Malone called, it was Frankie. He wanted me to hand over whatever I had saved up. He said he wanted to go sign into the place. When I said not until I had it all, he hung up on me. It's dawning on me he only wants the money, not help."

"Word on the street is he's into his dealer for megabucks. And if he doesn't pay up there'll be consequences. Don't act surprised. I've kept an eye on him. Until he signs himself in for treatment, and believe me, he isn't ready, no one can help him. He's a user both of people and drugs. You're a good person for wanting to help him…"

"He'll die if he continues…"

"He will, but that's on him—not my parents, his parents, or us. You have to face the fact he's a loser."

She sat in the chair by the window, tears streaming down her face. It broke his heart. "I'd never be able to throw one of our children away."

"And with God's help we won't have to. We have smart children, who were taught the difference between right and wrong. Please tell me you won't give Frankie any money."

"I won't, but I want to use the money I've earned for his rehab. When he contacts me, will you come with me to make him understand that's all we'll help him with?"

"Yes." He tugged her up off the chair, drawing her toward him until she fell into his arms. Still hurt she'd lied to him, Louie figured he had two choices: accept it or cause a further rift in his marriage. He swallowed his pride and decided on peace.

* * * *

Jake stormed out of McGuire's office. As he entered the bullpen, he ignored the summonses of several detectives, went directly to his own office and slammed the door behind him. IA had better rule in Louie's favor. He'd done nothing wrong. It wasn't the place to let his temper out, nor would it be any use on the case. Jake paced for several minutes in the small space. His strides ate up the area quickly, forcing him to turn as soon as he picked up momentum. Out of steam, he collapsed into his chair, placed his elbows on the desk and his head in his hands. It had been a hell of a day—one which he hoped would never be repeated. Would Mia be in constant danger for the rest of her life because of his job? After today, would Sophia ever again be the trusting, sweet woman he knew and loved?

With no answers in sight, he pulled out his files on the Carren case. Call him crazy, he'd rather work a murder than deal with the personal stuff. Most murders made sense if you could follow the killer's logic. Creeps like Malone didn't follow any logic. With his head ready to explode, Jake reread this morning's note from the killer. Someone knocked on his door and broke his concentration. Brown stood in the doorway with a file in his hand. Jake motioned him in.

"Sorry to bother you, LT."

"It's okay, Kirk. What have you got for me?"

"Is Louie's wife okay?"

"It's already made the rounds?"

"Yeah."

"She's good. What have you got?" Jake didn't want to discuss it.

"I've eliminated another suspect but wanted your opinion on my findings."

Jake took the file from Kirk and pointed to the seat in front of his desk as he started to read it. After a few minutes, Jake raised his eyes to Kirk's expectant ones.

"Good work."

"You agree?"

"Yes."

It seemed on the dates of two of the women's disappearances Pencer was the guest of two separate states. For Bartholomew he was in a Rhode Island jail for disorderly conduct. For Greene he was a guest of Vermont for driving under the influence.

"Why didn't these arrests show up in our initial searches?"

"We only ran Connecticut the first time around. I've broadened the search on Velky and McMichaels to search the national database and ran the whole list while I was at it."

"Close the door." Jake waited while Kirk did it. "What pointed you in Velky's direction?"

Kirk shifted in his chair. "I overheard you and the sergeant discussing him this morning."

"You had to be glued pretty tight to my door, Kirk, to hear our conversation."

"No, sir, I was coming to see you, and your door wasn't closed all the way when I overheard that part. I turned around and went back to my desk. I figured you didn't want anyone to hear what you were talking about." Upset at his own carelessness, Jake made a mental note to close his door all the way the next time. What if Walsh had overheard them?

"You figured right. Anyone else aware he's a suspect?"

"I'm not sure."

"Let's keep it quiet for now. Keep me in the loop on your search results."

Kirk agreed before heading back to his desk.

* * * *

While narrowing down the suspect list, Kirk Brown had hit on a new fact pertaining to Velky. Jake dialed Brown's extension.

"Kirk, the person we recently spoke about had a broken engagement. Redo your search with his name and McMichaels's for engagement announcements for the last ten years."

"Will—you need something, Harry?" Kirk asked, ignoring Jake. Jake waited for Kirk to return to the conversation.

"Sorry, he's been hanging around my desk the last couple of days."

"Did he see who you're searching?"

"No, I password protect my computer every time I get up." Kirk paused. "Sir, I'm going to sign out for my mandatory time off. I'll keep the searches running from home if that's okay with you?"

"Yes, please do."

Chapter 26

Jake kicked back in his chair. Harry Walsh, without realizing it, was stringing his own noose along with the mayor. Why Mayor Velky dealt with stooges like Walsh and Miller baffled him. Maybe there was a shortage of dishonest people and dirty cops with brains. He could only hope. It was John Velky's problem that he picked the stupid ones.

Mia's tense voice as she pleaded for help burst into his head. To calm the thought, he picked up the phone and dialed his house.

"Hello."

A little taken back when Officer Fisher answered instead of Mia, Jake recovered quickly. "Stella, how's everything there?"

"Everything's good."

"While you're on duty at my house, Stella, it's Jake."

"Okay, Lieu…"

"How's Mia?"

"She's hanging in there. I'll have her call you back when she gets out of the shower."

Mmm, Mia in the shower presented a lovely vision. Maybe he should head home.

"Are you there, Jake?"

Did he hear a smile in Stella's voice? "Yes, I'm here. I'm trying to calculate when I'll be home."

"Right," Stella chuckled.

"Shut up." Smiling, he hung up the phone. Stella was the right choice for protecting Mia.

Three things in his email caught his eye: an email from Gwenn, one from Clive Thomas, and one from Bill Samuels. Jake opened Samuels's email first.

Lieutenant, I was at the bar last night and the guy you wanted to talk to came in. I couldn't give you a call because the guy sat down next to me again. How should I handle it the next time?

Stupid son of a bitch! He could have excused himself and called it in. Were they playing games? Was Samuels involved somehow? He hated to do it to Timothy at Hard Rider again, but Jake needed his eyes and ears. Moving down to the next email, he opened Gwenn's.

Jake, number three has more childhood problems than previously thought. His school records detail cruelty in the classroom. He was also suspected of several acts of vandalism against some teachers, though they had no evidence to suspend him. Your second person of interest has a similar background. If we could meet up sometime tomorrow, I'll explain.

He put in a call to Gwenn to see if they could meet up tonight. She'd whetted his appetite. Which one had trouble throughout his school years? Moving on to his third email, Jake opened the pictures Thomas had attached. Splitting his screen, Jake pulled up the picture from the bar and the one from outside the station. No doubt in his mind they were the same person. He searched his Rolodex until he found Joel Bennett's extension. Voicemail picked up when he called. A quick check of his watch had Jake wondering where the time went. It was after ten o'clock. Bennett was on the day shift, not the evening one. He made notes on the pictures and sent them back with the two shots of his suspects so Bennett could work his magic. Hopefully, he'd be able to say which one resembled the disguised guy the most. The build was a little bulky for Velky but not for McMichaels, but he was sure the guy in the first picture was padded.

Jake switched off his light, closed his door and locked it. The bullpen had the night detectives on duty. He waved but didn't stop to speak to any of them. Jake pressed the Down arrow on the elevator. When the doors opened, Damien Dunn greeted him. Dunn wore a pair of jeans with snakeskin boots and a fringed cowboy shirt and hat.

"Going to a rodeo?"

"Funny. No, I'm going dancing. How's it shaking?" He spun around in front of Jake.

"It shakes, Damien. Can we meet up tomorrow? I want to see if you found out anything else on your end of things."

"Sure, is eight good?"

"Yes, why don't we meet for coffee at Phil's Coffee Shop?"

"Cool. They have the best bear claws."

In the police garage, Jake walked to his car and climbed in. He sat for a minute scanning the area and his mirrors for anyone or anything out of the ordinary. Nothing popped out at him. He decided to head home. At the entrance he reached for his phone and tried Gwenn's cell. It wasn't his night. Gwenn's voicemail picked up. He'd have to wait until tomorrow after all to get any answers.

Jake made three passes around his block before pulling into his driveway. Nothing seemed out of the ordinary. His departmental issue stuck out like a sore thumb, but he didn't care. Everyone in town knew they were the city-issued cars for the department. If not, his license plate WLKBY 10 was a dead giveaway. As he exited the car, he realized something was off. Movement in the woods caught and held his attention. Jake bolted across the street to the plainclothes officer on duty. His stomach dropped when he looked inside the unmarked car and found the man unconscious. He'd better be unconscious, or Jake was going to knock him out when he came to. A medicinal scent hit Jake in the face reminding him of a hospital. His guess, methyl propyl ether, but he'd have to wait until the lab confirmed it. Easy to acquire and fast acting, the choice of cowards. He pulled his handkerchief from his pocket and covered his own nose.

When he opened the door, a note floated out. In a quick one-handed motion, he grabbed the note with his left hand and held the officer upright with his other. A moan escaped from Officer Burrows's lips as Jake gave him a good shake.

"Carl, for God's sake, wake up."

"What happened?" Burrows tried to push up.

"God damn it. You were sleeping on the job, Carl." Jake's voice cut hard through his words.

"No, I wasn't. I swear."

Jake picked up Burrows's coffee cup and sniffed it. Nothing unusual, it smelled like coffee. "Where did your dinner come from?"

"Tooley picked it up at the diner on Highland."

Jake called for backup as he raced across the street to his house. He took the stairs two at a time. He pounded hard on the door until Officer Fisher opened it.

"What's going on? I heard you in the garage and then saw you bolt across the street."

"Carl's been drugged. Tooley's not answering his cell. Another team should be here shortly. I called it in."

"Jake, there's no one here. I checked the windows and doors before you came home."

"Let's check them again, Stella. I want to be sure."

Each checked a room and then rechecked. Jake didn't care if he was being anal. It was Mia's life on the line.

In the last place he checked, he found Mia. "The closet?" He smiled at her.

"Stella shoved me into it when you started banging on the door. I'm going to have to talk to her about my claustrophobia."

"So I outed you." Mia punched his arm but laughed as he intended her to. "Why don't you take a seat in the kitchen while I have a word with Stella?"

"I want to hear what you have to say."

He stuck his hands in his pockets. Jake felt the note. "I'll be right back."

"Where are you going?"

He pointed to the bathroom as he continued to walk down the hall. Once inside, Jake closed the door and locked it. He pulled a pair of gloves from his front left pocket and then proceeded to pull the note from his trousers. There was no way around it, his fingerprints would be on the note, but he didn't want to have them all over it. Carefully, he unfolded it. This time the killer had to have used computer script. It was too uniform to be anything else. The lab would verify his suspicions.

Lieutenant,

Sorry about your guy outside. He'll wake up shortly. It was a puff of sleeping gas, nothing toxic. The dentists use it all the time. I had to get creative to get the note to you somehow, now that you have them watching the station.

I'm disappointed you think I'd scare your girlfriend though she's quite attractive. What happened in Woodbury has nothing to do with me. Send her home and end this distraction. It's you against me. If you win you get the grand prize and it's not me.

The Groom

Jake hated the moniker. When they found him, they might be able to match the printout to his printer. Was the killer telling him the truth? If he didn't have anything to do with the intrusion into Mia's condo, then who was pursuing her? *It made sense. Why distract me if he's pitting himself against me?*

Mia was sitting on the bed with Brigh's head in her lap when he returned. He locked eyes with her as he stepped inside the room and closed the door behind him. Jake put on his stereo on low. In two long steps he stood in front of her and pulled her off the bed into his arms, which annoyed Brigh, who barely budged. He circled her around the room in an easy dance. All day he'd had an overwhelming need to hold her. Not only for her comfort but for his, too. Her safety was paramount to him. Jake hugged her closer as he rested his head in her hair. Her fragrance soothed him. It was pure Mia. He knew he only had a few more minutes of this peace before reality came crashing back. First, he'd need to update Fisher, then the captain. Was Nadia's killer telling the truth? If the Groom, for lack of a better term, didn't have anything to do with Mia's break-in, then who was pursuing her? Could it be related to the dead animals she'd received a few months ago? Even now his mind wouldn't rest.

"We have to go back out there," Jake said.

"I need you. Hold me for a few more minutes."

"Okay."

He didn't mind. How he wished he could stay in here with her forever. The song ended. Jake leaned away from her and took her chin in his hand. He placed his lips on hers in a sweet, gentle kiss before he trailed kisses over to her right ear, then whispered, "It's time."

Instead of speaking, she hugged him hard to her body and held on. He crushed her to him as the scent of lilies, her signature fragrance, filled his head. Her soft, silky hair rubbed against his lips. It gave him ideas not related to murder. Jake understood it was up to him to break the embrace as Mia tightened her grip on him. He reached behind his back and took her hands in his, brought them to the front and raised them to his lips.

"I love you. Do you feel any better?" It killed him to see the fright in her eyes.

"I'm all right. Can I sit in when you speak with Stella?"

"Yes." A thought struck him. "Mia, did you call your father?"

"No, I'm going to call him tomorrow about going there Saturday."

"I want you to call him right now. Your name is on the police report and a smart reporter will put two and two together. Call him before he reads about it."

Jake had two reasons for asking her to call him. If he was correct, her father would send out his own security to protect Mia and give her another layer.

"I thought they withheld a victim's name?"

"It's a home invasion, not a sexual assault. They do hold it back most times, but someone, for a few dollars or fifteen minutes in the limelight, will slip your name out there. It's the price of fame."

"I'm not famous."

"And you're not naïve, either."

She sat on the bed and pulled out her phone. He slipped from the room to give her privacy and took the opportunity to speak with Stella.

"What's this?" Stella asked when Jake handed her the note.

"A note signed 'The Groom.'"

"How'd he get the drop on Burrows?"

"The note said he used sleeping gas, but how did he get so close to the car without being detected?"

No matter how he turned it around in his mind, it bothered him. Burrows had to have been dozing off for a person to be able to sneak up on him. That didn't bode well with Jake. Until now, he'd liked and respected Burrows. But something was still off. He needed to speak with Tooley and see if he'd been drugged, too. If not, where was he?

"Do you want me to research the gas?"

"No, I'll do it. I'm going outside to talk to Tooley."

When he reached his front door his home phone rang. Jake turned back and picked up the receiver. "Hello."

"Lieutenant, you don't have a problem, she's too old for me."

The line went dead before he could reply. How in hell did the bastard get his home phone number? Jake thought hard and long, cataloging the places his home phone number appeared. It was in his personnel file. McGuire, the commissioner, the chief of police, Louie, and dispatch had it…and the Groom. Did the mayor have access to it? He could certainly get it if he wanted it, as could a dozen other people at the station. Jake grabbed the receiver and pressed *69 which, in Connecticut, could give the last caller's ID. It wasn't unexpected, but disappointment seeped into his bones when the operator stated the number was blocked.

Jake took his phone from his pocket and dialed Damien. Without waiting for a greeting Jake started talking when the call connected. "Damien, can the phone company trace a number with star-six-nine when it tells me it's blocked?"

"I'm sure they can. Not sure how long it would take."

"Could you?"

"No."

It was rare for Damien to admit he couldn't do something. "Thanks."

"You need me for anything else right now?"

"No."

"Good; my lady's in a loving mood and I might be late tomorrow."

Jake hung up. He was glad someone was having a good evening. He walked outside and circled around back behind his house. Tooley was returning to his car.

"LT, what's up?"

"Where were you, Tooley, for the last fifteen minutes?"

"I was in the house behind me. I heard a noise and went to check it out."

"Where's your radio?"

"It's on my belt. I turned it down to avoid being heard. Why, something happen?"

"Yes, something happened. Burrows's been gassed, and the suspect left me a note. I want a report on my desk first thing, explaining why you thought it was prudent to leave your post and cut communications on a stakeout."

"But my orders also were to keep an eye out on the houses behind me."

"Burrows could've been killed as well as everyone in my house." Jake didn't wait for his answer. He stormed back to his house.

"Where was he?" Stella asked.

"He was checking out the vacant house."

"He didn't hear the request for backup?"

"Claims he heard a noise and shut off his radio."

"It is procedure to lower the radio when entering a suspect's crib, Jake."

"I don't care, Stella."

Jake dialed Louie and started right in on him. "I thought you researched everyone you put at my house."

"Calm down, I did. What's up?"

"I'll tell you what's up. That idiot Tooley left his post and turned his radio off. The Groom was here and left me a personal note."

"Why did he leave his post?"

Jake filled Louie in. "Tooley did his job. If you'd remove your emotions, you'd see it," Louie said.

"I don't care. Mia was in the house!"

"I'll be right over."

"No need. Get me Tooley's complete file. I want everything on him. I especially need to understand his political leanings."

"I have the complete file. I'm not a damn rookie, Jake," Louie said, miffed.

Jake scanned the room. His eyes landed on Stella first, who stood at attention, and then his gaze fell on Mia's wide-open eyes as she searched his face.

"Get me the file, Louie." After hanging up, he turned and walked into the kitchen.

"It sounds like your officer was doing his job," Mia said.

"I need a drink."

"Look at me." She waited until he did. "I'm speaking as a doctor, not your girlfriend. It's been an emotional and trying day for everyone. You're taking it out on a poor kid who was only doing his job. I've seen your temper a couple of times and it's fierce. You should go back outside and apologize to Tooley."

"No. It would undermine my authority."

"No, you undermined your authority when you went off on him. Be the bigger man and apologize. I'd hate to have the kid who's out there protecting us holding a grudge."

Jake turned away from Mia and poured vodka into a glass with ice. "You want one?"

"No."

"I need a few minutes." He took his drink, walked down the hall, went into his study, and closed the door behind him.

He hadn't gone to his computer to research Tooley. He needed a few moments to calm down. He sat back in his recliner and closed his eyes. Too much had gone wrong today. It didn't help he hadn't had a minute to analyze anything. He was reacting on emotions instead of logical thought. If he wasn't careful the suspect would get the drop on him. He downed his drink and pushed out of the chair. It was time to put his tail between his legs and admit he was wrong. He walked into the kitchen and poured a cup of coffee. A chill hit his neck. Turning, he eyed Mia in the doorway.

"I'll be right back. You're right."

"Music to my ears," Mia said to break the tension.

Jake approached Tooley's cruiser. He handed the cup to the officer through the window while he read his full name on his tag. "I'm sorry, Jim, for blowing up at you, but this case has become personal. I understand you were only doing your job."

"Thank you, Lieutenant, for coming out, and for the coffee."

Embarrassed, Jake started to walk away. Tooley called out. "I never had a supervisor apologize before. I appreciate it."

"I admit when I'm wrong."

"Good night, sir."

Jake walked around front, crossed the street, and stopped in front of Burrows's car. "How do you feel?"

"Like an amateur."

"Any idea how he drugged you?"

"No, sir, the only thing I can come up with is he crawled under the car. But to do it he'd have to be real skinny."

Out of the dark comes some light, Jake thought. "You're probably right. No aftereffects?"

"No, sir… LT… I want to…to apologize…"

Jake cut him off. "Stay alert. If you feel funny, start clicking your radio. It will bring help."

Should he replace Burrows? Well, one thing was for sure, Jake wasn't going to be able to sleep tonight. Right or wrong, Burrows hadn't performed his duty. Carl's comment about the suspect got his mind whirling. He ran back into the house. Inside he grabbed the photos from the station and the bar from his briefcase. Jake dialed Clive Thomas's number. When the voice system picked up Jake left a message. Tomorrow he would check out Thomas's renderings.

"Jake, dinner's almost ready," Mia said.

"It's late and I'm not hungry. You and Stella eat. I'll be in my study."

Mia stepped into his path as he turned to leave the room. "Sit down and eat your dinner. It wasn't a request. It's not going to help anyone if you get sick."

"I'm not going to get sick. My body doesn't require constant food." Annoyed, he stepped around her.

"Fine, I'm heading home, then. I don't need your moodiness."

Jake stopped in his tracks. "You're not going anywhere."

"Really!" She batted her eyelashes at him and clasped her hands to the side of her face.

He choked on his laughter.

"Sit down and eat."

Jake sat, and shot a glance at Stella, who throughout the entire exchange had stood off to the side. Her snickers had him raising an eyebrow.

"I knew she'd win," Stella baited. "Big, bad, strong lieutenant taken down by a wily female."

"Shut up and eat, Stella," Jake said, with a smile tugging at his lips.

The rest of the night was uneventful. With Mia tucked in next to him, Jake relaxed enough to rest. Around four a.m. he quietly climbed out of bed.

"Huh? What time is it?" Mia mumbled.

"It's early. I'm going to the station. Go back to sleep."

Mia rolled over without another word. He hopped into the shower. The hot water beat at his tense muscles. The day in front of him pushed forward as he tried to keep it at bay for a little while longer. He dressed in the semidarkness and walked into the kitchen with Brigh at his feet.

"You're up early."

"It's my usual time," Stella said.

"Did you get enough rest, or do you need a relief?"

"I'm good. Don't worry about us."

"I'll check in later this morning." Jake turned to leave, his coffee mug in his hand.

"Mia's a lot tougher than you give her credit for."

"She is, but it won't stop me from worrying." He gave Brigh a pat, then opened the door leading to the garage and closed it quietly behind him.

Before he reached the station, Jake remembered he wanted to drive by Velky's house to scout out the area. Neither of McMichaels's residences fit the bill for the kind of work required to torture the women. He had to wait at least two hours before doing the drive-by. Velky got into work at seven. It was five fifteen. Jake pulled off to the side of the road to write down his thoughts. He didn't want to forget again. Somewhere deep down he believed it would tie the cases together—the missing women and Nadia Carren's murder, unless, of course, McMichaels had rented a warehouse to torture the women. He'd put Kraus on the search when he got into his office.

Louie charged at him when he entered the bullpen. Jake checked his watch, pointed to his office, and kept walking. After checking the water level, he grabbed the strongest roast he had and put it into the machine. As the scent of coffee filled the air his nerves evened out. When it finished brewing, Jake lifted the cup to his lips and took a sip.

"You're in early, everything okay?" Louie grinned.

"I can say the same, you got something hot?"

"I talked to the DA this morning. She's going to file charges against Malone for aggravated attempted rape. The captain said he'd call after the court appearance. Malone will get some jail time."

"You gave me a moment there yesterday." Jake stared at Louie over the top of his coffee.

"I gave myself one, too." Louie brewed a cup of joe for himself.

"You have anything new on the case?"

"Yes. First, here's Tooley's file. He's a good cop, Jake."

"I apologized to him."

Jake smiled at Louie's quizzical expression. "How come?" Louie asked.

"Because Mia made me."

Louie doubled over laughing. He grabbed the corner of Jake's desk to balance himself. "Welcome to the club."

"What club?"

"The 'I Got You by the Balls' club." Louie was still laughing.

"Are you through?"

"Not yet, I've waited years for this."

"Okay, then, I'll tell you the rest. She also made me eat dinner. Now, you can get it all out at once."

Jake sat patiently while Louie snorted and fought for control. It felt good to laugh. A few minutes later, Louie got serious, much to Jake's relief, and started talking murder.

When Jake finished updating him, Louie said, "You're still leaning toward Arnie?"

"Our two viable suspects are McMichaels and Velky. Out of the two of them, I'm leaning toward Velky. You?"

"I want it to be Velky because I despise the mayor, but I don't want to arrest the wrong guy."

"I agree." Jake said. "We'll go where the evidence leads and not where our emotions take us. Has Green gotten back to you on everyone's electronics courses?"

"He's completed his search on McMichaels and Pencer. I'm waiting on Dunn to finish up on Velky's online course search. It's more difficult to verify."

"Damien and I are meeting to discuss that issue. I'm also meeting with Gwenn this morning. She's dug up some information but didn't say on who. There was a reference to my number three suspect. I can't remember what order I gave her the names to research."

"What time are you meeting her?"

"My meet with Damien is at eight. Afterward, I'll call and connect with Gwenn."

Louie clapped Jake's shoulder. "Popular guy. You want me to meet up with Damien while you meet with Gwenn?"

"I could use some time out of here this morning to gather my thoughts in-between my meets. I want you to keep at the searches. Follow through with Brown and Green. Don't talk in the bullpen with Kirk or Joe. Use my office, especially if Velky's name comes up. Walsh has been nosing around their desks."

"I wanted to give you a heads-up. Around lunchtime I'll be taking a couple of hours of personal time."

Jake didn't ask why. After yesterday's incident he'd make an exception for Louie.

Chapter 27

At seven forty-five Jake walked into the coffee shop. The hair on the back of his neck stood up. He couldn't shake the feeling he had a shadow again. It couldn't be John Velky's man again. He scanned the restaurant but didn't recognize anyone related to his case. Damien was already seated and shoveling down a full breakfast of bacon, eggs, and pancakes. Somehow the guy stayed rail-thin. Jake slid into the booth opposite him. Damien had chosen the table in the far corner where he could see both the front and back doors. Once a cop, always a cop, Jake thought. He wished his back was the one against the wall.

He'd have to trust Damien to vet any problems or unwanted guests. "LT, you want to switch seats?"

Did the kid read minds? "I'm good, as long as you can stay alert while you eat."

"No problem."

"Eat your breakfast while I detail what I need. And remember, Damien, it's okay to say no."

"Shoot."

Back in his car twenty minutes later, he still couldn't shake the antsy feeling. Throughout his career his spider sense had kept him alive. Jake wasn't about to ignore it now. He took a detour to his next destination as he weaved his car through the streets of Wilkesbury, until he arrived in the industrial area. He pulled in between a paper mill and a hardware store and waited. Disappointed when no cars drove past the buildings, he pulled back out onto the street after ten minutes. He either had a smart pursuer or his instincts were off. He went with smart shadow.

A debate raged in his head. Guilt had him picking up his phone. He had asked a fellow cop to break the law. Where should he have drawn the line? Dunn had had no problem with his request. It told Jake in another life Dunn would've been a damn good hacker. Did he have the right to put the young detective's career on the line? Did the end justify the means? In his heart, he knew the answer. In this case, yes it did.

Now he was late for his meet with Gwenn. He'd better get a move on before he missed her.

* * * *

He spotted Gwenn in the back corner of the shop. A tall cup of coffee steamed in front of her while she wrote furiously into a notebook. The place was quiet, four customers besides Gwenn. Jake stepped to the counter, ordered a large cup before walking over to her table. Today she wore her hair up. Her bright blue suit drew his attention to her beautiful eyes. He smiled inwardly when she lifted those sharp eyes to him as she pierced him with a look. He took the seat to her right.

"You're late."

"Sorry, it was unavoidable. What have you got for me?"

"Let's start with McMichaels. He has a hunting lodge in Massachusetts."

"It didn't come up in my search. He fishes, does he also hunt?"

"Could be a fishing lodge, but who cares what men do in the woods? It's on a lake—water, fish, yeah, he could use it for fishing."

"But that's not the third one on my list, is it?"

She flashed him her award-winning smile. "You can't remember in what order you gave them to me, can you?"

"No, I don't. Yesterday got out of hand. Who was third on your list?"

"Velky."

"What did you get? We have the small animal torture and the vandalism against a teacher. Do you have more?"

"Yes. I spoke with a former neighbor who moved his family out of state because of young Velky."

"Spill it."

"Gee, I worked hard to unearth these facts, the least you can do is humor me." Gwenn faked a pout.

He balled his fists at his sides and bit back his impatient words. Instead he said, "Deadline here. He only gave me two weeks before he grabs another, Gwenn. I don't want her death on my conscience. Do you?"

"Oh my God! When and how did he notify you?" She started scribbling in her notebook as she threw questions at him. Jake held up his hand. "How much time do you have left? Have you pinned down which woman is in danger?"

She threw questions at him like a major leaguer in October. "We've kept the letter from the press for a reason. You can't release any information I give you until I say so. The brass decided it was for the best. I don't agree, but my hands are tied. I wanted you to understand why I'm not finessing here. I'm on the damn clock."

"Okay, but I get it all first."

"As we agreed, now give."

"Velky was picking on the neighbor's daughter. They were both ten. He was always making a grab for her or leaving her dead animals. She refused him when he asked her to the class dance in grammar school, for Pete's sake. The neighbor, Lenny Fishburne, said his tires were slashed five weeks in a row and his insurance company refused to pay for them after a while. During the day when she was alone, his wife got some nasty prank calls, even threatening her a few times. They didn't have caller ID back then. He was afraid—and these are his exact words—'That the Velky kid would sexually assault my daughter one day and I decided it was prudent to move away before the kid followed through.' He worked for a national company and put in for a transfer. And here's the clincher. She's a brunette with brown eyes."

Jake scribbled in his Moleskine as she talked. He was still upset Velky hadn't hit his radar until Damien found his juvie record. "Anything else?"

"A couple of his teachers passed him when he didn't deserve to be promoted because they wanted to get rid of him. He gave them, and this is a direct quote, 'the heebie-jeebies.' By the way, they were all women."

"Is this public knowledge or private sources? Where can I obtain it legally without questions? I'll need it all for a warrant to search his house and property."

"It's public. I'll send it to you."

"I'd rather keep you out of it in case he gets a heads-up."

"I can take care of myself, Jake."

"Please, let's handle it my way. Tell me where you acquired the information."

Gwenn supplied him with her sources and where he could vet the info. It took him two hours to run everything on his laptop and to follow through with the calls. On the way back to the station, he called Louie and told him to approach a judge and request a warrant on the harassment incidents and Velky's school records. He then told him to update the captain.

"Are you at the station or still home?" Jake said.

"Station, why?"

Jake filled him in. "I want you to run the McMichaels angle. Find out everything you can on the fishing house in Massachusetts. Who he brings there and how long he's owned it."

"I'll put it down to stress that you're telling me how to do my job." Jake didn't miss the sarcasm in Louie's voice.

On the way back, he made time to drive by Velky's house. It was located on the edge of town on a dead-end street. Two houses occupied the street, one a doll-size cottage badly in need of repair. The other reminded him of a large farmhouse. Velky's well-groomed house sat at the end of the cul-de-sac—white with black shutters, a wraparound porch, built around the turn of the century. His highly manicured grass and bushes surrounded the house which butted against the woods and hugged the property on three sides. Secluded, quiet—the perfect place to kill, Jake thought.

* * * *

"Lieutenant Carrington doesn't seem to be taking me seriously." He spoke aloud, pinning up pictures of the new Ciara on his basement walls.

He rubbed his stubbly chin as his mind wandered. *What should I leave on the body this time? It's obvious the lieutenant isn't as smart as people believe him to be. Whatever it is, it has to hit him in the face to keep this game moving. It should lead him to the other suspects.* Tires crunched on the gravel outside his house. *A car on this street? Coincidence? Couldn't be.* He took the steps two at a time. In the living room, he headed right to the front window.

"Damn it." He pulled up short when he recognized the city-issued sedan.

"Well, well, well, it's about time you started investigating. But what led you here?" He wrote down the license plate, WLKBY 10, and continued to observe the car. The sun's glare off the front windshield hid the driver's face but he knew it had to be Carrington. Pins and needles ran up and down his spine. Was he taking pictures of the property or observing? Why? Did the old bat next door call the police? Clammy hands quivered as he continued to peer out through the curtains. Why do a drive-by in daylight? *Nothing should have led him to me.* Maybe later he'd pay Mrs. White a visit. See if she had reported something. He hoped it wasn't her—he'd hate to have to dirty his hands and kill the old lunatic. What sent the lieutenant directly to his door? He snapped a couple pictures of the car with his cell phone. He couldn't believe it when Carrington climbed from his car and started into the woods.

"Asinine asshole—what the hell is he doing in my woods?"

He ran outside with his phone and snapped off a couple more shots. Maybe he'd be able to prove harassment with them.

Carrington spotted him. "Mr. Velky, right?"

As if he doesn't recognize me. "That's right. We met at my job. Can I ask why you're trespassing on my property?"

"I thought the city owned the woods. I hunt and decided to check out these woods for game."

It might be time to talk to my brother. "Lieutenant, do you have a warrant?"

"Why would I need a warrant to walk the woods?"

"Don't play games with me, Carrington. It's private property. You have beef with my brother, not me; remember that. I'm asking you to leave now."

"I'm not playing games, Arnie. I got an anonymous call to look for evidence pertaining to my case in the wooded area here. Do you mind if I continue to my search?"

"I do. If you want to search my property get a warrant. And FYI, I'll be speaking to my brother about this as soon as you leave."

The bastard hasn't taken his eyes off me. What the hell did he unearth? And what the hell would my brother do anyway? John would probably ask if he could put the cuffs on me personally.

"I'll be back, Mr. Velky. You can count on it."

He stood rigid until Carrington's car was no longer in sight. Then he rushed back into his house. A ball of lead filled his belly as he tried to think what had led Carrington to him. Methodically, he walked around the rooms as he scanned for items he might've left around belonging to the women. Satisfied nothing had been left sitting out, Arnie headed down to his basement.

Down here, in his workroom, there'd be evidence if they did an extensive search. He scooped up the large bottle of bleach and poured it in the bucket he kept down here. He added water, threw in a sponge and let it soak. Arnie squeezed it out and started scrubbing every surface. No way would he let Carrington win. He'd made sure he took care of the blood and trace evidence. He'd been careful. And blood degraded over time. The others didn't count. He couldn't be caught until he had Ciara in his possession. The bitch needed to be taught a lesson. Tears dripped down his cheeks. How could she have disappeared off the face of the earth? Maybe it was time to hire a private dick. Would it be worth the cost? Only if he found her—if not, he'd have to kill him.

* * * *

Jake drove down the street, turned at the corner, and pulled over out of sight from Arnie's house. Did he have exigent circumstances? Normally he'd say yes, but with the suspect being the mayor's brother, he'd err on the side of caution. Was Arnie destroying evidence as he sat inside his car? He'd bet his life's savings Velky was doing exactly that. He wrote down his impressions of Arnie. Nervous was an understatement. Jake needed to get into Velky's house. He noticed Arnie's front door was reinforced steel. He dialed Louie's direct line.

"Where's my warrant?" he demanded.

"I'm still waiting."

"Who's the judge?"

"Brenner. She was the only one available."

"Damn it, Louie, she supported Velky in the last election. She's stalling. Give me her number."

He wrote down the judge's number as he tried to figure out how to handle her. If he called Judge Warner, who hated Velky, would Brenner consider him to be overstepping his boundaries? Would he have to deal with Brenner in the future and would the snub ruin future cases? If it saved another life, he'd have to put up with it.

"Your Honor, it's Lieutenant Carrington," he said the minute she picked up.

"I spoke with your associate a couple of hours ago, Lieutenant."

"I'm aware, Your Honor, but I feel the suspect will destroy valuable evidence if I'm unable to get access to his property soon. Until today, he didn't realize he was a suspect."

"And how did he realize he was suspect, Lieutenant?"

"I drove by his street to survey the property. He came out and engaged me."

"Do you often antagonize a suspect?"

Freakin' bleeding heart… "Your Honor, it's standard practice for an officer to survey an area before a person of interest is approached in case he tries to escape. I personally did the survey so as not to have tongues wagging at the station. And I needed to calculate how many team members I'd require to search a property as large as his."

"I hear the annoyance in your voice, Carrington, but I'm trying to cover not only my ass, but yours, too. John Velky has some powerful friends. I want an honest answer to my next question."

Jake took a deep breath. "You have my word."

"Is he a viable suspect, or does this have anything to do with your feud with the mayor?"

"He's my main suspect. And no, it has nothing to do with the mayor. Arnie Velky's profession, his property, and his background are what led me to him. The last time I encountered him, he was wearing a necklace that matched a witness's description."

"You better be right, Carrington. I'll send the warrant to your email." She hung up on him without another word.

Jake also hoped he was right. If not, he'd committed career suicide. No judge in his or her right mind would ever work with him again. He shook it off and headed to the station to pick his team.

Chapter 28

Jake pulled up in front of Velky's house. The rest of the team parked along the street, while several SWAT team members filed into the woods like fog oozing over the grounds. The dogs and their handlers stood to the side and waited for the go-ahead to set up a grid and begin their work. Several Crime Scene Units waited on Jake.

Gun drawn and Louie to his left, Jake rapped his knuckles hard against the door. Several moments passed. No noise from the inside. An officer held the Enforcer, a battering ram for such an occasion to force open Velky's steel door. Jake watched as the man gathered his momentum and rammed the door once, then twice. It took four tries to dislodge it. The minute Jake stepped into the house he knew Velky had rabbited. Damn the freaking judge.

As he walked in he took a sniff of the air. "You smell that?"

"Yeah, bleach. He's gone," Louie said.

"Yep. Brownnosing bureaucrats. If the judge had done her job properly instead of worrying about covering her own ass we'd have had him. You take a team and clear the top floor. I'll work down here. When you're done we'll sweep the basement together. Put out the APB now while I call the captain and report in. He can update the brass."

Louie turned and walked out the front door to make the call.

After he hung up with Shamus, Jake started his search in the living room. With his UV light he scanned walls, furniture, floors, and rugs for body fluids. He'd leave the luminol testing to the crime scene techs. Smeared fluids appeared on the rug right inside the door. Jake dropped a marker for the CSIs and continued his search of the room. In the kitchen he found a pail of dirty water filled with sponges. He dropped a marker next to it.

* * * *

Louie figured they weren't going to find anything upstairs, but he left CSI Willie Phelps there to do his magic. He moved through each bedroom, shining his light into all the corners and closets before moving to the first floor. Everything seemed normal—in fact, a little too normal. There wasn't anything out of place, not even a speck of dust. He headed downstairs.

Louie stopped and listened while Jake talked to Alessia, the CSI tech who was working the living room. "There's nothing here or in the family room, Lieutenant, except for a small amount of fluid by the door." Louie stepped into the foyer.

The hallway walls had newer-looking paper than the upstairs, but still reminded him of a time gone by. His grandmother's house had all the walls covered, not painted. Was Arnie hiding something behind the new paper? He figured with Arnie gone the warrant covered everything.

Jake spotted Kylie Shaker, the head CSI, and walked over to her.

"Kylie, can you accompany us to the basement?"

"Sure. This house is clean. I mean *clean*. Like within the last several hours cleaned, you get my drift?"

"I do. Hopefully we'll find something in the basement."

"Let's get it done."

They sandwiched Kylie between them as they headed down the stairs, to protect her in case Arnie was hiding down there. Jake scanned the area as he led with his gun. Dear God, he needed to find something and ensure another woman didn't die because of his incompetence.

His eyes roamed the room and landed on heavy-duty steel rings placed a wingspan apart that had been screwed into the far wall—a matching pair were attached to the concrete floor. He feared what they'd been used for and shone his light on them. Nothing appeared.

Jake walked to the other side of the basement. A large wooden board rested across a set of Bilco doors. Weird, they were hung in reverse. They swung in, not out as doors leading to the backyard normally were hung.

"Kylie," Jake walked over to her. He squatted down to talk with her and pointed to the door. "Around the rings, can you test for blood in every crevice? And give me your first impressions?"

"I smell bleach. Lots of it, and it was used recently, let's say within the hour."

"I caught that. Also, make sure you get those doors." Again, he thanked the damn judge for taking her time. She had probably blown up his whole case.

Jake stood, walked away to let Kylie do her job. He went over to the worktables and drawers and started opening each one. Most were empty. A small, torn piece of photographic paper was stuck in the back corner of one drawer. He took it out and studied it.

His phone vibrated in his pocket. He noted the caller and put the phone back in his pocket. He'd check in later with Dave Guerrera. Maybe Dave would close Mia's case today.

"Lieutenant, can you come over here?" Kylie asked.

He started across the room. He reached Shaker's position and knelt next to her. "Whatcha got?"

"Traces of blood in the concrete, but I'm not sure I'll get enough to give me useful information. Like I said, it was recently hit with bleach."

"Try. If the cadaver dogs find something outside this will add to the evidence. Did you find anything else?"

"Not yet. If it's here, I'll find it."

Jake started back to the table and drawers when someone on the other side of the reversed Bilco doors pounded. "Hey Lieutenant, are you in there?"

"Yes."

"Come out here, please." Officer Kaitlen O'Malley's voice rocked. Charlie, her dog, whined at the top of the stairs, his hind legs stretched up and his face resting on his front paws. Jake knew finding bodies hurt the animals as much, if not more, than the humans they worked alongside.

He climbed the steps with O'Malley. Once in the backyard, the dog sat waiting instructions. O'Malley scratched Charlie's back a few times, which prepared Jake for the scene that lay ahead. As Jake stepped into the backyard he pulled up short. Little yellow flags blew in the wind. Not four, but eight. Who were the other women? How long had Velky been practicing before he left Nadia's body for discovery? Once again, the system had failed. If someone had paid attention to the signs, Velky could have received treatment at a young age, when his symptoms first appeared.

"How long will it take, O'Malley, to unearth one?"

"It's a slow, delicate process. It's in the anthropologists' hands now. Charlie and I only locate them. It will take as long as it takes. I've called for more forensic anthropologists to help with the dig."

"Are you sure it's human remains under the ground?" His eyes stung, a sharp pain shot through his heart at the waste of human life. Kaitlen placed a hand on his arm. He had to tuck away his feelings if a stranger could read his dark thoughts. "Thanks, O'Malley, I'm fine." Charlie nuzzled his nose under Jake's hand. His eyes never left the backyard. It had been transformed into a graveyard. He petted Charlie, happy Brigh was home and safe. Glad she didn't have to experience what Charlie had.

"Yes, I'm sure we have human remains. How long they've been there, I can't say."

The team continued to scan the grid they had set up. All in all, when they were finished, they found nine sets of remains. Five women had been reported missing with one's body already found. *Who were the others?* he wondered. *Were they local? Street people? Runaways? Hadn't anyone missed them?*

Jake pulled a burner cell phone from his belt. He sent the message he had prewritten an hour ago. Gwenn would be here momentarily with her cameraman. The impact of the find was in every face he turned toward. His heart heavy, he had to acknowledge sick, vicious people like Edward Arnold Velky existed in this world. It broke his heart, and without warning slammed Eva's battered body vividly into his mind, and the horror forever etched into his sister's features. He knew he'd need counselors to speak to the team afterward. Would he use them himself? Maybe this time he would. After these kind of events, even the dogs got counseling for their depression.

Gwenn arrived within ten minutes and took another five to set up. She had her cameraman scan the scene.

"Gwenn, please move back two feet." Jake signaled a uniform to make them comply.

She shouted, "Lieutenant, what have you found?"

"Please give some consideration to the families of these victims. What we've found are remains. Until we identify and notify each family, we won't be giving any statements."

His team had been at it for three hours and each wore a weary expression.

"Is the owner of this home a suspect?" The camera swung toward Velky's house.

"No comment."

Jake figured the comment covered both their asses and started to turn away. A thought banged into his head.

"Louie," he bellowed as he raced back down the stairs to the basement.

Louie ran into him at the bottom of the steps leading out. "What? You find something?"

"Yes, bodies. But that's not what hit me. Assign a team to continue the search here. Burke and Gunner are tied up in Watertown. I'm going to call Shamus in to supervise the scene."

"Why?"

"What's missing here, Louie?"

Louie looked around. "Beats me."

"The mayor. Let's do a wellness check on him and his family in person and post a guard for their protection, and one at his mother's place. I don't think Arnie will go after them, but his attitude is quite derogatory concerning John."

His patience running thin as he waited for McGuire to arrive Jake paced back and forth. Once he did, Jake and Louie rushed from the scene.

"Jake," Gwenn called.

"Not now, Gwenn."

She raced to his car. "Where are you going?"

"I can't say. When I can I'll call you."

He was torn about leaving the victims but finding and containing Velky was imperative, time was ticking down.

* * * *

John Velky answered the door when Jake knocked. Sweat dripped from John's brow. "Mayor, I'm sorry to bother you, may I come in?"

"No, everyone's sick in here." Velky hadn't opened the door more than an inch.

Jake's view was blocked. He turned to Louie and mimed writing. Louie pulled out his pad and scribbled on it. He held it up to the mayor. John Velky barely nodded his acknowledgment.

"I don't mind if everyone's sick, sir. What I have to say will only take a minute. Have you seen the news?"

"No, the television's been off." Jake clearly heard it in the background. "Listen, Carrington, this is my house and you can't come in. Now go away if you want to keep your job."

"Is your mother home or here?"

"What's my mother got to do with this?" John's voice squeaked.

"Please answer the question."

"She's here visiting her grandchildren."

Should he storm the place or back down? The arrogant Honorable Mayor John Velky's pale face emphasized his wide eyes filled with fear as his expression pleaded with Jake not to do anything that would harm his family.

"I'm sorry to have barged in on you. Please have your mother give me a call." He handed John his card.

As they turned he noticed the uniformed officer he had requested pulling up to the curb in his own car, not a cruiser. They walked to the car. Jake swore when he saw the young officer. Why the heck did they send a recent graduate from the academy? He scanned his name tag but didn't recognize the name.

"No questions. Meet us one block over on West Main Street by the park."

The kid didn't question him. Jake watched the rookie pull away before climbing in his own car.

"What do you have planned?"

"We can't storm the place. We'll approach from the rear of the house and try to find a way in. We'll call for backup but I don't want to spook him. We're not sure what he'll do or who he'll hurt."

One street over they waited with the rookie until support showed up. It had become a hurry up and wait situation. Once it arrived at five-thirty, Jake coordinated with the SWAT team about how they'd approach the house. After reviewing the layout of the neighborhood, SWAT decided they'd wait until they cleared the neighbors out, and it got closer to dark. The back side of the house lost the sun around six-fifteen. It would give them enough camouflage to proceed.

Jake shrugged into his Kevlar vest, as did Louie and the uniform. He wanted to go in without the vest for easy movement, but Louie had put up a stink. He put an extra magazine in his pocket before holstering his gun. He knelt, then checked his ankle piece. Satisfied, he and Louie crossed over neighboring yards with the SWAT team on their flank.

At the first window, Louie stood back in the shadows as Jake inched his way up and peeked inside. He signaled there were two occupants in the room and raised his hand about two feet off the ground to indicate children. One of the kids ran to the window. Jake put a finger to his lips and pointed to the lock. To calm them down, he showed the girl his badge. The window squeaked as he helped her push it open. He estimated they had a few seconds to get both girls out safely. Louie grabbed the first girl. Jake grabbed the second one as she perched on the sill. With her in his arms, he ran her to the edge of the woods. Jake passed both children to a team member as the girls cried for their mother.

He moved back into position and checked the next window. No one was in the middle bedroom. Inching along the wall, he came to the screened-in kitchen porch. Arnie Velky, with a gun in his hand, filled the window of the door to the house. Scrunching down further, Jake moved along the wall to a better position to view more of the kitchen. He spotted John and his wife at the table and Velky's mother by the sink. He signaled Louie—four adults. Jake waved his gun and pointed to the door. Would Arnie kill his family? Had he completely lost it?

He inched closer to the door in a crouch. The porch outside the kitchen was screened in, no solid walls. It wouldn't offer any cover. Jake motioned for Louie to hang back. Boards creaked as he stepped onto the porch. Jake eased the screen door back. He inhaled, waited, then moved to the kitchen door.

As he reached for the door and started to stand up, it swung open. "Welcome to the party, Jake. Drop your gun. Where's your partner?"

Wild eyes stared into his. Arnie Velky flashed him a grin.

"Arnie."

"Take a seat, Jake. I need to figure out what to do."

"Why don't you free your nieces?" Jake didn't give him the heads-up they'd removed the kids from the scene. "You have the mayor, what more do you need?"

"I'm running this show. Sit down and shut up."

Jake studied the mayor's disheveled appearance—neither John nor his wife was holding it together.

"Edward, put down your gun. You have no place to hide," said his mother.

"Shut the hell up. I told you not to call me Edward. Call me Arnie."

"Your name—"

Arnie interrupted her as he jumped across the room and jammed the gun under her chin.

All she was doing was igniting a fire. One Jake didn't need right now. "Mrs. Velky, please go wait with the children."

"Stay right where you are, bitch. Jake, I'm going to tell you again to shut up." Velky pointed his gun at Jake's head. "I'll never understand cops. Why the hell did you risk your life to come in here? You hate him as much as I do."

"I don't hate anyone. Politically, we don't see eye to eye. That's it."

Arnie pushed his mother aside and walked behind his brother, the gun in one hand, a butcher knife in the other. "You." He pointed to his sister-in-law. "Pull his head back by his hair."

When she hesitated, he nudged her with the gun. Karen Velky jumped up and yanked her husband's head back. "Jesus, Karen," John whined.

Arnie laughed like a loon. He slid his gun over Karen's cheek. The gray, sickly expression on Karen's face told Jake she'd lose her stomach contents if Velky continued. "Good job, dear." He placed the butcher knife under John's chin. "Now, Karen, you must hold his head back. If you drop it the knife will slit his throat and you don't want that. Do you?"

"Why, Arnie?" his brother pleaded.

"I'm freakin' sick of your superior attitude. Your snide comments, the insults, and most of all, I'm sick of how she favors you." He pointed the gun at his mother. "You've both made my life a living hell."

Arnie stared his mother down—neither flinched. Jake wondered how the woman held it together—arrogance, or an ingrained motherly thing most women seemed to be born with? Mrs. Velky kept her five-foot-three body erect. Like her son, the mayor, not one hair was out of place on her mostly gray head. Though her makeup was expertly applied it caked around her eyes, probably from hours of stress. Jake estimated he had an hour before she cracked.

"You're next, darling," Arnie said to Karen as he folded his lips over his teeth.

He turned to Jake. "Now, Jake. I didn't plan on you being here. I thought I had a few hours while you searched the place. What have you found?"

"The ones you practiced on," Jake said.

"I expected you back at the house sooner, what was the holdup?" The idiot carried on as if this was party conversation.

"The judge," he said in disgust. Arnie's lack of reaction, or any facial expressions, scared Jake. The man was over-the-top nuts. Could he bring him back?

"Don't you love politics? Blowhards like this one here make everyone's life a mess." Arnie jammed the knife closer to John's throat until a trickle of blood appeared. The mayor screamed.

Jake stood.

"Sit down, Jake. Don't be a hero for these people. They consider the likes of you and me as dirt on their shoes. Isn't it right, Your Honor?"

"No, it's not, Arnie," John Velky stammered.

"Would you like me to quote you on your opinion of the good lieutenant here?"

"I—I Arnie please—"

Their mother grabbed a knife from the sink. Arnie's hand jerked up then quickly down as he sliced into John's arm. Arnie ducked and fired his gun in his mother's direction. The bullet grazed his mother's temple. A high-pitched squeal cut through the kitchen. It was John, not his mother. Jake jumped up to help Mrs. Velky.

"Jake, I'm not going to tell you again to sit."

"I can't. I need to check on your mother. Look at all the blood, you might've killed her."

"Serves her right. She killed my father."

"Your father died from a heart attack," Mrs. Velky choked out.

"You lying bitch." Velky jumped over to where she lay on the floor and jammed the gun into her stomach.

The gun was un-cocked. Jake flung himself at Arnie and dragged him off his mother. Jake grabbed for the gun but Velky held on to it, slamming it down. Jake pushed to the side. The gun glanced off the side of Jake's head. An inch closer and it would have turned out his lights. Jake threw a right cross. It hit its mark. The crack of Arnie's nose splintering along with the sound of his curses was music to Jake's ears. Blood spurted everywhere.

"You bastard. You're going to pay for that. Why couldn't you mind your own damn business? I would have rid the world of them."

Jake sent another right jab into Arnie's jaw but Velky got his in first, clipping Jake on the jaw with the gun. Dazed, he fell to the floor. Jake tried rolling to his feet as dizziness and nausea flooded his body. Arnie kicked him in his right kidney and jabbed the knife into his stomach. The last thing he heard before he passed out was John's pleas for his life.

Chapter 29

Louie had his ear to the door and listened in while the SWAT team surrounded the house. He knew Jake would try to save everyone inside, whether Louie liked it or not. He turned the knob slowly, hoping no one saw the motion. He was ready to push in the door, his gun leading, when all hell broke loose.

While Jake rolled around on the floor with Arnie, Louie rushed the mayor, his wife, and mother out the back door as he signaled the SWAT team to enter the premises. Once Velky's family was safe, he charged back into the kitchen to help Jake. Arnie slammed Louie into the wall, and just before Velky landed his punch, Louie saw Jake on the ground, blood gushing from his stomach. Jake was trying to get to his feet. Rage built in Louie as he blocked Arnie's next punch. Louie brought up his knee, slamming it hard into Arnie's balls. As the bastard bent over in pain Louie threw a punch into his already shattered nose. Louie grabbed the front of Velky's shirt to steady the killer for his next punch. Someone grabbed his arm before he could finish the job.

"Sergeant, stand down."

With blood in his eyes, Louie turned toward the voice. He dropped Velky to the ground. "Yes sir."

The SWAT team lieutenant said, "We'll take it from here."

Enraged, Louie walked over to help Jake gain his balance as he stumbled to his knees. Halfway up, Jake passed out on him. He caught Jake in midfall before he hit the ground.

Right away, an EMT went to work on him.

"How is he?"

"Kidneys are bruised. He took quite a beating. His jaw might be fractured. X-rays will tell us that. It's the knife wound that concerns me. Pray it didn't nick an organ. There might be some internal bleeding. I have a team standing by at the hospital."

"I'm gonna ride with him."

"Okay, then let's move out."

* * * *

Louie paced the waiting room. He should be at the scene supervising the dig, but he couldn't leave Jake. The EMTs had done what they could for Jake before they took him up to surgery. Louie wanted ten minutes alone with Velky. It would be all he needed to teach the bastard a lesson. He plopped into one of the hard, gray chairs and hung his head in his hands to hide the tears. Several officers and detectives had shown up to keep vigil with him. Someone sat down next to him but he didn't want to talk—couldn't.

"Here's some coffee. Have you eaten?" Sophia asked.

"I'm not hungry. Did you call Mia?"

"Yes, she's at the nurses' station with Officer Fisher trying to pull information from the nurse. All the nurse said was it was going to be awhile. Why don't you get some fresh air with me?"

"I'm not leaving." He draped his arm around his wife. She placed her hand on his thigh.

Mia entered, clutching a handful of tissues. "They won't tell me anything. Oh my God, if anything happens to Jake it will destroy me," Mia said, sitting down beside Sophia. Tears ran down her cheeks.

"He'll be fine, Mia. Jake's tough," Louie said. Or at least he hoped he would be.

An hour later, Louie stared out at the empty waiting room. It was only him, Mia, and Officer Fisher left as they waited for news. Sophia had gone home a half hour ago to feed the children. Most of the officers offered to donate blood—Jake couldn't use it, but it made them feel useful. The hospital gladly took them one by one into another room and drained them. Louie lifted his head at the sound of footsteps. "Captain?"

"How is he?"

"I haven't heard anything yet. How's the recovery going?"

"Slow going. The chief is supervising it until I return."

"When he gets out of surgery, I'm heading over to Judge Brenner's house and give her a piece of my mind."

"No, you're not, Louie. It won't help," Shamus said, ever the voice of reason.

"He wouldn't be here if she'd given him the damned warrant in the first place. Politics—he's lying in there because of freaking politics."

"You need to clear your head. Take a walk around the hospital."

"I don't—"

"Now."

He had no choice. Louie walked outside the emergency room exit. He wished he had something to pound on. Lost in thought, he didn't hear Burke approach him.

"I'm heading up."

Burke's arrival gave him reason to head back in. As he and Burke walked into the waiting room, a doctor in bloody scrubs, Jake's blood, walked in and pulled down his surgical mask.

"Carrington family."

"That's us." Louie answered for both him and Mia.

"Mr. Carrington's in critical condition, and the next forty-eight hours will tell which way his body is heading. He suffered a bruised kidney and his jaw's severely bruised. He's lucky it wasn't broken or fractured. It will hurt for a couple of weeks when he speaks or eats. It's the same for the bruised ribs. Only time will heal that. We'll treat the pain. The internal bleeding—we stopped it, but he'll be closely watched. His only blessing was his attacker missed his vital organs. It can be touch and go, like I said, for the first forty-eight hours. But he's in good physical condition and support from his family will help him heal."

"No concussion?"

"No. He was lucky there, too. The blow glanced off his head. It gave him quite a bump. He'll have a headache for a bit, but it didn't contuse."

"When can I see him?" Louie asked.

"He's in recovery now. It will take about two hours before they'll let anyone up there."

Louie grabbed the doctor's arm when he turned away. "We need to see him now."

The doctor stared at Louie's hand before he gently removed it. The doc glanced over at Officer Fisher. "I'll take only the two of you up." He pointed at Louie and Mia.

"The officer needs to remain with Mia for her protection," Louie said.

* * * *

After seeing Jake, he left Mia and Stella with him and headed back to the scene with the captain. Jake would be out for at least a few more hours and Mia promised to call him with any changes. Louie stood at the edge of the property as he absorbed the travesty of it. Two morgue assistants walked by with what was left of victim number three. At this point they didn't have the identities of any of the women. DNA and dental tests would put names to each of them but it took time and there was a possibility some would remain unidentified. He hoped not.

"Captain, the scene is contained," Louie said. "I'm going to head back and start the interviews with the mayor and his family. I'll wait to interview Arnie Velky until we have a body count. I'm charging him now with the murder of Nadia Carren, other charges to be levied in the future."

"With Jake down, I'm going to assist in the interviews."

"I can—"

"Louie, I'm your partner on this case until further notice. Clear?"

"Yes. Let's head in."

* * * *

Back at the station Louie took a few minutes to collect himself before he entered the chief's office. Captain McGuire felt it was best to interview the mayor and his family there, so as not to traumatize them further. He bit back a curse. Not only would McGuire be there with Velky's family but the chief and commissioner were also in the room and seated.

"Your Honor, Chief, Commissioner," Louie looked at each one. "Mayor, I'll need to go through what happened. The where, the why, and when Arnie showed up. If at any time you're uncomfortable with this many people in the room, please tell me, Mayor, and we'll reduce the numbers."

The chief raised his eyebrows but otherwise no one made a gesture or comment.

"I'm going to ask your mother and wife to leave the room while we talk to you. Then I'll talk to each of them alone." When John Velky nodded, his wife and mother got up and left the room.

"He was going to kill us all, even the children," John said, his voice hitching.

"Your Honor, did you have any knowledge Arnie killed those women?"

"No, how could I? If this is a ploy to ruin me, it won't work."

"John," Louie switched to his first name, dropped rank. "This has to do with nine women who were brutalized and killed, not politics. What goes on in here will become part of the record, but it won't be released to the press. Understood?" He didn't give a shit who was in the room, the gloves were off.

"Your brother must have shown signs growing up. Once this investigation was underway you had to have your suspicions."

"I didn't. Not at first. I asked him last week at Sunday dinner if he had anything to do with it. He was too cocky and belligerent with me and my mother. Arnie has always been a little off. My father used to protect him, explain away his behavior. It's the reason my parents fought all the time. God, he was always in trouble in school. I knew something was up when most of the neighbors moved away without notice."

"How long ago was that, Mayor?"

"I'm not sure, probably three years ago. I can't believe he hated me this much. If I had known I would've tried to fix it. Right from the start my wife couldn't stand to be alone with Arnie. I thought she was overreacting. All she'd say was he gave her the creeps. When Ciara left him at the altar he snapped. He hasn't been the same since."

"Why did she leave him?"

"Maybe because he's nuts, a killer—hell, who knows? She never told him or left a note on the reason why."

"How'd he get you all together?"

"My mother visits the kids on the same day every week. Arnie's aware of that. He also knew when we'd all be home because I don't schedule any meetings when my mom's with us. We have dinner together before my mother goes home and on Sundays at my mother's place. Arnie only shows up for the Sunday meals and rarely stays past an hour. When he showed up here for dinner it surprised us. Once we were seated at the table he pulled out his gun and knife. He said before we died we had to understand why. Arnie was in the middle of his speech when Jake showed up. You saw the rest of it."

Louie took him through the fight and what put Jake into action. Then he took both the Mrs. Velkys through their stories. With little variation, they matched. He sent the family down to homicide to pick up their children. Officer Myers had had them in Jake's office since they were rescued.

He closed the door after they left. Louie scanned the room. No one spoke. He cleared his throat. "I'm going to head back to the hospital."

"Louie, we need to start talking to Velky," Commissioner Blake said.

"With all due respect, Commissioner, I've charged him for Nadia Carren's murder. I'll charge him on the others once we have a full body count. It will take a couple of days to put it all together."

"Sergeant, you're stalling, why?" Blake asked.

"I'm not. But if I was, it would be so my partner, Jake, can be in the room when we interview Arnie. Velky seems to think he has a connection with him. We'll get more from him if Jake interviews him."

"Why not have Jake do it from his hospital bed?" Blake asked.

Louie coughed into his hand to hide his smile. "That's mostly a television thing, Commissioner. We only interview there in extreme circumstances. If we did make an exception and do it there, it would give Velky power over the situation, and immense pleasure. It would also render Jake ineffective."

"Will the lieutenant be up to it?" Blake asked.

"I'd want the same thing, if it were me. Jake's one stubborn bastard. Give him two days and he'll be here. I'm going back to the hospital. If Jake feels he'll be ready, then he will be. Do any of you have any objections?"

"Louie, I—"

"Commissioner, as Louie stated, we don't have all the evidence yet. It would be prudent to collect as much as possible before we question the suspect," McGuire said.

Louie didn't wait for the commissioner to answer. He took off and headed back to the hospital.

* * * *

"Hey."

"I'll give you two a minute," Mia said. Before she left the room, she threw Louie a warning look over her shoulder. Like he'd upset Jake. *For Pete's sake. Women.*

"Hey yourself. What hit me?" Jake voice was weak and low.

"A gun. Arnie pistol-whipped you," Louie said, as he took Jake's hand, squeezed it, then dropped it.

"Damn, it hurts. Who'd have thought the little prick had it in him?"

"The small wiry ones seem to have an abundance of hidden strength. We're not questioning Arnie until we're sure of the body count."

"I'll be out of here in forty-eight hours. We'll question him together. In fact, I'm fine to go with you now." Jake tried sitting up. The stubborn Irishman winced in pain but kept trying until he fell back against the pillow.

"You'll be in on the interview, Jake, but you have to give yourself a couple of days. You're not leaving here until the doctor gives the okay."

"Who died and left you boss?"

"You," Louie said quietly, resting his hand again over Jake's. "Listen, it was touch and go from the scene to here. You're alive because you had great EMTs. If you try to leave this room I'll tell the officer on the door to handcuff you to the bed."

"Oh really." They stared each other down. "I'm good with that," Jake said after a couple of seconds and closed his eyes.

Satisfied Jake was going to make it, Louie left him in Mia's hands. At the station he prepared his questions, reviewed the evidence file and took a deep breath. Louie made notes and would drop off a copy with Jake before he went home and hit the sack. If he did his job right maybe they'd save the state some money and Velky would forgo a trial. *And yes, Louie, there really is a Santa Claus.*

* * * *

It took three days before the doctor released Jake. Black and blue from head to toe, he eased into his clothes with Mia's help.

"Jake, you're not going into the station. The doctor said to give it at least a week."

"Mia, I love you, but don't mother me." He knew he sounded cranky, even ungrateful, and decided to try another tactic. "In order to heal I need to close this case. Louie and I worked hard to solve this one. It needs to be us who close it."

She slipped his T-shirt over his head, gently took hold of his arms to put them in the sleeves. Jake sucked in a breath. Movement of his arms sent his stomach and ribs into spasms of pain.

"Take a pain pill."

"I can't. I need a clear head when we talk to Arnie."

"I don't see how it can be clear when you're suffering."

"I'll use the pain to my advantage."

"Men are idiots," Mia said as she bent over to pick up his boots.

He tugged on her shirt, overbalancing her into him, and regretted the move. He nibbled on her bottom lip. "I love you, too."

Jake walked into the bullpen with his arms around Mia for support. His detectives greeted them with catcalls and cheers. Kraus came over and raised a hand to slap him on the back. "You do that, Gunner, and I'll shoot you where you stand," Jake said through gritted teeth. His belly on fire, as if someone had stuck a hot poker in it, it took all his concentration to walk, never mind deal with a well-meaning tap.

Kraus dropped his hand to his side. Mia tightened her grip on his elbow. He whispered in her ear, "I can make it to my office from here."

She didn't let go.

"Mia?"

"Jake." She fluttered her eyelashes.

He threw her a lopsided grin. "Okay, you win this time."

He retrieved his voice messages as Mia stepped out of his office. The first started playing and stopped him in his tracks.

Chapter 30

"Lieutenant Carrington, my name is Ciara Black. I saw the news this morning and wanted to touch base with you. I was Edward Velky's fiancée. I'm embarrassed to say I left him at the altar. I should have left him sooner, but I was a coward. He had started doing little things which scared me. It opened my eyes. I'm…I don't want to go into them with you over the phone. I wanted to tell you I saw the news and will talk to you if you want. I've hidden for five years, fearing for my life because of him. He's stalked my parents as a way to try and locate me. Here's my cell. It's a burner. I wish I'd made the connection before this. Maybe those women wouldn't have had to die because of me."

Jake stared at his phone. He called her back. Ciara gave him a boatload of information to use against Arnie. He took a few minutes to line up his thoughts. One man had messed up many lives. Armed with information, lab reports, and Ciara's phone call, he went to Louie's desk to update him before they headed to the interview room.

It surprised him to find the mayor sitting with Arnie. Silently, he questioned John Velky's choice.

"No matter what else, Jake, he's my brother."

Arnie Velky held out his hands in a helpless gesture at his brother's comment.

During the interview, Velky toyed with them, his lawyer, and his brother until he was tired of playing. He fired his lawyer and dismissed his brother after he got his digs in.

"Arnie, you willfully fired your attorney. You understand this interview will continue and anything you say can and will be used against you in a court of law?

"Yes."

Then he started talking.

Nadia was the ninth victim. Jake scribbled each name as Arnie spoke in a monotone voice. In time, he'd be familiar with each one of victims, their likes and dislikes and the potential lives they could've had and enjoyed. Nine women in the prime of their lives, who wouldn't see their next birthday, or celebrate a wedding, childbirth, or anything else life had to offer. And this bastard in front of him still thought he had the right to do what he'd done. Velky explained all this to him as if he were talking to a child who needed clarity. With each description, Arnie's chest puffed out with pride, much to Jake's disgust.

"It took a while, Jake, before I was able to leave the bodies clean. I studied the masters, then devised my own method." It irked Jake how easily his name fell from Arnie's lips.

"You call them masters, Arnie, but each one was caught and sentenced to death. A master wouldn't have been caught."

It was a small pleasure to goad him. Jake took his fun where he found it. Velky started tapping his fingers on the table, and his voice took on a steel edge.

"If you want to hear the whole thing, I suggest you back off."

Jake noted it was between Velky and himself—Arnie all but ignored Louie.

"See, something snapped in me on my wedding day. Standing all alone at the altar, except for the humiliation, the pain, and the questions—I understood right then and there if she wasn't dead, I'd kill her."

"But you didn't, Arnie. You killed innocent women, and ruined their lives and their families' lives."

He waved a hand in dismissal. "What does it matter? Mine was ruined and no one cared. I saved those poor schmucks the pain I went through. Because once you marry them they become shrews."

"I see you have a high opinion of women. Let's discuss Ciara Black specifically." Velky jerked in his seat and set his leg irons rattling. "You see, I had a discussion with her before I came in to speak with you."

"You're a liar. I've searched five years for her..." He stared up at the ceiling then back at Jake. A smirk played at the corner of his lips. "Well played."

Jake watched Arnie gather his composure. He had to tuck the jabbing pain in his stomach out of his head before he continued. His breath backed up in his throat. When it settled down, he continued. "Five years, you're kidding? I found her in a day. Amateur." Jake taunted Velky, a tactic to keep him off balance.

"You did not!" Arnie pushed up from the chair but was yanked back by the chains on his legs. A single tear slid out of his right eye.

"I did. And she hates you as much as you hate her, maybe even more."

"You're a liar. What's she been doing all this time?"

"It's none of your business. She knew you'd come after her. She said it was child's play to avoid you. Only once in five years did you even come close."

"Arizona."

Jake sat back and swung his arm over the chair next to him and instantly regretted the move. "You're lucky nobody caught you sooner. She stopped in every police station and supplied them with your picture. She never gave her name."

"You're jerking my strings. There weren't any warrants out for me."

"She told them it was domestic abuse. A police department would be crazy to ignore it if a suspect came into their sights."

"You seem to be enjoying yourself. What if I told you your woman's still in trouble and there's no way to stop what will happen next? I've got the name of the guy jerking her around."

An empty threat, but it still fisted his heart and squeezed off his air supply. "You've got to do better than that."

It always amazed Jake how he could have pity for the nuts, though he'd never give them a pass, no matter what reason led them there. Somewhere in a psycho's life, something had happened and twisted them up. In Arnie's case, he claimed it was his mother. Jake brought up the incident with the girl from his childhood. The one he stalked—the teachers he'd terrorized. Each incident Jake presented, Arnie brushed them away as nothing.

"Don't you see, they all brought it on themselves, Jake? Each one went out of their way to make my life miserable. I couldn't fight back against my mother or brother, but I damn well wasn't going to take it from a stranger. And you, I loved how you and my brother fought. He hates you."

Jake had a rebuttal for each of his answers, though he didn't bother. He understood it would land on deaf ears. No matter, he'd make sure Edward Arnold Velky stayed in jail for the rest of his natural life, and his brother would never hold office in this town again.

The interview lasted eight hours, with breaks every couple of hours for Jake's sake. When he'd gotten all he was going to get from Arnie, Jake signaled for the officer to take him back to his cell. Exhausted, he sat in the interview room with Louie long after the officer led Arnie away.

"Another one off the streets," Louie said and started for the door.

"Yeah, hopefully the next one won't be worse."

"Now there's a wish." Louie shrugged. "How're you doing?"

"I'm in pain. I'll head home and take a pill to quiet it."

Jake's phone buzzed a missed call. He recognized Dave Guerrera's number and hit redial. Maybe this was the week for closure. He certainly hoped for Mia's sake it was.

"Speak to me, Dave."

"We have a fingerprint and a match from your CSI team."

Why the hell didn't they call me sooner?

"They sent me the info because it's my case, Jake."

"You read minds now?"

"No, but I heard your message loud and clear. I want to discuss how we're going to handle this."

* * * *

Damn! He'd get no rest tonight. Louie cut one of the pills in half for him to take the edge off. He ignored the doctor's orders and drove himself home. On the way Jake played out how he'd tell Mia. He knew she'd suffer once she learned the who and why she'd been targeted. He wanted five minutes alone with the guy. It was all he'd need to tune him up for what he'd put Mia through all these months. With his body in such poor shape he wouldn't get the chance. The criminal had all the rights. Before any evidence was presented the media portrayed the cops as the bad guys. And all because of a few cops who couldn't handle stress or thought they could get away with anything. It made a good cop's job more difficult. A headache pounded away at his frontal lobe as his ribs drilled knives into his sides with each movement. Jake rubbed his side with his left hand while steering with his right, sucking in a breath every time he moved the wrong way. He had ignored Louie's offer and drove himself home, regretting the decision as he hit each bump or pothole.

Flipping on his right-turn signal, he turned onto his street and pulled into his garage. He sat for few minutes, still playing with Dave's idea. Did Mia need to face down her stalker? Though it killed him, he knew she had to make the decision, not him. Resigned, he unfolded himself out of the car. Who knew climbing four little steps could be such a chore? He inhaled, exhaled, before he stepped into his foyer. The television was on a cooking show, but neither Mia nor Stella was in the room watching it. Weird. Brigh hadn't come running to greet him. He unlatched his holster with care and opened the closet door in the foyer and placed his gun in the safe. A coarse breath caught in his throat as his ribs throbbed when he reached up to open his safe. The limited range of motion had him proceeding with caution. Jake stuck his guns inside, twirled the dial to lock it as the fragrance of something wonderful filled his head and the hunger hit. It had been days since he had an appetite. He'd been involved in his own thoughts when he came into the house and the aroma hadn't filled his senses.

"Something smells good, what is it?" he asked, walking into the kitchen. Mia pointed to the television. "That."

"And what is that?" He leaned in and kissed her.

"Sweet and sour salmon, with pineapple chutney on the side, served with dirty rice."

With tongue in cheek, he said, "I'm living the dream. A man could get used to coming home to a hot meal and two beautiful women cooking for him each night after work." Mia gave him a light tap on his shoulder. He held in the grunt.

"Don't get used to it, buddy."

Shaky on his feet, sweat trickled down his brow as he lowered himself into the kitchen chair and watched Stella's and Mia's choreographed efforts. Mia poured him three fingers of Jameson, then thought twice about it.

"Did you take a painkiller?"

"Only half of one, but I don't want the drink." Mia took the glass away. At the sink, before she poured out its contents, she took a long sip.

Stella stirred the rice. Somehow in all this mess, the women had become friends. Jake figured they both had good taste.

"Dave called again. I spoke with him. He has a fingerprint from the alarm inside your front door. There was a match." He eyed Mia as she processed the information.

"Are you going to tell me who it is?" She tapped the wooden spoon in her hand against the palm of her other hand. *Don't kill the messenger,* he thought.

"Yes, but first Dave wants to give you a chance to face down the suspect. Do you want to?"

"Can I punch him?" Mia sat down beside him, laid the spoon down. He took her hand in his and raised it to his lips.

The corner of his mouth tugged up. *That's my girl,* he thought. "No, it's not allowed."

"Who was it, Jake?"

He told her. Mia's jaw dropped. She tightened her grip on his hand. Pain shot up his arm, resounding throughout his body. For the most part he hid his reaction and worked his hand loose.

"Why?"

Chapter 31

Mia had insisted on driving. On the drive to her condo she debated if she was doing the right thing. Jake had refused to advise her. The shock had worn off and in its place anger had taken hold.

"Why won't you give your opinion?"

"It's for you to decide."

"Come on, Jake. I'm serious."

"So am I. If this gives you closure, then yes. If not, you have to decide what will."

"Hmm."

"There's Dave's car. Are you all set?"

"Yes, as set as I'll ever be. Are you going to be okay? You're pale," Mia said.

"Once this is over, I'm going to go home and sleep for a week. Let's go in and get it done."

Dave opened the front door and let them in. Mia scanned the number of police officers in the small space. In the living room, off to the left side of the big picture window, stood two men. She spotted another down the hallway, gazing out the slider into her backyard.

"That's a lot of officers to take down one person."

"It's a precaution. I want you safe," Jake said.

Mia walked to the kitchen, picked up the wall phone, and pressed in the number she knew by heart. It was a small town. After this afternoon, when she took down a well-respected resident, how would she, an outsider and a New Yorker to boot, be received? *Ah, maybe it was time for a change.*

Her hand trembled as she hung up the receiver. "It's all set. They'll be here in ten minutes."

"You don't have to be here for this," Jake said, taking her in his arms. She wrapped her arms around his waist and held tight.

"I need to be." His hands soothed as he rubbed them up and down her back. She never wanted him to let go. She lifted her eyes to his and searched his face. "What?"

"I want to protect you, Mia, which irks you. Dave will take them right in when they arrive, you won't have to do anything."

"You're infuriating. When I want you to interfere you don't," she said with a thin-lipped smile.

"That's because I love you." Laughter shone in his eyes, but she was glad he was smart enough not to laugh aloud.

Ten minutes seemed like ten hours as she waited to face her stalker. The bell chimed throughout the house. "Showtime," she said, her voice pitched a bit too high, as she walked to the door and pulled it open.

"Oh, Mia, I was afraid for you after I heard what happened. Are you okay?" Piper rushed over the threshold and hugged her. "I picked up my husband like you asked. What's going on?"

Mia showed them into her living room. "Do you want something to drink?"

"No," Daryl and Piper said in unison. Daryl hadn't taken his eyes off Mia since she opened the door but jerked when he caught sight of the men in the room.

"Piper, I want to start by saying I'm sorry, truly sorry."

"For what?"

Mia ignored her and turned to Daryl. "The police recovered a fingerprint inside my alarm box." She watched her words land.

"There's no way they found anything," Daryl declared.

He'd practically admitted it. It was time to tighten the noose. "Technology is a grand thing, Daryl. They were able to match the prints to the military database." She stared him down. "Your prints were found on the box."

"No way, I wore gl—" he stopped midsentence, stared her down.

She ignored him, turned toward Piper. "I'm sorry for this, Piper. The prints belong to Daryl. He's the one who's been leaving me dead animals. He's also the one who broke into my home and scared me half to death this week." Turning back to Daryl, she asked, "You broke a priceless vase. Why?"

"You're nuts. That's what you are. Don't you see, Piper, she heard we're getting counseling. She doesn't want to see us together. What kind of friend is that?"

"You're wrong, Daryl. I was happy when Piper told me you were trying to work it out. She's a lot more forgiving than I'd ever be. Once again you've ruined it."

"You bitch. You'll not see another day." He jumped off the couch and grabbed Mia by the neck. Piper let out a bloodcurdling scream as she jumped on Daryl's back and tried to pull him off Mia.

A red rage filled Jake as he ran into the room with Dave and the other officers. His pain pushed to the background, he got to Mia first. He pulled Daryl off her then spun him around and planted his fist, twice, in the man's face. Before Daryl fell back, Jake pulled him forward and pushed his face toward Mia. She wound up her arm, tightened her fist, locked her thumb over her fingers and threw her weight into the punch as she smashed her fist into Daryl's nose. Jake turned him around and planted another in Daryl's stomach.

"Jake," Dave said as he stepped between them and grabbed Jake's fist before he planted another. "Take care of Mia."

His breath came in short bursts as the pain shot through his body, the rage clearing as he turned toward Mia. "Are you okay?"

"It burns. Did he leave marks?" she said, her voice hoarse from lack of air. "You've opened your wound." She pointed at the blood on his shirt.

"Yes, but they'll fade. Did you get your closure?"

"Yes and no." She turned toward Piper, who sat on the couch with her head in her hands. Sobs racked her body. "Piper?" Mia sat beside her.

"Stay away from me. I never realized just how much you hated him. But to set him up is low. He's right. You're a bitch. I only have one question. Why?"

Piper's words landed as if concrete blocks smacked her on the side of the head. A wave of nausea stuck in her throat. Mia couldn't breathe. Mia wrapped her arms around Piper as she hugged her by way of an apology. "I'm sorry, Piper. I hope someday you come to terms with what he did."

She pushed out of Mia's arms and stood. "Don't ever come near me or my family again. Do you understand?"

Overwhelming pain gripped her heart. Her best friend in Connecticut had cut her loose. "More than you'll ever understand, Piper. I suggest you get some counseling."

"Screw you."

Shocked, Mia stared after her as Piper rushed from the room.

* * * *

It took a while, but Mia answered Dave's questions. She made her statement in the living room while Jake made his in the kitchen. After giving his statement Dave had an EMT check out Jake and rebandage his wound. Dave had put Daryl in his car, handcuffed, and Piper in a cruiser until he could take her statement. Mia wondered what Piper would say. It seemed like an open-and-shut case to her, but Jake warned her there was no such thing once lawyers got involved. Jake spoke quietly with Dave by the front door. Her eyes never left his as he finished up with Dave and walked toward her.

Jake took a strand of her hair in his hands—a simple gesture. It calmed her stomach and filled her heart. "Do you want to stay here tonight or at my place?"

"I don't think I'll ever want to stay here again, Jake."

"Let's give it a few days and then talk about it. Are you hungry?"

"I could eat. You choose the restaurant because there aren't two beautiful women who will cook for you tonight. You're stuck with only one."

"I like being stuck." He took her chin in his hand, bent down and gently bit her lower lip. "Let's go home."

All the Dirty Secrets

Don't miss the next exciting Jake Carrington thriller by Marian Lanouette!

Coming soon from Lyrical Underground,
an imprint of Kensington Publishing Corp.

Keep reading to enjoy a preview excerpt . . .

ALL THE DIRTY SECRETS

A Jake Carrington Thriller
by
Marian Lanouette

Chapter 1

Shouldn't marriage come with an expiration date? Darcy wondered, twisting her wedding band as she stood in front of the full-length mirror in her lacy lingerie, alone and afraid to emerge from the dressing room.

"Mrs. McGuire, are you ready?" photographer Melinda Mastrianni asked from the other side of the door.

"Almost," Darcy said.

What am I doing here? This was a stupid idea. She was not an indecisive person. As CEO of Calindar Industries she implemented decisions daily that made or broke companies. But this was new to her.

The evil mirror magnified every one of her flaws as she stood under the harsh fluorescent lights. *Would Shamus only see the imperfections? It's not like we don't have enough on our plates—he the department, me the business. With the kids off at college, it seems like we have nothing to talk about anymore. I should've booked the usual anniversary trip instead of doing this. My lord, I'm practically nude.*

A gentle knock at the door had her chest tightening as she twisted away from the mirror. "Yes?"

"It's all right if you've changed your mind," Melinda said through the door.

"No, I'm—give me a minute, please." She was what she was—a fifty-one-year-old woman with three grown children in college. What was she thinking when she scheduled this? She fluffed her brunette bob, wet her lips, closed her eyes, and inhaled deeply to calm her nerves as she hoped for the best.

Callie Blake's photos were gorgeous. She said she had gotten fabulous results with them. Her husband Todd had gone gaga over them. *What am I afraid of? Rejection? Ridicule? What happened to the young, carefree couple who couldn't keep their hands off each other? Was hunting for the spark again too much to ask after twenty-six years of marriage?*

Darcy shoved the foreboding thoughts to the back of her mind, squared her shoulders, and marched out of the room in her red stiletto heels, red lace bustier, and black fishnet stockings.

"I'm ready, Melinda."

"Let's start with you on the chaise longue."

She walked to the green velvet seat and sat down, not sure what to do next. "Darcy, think *alluring*. These are to entice your husband. Now, stretch out on your right side, bend your left leg over your knee and draw it up halfway. Great. Lean further back into the seat, place your right arm against the back of the cushion and drop your head into your hand." Melinda walked over to her, adjusted her position. "You're doing good, think *movie star glamour*. Here, relax your arm and let me pose it."

Darcy felt foolish. What harm could it do? An innocuous picture, it was nothing more. A ludicrous thought struck. What would the board members of her company think of these racy shots of their CEO? Like they'd ever see them—no, these were for Shamus's eyes only.

"I'm going to take a few shots to adjust the lighting to your skin tone. Relax, these won't count."

She let her mind wander to Shamus. His last case held his full attention. Even when he was home, he was absent. She had started to ask if she'd be better off with or without him. Was she using the time commitment or the children to hold it together? No, she loved Shamus. How he reacted to these photos would give her the answer she needed. Did he love her or not? Were they together because of habit or love?

"I'm sorry, I didn't hear you," Darcy said.

"The lighting is perfect, so let's begin. Forget I'm even in the room. You're a beautiful woman. These pictures will capture all the glory of Darcy."

Melinda moved around the room as she snapped away. She'd climb up on a ladder and shoot downward, then she'd lie on the floor and shoot upward. The session took an hour and a half. Melinda had her at ease after the first ten minutes. She started to pose without being told. Melinda offered encouragement throughout the session. By the end of the shoot, Darcy felt glamorous. When Melinda put down her camera, Darcy picked up the robe draped over the chair and put it on.

"Oh, these are wonderful. I'm sure you're going to love them. And remember, this is digital photography. It gives me the ability to enhance as much or as little as you want," Melinda said.

Darcy watched Melinda work over her shoulder as she uploaded the photos from the shoot. The more she stared into the screen, the sadder she got. She'd aged over the years; though she lost the weight, childbirth did a number on her body. She still had time to book the trip and burn the photos.

"Darcy, these are the raw pictures. Let me show you how this works."

After a few minutes, she was transformed from old to glamorous with Melinda's magic wand. Would she show Callie the pictures or keep them private? Callie had convinced her they would liven up her marriage. It amazed her when she learned she and Callie were both in the same boat. Inattentive husbands must be the curse of longevity. After she picked out the photos she wanted printed, she stood and headed back to the dressing room.

"Darcy, before you get dressed, I have a male model here if you want to pose with him. I won't show his face, but it might add some spice to add him to the shoot."

A man in his late thirties walked out from the second dressing room. His black hair was slicked back, his muscles bulged under the short-sleeve robe he wore. A rush of adrenaline brought back Darcy's apprehension. She didn't sign up for this. After years of assessing people and their motives, she had a sense something was off. This guy exuded pervert vibes.

"No, I'm not interested." As she turned away, Melinda laid a hand on her arm.

"No problem. I thought you wanted spicy shots for your husband. Nothing makes a man hotter than another man desiring his woman," Melinda said.

* * * *

Why today of all days? Callie turned her back to the door as she wiped her eyes with the saturated tissue, the letter clutched in her manicured hand. She'd been staring at it for hours, waiting for it to burst into flames. In seconds she'd have to confess her foolish actions to her husband. She rested her elbows on the vanity and dropped her head into her hands. *What am I going to do? Todd's going to kill me when I show him this*. As if on cue, Todd walked into their well-appointed blue-and-gold bedroom.

"I'm sorry I'm late. I'll jump right into the shower and then we'll head out," Todd said, tugging his shirt from his pants.

"It's not a problem. We have plenty of time," she said, not able to meet his eyes. It must have been something in her voice. The man knew her too well. At the bathroom door Todd stopped, turned, then backtracked to the vanity.

"What's wrong?" he asked, lifting her chin up to search her tearful eyes.

"Oh, Todd." She burst into tears, her mascara running down her face. She didn't care about the ball or anything else at this point.

"What?"

She turned from the mirror, stood, and handed him the letter along with the pictures. She gripped her left arm at the elbow as she waited for the yelling and screaming to start.

He dropped down on their king-size bed and read the letter, then viewed the disgusting pictures. Todd gaped at her with his *what have you done now* look.

"These are exactly like the ones you gave me except for the man in them. Who is he?"

"They are, but I never posed in a bedroom, Todd, you have to believe me. Someone doctored those." She pointed to the photos in his hand. "It has to be the photographer."

"I'll take care of the situation, but I need time to think it through. Who is he?"

"I don't know, but you can bet I'm going to confront the photographer tonight and ask her what she thought she'd accomplish with them."

"No, you won't. I'll handle this. You better finishing dressing while I shower," Todd said.

She'd worked so hard on the charity ball and auction. It had been billed as the social event of the year. Before this afternoon, all her energies had been focused on the event. It had consumed her. Now…she just wanted to hide her head in the sand.

The vein at Todd's left temple throbbed, a sign he was holding back his temper. After the door closed, she heard music scream through it. Callie walked up, put her ear to the door, and listened. The shower water along with the music created a strange cacophony. Then it came—what she had been waiting for.

"Of all the stupid, ridiculous things she could've done, why this?" Todd said, his words muffled but distinguishable through the thin door.

Pounding on the shower wall followed his words. Tears streamed from her eyes. Her husband thought her stupid. It was innocent. A special gift was all she had wanted to give him. *It's not like we're rich. Why me? What will the blackmailer gain by targeting me? He had to know he'd have the whole police force after him with this move.*

Two children in college, a mortgage, and contributions into the pension plans with a single salary hadn't given them the opportunity to invest big. Tonight they'd have to act normal, as if life was great.

And of all the degrading things in life, she now had to open up their private life to Shamus, so he could investigate the crime. Callie hoped

Shamus would be able to keep the press at bay, stifle her husband's embarrassment, and save his career. She understood that somehow, this was going to spiral downhill.

* * * *

In the mirror Jake watched Mia slip into her blue gown as he tied his bow tie. How she ever conned him into going to this thing tonight baffled him. It was his wish to leave today for Vermont; now they'd need to get an early start tomorrow to enjoy the three days at the mountain. He spun back to the closet, pulled the jacket off the hanger, and eased into it. Jake ran his fingers over the rich fabric. Mia had bought the suit for him. Its slim fit was comfortable, but as he adjusted the waistband, his stomach where he'd been stabbed reminded him he wasn't fully healed. He'd done too much today, and the day wasn't over.

"Can you zip me up?"

"I'd rather be zipping it down and off," Jake said.

"Keep that thought for later." She turned her head over her shoulder. "It'll be hard to keep my hands off such a dashing figure of a man."

"It reminds me of James Bond." He shot his cuffs.

"Exactly, handsome and elegant."

Jake ran his finger over her bare shoulders and traced the heart-shaped neckline of the dress over the tops of her breasts. The corner of her mouth lifted, and her eyes twinkled as the royal-blue gown emphasized the expressive ocean blue of her irises. He ran his hand through her silky black hair. She swatted it away.

"You'll muss it, stop," Mia said, stepping back. He loved how the gown hugged her hips and flared at the bottom. "It's time to head out. Wait, let me adjust your tie, it's crooked. Lord, I love the look of a man in a tux. Who knew you could clean up so nicely?" she teased as she patted his cheek.

He stood patiently while she fussed. When she finished he brought her hand to his lips. "Thanks for sticking with me these last few weeks. I know I haven't been the best patient."

"Ah, an understatement, and you're welcome."

A smart man, he bit back his quip and held up her coat.

* * * *

Edwina Dunstan took her time. She wasn't in a hurry to see Linden. He'd started to bore her, but he had a purpose. She needed him in order to bring down her lying, cheating husband once and for all. She was tempted to bring Linden to tonight's charity ball instead of Cedric, but even for her it would be pushing the envelope.

As she entered the hotel lobby Edwina scanned the place for a familiar face. She didn't care if she was caught in the act. The prenup didn't damage her in anyway, only Cedric, who'd leave the marriage with only the clothes on his back. Jimmy Nelson, the private detective she'd hired last year, had plenty of pictures and hotel receipts; he'd also obtained a copy of the lease on Cedric's mistress's apartment to prove his infidelity. And copies of the checks he'd used to pay for her apartment each month.

She couldn't wait to confront Cedric with them when she threw him out on his ass. The next person she had to bring on board before she could move forward was her father. She not only wanted her husband out of the house, she wanted him out of the bank her family owned. Stripped bare; let's see what woman would want him then?

Linden had texted her he was in room 412 waiting for her. With a gentle knock she waited for him to open the door. He answered, wearing jeans and a T-shirt. Normally they met during the week around lunchtime. He'd wear well-cut suits, the traditional uniform for his banking job. It was a yummy change, but in the standard way—not too pretty—not too anything. His dark brown hair and heavy brows in the same color framed a square face and a nose that had been broken—playing hockey, he'd said. As she studied him, she wondered why she'd never noticed his averageness before. Even his name, Linden Smith, didn't make an impression.

"I've waited all day for this," Linden said, as he took her in his arms.

"Me too, but I don't have a lot of time. I need to get to the hairdresser at two thirty."

"Why didn't you push it out?"

"Don't whine, it's unbecoming. We have two hours together. Let's not waste them," she said, as she started to unbutton her blouse. He pushed her hands away to do it.

Thirty minutes later, she bit the inside of her mouth to keep from laughing. They hadn't needed the two hours; the man finished well under the time constraints. Sex had become routine with Linden, the excitement gone. If she hadn't needed him, she would have moved on.

It's now or never, she thought.

"Do you have access to all the accounts in the bank?" Edwina asked, twirling a clump of his chest hair around her finger as she snuggled closer to him.

"Yes, why?"

"I need you to check if Cedric opened an account at your bank in his name or in the name of Rosie Riverton."

"I can't give you that information, honey."

"You want us to be together, don't you?" she asked, tilting her head up to meet his eyes, her meaning clear.

"I do, but if it got out I passed off confidential information, my career would be ruined. I'd never be able to work in banking again."

She rolled away from him, the sheet firmly in her hand as she held it to her chest. "No problem, I have other ways of doing it."

"Come back, Edy. Please understand you're asking me to compromise my principles."

"Oh, but your principles let you screw another man's wife," she said as she scooped up her clothes on her way to the bathroom. Over her shoulder she said, "You're exactly like him. Why didn't I see that before?"

He jumped from the bed, took her gently by the shoulders. "It's different."

"No, it's not. It tells me women are not important to you, only your career is. It also tells me you have selective ethics."

She'd tempered her words with just enough heat. *That ought to make him decide what's important.* She'd give him a couple of days. One way or another he'd do her bidding. She slammed the door in his face. A few minutes later, dressed, her purse slung over her shoulder, her coat draped over her arm, she walked out of the room without a good-bye.

* * * *

Todd stepped from the bathroom, a towel wrapped around his waist, his lips pursed. Callie tracked his movements as he reached into the closet for his tux, stopped, and rubbed his chin.

"I love you, Callie, you know that, but I can't believe you posed for those pictures without running it by me first," said Todd.

"I thought I'd surprise you." Callie wiped her nose with the tissue. "I never thought… What are we going to do?"

"Nothing. I'll take care of it. You can't pay a blackmailer. If you do, it will never end." Todd shrugged into his jacket. "Are you having an affair?"

"Oh my God, Todd, I'd never cheat on you. I only posed to spice up our marriage."

"I didn't know we needed it," he said, his brows knitted together. This was all her fault.

Callie wrung her hands. "You've been so busy at work, I just thought…" Would he be forced to retire if the pictures went public? The calm he showed on the outside was a facade, she understood. After twenty-seven years of marriage, she knew when his temper reached the boiling point, it was smart to move out of its range.

When Todd opened his arms, she fell into them. "If you don't fix your face, your guests will be questioning you all night. Is that what you want?"

"No."

"Don't tell anyone about the letter. I need to think about it first, before I approach Shamus, understand?"

"Yes," she said, her shoulders slumped, the boning in her red backless dress digging into her ribs as it cut off her breath. She wanted to ask Darcy for advice. Her stomach rocked back and forth. *I probably should tell Todd I already went to the bank today and withdrew the money.*

"Callie, even with the tears you're stunning." He took her chin in his hand and kissed her. It gave her hope things might work out.

* * * *

"Are you sure this gown is right for tonight?" Sophia Romanelli asked Louie for the fifteenth time.

"I told you, you're perfect," he said. What was it with women? Sophia should be confident. She'd be the prettiest woman in the room.

"At least we're sitting with Jake and Mia."

"*Amante*, relax. There's nothing to worry about unless you make us late," Louie said, using his Italian pet name for her to try to calm her down.

"Louie, we're sitting with the commissioner and his wife, as well as your captain and his wife. Darcy McGuire is head of an international company. What do I have in common with these people? I don't want to sound ignorant."

"How could you? I'm telling you, they're normal people. You're going to have a blast. It's not as if it's your first time socializing with them."

Sophia had been carrying on for over an hour. Louie was ready to give up. Every time there was a function with the brass, her nerves took over.

"Let's get a move on it, the babysitter's already downstairs."

He went down to the living room to give the babysitter her instructions. Sophia had hired the girl next door to sit because she didn't want their teenage son, LJ, to cancel his date. It would be the neighbor's first time sitting for them. He crossed his fingers there'd be no problems.

All the Deadly Lies

Homicide detective Jake Carrington takes murder personally . . .

The victim was bludgeoned, stripped, and left for dead. Shanna Wagner deserves justice—and there's no better cop than Lieutenant Jake Carrington to find her killer. The brutality of the crime reminds Jake of his sister's murder seventeen years ago, and the remorseless man responsible, now up for parole.

Then another woman is killed—and Jake goes dangerously close to the edge. He'll have to face his personal demons and focus his formidable skills if he hopes to stop a vicious murderer from striking again—and hold on to his career, and his life . . .

All the Hidden Sins

When it comes to crime, homicide detective Jake Carrington plays for high stakes . . .

Assigned a missing persons case, Lieutenant Jake Carrington investigates a local Mob boss. The trail goes cold, but the Mafioso isn't taking any chances, and soon the heat turns up from another quarter. Turns out there's more than one dangerous suspect . . .

Kyra Russell is drop-dead gorgeous and Jake is only human. But despite their mutual attraction, Jake's suspicion deepens when he learns about her gambling problem—an addiction that cost her both husband and son. Even more disturbing is Kyra's day job. She runs a crematorium—and it's tied to the Mob. Now Jake will have to navigate a firestorm of treachery to get to the truth . . .

Previously published as *Burn in Hell*

Acknowledgments

Without editors no book would be fit for readers.
I'd like to thank my wonderful editors, Michaela Hamilton
and Shannon Plackis from Kensington.

About the Author

Photo by Brenda Piel, Apielig Pictures LLC

A self-described tough blonde from Brooklyn, **Marian Lanouette** grew up as one of ten children. As far back as she can remember, Marian loved to read. She was especially intrigued by the *Daily News* crime reports. Her Jake Carrington thrillers are informed by her admiration for police work, her experience in running a crematorium, and her desire to write books where good prevails, even in the darkest times. Marian lives in New England with her husband.

Visit her on Facebook or at www.marianl.com.

Printed in the United States
by Baker & Taylor Publisher Services